Beau gently touched her shoulder. "Alicia, you don't have any reason to be embarrassed. You didn't do anything wrong."

"But it feels like I did, Beau! It feels like I did."

And suddenly huge tears were rolling down her cheeks. Another man probably would have fled, but Beau had never fled from anything. Cursing himself for a fool even as he did it, he gathered Alicia close and hugged her, rocking her gently.

She cried for a long time, but he figured it was good for her. She'd been holding an awful lot inside for an awfully long time, and now she was letting it out. He didn't mind that in the least.

But he did mind how good she felt in his arms. It had been a long time since he'd held a woman close. He'd forgotten how good it felt.

He was in trouble now, he thought. Deep trouble.

❤ ❤ ❤ ❤

"Rachel Lee's Conard County is a place where every romance reader's dreams come true in the most wonderful of ways."

—Melinda Helfer, *Romantic Times Magazine*

Watch for these upcoming Rachel Lee titles:

A CONARD COUNTY HOMECOMING
A two-in-one collection of your favorite
Conard County stories:
MISS EMMALINE AND THE ARCHANGEL
IRONHEART
August 1999
Silhouette Books

INVOLUNTARY DADDY
A brand-new Conard County novel
October 1999
Silhouette Intimate Moments

RACHEL LEE

wrote her first play in the third grade for a school
assembly, and by the age of twelve she was hooked on
writing. She's lived all over the United States, on both
the East and West coasts, and now resides in Florida.

Having held jobs as a security officer, real-estate agent
and optician, she uses these experiences, as well as
her natural flair for creativity, to write stories that are
undeniably romantic. "After all," she says, "life is the
biggest romantic adventure of all—and if you're open
and aware, the most marvelous things are just waiting
to be discovered."

RACHEL LEE

CONARD COUNTY:

Boots & Badges

Silhouette Books

Published by Silhouette Books

America's Publisher of Contemporary Romance

SILHOUETTE BOOKS

CONARD COUNTY: BOOTS & BADGES

Copyright © 1999 by Harlequin Books S.A.

ISBN 0-373-48383-X

The publisher acknowledges the copyright holders of the individual works as follows:

LOVING YOU IS EASY
Copyright © 1999 by Susan Civil-Brown

WHERE LOVE LIVES
Copyright © 1999 by Susan Civil-Brown

YOU LOVING ME
Copyright © 1999 by Susan Civil-Brown

LEARNING TO LIVE AGAIN
Copyright © 1999 by Susan Civil-Brown

This edition published by arrangement with Harlequin Books S.A.

® and TM are trademarks of Harlequin Books S.A., used under license. Trademarks indicated with ® are registered in the United States Patent and Trademark Office, the Canadian Trade Marks Office and in other countries

Look us up on-line at: http://www.romance.net

Printed in U.S.A.

CONTENTS

CONTENTS

"Loving You Is Easy"
Chapter 1

Her fever was coming back.

Melody Dreyfus clutched the steering wheel tighter as a shiver ripped through her and clenched her teeth so they wouldn't chatter.

The night was moonless, and the black ribbon of highway stretching before her disappeared at the end of her headlight beams. The white line along the shoulder had taken on a life of its own, weaving, shimmering and sometimes disappearing, making her feel as if she were driving into a yawning black hole.

She was freezing and burning up all at once. Just a few more miles, she told herself as another shiver racked her. Just a few more miles. But keeping the car on the road was becoming more difficult with each passing moment.

Sometimes she thought she saw shadows jump up in front of her, and she jammed on the brakes, but there was nothing there. A few miles back she was sure she had seen a dark horseman gallop toward her, but between one eye blink and the next, he vanished. In some corner of her mind, she realized she must be hallucinating, but she couldn't stop the car here on this deserted stretch of road. She had to keep going.

Reaching out with an icy hand, she turned the heater up. It was the fever. She knew that. Three aspirin tablets taken a few hours ago had helped control it, but the effect was beginning to wear off now. It was just a fever, she told herself. No big deal.

Just a few more miles.

Every bone in her body was aching, and she was beginning to feel strangely disconnected, as if her brain were floating on a restless sea. She had to force herself to concentrate on the road, had to keep reminding herself that she would be there soon.

All she had to do was hang on for a few minutes more. A few miles more. Then she could find Alicia.

That was all that mattered. She had to get to Alicia before Harold or his men did.

Deputy Virgil Beauregard—known to his friends as Beau—emerged from Kat's Bar and Grill into the cool, dry late-summer night air of Conard County, Wyoming, and stretched hugely, feeling more content than any man had a right to feel. Kat's was a roadhouse, little more than a bar with a half-dozen rickety tables that catered to cowboys and chance travelers along the state highway, but Kat sure made damn good coffee.

The only vehicle in the lot was his tan Blazer with the sheriff's star painted on the side in gold. Seeing as how it was late, and it was a weeknight, that wasn't surprising. Kat's got most of its business on the weekends.

He settled his Sam Browne belt more comfortably on his narrow hips and climbed into his Blazer. He picked up the microphone to tell dispatch he was back on the road, then turned to drive out of the rutted parking lot. Headlights were approaching from the east, so he braked at the edge of the lot and waited.

His mind was far away tonight, he realized, feeling a familiar wistfulness. These long night patrols had a habit of doing that. Too much time to think and usually not enough to do. Unless some rancher got drunk and got to hitting his wife or acting up, he didn't have much to occupy him except the occasional speeder.

The approaching car whizzed past him, and it didn't take Beau a split second to realize it was going like a bat out of hell. After sixteen years as a police officer, he was as good as a radar gun at estimating the speed of a vehicle. That car was doing eighty miles an hour.

Which was too damn much to ignore. This close to town, the limit was posted at fifty.

Sighing, he tromped down on the accelerator and set off in pursuit.

It took him a mile to catch up to the car, which had slowed down. The driver had probably noticed Beau's car as he had whizzed by in front of Kat's. Beau was a reasonable man, willing to let it go now that the driver was observing a much safer speed, doing about forty as the speed limit went down to forty-five. He figured he would follow for a few minutes, to make sure the driver was going to continue to obey the law.

"Hell," he muttered when the car in front of him crossed the center line, then veered back. A second weave convinced him he couldn't let it go. Turning on his flashers, he pulled up close to the car's bumper. The car weaved a couple of more times, then braked to a sudden halt in the middle of the lane, nearly causing Beau to rear-end it.

Drunker than a skunk on Saturday night, Beau thought with disgust. He picked up his microphone and told the dispatcher he was making a traffic stop, giving her the license number, make and model of the vehicle.

Then he picked up his flashlight, climbed out and walked up to the driver's side of the stopped car. The window was still rolled up, and he couldn't make out what was inside. Feeling instantly edgy, he switched on his flashlight and pointed it in at the driver. A woman sat behind the wheel, her eyes closed.

Drunk for sure. He rapped on the windowpane, and she stirred, looking blearily at him. Young and pretty, he thought, except for her sunken eyes. Dark hair, and skin that looked far too pale against it.

"Roll down the window," he ordered.

She reached out a hand, touched a button, and the window rolled down.

"Do you have any idea how fast you were driving back there?" he asked her.

She shook her head, just a small movement.

"License and registration, please."

"Oh." She blinked, as if just becoming conscious, then shivered visibly. He'd seen shivers like that before, he thought as he watched her paw at her purse. It was a hypothermic shiver, the kind that rattled the bones—only it was too warm for her to be hypothermic.

"Sorry," she said. Her voice was thin, crackling, strangely dry. She passed him her license with a shaking hand.

He didn't smell alcohol. As their hands brushed, he felt how hot and dry her skin was. Taking her license and registration, he leaned down and looked more closely at her. Tremors were shaking her entire body.

"Lady," he said, "you're sick."

"It's just a fever." Her teeth chattered as she spoke. "I've got to find Alicia before *he* does."

"You can't drive in this condition."

"You don't...understand. I've got...to find Alicia..." The words trailed off as another shudder ripped through her. He could hear her teeth chattering even over the cacophony of the crickets.

"Alicia's gonna wait," he said, making up his mind. Reaching inside, he opened her door. "Come on, I'm taking you to a doctor."

"No! Alicia..."

He took her hand and tugged gently. "Come on," he crooned. "We'll go find the doctor, then you can find Alicia. I promise."

That seemed to soothe her. Still shaking, she swung her feet out of the car and stood. In the light from his blue-and-red flashers, she looked even more ghastly.

"Come on," he said coaxingly. "You get in my car, and I'll drive you into town."

She took only two steps before she collapsed.

The daylight brightness of the emergency room entrance of the community hospital was nearly blinding after the absolute darkness of the Wyoming night. Beau squinted against it as he walked through the pneumatic doors with the woman in his arms.

"What happened?" Carol Tate asked. She was a red-haired, green-eyed beauty just like her mother, and Beau might have taken a second look if she hadn't been the sheriff's daughter. Heck, he'd known her since she was six, and he felt like her uncle. After so many years thinking of her as a child, he was having just a wee bit of discomfort getting used to her in her role as registered nurse.

"High fever. She was a little delirious and collapsed a few minutes after I stopped her. Keeps talking about having to find somebody named Alicia."

Carol helped him get the woman on a gurney. "Any ID?"

"Out in my car. I'll get it."

As Beau was walking back out, Dr. Adam Roth came out of the cubicle where he'd been stitching up a minor scalp laceration. He was a relatively recent arrival in Conard County, an attractive man of thirty who'd made the decidedly odd choice to practice his profession in a place where very little exciting happened. Carol figured it had to do with his antiquated style of practice. The man made house calls, for gosh sake. He was a good-looking, pleasant man, though, and he'd caught her eye the minute he'd arrived. Unfortunately, it hadn't worked out.

"What's this?" he asked as Carol wheeled the woman on the gurney past him into the other cubicle.

"Looks like fever and dehydration."

Adam took a moment to examine the patient. She appeared about as dry as parchment, and her eyes were sunken, dark circles. She was mumbling quietly to herself, and shivering. "Definitely dehydration," he agreed. "Let's get her started on some fluids stat."

"You got it."

He turned and went back in to his laceration patient, an eleven-year-old boy who'd been fooling around with his older brother and had managed to fall off the top bunk bed and cut his scalp on a toy truck. His mother was sitting beside the gurney, looking uncertain as to whether she should be angry or relieved.

"Buck's head is going to be just fine, Mrs. James," Adam told her. "The carpet in his bedroom is another matter."

The woman nodded. "There was so much blood!"

"Scalp wounds always bleed heavily. He doesn't appear to have a concussion, but just to be safe, keep an eye on him. If you can't wake him up easily, or he seems to get confused, bring him right back in. Otherwise, just bring him to the office in a week to get the staple pulled, okay?"

She nodded.

"As for you," Adam said to the boy, "next time, fall off the lower bunk, will you?"

The kid grinned shyly. "It wasn't so bad."

"You were lucky. No more wrestling on the top bunk, sport."

In the other cubicle, he found that Carol had started the IV.

"Her temp's 104 degrees," Carol told him. "Blood pressure is one hundred over seventy, pulse is ninety-six."

"What's her name?"

Carol reached for a handbag that was sitting on the chair in the corner and opened it. Right on top was a driver's license. "Melody Dreyfus. Minneapolis. Beau said she was shivering violently when he stopped her, but she's not shivering anymore."

"Maybe good, maybe not." Bending over the gurney, he looked at the young woman's face. "Melody. Melody, can you hear me?"

Her eyes fluttered open, revealing irises so blue they were almost violet.

"Melody, I'm Dr. Roth. I need to ask you some questions, okay?"

She licked her dry lips and managed an infinitesimal nod.

"Are you allergic to anything?"

"No." Her answer was a mere breath of sound.

"How long have you been sick?"

She shook her head.

"Diarrhea?"

"Yesss."

"For how long?"

Her brow furrowed. "Two...three...days..."

That hardly surprised him, given her dehydrated state. "We've got you on an IV," he told her. "You're severely dehydrated. Do you have any chronic health problems?"

"No."

"Just this diarrhea and fever, then?"

A small nod.

"You're going to be fine. You just need some fluids and rest."

"Alicia..."

"Do you want me to call Alicia for you?"

She shook her head.

"Anybody else?"

Carol spoke. "There's a card with a phone number on it in her purse. A Harold Dreyfus."

Adam looked down at the woman. "Do you want me to call Harold?"

"No!"

The woman's response was almost shocking in its vehemence, and there was no mistaking the fear in her blue eyes. "Okay," he said swiftly, wondering what the hell was going on. "Okay. I won't call Harold."

"Don't call anybody!" Her voice cracked, but there was no mistaking her insistence. "Nobody. I can pay for this...."

"I'm not worried about getting paid," Adam said gently. "It's okay. We won't call anybody. And you're going to feel a whole lot better in a couple of hours. Just relax and let us do a few tests."

He ordered up the tests, told Melody he would be back to check on her, then headed for the lounge. The community hospital didn't have a full-time emergency room doctor because it didn't need one. The physicians in Conard County took turns being on call for emergencies, and everyone figured that for such a small population, they were lucky to have a hospital. Most nights when he was on call, Adam's phone didn't even ring.

Tonight was going to be different. He wasn't going home until he was sure that Melody Dreyfus was out of danger. Settling onto the couch, he put his feet up on the coffee table and closed his eyes. Not having many evening emergencies didn't mean he didn't spend long days seeing patients for routine problems and the injuries that seemed to go hand in hand with life on a ranch.

He'd added to his burden by making house calls, too. Not for everyone, of course, but when a rancher called in to say he had four kids down with something, it struck Adam as making more sense for him to go out to the kids. So he tried to complete his office visits by two, then made house calls as necessary, and finished up his day with hospital rounds if they were needed.

In the past few days, he'd been unusually busy. Strep throat had broken out among the five- to seven-year-olds. Since school wasn't in session, and since most of these kids lived on ranches, he assumed the strep was being passed around in Sunday school. And since most of the sick kids had been in Sunday school just this past weekend, he figured he was going to get another wave of the illness before long. He just hoped he could clear it up before school reopened in three weeks.

Carol poked her head in. "Melody Dreyfus's fever has dropped a little. Want me to go ahead and admit her?"

"Yeah. She's probably going to need to be on IVs for twenty-four hours. And we don't want to let her go until that diarrhea clears up."

Carol nodded. "Consider it done."

"Thanks, Carol."

"No problem."

He watched her go, half wishing that things had worked out between them. They'd dated a few times, but something had been missing, and by mutual agreement they'd returned to friendship.

When he'd decided he wanted to practice general medicine in this backwater because he loved the wide open spaces and the mountains and the opportunity to get away from it all merely by walking out his back door, he'd forgotten to consider that there weren't a whole lot of eligible young women around.

Conard County was a great place for a married man, but for a bachelor...well, it was beginning to seem that he was going to have to get used to loneliness.

He found himself thinking of the young woman with the blue eyes who was even now being admitted; then he brushed the thought away. Harold was probably her husband. Besides, she was from Minneapolis, and just passing through.

Maybe, he thought wryly, it was time to go home for a visit and let his mother unleash her frustrated matchmaking skills.

The thought of the chaos that would probably ensue actually made him grin.

It was nighttime, and she was in a hospital. Melody remembered that much. She hated being in hospitals. She'd hated it ever since her sixteenth birthday, when an auto accident had changed her life forever.

Lifting her left hand weakly, she looked at the tape that was holding the IV needle in place. If she had believed that she would have the strength to rip that needle out of her arm and get out of bed, she might have done it. She hated hospitals more than she could say.

And even more, she hated being unable to do what she'd set out to do. She had to find Alicia.

Feeling around, she found the controls and raised the head of her bed. The blinds in the windows were closed against the night, and the only illumination in the room came from the baseboard night-light.

What had become of her car? Had the policeman left it beside the road? How long was she going to have to be here? But even as she considered trying to sit up all the way, another shiver passed through her, and with it a wave of fatigue that left her feeling limp. Of all the times to get sick with some stupid flu!

Tears of frustration and exhaustion squeezed from beneath her eyelids, and she dashed them away. Never, not once in her life, had she managed to do anything right. She always managed to screw up somehow. And every time she did, Harold recited the whole litany of her screwups, beginning with the car accident. Boy, wasn't he going to give it to her over this one.

"What," he would ask in his sarcastic way, "ever possessed you to think you could drive across two states all by yourself? Haven't you learned anything? Mel, you're one of life's incompetents! You mess up everything you do!"

And he would be right, she thought dismally as another tear seeped out. He would be absolutely right. Anybody else in the world could have made this trip without any problems, but not her. No. So what if she'd managed to avoid having an accident or a breakdown? She'd still managed to get herself hospitalized with *diarrhea*, of all things. Why couldn't it at least have been some respectable kind of illness, instead of something that should only happen to a child?

She couldn't even get a traffic ticket like anybody else! Oh no, she'd had to collapse in the cop's arms!

And Alicia was still out there somewhere, not knowing she had a friend left in the entire world.

The door to her room opened, and a tall man wearing a checkered shirt and jeans walked in. He was ordinary looking, Mel thought, with dark brown hair and dark eyes, and pleasant features. But then he smiled, and he didn't look ordinary anymore. It was the warmest, friendliest expression, and Melody found herself wishing she could just crawl into that smile and have a good bawl.

"You're looking better," he said. "I'm Dr. Roth, remember? I saw you in the emergency room."

Melody's memory of the emergency room consisted of bright

lights, voices asking her questions, and needles poking into her. She didn't even retain much of a memory of how she had gotten out of her clothes and into a hospital gown.

"You probably don't remember much about it," he said, answering his own question. He reached for her right wrist, taking it in a gentle, warm grip, and looked at his watch as he took her pulse. "Much better," he said, and released her.

Melody was sorry when he let go. It was ridiculous to feel that way, and she knew it, but it had been a very long time since anyone had touched her that gently, and his skin had been warm, besides.

"You're still feverish, though," he continued. "Has anybody taken your temperature in the last hour?"

"I don't know. I just woke up."

"I'll get somebody to do that then. Any cramping? Do you need to go to the bathroom?"

Melody shook her head.

"That's good. We gave you something to slow down the diarrhea, and something for the fever. This is probably going to shock you, but from your test results, I'd say you have some kind of intestinal virus."

He was trying to be funny. She could see it in the crinkles around his eyes, and she felt herself responding with a little smile.

"I knew that would grab you. This will probably sound like bad news, but I can't even tell you what kind of virus. Terrible, isn't it? But the good news is that if it's something we haven't bothered to name, the chances are you'll live."

A tired little laugh escaped Melody. "Count on me to get an anonymous virus."

"Hey, that's the only kind to have. Trust me. The ones we trouble to name tend to do really ugly things. Anonymous is better."

"I'll take your word for it."

"Good. I wouldn't want to have to pull out a textbook to prove my point. That would involve driving across town to my office, finding the darn thing, then bringing it back here, and considering that it's three in the morning, I'd rather pass. Of course, if you want to read some gory stuff tomorrow, I'll be glad to oblige."

"No thanks. How long do I have to stay here?"

He reached out and pulled a chair away from the wall and closer to her bed. Sitting so that he was just below her eye level, he gave a little shrug. "Another night, probably."

"Oh, I can't!"

"You don't really have any choice, Ms. Dreyfus. You came in here seriously dehydrated. That knocks your whole system out of whack, you know. Electrolyte levels change, organs stop functioning properly. It's worse than just being thirsty on a hot day. So basically, I'm going to keep you right here until everything is back to normal. You're getting fluids and electrolytes in that IV, and you're going to keep getting them for at least another twelve hours, maybe longer. And then I want to watch you for a while after you get off of them to make sure everything is okay again."

He jerked his thumb toward the door. "Want to see your test results? The numbers are all wrong." He tsked and shook his head. "I'm afraid you didn't pass with flying colors. You didn't even come close. In fact, you were dangerously near...unpleasant consequences, shall we say. So tell me, what is it like to drive across Wyoming in the dead of night on nothing but sheer willpower?"

She looked at him for a moment, then cast her gaze down, feeling inexplicably shy. "Confusing," she said finally.

"Why doesn't that surprise me? Were you hallucinating?"

"I...think so. I saw a black horseman come galloping toward me, but when I blinked, he was gone." She stole a look at him and found his pleasant face had turned grave.

"I think your subconscious was trying to tell you something," he said. "Next time, listen."

She nodded, wondering why she was always so abysmally stupid.

"And when you have diarrhea," he continued, "you need to drink at least a pint of water an hour. A whole lot more than normal. I guess, since you were on a long road trip, you didn't want to drink all that much."

She nodded, feeling embarrassed.

"Well, if it ever happens again, you'll know how to avoid trouble. Most people don't realize how serious this can be."

"I do now," she said quietly.

"Don't feel bad about it." He leaned forward and touched her hand lightly. "This was an easy mistake to make. Is Harold your husband?"

She was startled by his abrupt change of subject and looked at him, wondering what he was getting at. "No." Then panic hit her. "Is he here?"

Adam frowned. "No. Why? Are you afraid of him?"

"Not...really." She wasn't afraid *of* him. But she was afraid *for* Alicia. "Why do you want to know about Harold?"

He spread a hand. "How about that you've been very ill, that his card was in your purse, that you have the same name, and when most people wind up in the hospital, they want their families notified?"

"I don't. He's...just my brother."

"Okay. Is there anybody at all you want me to call?"

"No. Nobody."

"Not even this Alicia you're so worried about?"

Melody shook her head. "I don't know how to get in touch with her. That's why I'm worried. She used to live here, so I'm hoping this is where she'll come."

"She's running away?"

She looked down at the sheet and saw that she had twisted it into a knot. She really didn't feel comfortable discussing a family matter with a stranger.

"It's none of my business," he said, when the pause grew too long. "I wasn't trying to pry. Or maybe I was. You have to admit, the little bits you've thrown out are enough to make anyone curious."

And somehow she found herself smiling at him again.

"That's better," he said approvingly. "Well, I'm going to go get the nurse to come take your temperature and blood pressure again. Then you're going to curl up and get some rest, and I'm going to go home and look for my bed. Assuming I can remember where it is. It's been so long since I last saw it...." He made a wry face, rose and headed toward the door. "I'll check on you again in the morning. Good night."

She was surprisingly sorry to see him go.

Chapter 2

A ray of early morning light slipped past one of the blinds and fell across Melody's eyes. She squinted at the sudden brightness, waking up reluctantly. She had been having such a nice dream, something about fields of wildflowers and a friend who really liked her. Not that she had any friends like that, except for Alicia.

Alicia!

In an instant she came fully awake, her heart pounding with adrenaline. She had to find Alicia.

But she was still taped to the IV, and when she sat up her head swam, telling her that she wasn't yet ready to climb out of this bed—unless she wanted to be stupid and collapse again.

She was trying very hard not to be stupid. So far, she had only seemed to mess up more, but that didn't mean she was going to give up trying to be smarter. And right now, being smarter meant staying in this bed until the doctor said she could leave.

"Good morning!" A cheerful-looking woman with graying hair entered the room. She was wearing white pants and a loose white V-neck top that indicated she was an employee of the hospital. When she drew closer, Melody could see her name tag: H. Redden, R.N. "How are you feeling?"

"Much better, thanks," Melody answered. It was true, and besides, she had been taught from a very early age not to complain about anything, not even about feeling a little dizzy.

"Well, you're looking pretty good," the nurse agreed with a smile.

Melody waited patiently while Nurse Redden opened the blinds, took her temperature and blood pressure, and made notes on her clipboard. Then she asked, "How soon can I leave?"

"Dr. Roth will need to decide that. I can't say exactly when he'll be here this afternoon, but I'm sure he'll want to check on you just as soon as he can." She gave Melody's leg a friendly pat, then headed for the door. "Breakfast is on its way. Unfortunately, you're not allowed to have the stewed prunes, so I guess you'll have to settle for eggs, fruit and a blueberry muffin that would give any serious dietician a fit."

Melody watched the door close behind her and wondered if everyone at this hospital was a comedian.

Rolling onto her side, she looked out the window. Nothing was visible for miles but gently rolling ground, grasses waving in the wind, and mountains at the very edge of the world.

She wished she had a book to read. The thought of turning on the television in the daytime made her shudder. That had always been forbidden in her home, and even now, at the advanced old age of twenty-five, when she ought to be able to make her own decisions about such things, she still felt guilty for turning the tube on before the evening news.

Sometimes she cheated and watched one of the daytime talk shows when she was home alone, but they always made her feel uneasy, as if she were looking through someone else's window at things she wasn't supposed to see.

But maybe that was better than staring out this window all day, worrying about Alicia and watching the shadows change as the sun moved. *Watching grass grow.* That was what Harold would have called it. He would have insisted she do something to improve her mind.

Feeling a small spark of defiance, Melody rolled onto her back and stared at the patterns of light and shadow on the ceiling. That was even less productive than watching grass grow.

Five minutes of that was enough to make her feel like screaming. Finally, in frustration, she sat up and swung her legs over the side of the bed. At least she could take herself to the bathroom!

But as soon as she was fully upright, that struck her as a stupid idea, because the dizziness washed over her again. After a few moments it passed, but she decided it might be foolhardy to try to walk to the bathroom on her own.

Nurse Redden came back and cheerfully held her arm as she went to take care of nature. A few minutes after that her breakfast arrived, looking more appetizing than she would have believed possible for hospital food. Especially that illicit blueberry muffin, which was almost as sweet as cake. After breakfast, she graduated to the armchair in the corner of her room and decided it was entirely possible she could talk Dr. Roth into letting her go this afternoon.

When the knock finally came on the door, she was ready to get down on her knees and beg Dr. Roth to let her out of here. But it wasn't Dr. Roth who pushed the door open, it was a tall, attractive man in a police uniform.

"Ms. Dreyfus? I'm Deputy Beauregard. I'm the one who stopped you on the road last night and brought you to the hospital."

She looked up at him, feeling very small, very vulnerable and very alone. Maybe she should have called Harold after all. Nobody intimidated Harold. "Do you want to give me a ticket?" she asked, hoping she hadn't done something terrible that she couldn't remember.

He shook his head, venturing a smile. "No, ma'am. Considering how sick you were, I wouldn't dream of it. No, I just wanted to see how you're doing, and to ask you a couple of questions."

She nodded, still feeling wary. *A couple of questions* might mean almost anything.

He sat facing her in the other chair. "I also brought you a book," he said, holding out a brand-new paperback. "I figured being in the hospital is bad enough without being bored on top of everything else."

She took it from him, touched by the kindness of a total stranger. "Thank you."

"I didn't know what you'd like, but that's got a little bit of everything. Romance, adventure, suspense. I thought it was pretty good."

This time she smiled at him. "Thank you very much."

He shrugged, as if embarrassed. "It's nothing. I also figured you'd want to know about your car. I had it towed here to the hospital, so it's waiting outside for you when you leave."

Once again Melody tried to express her gratitude, and once again he seemed embarrassed and shrugged it off. "Just trying to be a good neighbor," he said.

She decided to let him off the hook and change the subject. "You said you wanted to ask me some questions?"

"Well, one question, really. Last night you seemed awfully worried about somebody named Alicia, and you said you had to get to her before *he* did."

Melody felt her cheeks heat uncomfortably. Good heavens, had she been babbling about private family matters to every stranger she saw?

"I just wanted to know," Deputy Beauregard said, "if this was something I ought to be concerned about as a lawman."

"I don't...I don't think so."

He looked closely at her and nodded, but she had the definite feeling that he wasn't quite satisfied.

"Well," he said after a moment, "if you change your mind about that, just let me know. Here's my card."

Melody accepted the business card, feeling surprised that policemen carried them. But then, what did she know of policemen? Her last dealings with them had been after the accident.

"Thank you," she said again.

"My pleasure. Enjoy that book, now." With a friendly wave, he departed.

Melody looked down at the book in her lap. *Shadows of Lies* by Cris Brown. By the time she finished the prologue, she was thoroughly hooked.

It wasn't until nearly two hours later that she realized she should have asked Deputy Beauregard if he happened to know if Alicia was in town. After all, Alicia had always described Conard City as a place so small that everyone knew everyone else's business.

God, she was stupid! Harold was right. She messed up everything.

Adam Roth said goodbye to his last office patient of the day and looked at his watch. One-thirty. He needed to get over to the hospital and see how Melody Dreyfus was doing. By now she was probably wondering if he'd forgotten all about her.

"You're done," said the receptionist he shared with Dr. MacArdle and Dr. Randall. "No house calls today." Jolene was a motherly looking woman of about forty who treated all the doctors as if they were errant little boys.

"Wow." He leaned one elbow on the counter and tipped his head back to ease the tension in his neck. "Free time. What do you suppose I ought to do with it, Jolene? Go hiking somewhere? Read a book? Take a nap?"

"I vote for the nap," she said tartly. "You look plumb awful. What'd you do? Sit up half the night with some drunk having the DTs?"

"It was some woman suffering from severe dehydration."

"I hope for your sake that she was young and pretty—and unmarried."

He looked down at her, a mock frown on his face. "I don't fool around with my patients."

"I know, but a little fantasy never hurts. And you need to quit living like a monk."

"You sound just like my mother."

Jolene shrugged. "Mama knows best."

"Don't tell her that. Last time I was home, she set me up with a blind date every single night. And every single one of the women couldn't seem to understand why I'd want to practice general medicine in Wyoming, rather than have a lucrative practice in L.A."

"Why would you?"

He sighed but noticed that there was a twinkle in her eye. "Because I *like* it here."

"Tsk. What a waste, when you could have a Beverly Hills practice."

"My mother would agree with you."

"Maybe mamas *aren't* always right."

He felt himself grinning. "That's a major concession, Jolene. Be careful, or I might start taking you with a grain of salt."

"With a very *large* grain of salt, Doctor. That's the only way to take me."

"Well, I'll go over to the hospital to check on the Dreyfus woman and then consider that nap. Call me if you need me."

"Doc MacArdle can handle anything that comes up. Don't feel tied to your telephone. You just get your sleep."

"Does he know you're volunteering him?"

She shrugged. "Sure. I volunteer *you* all the time when *he* needs sleep. Now scat."

He scatted.

It was a beautiful day, so he walked over to the hospital just to enjoy the warm, dry air and sunshine. When he started out, his thoughts revolved around what he was going to do with his freedom for the rest of this beautiful afternoon, but by the time he arrived, his thoughts had centered on Melody Dreyfus.

There was something she wasn't telling him. Of course, that was to be expected, since she didn't know him. Why should she tell him anything that didn't relate directly to her medical condition?

But the fear he'd seen on her face in that unguarded moment when he had suggested calling her brother wouldn't leave him alone. And she was worried about someone named Alicia. It might be nothing major at all, of course, but he couldn't quite believe that.

The problem was, how to get her to talk so he could reassure himself that everything was all right?

It was questions like that, and involvement like this, that had led him to Conard County to practice medicine. He had discovered during his internship and residency that he wasn't happy when a frantic pace kept him from seeing his patients as people. When he had realized that they had become nothing but chart notations and individual body parts, he had decided that a major change was necessary.

Here, he had found exactly what he wanted. Last night, when he had treated the boy with the scalp laceration, he had known everything about the family and the child. He didn't have to wonder if he was hearing some story to cover abuse, because he'd seen those bunk beds, he'd been treating that child and his siblings for two years now, and he knew the parents. You couldn't find that kind of peace of mind in a big-city practice.

He waved to nurses and orderlies as he walked through the small hospital and was able to greet them all by name. There were, of course, some facilities he wished they had. Too often serious heart attacks or severe trauma meant that patients had to be transported elsewhere, that all he could do was try to stabilize them so they would survive the journey. And serious, complicated cases often had to be referred out, or wait for one of the specialists who came here one day a month.

On the up side, though, he got to deal with every kind of medical problem, rather than being limited to a narrow specialty. And he got to take care of all these people once the specialists were done working their specialized arts.

Then, too, he got the occasional unexpected afternoon off like this one, a gift of time from the universe to spend however he chose.

And he would get to see his patients grow up and grow old, the way Dr. Randall and Dr. MacArdle did. There was no price tag you could put on that.

On the other hand, it was beginning to look as if he were going to spend the rest of his life alone, because no woman seemed to want to settle in this backwater.

Oh well.

He picked up Melody Dreyfus's chart from the station and entered her room. She was sitting in a chair in a shaft of warm sunlight, reading a paperback book. When she heard his approach she looked up, and then a beautiful smile dawned on her face.

"Can I go now?" she asked.

The question surprised a laugh out of him. "I guess you *are* feeling better."

"I feel great. No diarrhea, no fever, no nothing. Good as new."

He glanced down at her chart, pretended to mull it over, frowning and making little *uh-hum* noises in the back of his throat. "Well..." he said finally, drawing the word out as he looked at her. She leaned forward with obvious eagerness. "I guess so."

"Really?"

It was like watching the sun rise over a cold, gray world, he found himself thinking in bemusement. This woman was incredibly beautiful now that she was no longer sunken and drawn from dehydration, and her smile would have made Helen of Troy envious.

And where were these ludicrous thoughts coming from? "Really," he said, his voice coming out a little hoarse.

"Oh, good!" She actually clapped her hands. "How soon?"

"Well, I'll need to have the nurse remove the IV, but then you can go. But you have to promise me that if you start to feel sick again you'll give me—or another doctor—a call."

"I promise."

"Good. I'll go get the nurse." But he didn't move. If he let her go now, he might never see her again. How did a doctor hit on a patient, anyway? Not that he really wanted to hit on her. He just wanted to find out the answers to the mysteries in those incredible violet eyes of hers. He wanted to know about Alicia, and about Harold.

But he didn't want to hit on her. She was just passing through, and like all the other young, unmarried women he met, she probably wanted to lead a life full of luxury and social activities, and wouldn't be at all interested in a doctor who preferred the back of nowhere, who liked to spend his time hiking and camping, and who probably would never manage to make much more than a living wage.

But he *did* want some answers.

She was looking at him questioningly, as if wondering why he was glued to the spot when he'd told her he was going to get the nurse. That was when he blurted, with none of the savoir faire he usually displayed, "Say, I have the afternoon off. Can I buy you lunch?"

Her eyes widened, darted away and then came back to him almost shyly. He hadn't known many shy women, he thought inanely. There was something to be said for it, though, because he felt a surge of protectiveness toward her that was out of all proportion to the situation. All of a sudden, he felt very *manly*—which was a feeling he hadn't much cared about since he'd gotten buried in work during his first year of medical school. Or at least since he'd matured enough to realize that being manly was somebody's idiotic idea of being a jerk.

But *this* feeling was...good. There was no other word for it. It wasn't a breast-beating, jungle-hollering feeling, but something more...*caring*.

"Don't be afraid to say no," he heard himself tell her. "I don't bite, kick or scream. I can take it."

Her shy look blossomed into a shy smile. "I'd like to have lunch with you," she said uncertainly. "Maybe you can help me figure out how to get started."

"Started?"

"Finding Alicia."

Well, what do you know? he thought happily. It was going to be easy to get his answers after all.

Chapter 3

Adam hadn't brought his car with him, and he refused to impose on Melody, so he gave her directions to the City Diner and promised to meet her there in twenty minutes.

Melody wondered if he was afraid to drive with her so soon after she had been seriously ill but had to admit she was relieved not to have him in the car with her. Since the accident, she'd been unwilling to drive anyone else around. Having Dr. Roth in the car with her probably would have made her so nervous that she would have driven into a light pole.

Driving in Conard City was a lot easier than driving around Minneapolis, though. Even at its heart, this small town felt like a quiet residential area. There were cars on the streets, but traffic was thin compared to what she was used to. She pulled her little car into a parking slot right in front of the diner without any difficulty at all. It was nice, she thought, not to have to drive around huge city blocks while waiting for someone to vacate a space.

Across the street from the diner was a small white-steepled church that made her think of Currier and Ives and falling snow. On either side of her were little storefront shops—a shoe repair, a beauty shop, a barber, a dress shop, and even a small bookstore that sold both new and used books. It seemed to be the kind of place where you could park your car and do everything you wanted to do within a short walking distance.

What intrigued her, though, was that these shops were not chain stores. Unlike malls, which had almost exactly the same businesses no matter where you went, this town had its own character. Melody decided that a person could move here and in a very short time become known by name to all these shopkeepers. How very different from city living where, even if you went to the same store a dozen times, you were just another faceless, anonymous person in the crowd.

Of course, she imagined there was probably a downside. In a town like this, everyone would know about her accident and about what was wrong with her. They would even know just how stupid she was.

Standing there in the warm sunshine, however, she found herself feeling wistful. Harold thought it was enough just to have a family. For the first time, Melody wondered if he was wrong.

She felt guilty for the thought almost as soon as she had it and scolded herself for ingratitude. Harold had been good to her and had taken good care of her long after most brothers would probably have booted her out and told her to stand on her own two feet. He reminded her of that fact often enough. He still tended to think of her as an invalid, though, but he was right about that. She would never be perfect again.

Not that she ever had been perfect, she reminded herself. Since earliest childhood, she had been stupid and silly. In fact, this whole trip had been stupid and silly, and all she had managed to do was get herself put in the hospital again.

But what about Alicia?

The thought gave her a pang. What did it matter, she asked herself, if she had been silly? Alicia needed *someone*. And since she was already here, Melody decided that she might as well continue, in her bumbling way, to look for her sister-in-law.

A battered-looking four-by-four pulled into the parking slot next to her car, and Dr. Roth climbed out with a smile.

"You should have gone on in," he said. "I didn't mean for you to wait outside for me."

Of course, she thought, feeling dumb. She should have thought of that. She looked down for a moment, and when she looked up again at him, she felt as if her smile wobbled. "I'm sorry," she said automatically.

"What for? I'm sorry I didn't make myself clear. It's my fault you've been standing out here when you're still not perfectly well."

"Oh, I'm fine," she hastened to assure him. She really didn't want him to think she was still sick. She hated it when people thought she was weak, even if she was.

"Well, no matter," he said with a smile. "It looks like you survived. Let's go in."

Melody had never eaten in a place like the City Diner in her entire life. Harold wouldn't dream of eating in any place that didn't have linen tablecloths, and certainly not one that had vinyl-covered chairs and booths, and paper napkins in a dispenser on each table.

But the smells that filled the diner were delicious, and sitting in a booth facing Adam Roth felt like an exhilarating act of defiance.

A dour woman slapped plastic-covered menus down in front of them. "I haven't started cooking for dinner yet," she said, "so you'll have to take your pick from the lunch menu."

"That's fine, Maude," Dr. Roth said. "Lunch is all we want."

"Coffee?"

Dr. Roth looked at Melody, who said hesitantly, "May I have tea, please?"

The frowning woman looked at her as if she'd just committed a major solecism.

"I'm sorry," Melody said swiftly. "If tea is too much trouble—"

"Ain't no trouble at all," the woman said gruffly. "Folks around here drink enough iced tea to float a battleship. I was just waiting to know if you want it hot or cold."

"Hot, please."

"Easier than making a decent cup of coffee at this time of day," Maude grumped. "Can't hold me responsible for it being too strong."

She stomped away, leaving Melody to feel as if she'd missed something, or had misbehaved in some way.

"Don't mind Maude," Dr. Roth said. "She talks to everyone that way. You get used to her."

Melody didn't think she would be here long enough to do that, and her picture of a friendly town with friendly shopkeepers began to alter slightly. Maybe being anonymous to indifferent salespeople was actually preferable?

Harold certainly wouldn't have tolerated this kind of service, but Melody decided to just treat this all as a great adventure, the only one she would probably ever have.

But now she was faced with the much more pressing problem of making conversation. She couldn't think of a single thing to say, even though she thought wildly, trying to come up with something. Before she succeeded, her tea was placed in front of her with a thud, just a mug of steaming water accompanied by a saucer with a teabag on it, and a wedge of lemon.

"What'll it be?" Maude asked.

Melody looked helplessly at Dr. Roth. She hadn't even looked at the menu yet.

"Can we have a couple of minutes, Maude?" he asked. "Melody's not familiar with your menu."

Maude nodded and glared down at her. "If'n you're one of them females that eats like a bird, just order a half portion. I hate to be throwing good food away."

Melody nodded obediently, and Maude stalked away once again. She found Dr. Roth looking at her with something like concern, and she managed a little laugh. "She's overwhelming."

"She works hard at it," he agreed.

"Well, I'd better read the menu in a hurry."

He laughed, but picked up his own.

When Maude returned a couple of minutes later, they were able to give their orders.

Then there was no excuse not to make conversation. Melody licked her lips nervously and wished she were more like Alicia, confident and outgoing. Life would be so much easier.

"Tell me about Alicia," he said.

"She's my sister-in-law."

He nodded encouragingly. "Harold's wife, by any chance?"

Melody nodded. "They've been married two years. Alicia is...well, she's like sunshine. She's blond and gorgeous. She used to be a model, before she married Harold, but he didn't like her working once they got married."

"How did Alicia feel about that?"

Melody shrugged. "She didn't say anything about it. But...I kind of felt she wasn't really happy not working. Harold has lots and lots of money, so it wasn't as if she needed it, but...I think she liked being busy. Busy and important.''

Adam looked at her across the table, wondering how much of what Melody had just said reflected her own feelings rather than Alicia's. He had a feeling Melody Dreyfus had never felt important in her life.

He pulled back to let Maude slam their plates down in front of them, then asked, ''I take it she was a successful model?''

''Oh, very. She used to be in the newspapers all the time, and in catalogues. Before she got married there was even talk that she might go to New York or Paris.''

Adam nodded. ''It couldn't have been easy for her to give up that kind of career.''

''Like I said, she never complained about it. And that's what women do, isn't it? Get married, stay at home and have babies?''

''I suppose there are some who still do it that way.''

Melody gave a little shrug.

''So, why are you out here looking for Alicia?''

She looked down at her chef salad. ''Three days ago Harold was served divorce papers. And nobody's seen Alicia since two days before that.''

''Do you think she's hurt?''

''I think she ran away.''

Adam leaned forward, resting his elbows on the table and thinking about that. What she'd left unsaid spoke volumes to him, as did her tentative manner and her quickness to apologize. ''Do you think Harold abused her?''

Melody gasped and paled. ''I...I...don't know.''

Which was a far cry from the denial he would have expected, Adam thought grimly. He used his cheeseburger as an excuse not to say anything while he turned things around in his mind. The last thing he wanted to do was frighten this sweet little bird away by telling her what he suspected was wrong with her life.

He watched Melody pick at her salad while he ate half his burger and noticed the way her eyes kept darting around, as if she feared attack from some quarter. It was on the tip of his tongue to ask whether Harold had abused *her,* but he bit the words back, swallowing them with another mouthful of food.

''So,'' he said finally, ''where do you think Alicia went?''

''Here.''

"Here?" That made for an interesting avenue to keep this conversation going, he thought. And maybe, in the course of listening to her talk about Alicia, he would learn more about her relationship with her brother. "Why here?" He gave her a rueful smile. "I have it on excellent authority that no one ever comes here on purpose—with the possible exception of myself."

A smile curved her mouth, and he found himself thinking again how beautiful she was. Not beautiful like the models in magazines or like a movie star, but beautiful in a shy, quiet, understated way. In fact, it was that smile of hers that transported her from nice-looking to stunning.

And this was a direction he didn't want to take, he reminded himself. This lady would leave town in a few days and go back to all that money in Minneapolis. At least he assumed she had money. Even the casual clothes she wore right now reeked of it, as did the quarter-carat diamond studs in her ears.

"Alicia grew up here," she said.

"Really?" The news snagged his attention back to the subject at hand. "But she left some time ago?"

Melody nodded. "Right after high school. That would have been six years ago, I guess."

"So she's your age?"

"I'm a year older."

"How old is Harold?"

"Forty-three."

He raised a brow. "That's quite an age difference. Between you and him, I mean."

Melody colored faintly, as if she were about to say something embarrassing. "Actually, he's my half brother."

"Oh." He didn't really understand why he should feel as if he'd asked an indecent question, but somehow he did. Melody's reaction, he supposed. "But the difference in ages wasn't a problem for him and Alicia?"

"I don't think so." Melody looked down at her salad, plucked out a sliver of cheese with her fork and looked as if she couldn't quite make up her mind whether to eat it. Finally she put her fork down and looked at him.

"Harold's very youthful," she said, by way of explanation. "Very handsome, very dashing. Women are always attracted to him."

He nodded encouragingly. "So you don't think she left him because the age difference became a problem? That's what I was trying to get at."

"No. It wasn't that. They already knew the same people when they met. And Alicia—well, she always seemed older. Most people would guess she was thirty or so, I think, from the way she acted. And they liked the same things. Or at least they seemed to."

He watched her look away, as if she were losing herself in thought.

"Melody," he said gently, "why do you think Alicia ran away?"

Her gaze came back to him, and she looked so sad. "I'm not sure," she said, her voice little more than a whisper.

"But you have an idea."

She nodded.

"Did he hit her?"

He got a different answer this time. "I...don't know. But I think...maybe he did."

"Why do you think that?"

"She...she had a lot of accidents in the last year. And Alicia isn't clumsy at all."

After they finished lunch, he insisted she accompany him to the sheriff's office.

"But they can't do anything," Melody protested hesitantly.

"They can keep an eye out for her."

"Why should they? I don't have any proof she's in danger of any kind, and she's an adult, so she can't be a runaway."

He held the door of his car open for her and noticed the automatic way she climbed in, as if it would never occur to her to refuse. He paused before closing the door.

"If she grew up here," he said, "the sheriff probably knows her. What's more, this is a small town. The police here aren't too busy to keep an eye out for Alicia. They're also not too busy to keep an eye out for your brother, if he decides to come looking for her around here. The more people who are aware of the situation, the better for Alicia."

Her hands twisted in her lap. "Harold probably won't come after her."

"But you're worried about it."

She bowed her head and nodded.

"So we'll do what we can. It's okay, Melody. I'm not asking you to file charges or anything. I just want you to let the local law help you look for her."

She released a pent breath, as if giving in. "Thank you, Doctor."

"My name is Adam, and there's no need to thank me. I want to help in any way I can."

The sheriff's office was little more than a block away, in a corner storefront across from the courthouse square. The Victorian gothic courthouse overlooked lush lawns and gardens full of flowers. Iron benches were occupied by people enjoying the pleasant afternoon. Some read books, some sat and chatted with one another, shopping bags by their feet.

By contrast, the sheriff's office seemed deserted except for one scrawny, leathery-looking woman who sat at the dispatch console smoking a cigarette.

"Good afternoon, Velma," Adam said. "Is Nate around?"

"Tucked away in his office trying to do paperwork again," Velma said, blowing a cloud of smoke. "The way that man hates the stuff, you'd think he'd give up being sheriff and go back on patrol."

"I can't imagine anybody else being sheriff around here."

Velma cackled. "They ain't nobody else damn fool enough to want the job. Go on back. He'll be glad of any excuse to stop filling in the blanks."

They found Nate Tate sitting behind a desk stacked high with paper, looking like a man who wished he was anywhere else. When he looked up, though, he smiled broadly. An attractive man of around fifty, he had deep creases around his eyes and a permanently suntanned face.

"Adam! What brings you to my den?"

Adam made the introductions. "Melody has a little problem."

"Well, take a seat and tell me about it. Either of you want coffee? I won't guarantee it isn't old and about as thick as mud, though."

"No thanks," Adam said, and Melody echoed him.

"Probably wise," Nate said. "God knows when somebody brewed it. For all I know, it hasn't been touched since this morning. So what's your problem, Ms. Dreyfus?"

Melody hesitated. Adam had made it so easy to express her fears, but sitting here in this official setting, across from an utter stranger, she was afraid she would sound as if she were crazy. "I'm...um...looking for my sister-in-law. She disappeared two days before divorce papers were served on my brother, and she hasn't been seen since."

Nate Tate nodded thoughtfully. "Why do you want to find her?"

"Because I want her to know I'm still her friend. And I'm afraid she might need money. Everything was in my brother's name...."

He nodded again and reached for a piece of paper. "Would she have any reason to want to hide from your brother?"

Melody hesitated, looking at Adam. He gave her an encouraging nod. "Well," she said awkwardly, "I'm not really sure. But she might have."

Adam spoke. "Melody says her sister has had an unusual number of 'accidents' in the past year."

Nate sighed. "I've seen a whole lot of that in my life." He narrowed his eyes at Melody. "If you find your sister-in-law, are you planning to tell your brother where she is?"

The thought had never occurred to Melody, and she was shocked that anyone could think such a thing of her. She had to remind herself that this sheriff didn't know her. "Of course not! I just want to help her. She's my *friend*." Her only friend.

Nate nodded. "What's she look like?"

"She has long blond hair, green eyes, about five foot ten and 110 pounds...." Melody trailed off. "I have a picture of her." She opened her purse and pulled a photo out of her wallet.

Nate took it from her and looked at it. "I know her," he said. "This is Alicia Barstow!"

Melody felt her heart race. "Barstow was her maiden name. She's Alicia Dreyfus now."

"Well, I'll be damned," Nate said, still looking at the picture. "She was my daughter Carol's best friend from the time they were five. I don't know how many times she spent the night with Carol. The two of them would be up until dawn, giggling."

"Carol's your daughter?" Melody felt a fresh rush of adrenaline. "Alicia talks about her all the time. That's why I thought she would be coming here, because of Carol."

Nate looked at her and nodded slowly. "How many days has she been missing?"

"Five."

He shook his head, his expression darkening. "For your brother's sake, Ms. Dreyfus, I hope nothing has happened to her."

And for the first time Melody admitted to herself a fear that she hadn't wanted to face before. She was terrified that Alicia hadn't run away, that Harold had found out about the divorce before the papers were served.

She couldn't say why that terrified her. She didn't think of Harold as violent. At least, not physically. He had a tongue that could cut steel, but that had been the extent of it—at least to her knowledge.

But she feared for Alicia anyway.

"We'll definitely keep an eye out for her," Nate said, passing the photo back. "I think all my people knew Allie before she moved away, and they'll all take a personal interest in her welfare."

Five minutes later, out on the street, Adam smiled down at Melody. "That's the advantage of a small town," he said. "They'll take care of your sister-in-law."

She looked down at her toes and tried not to give in to a sense of doom. "If Harold doesn't find her first."

Chapter 4

"Are you going to stay in town a while then?" Adam asked.

Melody hesitated. She hadn't really thought about that, she realized. In her haste to pursue Alicia and make sure she had some money, she hadn't even thought about what she was going to do once she got here. Harold was right; she was stupid.

What had she thought was going to happen when she arrived? Had she believed she was going to drive down the street and see Alicia right away? Or just call directory information and get her phone number? She could have done that from Minneapolis.

"I'm so stupid," she heard herself say to Adam, the way she often did to Harold to forestall his cutting criticisms. "I never even thought about what to do once I got here."

Adam turned to face her, and his expression was both gentle and sad. "You're not stupid, Melody. You were worried about Alicia and didn't think about anything except trying to help her. I can understand that."

She hardly heard him. "What did I think I was going to do? Drive up and down the streets looking for her?"

"You thought you were going to do exactly what you just did. You went to the police, and now they'll find her and tell her you're looking for her. The only question I have is, are you planning to stay in town for a few days? If so, I need to show you where the motel is.''

Melody tipped her head back and looked up at the cloudless blue sky. "I'm worried," she said. "I got here in two days. Why would Alicia take longer?"

"Maybe she's taking more time about it. Maybe she thinks this is the first place Harold would look for her, so she doesn't want to get here too quickly. Maybe she's following an indirect route so he can't find her along the way."

"Or maybe she's decided to go to London and start a whole new life." Feeling glum, Melody lowered her gaze from the sky to Adam. He looked like such a nice person, she thought. Everything about him made her want to trust him. And she didn't think he was pretending the concern she saw on his face right now.

"*Can* you stay for a few days?" he asked.

"Oh, sure. I could stay here forever if I wanted." And if Harold didn't find her and invent some reason to insist she come home.

"Well, then," Adam said, "it's settled. Let's go get your car. I'll show you to the motel, and you can wait while the Conard County Sheriff's Department does its job. Nate'll find Alicia, you know. Even if she doesn't come here. You got him worried about her."

"Really?" She felt a surge of hope, even as expected tears began to prickle her eyes. She was feeling tired and very much alone all of a sudden, and was beginning to wonder if she had accomplished anything at all by coming here.

"Really," Adam said firmly. "Nate's not the kind of person to forget about something like this."

Just then a sheriff's Blazer pulled up in front of them, and Virgil Beauregard climbed out. He smiled, tipping his hat to Melody. "Glad to see you're up and about, Ms. Dreyfus."

"I'm feeling much better. And thank you again for the book. I'm really enjoying it."

"My pleasure." He shook hands with Adam. "Is something wrong?"

"No," Adam said. "We were just telling Nate about Melody's sister-in-law. She seems to be missing."

"I take it that's the Alicia you were so worried about," Beau said to Melody.

She nodded, wondering what he must think of her for not telling him this earlier, when he had asked. But if he thought anything at all, his expression didn't betray it. "I hope we can help you find her," was all he said.

Then he said goodbye and disappeared into the sheriff's office.

They got Melody's car, and Adam led the way to the Lazy Rest Motel. It wasn't the kind of establishment Melody was used to, but she didn't say anything. She doubted very much that there was a Hyatt or a Marriott tucked around here somewhere.

"The rooms are clean," Adam said as he helped her carry her bags into the room. "The decor may be prehistoric, but the maids are good."

Melody had never been in a hotel room with knotty pine walls and throw rugs on a wood floor, and the sink didn't even have a cabinet under it to hide the water pipes. Harold, she thought, would have a fit. The thought made her grin.

"What's so funny?" Adam asked.

"Nothing." She would have been embarrassed to tell him. He might think she was a snob.

He hesitated at the door, and after a moment turned to her. "Can I take you out to dinner tonight?"

Her heart leapt, even though she knew nothing could ever come of it. The wise thing to do, she told herself, would be to say no and prevent any possibility of having to tell him the truth about herself. But she was all alone in a strange town, and he was the only person she knew. She did not, however, want him to feel obligated. "You don't have to take care of me, Adam. I don't want to be any trouble."

Again that sad, concerned look appeared on his face, but all he said was, "I'm not taking care of you, Melody. I'm getting to know you. I'll pick you up at five, okay?"

Five seemed early, but this was the country, she reminded herself. "I'll be ready."

Then he was gone, and she was all alone in the strange motel room, with nothing to think about except what Harold was going to say when he heard what she had done.

Melody half expected they would go to Maude's, or some place like it, for dinner. Instead, Adam drove them nearly a hundred miles to an out-of-the-way restaurant with a surprisingly sophisticated menu.

"This is one of the best-kept secrets around here," he said. "The owner used to be a chef for a major restaurant, but he decided he wanted wide-open spaces and fresh air, so when he retired, he left the city and opened this place. It's a curious form of retirement, if you ask me. Now he not only has to spend most of five days of the week cooking, but he's got to run the business."

"But he's the boss," Melody said. "That probably makes all the difference."

He looked at her across the snowy tablecloth, and she had the feeling he had heard far more in what she had said than she had intended.

After a moment he spoke again. "Being the boss *does* have advantages."

"Of course it does. You get to make your own decisions, and you can have everything the way you want—within reason, of course."

"Do *you* have everything the way you want, Melody?"

The question took her by surprise. She wasn't quite sure how to take it. "Well, of course I have everything I want."

"I didn't ask that. I asked if you have everything the *way* you want."

She looked down, studying the way the light gleamed off the polished silverware. "Nobody has everything the way they want," she said finally. "There are other people to consider."

"Yes. Of course. There are always other people. Which other people do you consider?"

She felt herself poking her chin out defensively. "What people do *you* consider?"

"My patients. My friends. The people who work for me."

"Not your family?"

He smiled crookedly. "My mother would tell you I'm a thoughtless son."

"Why's that?"

"Because I refuse to come home to Los Angeles where I can make more money, find a suitable wife and settle down to giving her grandchildren."

"But you won't listen to her."

"Of course not. This is *my* life."

Melody thought about that. She wondered how you decided where your own life began and your responsibilities to others left off.

"What about you?" Adam asked. "Who do you consider?"

"My family."

"Just your family?"

She shrugged one shoulder. "There really isn't anyone else."

"You don't work?"

That question always embarrassed her. "No. Harold doesn't want me to."

"Why should Harold have anything to say about it?"

"He's my *brother*," she said, wondering if he were obtuse. Of course, after what she had suggested about Alicia...she felt herself grow defensive. "He's been very good to me. I owe him a lot."

"So what exactly is it you do for him that you couldn't do if you had a career?"

Good question, thought Melody, looking down again.

"I'm sorry," Adam said. "It isn't any of my business."

That let her off the hook insofar as answering him went, but she couldn't stop thinking about the question anyway. Why *was* Harold so insistent that she not work? And what *did* she do for him that she couldn't do if she had a job?

Somehow she felt the answers to those questions would change her forever.

They dined on broccoli soup, thick, juicy prime rib, baked potatoes and the best salad Melody had ever tasted. Adam steered the conversation into safer channels, talking about hiking in the nearby mountains.

"There's an old ghost town on Thunder Mountain I'd like to show you sometime. Back in the 1880s, apparently somebody found gold up there, and for a while there was a lot of mining activity. A lot of the old buildings and the derricks over the mine openings still stand. It's kind of spooky, but fascinating. One of the things that really awes me, though, are the slag heaps. The thought of people moving all that dirt out of the ground with nothing but shovels and pickaxes, and maybe a mule to pull the buckets up from below, just blows my mind."

"I'd love to see it," Melody said, wondering what he meant by *sometime*. He had to know she was going back to Minneapolis, because that was where she lived. Nor did she want him to be interested in her, because she didn't want to have to do all the explaining about what had happened.

Liar, whispered a mocking voice in her head. She wanted Adam to be interested in her. She wanted *somebody* besides Harold to be interested in her. She was only human, after all. Just because it could never happen didn't mean she didn't want an ordinary life, a husband and children. It didn't mean she didn't wish someone would fall in love with her.

But all wishing for those things could do was make her unhappy, so she pushed the yearnings aside with practiced determination. She and Adam could never be anything but friends. Period. But friendship was definitely something she could use more of.

Adam was very open about himself, and full of stories about things he had done. By the time he took her back to the motel, she felt as if she knew him as well as she had ever known anyone outside her family. Maybe better.

And never in her life had she felt farther away from someone she knew.

Adam spent a restless night. He was experienced enough to recognize that Melody Dreyfus was getting under his skin. He kept having the worst urge to snatch her up into his arms and promise that he would protect her forever.

The juvenile idea made him laugh into the darkness of his bedroom. He was old enough to know that nobody could protect another person from everything. He was also old enough to know that whatever problems Melody had, she needed to solve them herself. Apparently she already had a protector in her brother, and all that protection didn't seem to be doing her a damn bit of good.

Of course, he had a very strong feeling that Harold's protectiveness was purely selfish. Melody's brother was probably a control freak, and all that mattered to him was keeping people firmly under his thumb even if that meant getting violent, as Adam suspected he had with Alicia. Controlling people made him feel powerful and important, one great big ego stroke. It didn't matter what he made them do, it only mattered that he could *make* them.

Apparently, Alicia hadn't been as amenable to his control as Melody. But Melody had grown up with the guy. He'd probably been training her since birth. But now Melody had struck out on her own, and Adam greatly feared Harold's reaction.

Disgusted, Adam sat up and threw the covers back. He turned on the bedside light and reached for the novel he'd started months ago and still hadn't found time to finish. But the story couldn't hold his attention.

What held his attention was the memory of Melody's blue-violet eyes and the way her smile lit up her whole face. And, to be perfectly honest about it, he found himself remembering her very neat figure, which not even her loose, casual clothes could entirely hide.

He felt a stirring in his loins and wondered if he ought to resort to a cold shower, or maybe a long walk.

But his mind kept straying right back to Melody's figure. Not too busty, but just what he liked. Gently curved hips, the kind a woman should have. A long, slender neck that seemed to beg for a kiss. And her mouth—well, he'd found himself staring at her mouth tonight like a starving man. Her lips looked so soft and inviting, and they were very mobile in ways that made him think of all the things they *might* do.

God, he had it bad.

Finally, reminding himself of all the reasons why he didn't stand a chance with Melody Dreyfus, he pounded his pillow into a more comfortable shape and forced himself to read himself to sleep.

Across town, Melody was spending a restless night, too. By now Harold would be seriously worried about her. She really ought to call and tell him that she was all right, but he would demand to know exactly where she was and what she was doing, and she'd never been able to lie to him. And once he found out, he would order her to come home at once, and she honestly didn't know if she had the courage to tell him no.

She'd certainly never managed to refuse him before.

But the thought that he might have reported her missing began to gnaw at her. What if people were looking for her? What if he was really worried about her?

But she honestly couldn't imagine Harold losing any sleep over her. He might be irritated that she'd decided to leave—in fact, he was probably furious that she'd done so without consulting him. Never before had she done a thing like this on her own, and the little note she'd left on his desk, about needing a short vacation by herself, had probably infuriated him more than it had worried him.

Time and again she reached for the phone, thinking that since it was getting late he probably wouldn't answer but would let the machine take the call. Unless, of course, he wanted to yell at her.

And she was most definitely not in the mood for that.

Lying back on the bed, she stared up at the yellow pool of light the lamp cast on the ceiling and thought about what she was feeling.

Being this far from Harold was making her more than a little defiant, she realized. At home she never would have dreamed of trying to avoid his wrath, because it would only make him angrier. At home she never would have made the decision to go out to dinner with Adam without consulting Harold first.

And Harold would unquestionably have said no, reminding her of all the reasons why she couldn't risk becoming involved with a man. Harold was good at that, good at reminding her of her limits.

He was certainly going to call her all kinds of a fool for taking this trip by herself and becoming ill enough to need hospitalization, but she felt another spark of defiance at the thought. Actually, she told herself, she had managed quite well for someone who had never taken such a long road trip before, and someone who, other than the accident when she was sixteen, hadn't been ill a day in her life. And Adam didn't seem to think she had been stupid for not realizing that she was becoming dehydrated.

Which brought her right back around to thinking about Adam. He was so nice, and so handsome, and what could it possibly hurt to hug her pillow as she drifted off to sleep, thinking about what it might be like if Adam Roth loved her?

It was an innocent little fantasy, and surely she was entitled to her dreams.

But a little while later she climbed out of bed and went into the bathroom. Standing before the tarnished full-length mirror on the back of the door, she pulled off her nightgown and looked at her nude body.

The scars had faded with time, until they were silvery against the warmer tone of her skin. But they were still there, and they were still ugly.

Then, as her throat tightened, she pressed her hands to her belly, over the worst of the scars, and gave in to scalding tears of hopelessness.

Chapter 5

In the morning, Melody gave in and called Harold. She figured the longer she waited to face the music, the worse it was going to be. Harold was good at stewing himself into a real storm, given time. It was far better to get the explosion over with quickly.

"Where the *hell* are you?" he barked as soon as he heard her voice.

Melody felt her stomach sink the way it always did, and she was tempted to try to placate him. But no, she told herself. Once she started doing that, she would find herself promising to come straight home. "I left you a note."

"A note! Do you think that pathetic excuse of needing a vacation satisfied me? You didn't tell me a damn thing about where you were going, or when you'd be back. Or even why you left without asking me."

Without asking him? How very like Harold, she found herself thinking with an unusual flare of anger. "I'm twenty-five, Harold. I hardly need to ask permission to go away for a few days. I even have my own money to pay for it."

"That money is from your trust account, which *I* oversee! If you're going to become irresponsible, I'll see that you get no more of it."

She felt herself flinch at his angry, threatening tone, but she forced herself not to back down. One of these days, she reasoned, she had to stand up for herself, and this was as good a day as any to start. Especially when she could hang up the phone any time he got too nasty. Taking her courage in her hands, she said, "Only until I'm thirty, Harold."

"Thirty is still five years away, miss, and I can tighten your leash until it hurts."

"Why? Just because I decided to take a vacation for the first time in my entire life? You take vacations all the time, Harold. Why shouldn't I?"

"What in the world has come over you, Mel? You sound like an absolute shrew!"

"Quit browbeating me, then."

"I'm not browbeating you! I'm concerned about what's best for you. What am I supposed to think when you just disappear without any explanation? You could at least have discussed it with me beforehand."

"Why? So you could tell me I couldn't go?"

He fell uncharacteristically silent. When he spoke again, his tone was slightly more conciliatory. "I wouldn't have said you couldn't go."

"Really?" She hesitated, uncertain how to interpret that. "I just didn't want to fight with you about it."

"There wouldn't have been a fight if you'd discussed it with me first. Now, where are you?"

"I'm just driving around, stopping wherever I feel like it," she managed to lie. "I'm not even sure what town I'm in."

"Well, give me your number, so I can call if I want."

So he could trace her, she thought. No way. "I'm leaving here this morning, Harold."

"Oh. Well, then, call me tonight and let me know where you stop, so I don't have to worry about you."

She didn't answer, refusing to make a promise she didn't intend to keep.

"Why *did* you go off like that?" Harold said finally. "Why this sudden need for a vacation? Something like that just doesn't come over a person without warning."

Now he was going to imply she was crazy. She'd been this route with him before, when she did something he didn't approve of but refused to admit she was wrong. "I'm sorry I worried you, Harold." Which was as much of an apology as he was going to get from her this time, she promised herself. "Hearing that Alicia is divorcing you upset me."

"Upset *you*? What have you got to be upset about? She isn't *your* wife."

"She was my friend, Harold. And you're my brother. Of course it upset me."

He gave a frustrated sigh. "The damn bitch just doesn't know when she has it good. Don't you worry. She'll change her mind."

Something about the way he said that made a chill run down her spine. How was he going to change Alicia's mind? She didn't want to know.

"Why don't you just come home right now?" Harold suggested. Actually, it sounded more like an order. Everything Harold suggested sounded like an order. "All this mess will be taken care of shortly. There's no need for you to be running around the country."

How could he know it would be taken care of shortly? Her stomach flipped over. "Has Alicia called you?"

"Not yet. But she will. Come home, Mel."

"I think I want to take a little more time for myself, Harold." Feeling that she was being too selfish, she added, "I'm sorry if that disappoints you."

"Look, you're being silly," he said sharply. He called her silly all the time, unless he was calling her stupid. "Whatever you think you need to deal with about my divorce, you can deal with it at home."

Was she being silly? The possibility began to gnaw at her, and she wavered, as she always wavered when Harold pointed out that she was being dumb. But then she thought of Alicia, and her resolve stiffened. "I'm going to take a few more days, Harold. I don't see why that should be a problem for you."

"But I need you here now!"

Did he? She wavered again, wondering if he was really crushed by the divorce papers and needed a shoulder to cry on. But the thought of Harold crying on anyone's shoulder was so ridiculous that she banished it instantly. He often said he needed her when she wouldn't yield to his arguments, she realized. And she always caved in. But not this time.

"No, Harold," she said, as firmly as she could manage. "I'm sorry. But no."

"Damn it, Mel, I can find you wherever you are and bring you home. Don't make me do it."

"You can't find me," she said.

"I can get the phone number—"

For the very first time in her life, Melody interrupted him. "It won't matter," she said quietly. "I'll be out of here in ten minutes. I'll be out of this town in fifteen. You can't find me, Harold. So don't even try."

When she hung up the phone, she was shaking like a leaf in a storm, but she felt better than she had felt in her entire life.

Then she went to ask the motel office to move her into a different room, and to ask them to tell any man who called looking for her that she had checked out. She received a raised eyebrow, but no questions were asked.

It was surprisingly easy to take control of her own life—when Harold was several hundred miles away.

Adam fought with himself most of the day, but by five o'clock his last house call was made—the strep epidemic seemed to be on the upswing again among the youngsters—and he picked up the phone at his office and called Melody.

"She ain't here no more," said Lucinda Schultz, who owned the motel with her husband.

"What?"

"Checked out this morning."

Adam felt his heart turn over. "She said she was staying in town for a while."

"Not what she told me."

"Lucinda, this is Adam Roth."

"Oh! Hi, Doc."

"Miss Dreyfus is a patient of mine. Did she happen to say why she checked out?" He was being a fool, and he knew it, but somehow he refused to believe that this woman had walked out of his life as unexpectedly as she had come into it. And she hadn't even said goodbye!

"Well..." Lucinda hesitated.

Adam forced himself to wait, but he was drumming his fingers impatiently on his desktop, even as he wondered why it mattered why Melody had up and left. If she wanted to see him again, she would have left some message, called the office...anything except vanish without a word.

"Actually, Doc," Lucinda said finally, "she's still here. But she told me if a man called to say she was gone and had me move her to another room."

"Which room?"

"I don't know if I ought to be saying that."

"Thanks, Lucinda. I appreciate it." He hung up the phone, his mind racing over the events of the evening before, as he wondered wildly what he had done to give this woman such a distaste for him that she would want him to think she'd left town. Even to the point of changing her hotel room?

He didn't exactly see himself as a Robert Redford or a Brad Pitt, the kind of man any woman would want. But surely, despite the fact that he was merely mortal, he hadn't done anything to deserve this? Hell, he hadn't even tried to get a good-night kiss— and he'd been regretting that oversight all day.

"Damn!"

Maybe she was just a flake. But he didn't want to believe that, either. From what he'd seen, she was entirely too sensitive to treat anyone this insensitively.

Ergo, he wasn't the problem.

Harold! Her brother. He would have bet his next year's income that her brother was the person she was hiding from.

"Damn!" He swore again, then rose from his chair and headed for the exit.

Jolene was still at her desk, handling the last few patients for the other doctors. He hurried past her to the side door that the staff used.

"Good night, Doc," she said cheerfully.

"Mmm," he replied, hardly hearing her.

He climbed into his battered four-by-four and drove straight for the Lazy Rest Motel as fast as the law would allow. Naturally the town's one stoplight caught him, and he drummed his fingers impatiently on the steering wheel as he waited for the light to decide if it was ever going to turn green again. Finally it took pity on him and let him go.

When he reached the motel, he felt a sudden upsurge of relief and an almost fierce joy. Melody Dreyfus would make a lousy secret agent, he thought with amusement. In the otherwise empty parking lot, her car, parked before the unit on the far end, stood out like a beacon.

He pulled in beside it and went to knock on the door.

Moments later, the door opened a crack and one of Melody's eyes peered cautiously out.

"Adam!" she said with surprise and opened the door wide.

"Sorry to turn up unannounced," he said with a smile, feeling much better now that she'd opened the door all the way to him. "Your gatekeeper told me you'd left town, but I saw your car in the lot." He wasn't going to get Lucinda Schulz in trouble for revealing that Melody was still here.

"Oh. Oh!" Color flooded her cheeks. "I'm so sorry! I didn't even think of you when I told Mrs. Schulz to say I'd left. I was thinking of Harold. He threatened to come get me."

Adam frowned. "What the hell business is it of his?"

"Everything I do is Harold's business." She stepped back. "Won't you come in?"

He entered her sanctum, feeling privileged to be invited. When she closed the door behind him, he heard her turn the dead bolt.

"I guess I should park my car elsewhere," she said. "I'd almost bet he had my call this morning traced so he'd know where I was. I told him I was leaving, but he probably wouldn't leave it at that."

Adam sat in one of the chairs at a small round table. "Why'd you call him?"

"So he wouldn't worry about me."

He looked at her, thinking that this woman was entirely too good to a brother who apparently terrorized her into submission. "Why would he force you to come home?"

Melody sat on the end of the bed and looked down at her hands. He could see the slow burn of color in her cheeks and had to batter down an urge to go to her and hug her.

"He doesn't think I should be wandering around the country by myself." She gave a little shrug. "He's overprotective. He doesn't think I can take care of myself."

Which, Adam thought, was a kind spin to put on nothing but a desire to control. "You seem to be managing just fine to me."

Her head lifted, and she smiled at him, as if his comment truly pleased her. And that made Adam even angrier. This woman, this beautiful, *kind* woman, ought to be used to compliments far more extravagant than that. The fact that she could take his simple assessment of her abilities with blushing pleasure told him just how much Harold had undermined her.

It was a very good thing Harold wasn't within reach right now. Adam wasn't a violent man by nature, but what he was feeling just then bordered on mayhem.

"You're a perfectly capable woman," he said to her. "I can't imagine why you think otherwise."

"You don't know me very well. Harold says—"

"*Damn* Harold! If you ask me, he doesn't know you at all."

"You haven't known me very long, Adam," she said quietly. "I do stupid things all the time."

"Who doesn't? What none of us needs in our life is someone who points those things out exclusively and ignores everything we do that's right!"

She thought for a few moments, then nodded in agreement. He felt as if he'd just achieved a major victory.

"Listen," he said, throwing caution away, "why don't you come over to my house for dinner? I was thinking about making a stir-fry, and I could sure use some help running the food processor."

She looked at him with evident surprise. "You have a food processor?"

"Well, of course. I have a microwave, too. I'm all set up to make cooking as easy as possible, because I hate it. Besides, I don't usually have a whole lot of time to potter around in the kitchen."

She smiled then and nodded. "I'd love to help you cook a stir-fry."

Oh, thought Adam, could life get any better than this?

And as soon as he had that thought, he realized he was headed for serious trouble.

"I don't really know much about cooking," Melody warned him as they stood in his kitchen. He'd pulled a couple of chicken breasts out of the freezer and was thawing them in the microwave. "We have a cook at home."

"Well, I can see I'll have to remedy that," Adam remarked with a grin. "We had a cook, too, when I was at home, and the biggest shock of my life was getting my own place and discovering I didn't even know how to make coffee."

A laugh escaped her. "So what did you do?"

"I bought a cookbook and appealed to a girlfriend to help me out. Turns out it isn't that difficult once you penetrate all that arcane language. I don't claim to be a chef, but I can cook the basics well enough to eat."

"Stir-fry isn't basic."

"Yes, it is. It's one of the easiest things you can make. It just takes a little extra time."

Once he had the chicken sliced into thin strips and marinating in light soy sauce and hoisin sauce, he showed Melody how to run the food processor. Despite all the intimidating pieces, once it was put together, it turned out to be simplicity itself. She began to have a really good time running mushrooms, green peppers, broccoli and green onions through it. There was something very satisfying about shoving in all those big pieces and watching them turn into paper-thin slices.

The stir-frying, as he had promised, was simplicity itself, and they took turns at it.

Melody finally screwed up the courage to ask him about himself. "You grew up in the lap of luxury, too?" she asked.

"I guess you could say that. My dad's a movie producer, and before he and Mom divorced, life was easy."

"How old were you when they divorced?"

"I was in my second year of college. Twenty, I guess. Mom's still comfortable, but she does her own cooking these days."

"Did that upset you a lot?"

"The divorce? Nah. They'd hardly spoken a civil word in years. I figured it was a relief for all of us. At least now, when I go home for Christmas, I don't have to listen to the two of them arguing about everything from whether the turkey is too dry to whether Dad let the wine breathe long enough."

Melody gave a quiet laugh. "I think I'd like a household where people argue sometimes. At home, nobody argues."

"Nobody argues with Harold, you mean."

She darted a quick look up at him, ready to defend her brother, but the gentleness she saw in his expression made her decide to be honest. "I guess you could say that."

"I *am* saying it. Melody, you haven't said a whole lot about Harold, but what you *have* said leads me to believe he's a controlling son of a bitch. Does he ever let you do anything you want without his seal of approval?"

She looked down at the bowl of broccoli. "I have a tendency to get myself into trouble."

"That's Harold's opinion, I imagine. What about *your* opinion?"

"Well, I managed to get so sick I needed to be hospitalized, all because I didn't have the sense to drink enough."

"Crap." He said the word bluntly. "I see dehydrated patients all the time. People who work out in the sun too long without drinking enough, people who get diarrhea and don't drink enough, kids whose mothers didn't realize how dangerous a case of the runs could be...it's hardly uncommon, Melody. I guess that makes you just about as dumb as most of the people on the planet."

She stole a look at him from the corner of her eye, and began to smile. Adam made her feel so *good* about herself.

"In fact," he continued firmly, "the only stupid thing would be if you kept getting dehydrated again and again because you didn't learn from your first experience."

Her smile bloomed fully, and she began to feel light as air. But almost as soon as she began to revel in the feeling that she was as good as anyone else, she remembered the accident.

If Adam ever heard about that, she thought, he would think she was as stupid as Harold said she was.

Chapter 6

After they finished up the dinner dishes, Adam suggested they watch a movie.

"The thing about living here," he told her, "is that we only have one movie theater, and it only runs one movie at a time, so a VCR becomes essential if you like movies."

He had quite a collection of tapes. "Almost as good as a video rental place," she told him.

"I've been collecting them for years." He held up a copy of Hitchcock's *Rear Window*. "This was my first purchase, and I'm so glad I have it. For some reason you can't get it anymore."

"I love that movie. Can we watch it?"

They settled on a comfortable, if battered, sofa, put their feet up on the coffee table and watched Jimmy Stewart work his particular magic.

At some point Adam slipped his arm around Melody's shoulders and drew her closer. She found herself nestled comfortably against his side, and she forgot all about the movie.

Her heart started racing, even as her entire body grew languid. Except for a couple of awkward groping sessions when she was fifteen, nobody but her mother had ever held her. She had never imagined how *good* it could feel to have an arm around her shoulders, or how powerfully satisfying it could be to feel a man's warmth and strength against her.

Her mind wandered off into a hazy fantasy of what might have been if she weren't so badly scarred. She wondered what it would be like to be kissed by him and touched by him. She wondered if her senses would sing, the way she had read about, or if reality would be more ordinary. Would she feel embarrassed if he touched her breasts? Or if he wanted to look at them? Would she even let him, if he tried?

Of course not, she thought with a painful tumble back to reality. She didn't want him to see her scars. She didn't want *anyone* to see them. And she certainly didn't want to have to explain them, or explain about what was wrong with her now.

"Melody?"

His voice sounded deep, even a little sleepy. She looked up at him, afraid he was going to say she needed to go home so he could get some rest. His eyes looked sleepy, too, but something in them made her catch and hold her breath.

Her heart began to pound in a slow rhythm, unlike anything she had ever felt before. At her center, she felt a deep heaviness begin to grow.

"Melody," he said again, huskily, and bent his head to kiss her.

Oh, wow! The thought exploded in her brain as his warm mouth met hers and pressed with gentle insistence. This was nothing like those few, wet, awkward kisses she had shared with that long-ago high school boyfriend. Adam knew what he was doing, and the difference exploded along her nerve endings the same way wonder exploded in her mind.

Long-dormant needs began to pulse in her even before he deepened the kiss. She had never dreamed a man's mouth could feel so warm or so gentle, so sure or so knowing. She had never imagined that the mere touch of a man's lips to hers could light a conflagration that threatened to consume her.

Unconsciously, she tipped her head back, mutely asking for more. He obliged at once, swooping in like a hawk to claim the warm depths of her mouth with his tongue in a gentle, plunging motion that soon had her entire body gently moving in time to his thrusts. It was as if all that she was had become centered in the warm cavern he pillaged so gently.

She felt him move a little, felt herself pressed deeper into the back of the couch as he twisted so that he was leaning over her. His kiss became more insistent, and she reveled in it.

He wanted her. He truly wanted her! The impossible was actually happening, and her heart soared with delight and thrilled pleasure. Adam wanted her.

Then his hand covered her breast, squeezing gently. Shockwaves of pleasure ran through her, reaching to her center, where they exploded in a clenching pulse of need.

And that was when the panic struck her.

She couldn't let this go any further! Fear froze her brain and erased all the pleasurable sensations in her body. No. No! If this went any further...

Suddenly wild with fright, she pulled her mouth from his, wrenched her body away and somehow came to be standing across the room from him, panting and looking like a wild thing trapped.

Adam looked at her, confusion giving way to concern. "Melody?" he said hoarsely. "Melody? Did I hurt you?"

She shook her head. Now that she was free, and safe, mortification began to fill her. She'd teased him, she realized. She had promised him something she wasn't willing to give.

In the background, Jimmy Stewart tried to convince his friend the cop that he wasn't crazy.

And worse, Melody thought, Adam was feeling as if he had done something wrong. "You didn't...you didn't hurt me," she managed to say shakily. "It's not you. It's not you at all. It's *me*."

He continued to stare at her, saying nothing for a minute, but finally he nodded. "Okay," he said. "Relax. I won't touch you again. Just tell me what's wrong. Please."

She turned her back to him, not wanting to look at what she could never have. It hurt too much.

"Melody, please. If you won't tell me, I'll have to assume I did something that hurt you or offended you."

She didn't want him to think that. It wouldn't be fair to him at all.

"Really, it's *me*," she said again, her voice quavering, hoping he would leave it at that.

But he didn't. "What's *you?*" he asked. "Just tell me, so I can understand."

She was staring at the wall, and on that wall was a picture of Adam with a much older woman who looked so much like him that she must be his mother. Melody's mother had died when she was twelve, and Harold had become her guardian. As many times as she had missed her mother, she had never missed her more than she did right now. She needed someone she could talk to about this—about all of this—and there was no one, especially with Alicia missing.

"Melody..." Adam's voice was gentle, and it was that gentleness that undid her.

Tears filled her eyes, and she hugged herself tightly. She had to be honest with him, she realized. Only the truth would keep him from being hurt. And she didn't want to ever hurt Adam. "I'm sorry. I..." She hesitated. Telling him about herself was difficult, because it would leave her so very vulnerable.

"Melody," Adam said quietly, "unless you're an ax murderess in hiding, I don't think there's anything you could say that would make me think badly of you. So just spit it out."

"It's just that..." She had to draw a deep, shaky breath to continue, and a hot tear rolled down her cheek. "I'm ugly."

"Ugly?" He repeated the word almost disbelievingly, yet with a kindness that kept her from taking offense.

"Ugly." She had to force herself to say it again.

"Tell me how."

"I, um, had an auto accident when I was sixteen." She drew another trembling breath and felt her fingers dig into her upper arms. "It was all my fault. I was driving too fast on icy roads, and when I started to skid I hit the brake hard. I was so *stupid!* I knew better...."

"A lot of people have made that mistake," Adam said. "I still make it sometimes. It wasn't stupid."

"Yes, it was. But that...that doesn't matter."

"How badly hurt were you?"

"I was in the hospital for a long time, and then I had to have physical therapy." Memories filled her, reminding her of the time when she had thought she would never walk again. "I broke my back."

"My God!"

"It's better now. Really. But...I have all these...scars...."

All of a sudden his arms were around her. He turned her gently to face him, then wrapped her in his strength, in a tight hug that made her feel so incredibly safe. "It's okay," he whispered against her hair. "It's okay, Melody. I've seen plenty of scars. I'm a doctor, remember? I see them when they're still open wounds, and I see them when they're all red and puckered, and I see them when they've faded away to silvery lines. They're not ugly. They're injuries."

"But..."

"Shh..." He brushed her hair gently back from her face and kissed her on the lips. "If that's the only reason you wanted to call a halt, forget about it. But if there's something else, tell me now, before I pick you up off your feet and carry you to my bed."

Her heart jumped. She looked up at him, feeling amazed as all her fears began to fade. But, some mocking voice in her head reminded her, he still hasn't *seen* them. And she remembered all too clearly standing in front of the mirror in the bathroom at the motel, and how ugly she had felt.

"Time's up," he said, and before she understood what he meant, he swept her up into his arms and began to stride purposefully toward his bedroom.

"It's like this," he said. "Scars are the marks left by life and experience, just like lines in the face and sagging underarms and droopy jowls. I've got this really great scar on the back of my calf from when I was a kid and managed to go sliding across a rusty nail that was poking out of an old board. There's a scar on my thigh from a rug burn when I was fooling around with a friend. Then there's the one from my appendectomy when I was fourteen. We won't even talk about all the assorted little ones from various bumps, bangs and dings. I've even got this tiny, jagged-looking one from when a saw slipped and sliced my hand. Lots and lots of scars."

"But—" Before she could complete the thought, he put her down on his bed, and she found herself looking up at him as he stood over her, smiling.

"I'll show you my scars," he said coaxingly, "if you show me yours."

Panic was fluttering in her heart, and she felt as if she were standing on the very edge of a cliff. She could step back and be safe, or she could step out and possibly fly.

And oh, how she wanted to fly! The yearning was so strong

she ached with it. She wanted Adam more than she could remember ever wanting anything, and if she didn't take this risk, she just knew she was going to spend the rest of her life regretting it.

Nothing could come of it, of course. Once he learned the full extent of her injuries, he wouldn't want any more from her than this night, or maybe a few nights before she went home.

There was more at risk than that he might be appalled by her scars. There was the risk that she might give him something she could never get back. There was the risk that, when she left, she would leave with a broken heart.

But this opportunity would never come again. Of that she was sure. Never again would she want someone in the way she wanted Adam right now. And if she said no, Adam would never again look at her the way he was looking at her right now.

It was, she decided, worth the risk of plunging to the rocks below, if only to know that she hadn't missed the opportunity to fly.

Mutely, she lifted a trembling hand.

Adam suddenly grinned and leapt onto the bed beside her, causing the mattress to bounce. She cried out with surprise, then found herself laughing at his exuberance.

Still smiling, he gathered her close and showered her face with soft kisses. "Thank you for trusting me."

His understanding of what was involved for her made something inside her melt. Tentatively, almost afraid of her own boldness, she reached up to touch his hair, then his cheek.

His smile deepened. "Feel free," he said huskily. "I like to be touched."

And so did she, she was discovering. She especially liked having his arms around her. But then he stole her mouth in a kiss that left her breathless, that sent her mind spinning away to places it had never visited before, places that lifted her up and filled her with exultation.

This time, when his hand cupped her breast, she let herself feel only the heated pleasure that poured through her in response. When he squeezed gently, a gasp escaped her lips, and her entire body arched toward him. It was, she thought dimly, better than anything she had ever read about.

Through her clothes, his hands began to learn her body. With gentle yet firm strokes he traced her contours, from her aching breasts to her yearning thighs. Each touch seemed to soften her more, until she felt more open than she would have believed possible. And each touch carried her higher on the crest of desire, until her fears seemed silly and far away.

He tugged her blouse out of the waistband of her slacks, and she moaned softly as she felt his warm, dry palm stroke her midriff. A prickle of fear penetrated the fog of pleasure, as she realized he surely must feel some of her scars. But he didn't stop stroking her; in fact, he betrayed no awareness at all of her scars. She relaxed again, giving herself up to him.

His hand slipped upward, and almost before she knew what he was doing, he released the front catch of her bra and her breasts spilled free. The sensation was unexpected, but wonderful, making her feel surprisingly wanton and bold.

But then he touched her there, lightly brushing against her aching nipples, and showed her what an incredible instrument of pleasure her body could be. He lingered there, brushing gently, sometimes squeezing gently, first one breast, then the other, until she heard her own panting breath and felt her fingers dig into his shoulders as if she needed to hang on for dear life.

"I'm going to take your blouse off now," he whispered.

She nodded, past caring about her scars, past caring about anything except the driving need he was building in her with touches that seemed to paint fire on her skin.

Her blouse opened, fell away. She hardly even noticed how that happened, except she thought that she helped him. Before she could start thinking again about what she was doing and the risks she was taking, his hot mouth closed over her breast and began to suck gently.

Never had she imagined that anything could feel this exquisite. Ribbons of longing seemed to stretch from his mouth to her core, and her entire body seemed to pulse in time with the gentle motions of his lips and tongue.

By the time he unzipped her pants, she was eager to help him push them away.

And then, for the first time in her life, she lay utterly naked with a man—and discovered the exquisite sensation of feeling his clothing brush against her as his hands wandered freely over her, finding every hill and hollow of her. Small whimpers emerged from the back of her throat as his hand moved lower, circling in on her womanhood. She ached there, she throbbed there, and she felt she couldn't take the suspense another moment. Without even realizing she did it, she parted her legs and thrust her hips upward, begging for touches where he had not yet trespassed.

He granted her wish. A long, low groan escaped her as he cupped her femininity and pressed, answering the ache inside her with the pressure of his hand. More...she needed more....

But he teased her, sliding his hand away, returning after a few moments to give her butterfly touches that were taunting but unsatisfying. Again and again, as he sucked gently on her breast, he teased her between her legs with knowing fingers.

Frustration built in her, and impatience, along with the heady flood of desire. Mindlessly she tugged at his clothes, needing him to be as naked as she. Needing him to come to her and fill her.

He rose up for a moment, but before his absence could sweep away the desire that held her in thrall, he was back, and she felt his warm skin against hers, with nothing between them now.

She had never, ever, felt anything better than that. The sensation was exhilarating, filling her with wonder and joy. Blindly, she tugged on him, needing to know the answer to all the questions he had awakened in her.

"Melody." He whispered her name.

She almost groaned with frustration. He couldn't possibly want to talk right now, could he?

"Melody..."

She opened her eyes reluctantly and found his face inches above hers, his gaze concerned.

"Have you ever done this before?"

She shook her head mutely and found herself hoping against hope that he wouldn't stop *now*.

He brushed a kiss on her parted lips. "I'll be careful," he promised huskily. "It may hurt a little...."

It hurt a lot. He penetrated her in one swift movement, and the shock of the sharp pain lifted the fog of desire that had blinded her to everything else. But he was within her now. It was done.

He didn't move, waiting for the pain to subside. He sprinkled kisses on her face, on her throat and across her breasts, murmured soothing nonsense that she hardly heard, and little by little the hurt went away. And as it vanished, her hunger for him returned, stronger now that he filled her, a need that went far beyond the physical, a need that seemed to reach to her very soul.

The sparkling explosions of desire hadn't vanished. Now, as she lifted her hips almost tentatively to feel him even deeper within her, they returned, hopping along her every nerve ending, making her helpless to do anything except ride their rising rockets.

Higher and higher she climbed with him, seeking something she knew must be there but didn't know how to find. Desperation began to gnaw at her, as she started to wonder if she was going to spend forever in this strangely painful, pleasurable limbo.

Then, as if he knew, Adam reached down between their joined bodies and touched her. Completion caught her, sweeping her up and over almost before she knew it was happening.

And then, as she settled drowsily back to earth, she felt Adam follow her.

Never in her life had she felt so powerful. Or so whole.

Chapter 7

Melody started to sit up, then remembered that she didn't know where her clothes were. She didn't think she was ready to walk across the room naked while Adam watched.

As soon as he felt her move, Adam tightened his arms around her. "Don't go," he mumbled drowsily. "Stay with me."

A bubble of joy rose from the pit of her stomach. He had been so quiet since they made love, dozing on and off with his arms around her, and she had become afraid that she had disappointed him.

"I need to go to the bathroom," she said, feeling shy.

"If I try very hard, I might be able to let you go that far."

She smiled happily but didn't move. There was still the nakedness problem, and she couldn't imagine how she was going to handle it. Ask him to keep his eyes closed? That seemed silly now.

"Mmm," he said, nuzzling her shoulder. "You smell so nice. You feel so good. Why don't we just stay here in bed together for the next twenty years or so?"

Her heart took a soaring leap, then crashed when she remembered. He wouldn't want that when he learned the truth about her. Nobody would.

She closed her eyes against the stab of an old pain, a pain she had grown used to—until now. Because of Adam, it had grown fresh again, fresh and more agonizing than ever. But what had she expected? she asked herself dismally. She'd taken a bite of the apple, and now she would forever know what she was being denied.

"The bathroom," he said abruptly. All of a sudden he was gone from her side, leaving cold emptiness behind. Through eyes that were aching with unshed tears, she watched him pad naked across the dimly lit room and paw around in his closet. She wished she could be so unselfconscious. But Adam had a beautiful body. Why wouldn't he be comfortable in nothing but his own skin?

When he returned, he had a baggy red sweatshirt.

"Pull this on," he suggested, dropping it onto her stomach. "I'll even leave you alone while you do it, so you don't have to feel shy."

On his way out of the bedroom, he grabbed his jeans from the floor. Then the door closed gently behind him.

He had understood her modesty. Somehow that made her ache even worse.

It wasn't fair! The childish cry rose inside her and forced the lurking tears to spill over her lower eyelashes and run down her cheeks. It wasn't fair. Of course it wasn't. Life never was.

But she didn't move for several minutes, unwilling to make a full return to the reality of her situation. Finally, though, feeling old and weary, she sat up, pulled on the sweatshirt and went to the bathroom.

Nothing had changed, she told herself. She had seized an opportunity that might never come again, and she had done so in the full knowledge that it could never be anything else. All she could do now was wring every ounce of pleasure out of this night and pay the piper later.

By the time she emerged from the bathroom, she had swallowed her sadness and was determined to enjoy every single moment she was allowed to have with Adam.

He still hadn't returned to the bedroom, though. Finally, wondering if he'd taken flight, and afraid that that wasn't merely a fanciful fear, she went to look for him.

He was in the kitchen, making sandwiches, and greeted her with a big smile. "I'm starving," he said. "Stir-fry always goes through me quicker than...never mind. I feel like I haven't eaten a thing all day. Hungry?''

She nodded and sat on a bar stool across the counter from him.

"You look beautiful in red," he remarked as he spread mayonnaise on rolls. "Why don't you keep that sweatshirt? I like the idea of you wearing something of mine."

Her heart lurched, and her eyes flew to his face. What she read in his gaze nearly deprived her of breath. She had to tell him the truth, she realized. But not yet. She couldn't bear to do it yet.

He looked down and went to work layering turkey slices on the rolls. "Why do you look so frightened?" he asked.

The question sounded casual, but she didn't think it was. Her hands tightened into fists on her lap, and she couldn't think of any way at all to answer him, short of blurting the appalling truth.

"Are you engaged to somebody else?" he asked.

"No."

"Married?"

"No."

"Scared to death of spending the rest of your life in this godforsaken backwater?"

That question slammed into her like a freight train. He couldn't really mean what he was implying...could he? "N-no."

"Well then," he said cheerfully, "unless you think I'm a serial killer in disguise, there isn't anything to fear, is there?"

He didn't know. And she wasn't about to tell him. Not tonight. Please, she thought desperately, just let me have tonight.

He put lettuce and tomato on the sandwiches, then cut them in half and placed them on plates. Then he poured two glasses of milk. "I hope you don't hate milk."

"I love it."

"Good. I drink gallons of the stuff. You could say I'm addicted to it. But I absolutely hate eating in bed, so do you mind if we eat out here?"

She shook her head, watching him with hunger and yearning as he filled a bowl with chips and put it on the counter between the plates. She didn't want to eat food, she realized. She wanted to devour *him.*

He sat on the stool beside her and toasted her with his milk glass.

They ate in silence. It would have been a comfortable silence, except that Melody couldn't stop being afraid. Not of him, but of herself. Well, maybe of him, she admitted. She *was* a little afraid of how he would react to the truth about her.

On the other hand, maybe he would never have to know. Maybe all he wanted was this one night with her, and tomorrow he would put the distance between them again. Men were like that. Harold had often warned her about it, telling her that since no man could possibly want to marry her, she had to be wary of men who simply wanted to take advantage of her.

But she didn't feel that Adam was taking advantage of her at all. She had wanted this at least as much as he had, and maybe even more. He could probably have any woman he wanted, after all, while she couldn't expect to ever have this happen to her again.

But that wasn't the only reason why she wanted to be with him, she realized with a jab of unease. Her emotions went far beyond the desire to have a thrill. In fact, it would be so very easy to come to care for him more than she had ever cared for anyone in her life. Too easy. She had the feeling it could happen between one breath and the next.

"No news on Alicia?" he asked presently.

She shook her head. "I called the sheriff this afternoon, but they haven't heard a thing. Sheriff Tate said he really thinks that if Alicia comes back, she'll call Carol."

"Probably."

"Maybe I was wrong." Melody put down her sandwich and faced a fear she had refused to consider before. "Maybe she isn't coming here."

He looked at her, his gaze kind. "It's possible."

"But what if...what if something has happened to her?"

"Don't be too quick to assume that." Reaching out, he covered her hand with his and squeezed. "She may have just decided to stay out of the way for a while. Maybe she's worried that Harold would think to look for her here, too."

"I guess. Yes, he probably would. She used to talk so nostalgically about this place."

He nodded. "If you noticed it, then Harold probably did, too. So maybe Alicia figures it would be best to let him cool off for a couple of weeks before coming back here."

"I hope so. I'm just so worried she's gotten into trouble. And I don't think she has any money at all."

"Why not? I thought she worked as a model at one time. Even if she didn't want to take your brother's money…"

Melody shook her head. "Harold invested all her money. I think all of it's in *his* name now."

"She *let* him do that?" He sounded appalled.

"You don't know how hard it can be to say no to Harold."

"I'm beginning to get an idea. So let me see if I've got this straight. This brother of yours is a penny-ante terrorist who needs everyone and everything to be right under his thumb."

Shock caused her to draw a sharp breath. Her instinct was to defend Harold, but even as she opened her mouth to do so, she realized the justice of what Adam had said. Her brother *did* terrorize people, and he *did* insist on controlling everything. She even remembered how he had taken control of Alicia's money.

"He said he could turn a huge profit on her investment," she said weakly. "He told her that she would be a fool if she didn't let him do it." In fact, Harold had used far stronger words than that and had kept up the pressure on Alicia unceasingly until she gave in.

"Harold thinks everyone but him is a fool, doesn't he?"

Melody nodded reluctantly.

"Hell." Adam pushed his plate aside and swivelled so that he faced her. "So he intimidated her, undermined her confidence in her judgment and managed to get control of all her money."

Again she nodded. Her stomach turned over as she considered what he was saying. All this time she had been making excuses for Harold and believing the best of him, but now she could see all too clearly that she had been willfully blind to what he was doing. "That's…that's part of the reason I want to find her," she admitted to Adam. "Because she doesn't have any money. I've got enough to help her out, money that Harold doesn't control."

"How'd you ever manage that?"

She shrugged. "I don't spend my full allowance. I put most of it in a bank account he doesn't know about."

He cocked his head, looking curiously at her. "Why did you do that?"

"I'm not really sure. I just did. Anyway, I don't have nearly enough to reimburse Alicia for what Harold took, but I have enough to help her until the divorce is final. I think the court would give her her own money back in the settlement. Wouldn't they?"

"Maybe. One would hope so."

He reached out and touched her chin with his fingertip until she lifted her gaze to his. "Fly, little bird," he said softly. "Fly. You have wings, and they're stronger than you think."

Pleasure and confusion filled her. She wasn't quite sure what he meant, but the way he was looking at her and touching her made her happy.

He continued to stare into her eyes for a moment, then he dropped his hand and turned back to his sandwich. "So," he said slowly, examining the leaf of lettuce that stuck out from the roll, "what are you going to do about Harold?"

"Do?" She had never thought about *doing* anything about Harold. Most of her life had been spent trying to keep him happy.

"Yes, *do*." He tucked the escaping lettuce back into the roll. "Are you just going to go home again after you find Alicia and let him take control of you again?"

Two days ago she would have answered that of course she was going home. It *was* her home, after all. But suddenly she wasn't sure about that. "I...don't know."

He nodded. "Good."

"Good?"

He smiled crookedly at her. "Well, I have to admit to a personal interest here, Melody. If you decide to go home after you find Alicia, I'd like to be sure that it's what *you* really want to do."

Why in the world should that matter to him? she wondered. But somehow, it was nice that it *did*.

In fact, she realized with a twinge of trepidation, he was making her feel more cared for than she had ever felt in her life. That was a nice thing, but it was also a dangerous thing, because she could easily come to crave it.

Afraid of the direction this discussion was taking, she turned her attention back to her sandwich. Adam was making her see things in a different way, and she didn't know if she was ready for all the consequences of that.

Yes, she chafed under Harold's control at times, but she really wasn't sure what she would do without him to look after her. She knew she wasn't capable of taking care of herself. Harold was always quick to point that out to her.

But what if Harold was wrong? She had come all the way to Wyoming without his aid, and except for her dehydration she had managed very well. Maybe she was far more capable than she believed.

She felt a surge of confidence until she remembered what she was doing right now. Not only had she managed to nearly kill herself by getting sick, but now she was spending the night with a man and getting her emotions all tangled up in a relationship that couldn't possibly survive.

Harold would tell her she was being a fool, and there wouldn't be much she could argue in rebuttal. She *was* being a fool. She was wading in deep waters where she might well drown. Didn't she know any better?

"What are you thinking?" Adam asked. "You look so sad."

She shrugged and picked a small piece off her roll. "I was just thinking about all the mistakes I've made."

"Mmm. Well, there's nothing wrong with making mistakes."

She looked at him, surprised.

He shrugged a shoulder and gave her another one of those crooked smiles. "Hey," he said, "mistakes are how we learn. If we never make any, we never grow."

Melody hadn't thought about it like that before, but what he said made sense. Maybe she wasn't stupid after all. Maybe she just needed to make her own mistakes so she could grow.

All of a sudden, she was smiling. "You're right," she said.

"Sometimes," he agreed. "But, hey, I've made plenty of mistakes of my own."

"You?"

"Yes, me. I know it's impossible to believe, since I'm such an exemplar of manhood, but yeah, I've screwed up lots of times. And I'm not just talking about little mistakes. I've made some really scary ones."

"Such as?"

"Well, when I was an intern, I diagnosed a myocardial infarction—that's a heart attack—as indigestion and sent the guy home with antacids."

"Ooh. What happened?"

"The patient figured I was too wet behind the ears to know what I was doing and came back fifteen minutes later, demanding to see a real doctor."

Melody winced. "You must have been so embarrassed."

"I was horrified. That man could have died because of me. And there were other things. But that's how you learn. That's why doctors have internships and residencies. There's supposed to be somebody watching over our shoulders to catch our mistakes and teach us something.''

He shook his head and gave her a rueful smile. ''So the next time I erred on the side of caution and had a case of indigestion in the intensive care unit before the resident sorted me out. But as the resident said later, at least that time I didn't almost kill the patient.''

He reached out and took her hand. ''I've learned more from my screwups than I've ever learned by doing something right. The only fool is one who doesn't learn from his mistakes.''

Melody turned that thought around and decided to tuck it away for future reference when Harold started telling her how stupid she was again.

If, she thought with a surge of defiance, she ever gave Harold another opportunity.

Chapter 8

Adam decided he was losing his mind. He and Melody had spent three nights together, and now all he could think about was her. Jolene was teasing him about his absentmindedness, he had to keep asking patients to repeat the simplest things, and he had no doubt that word was getting around the county that Doc Roth was losing it.

Well, he *was* losing it. How could he do anything else, when he had found the woman of his dreams, yet she was remaining as elusive as the wisps of cloud in the morning sky?

There was something she wasn't telling him. He was sure of it. He could see it in the way shadows sometimes darkened her incredible eyes, or in the way she would suddenly look sad, all without reason.

She probably didn't want to tell him that the last thing on earth she would ever do was move to this godforsaken rural county and live on a shoestring. And why should she? he asked himself honestly. She was used to having money, used to the diversions of city life. This place must bore her to tears.

So he kicked around the idea of uprooting himself and moving to Minneapolis when he should have been listening to Mrs. Hutchins's complaints about her sore knee. He tried to envision himself living in a city again when he should have been telling Mr. Barton to give up the cigarettes if he didn't want to be on oxygen within the next couple of years. And he realized he couldn't do it about the time he should have been telling Tammy Wolf that having safe sex meant more than taking birth control pills.

He had moved here for the slower pace, for the mountains and the clean air and the wide-open spaces. He had moved here because this place comforted his soul.

But he had to stay because it had become his home. He had sunk down roots and made good friends, and he belonged here in a way he had never belonged anywhere else.

If he went to Minneapolis, something inside him would die, and that wouldn't be fair to either him or Melody.

But asking Melody to move here and give up her home and friends wouldn't be fair, either.

So he was losing his mind. It didn't seem possible, but he had managed to fall head over heels in love with her in just a few short days.

So he started thinking about moving to Minneapolis again, a prospect that filled his heart with lead. But so did thinking about losing Melody.

In the end, he decided to tell her that he loved her, and that, if she wanted, he would move to Minneapolis to be with her. One way or another, he was going to uproot his heart.

But losing Melody would inflict the worse wound by far.

Unaware that Adam was losing his mind, Melody spent the day wandering around town. There was still no word of Alicia, and she began to think her sister-in-law had decided to hide out in some far more exotic place.

Instead of worrying about something she could do nothing about, she had spent the time while Adam worked prowling the streets and little shops of Conard City. She was a stranger, which caused people to take notice of her, but they didn't treat her stand-offishly.

More than once a shopkeeper engaged her in lengthy conversation about Minneapolis and what she thought of the local area. By the time she walked out of a store, she felt as if she had made a friend.

Late in the afternoon, she sat on a bench in the courthouse square to soak up the warm August sun. She hadn't been there more than ten minutes, enjoying the gentle breeze and the way the sun made her skin tingle, when an old man sat down on the other end of the bench.

She turned to smile at him.

"You're Doc Roth's gal, aren't you?" he said.

Melody felt a shiver of surprise, followed by unmistakable pleasure. "I've been seeing him," she agreed cautiously.

He nodded, satisfied. "He needs a good woman. Young guys kick and scream about marriage, but that's foolishness. We were meant to go through life by twos. And life gets awful empty when you don't have nobody."

She nodded, wholeheartedly agreeing with him, but equally certain that she was going to go through life by ones. Alone. The shadow of looming loss took some of the warmth out of the day, but she forced herself to ignore it. Whatever the consequences of her involvement with Adam, it was something she had gone into with her eyes wide-open. All she could do now was take Adam's advice and learn from her mistakes.

"Checkers?" the old man asked. From a pocket inside his battered suit jacket, he pulled a magnetic checkerboard and opened it up on the bench between them.

"I've never played," Melody admitted.

"Really?" He looked astonished at that. "Well, it's simple enough. I'll teach you."

So, as the afternoon waned, she sat on a park bench and played checkers in the warm sunshine with an old man whose name she didn't even know.

And she wondered why she couldn't just stay here forever.

By the time Melody arrived at his house for dinner at six-thirty that evening, Adam was not only losing his mind, he was a nervous wreck. He'd bought a linen tablecloth at Freitag's on his way home, and a couple of candles and candlesticks. His indifferent china looked out of place in such an elegant setting, and he spent a few frantic minutes wiping water marks off the flatware and water glasses.

Damn, why hadn't he ever bought anything better than this? he wondered as he waited for the doorbell to ring.

He had a small roast in the oven, which should be done at seven. Except that, as his mother had warned him on the phone not twenty minutes ago, he'd better check it frequently, because small roasts could be difficult to cook just right.

Thanks, Mom, he thought now. He didn't need to hear how difficult it could be; he just needed to know how to do it right.

There was a salad cooling in the fridge, and he'd decided to microwave the baked potatoes, because his mother had said that an hour in the oven at 325 degrees wasn't likely to cook them.

"Eight to ten minutes," she told him. "Depending on the wattage of your microwave."

Damn, why couldn't cooking be precise? Why did it have to have all these astounding gaps between done and ruined?

"And when," she had asked in conclusion, "are you going to bring this young lady home to meet me?"

"I don't know, Mom. Maybe never. There's a distinct possibility that she may not want to spend any more time with me."

His mother sniffed. "Anybody would love you, Adam. You're a catch."

He didn't want to be "a catch." He wanted to be more important than anything else in the world to one woman, and *not* because he was a *catch.* "You know, Mom, many women have disagreed with you."

"Only because you refuse to come home, where you could make some decent money."

He had decided to end the conversation right there, before she dug up all his doubts and shoved them down his throat, where they would probably stick and suffocate him to death before he could screw up his courage to tell Melody what he felt.

The doorbell rang, and panic rooted him to the spot. Oh, God, she was here. The time when he had to put everything on the line was bearing down on him like a stampede. He wasn't ready for this!

The doorbell rang again. He took a couple of deep breaths to calm himself and went to let Melody in.

She looked even lovelier than usual tonight, he thought. Sun had kissed her cheeks and nose, giving them heightened color, and her eyes held a happiness he had never seen in them before.

"I had a wonderful day!" she told him exuberantly. "I wandered all over town and met so many nice people. And a really neat old man taught me how to play checkers."

He blinked at that. "You didn't know how to play before?"

She shook her head. "I never had the opportunity. Harold thought that if I was going to play board games, I ought to play chess." She wrinkled her nose. "I hated it."

He could think of a lot of things to do to Harold right then, but none of them were legal.

"Something smells good," she said appreciatively.

"I'm making a roast. Dinner will be ready around seven."

"Great. All that fresh air and walking has made me really hungry."

He glanced at his watch. "Well, I've got nearly twenty minutes before I have to put the potatoes in, so why don't we sit in the living room. Would you like something to drink?" Anything to postpone the dreaded moment.

"No, thank you. I'm fine." She smiled at him again and sat on the couch.

He sat next to her and finally gave in to the urgent need to put his arms around her and kiss her. He could feel her melting against him, but he couldn't quite give in to the moment, because of the sword hanging over his head.

Maybe he didn't have to bring this up tonight? Maybe he could just let it go for a few more days? But even as he had the cowardly thought, he knew he couldn't. What if Alicia turned up tomorrow and Melody left before he could talk to her? No, he had to bite the bullet now.

He lifted his head and looked down into her eyes. She was smiling faintly, looking a little dazed and very sexy. Not now. Talk first.

"Melody?"

"Mmm?"

"I love you."

He had thought he'd prepared himself for every possible reaction, but he wasn't prepared for the fear and anguish that suddenly shattered her smile. He wasn't prepared for the way she wrenched away from him and kept going until she was standing across the room from him, shaking.

"I'm sorry," she said. "Oh, God, I'm so sorry...!"

Sorry? His heart plummeted to his toes and it was a moment before he could speak. "Um...you're not responsible for my feelings," he managed to say finally. "You don't have to apologize—"

"Yes, I do," she cried out. "Oh, God, yes I do! It's my fault..."

Her *fault?* Now he was really at sea. "Melody, nothing's your fault. People date to see if they click. I thought we clicked, but you don't. It happens. You didn't do anything wrong." And he would like to kill Harold for making this woman feel she was responsible for everything.

"Yes, I did," she said, as huge tears rolled down her cheeks. "I did something very, very wrong."

"What could be so wrong?" He wondered why he didn't just end this conversation before it grew any more painful for both of them, but some stubborn hope kept him going. Maybe there was something he could say or do to change her mind. He clung to that straw of hope as if it were a lifeline.

"I lied to you," she said brokenly. "I lied to you."

Lied? His mind began a frantic search over the past few days, trying to remember everything she'd said. "You mean you really are married?"

"No."

"Engaged?"

"No! It's worse than that."

He couldn't imagine anything worse than that. "You're wanted in fifty states for murder?"

"No." She shook her head almost violently. "It's not funny, Adam."

"No," he agreed gravely, "I don't think it is. Just tell me, honey."

She turned her back on him, and he began to really believe that he had lost. His chest tightened until it ached. "Melody?"

"I...I can't have children."

"You can't have children?"

"No. I can't. Not ever. I don't have...the equipment."

"I see." He waited a moment, then rose from the couch and went into the kitchen. Once there, he gave a huge sigh, wiped his hands across his face and wondered how the hell he was going to deal with this.

Out in the living room, Melody collapsed on the couch and gave way to her tears. He could hear them all the way out here, and the sound of her anguish galvanized him. He hurried back into the living room.

"Melody?"

Another sob escaped her, and her shoulders shook.

"Melody, you didn't lie to me."

"Yes, I did," she said brokenly. "I wasn't honest. I should have told you."

"Why? Do you tell people something like that as soon as you meet them?"

"This was different."

"Now it's different, and now you told me. But you didn't lie to me. I don't remember asking you to pass a physical exam before we started dating. I don't even remember asking you if you could bear children."

"But..." Her voice trailed off. She drew a couple of shaky breaths and lifted her tearstained face. "I should have warned you."

"Why?"

"So you wouldn't fall in love with me!"

"Oh." Suddenly it was all very clear to him, and with clarity came a strong surge of hope and an even greater surge of determination. "Listen, little bird," he said firmly, "if I'd wanted a brood mare, I'd have gone to an auction."

Her eyes widened, and she sniffled. "Wh-what?"

"You heard me. If I was all that concerned about your breeding capabilities, I'd have checked them out. I didn't fall in love with you because I had visions of a houseful of rug rats. I fell in love with *you*. And all I want from you is your *love*."

He saw hope begin to brighten her face and decided it was safe to sit beside her. Pulling a tissue out of a box on the end table, he began to gently wipe away her tears. "I just want *you*," he repeated quietly. "Kids...well, the world is full of kids who are already here who could use a good mom and dad. If we decide we want children, we'll find some little waif who needs somebody to love him or her. Hell, we'll find a dozen little waifs, in every color of the rainbow. Kids are easy to come by, sweetie, as long as you're not attached to the idea that they have to be your own flesh and blood, or that they have to look a certain way, or that they have to be 100 percent perfect. Me, I like kids. I'll take 'em in any size, shape or condition. And they'll be mine because I love them. Just the way I love you."

She had been holding her breath through this speech, and now she let go of it in a long, shaky sigh. "You mean that?"

"I've never meant anything more in my life." He hesitated. "Was it the accident?"

She nodded.

"I suppose Harold has been telling you no man would want you because you're not perfect."

She caught her breath again. "How did you know?"

"Harold's influence is written all over you. Remind me to give him a good kick in the head sometime."

A fleeting smile lifted the corners of her mouth.

"I love you, Melody. And all I want to know is that you love me, too."

All of a sudden she threw her arms around his neck and hugged him as tightly as she could. "I do," she said, sobbing a laugh. "Oh, God, Adam, I love you so much!"

He squeezed her back, rocked her gently and felt a great wind of relief and joy blow through him, sweeping away all the fear and tension. She loved him. Everything else could be worked out.

"I want to marry you," he said into her hair. "I realize you probably don't want to live here, so I'll make arrangements to move to Minneapolis—"

And suddenly everything was going wrong again. Instead of telling him yes, she was pulling back from his embrace and almost glaring at him.

"No," she said.

"No?" Oh, God, she didn't want to marry him!

"Absolutely not!"

"But...if you love me, why don't you want to marry me? I can make more money in Minneapolis."

This time she reached out and covered his mouth with her hand. "No," she said gently. "You love it here."

"But I can—"

She pressed her hand more firmly against his mouth. "Shh, Adam, you're staying right here. And so am I."

He was so used to women objecting to this place that it took him a moment to comprehend. "But you must want to go home."

She dropped her hand from his mouth, shaking her head. "No.

I love it here. I was thinking just this afternoon that I'd love to stay here forever.''

Suddenly the last cloud was gone from his horizon, and his life was full of sunshine. "Really?"

"Really."

The time for words was past. He swept her up into his arms, holding her as close to his heart as he could get her. "I love you," he said huskily. "I love you more than I can ever tell you."

A long time later, he lifted his head and sniffed. "Oh, no! The roast!"

Jumping up, he ran out to the kitchen and pulled the pan from the oven. His three-pound roast now looked about half its original size. "I ruined it."

Melody, who had come into the kitchen behind him, started to laugh.

"What's so funny?"

"I guess this is where we learn from our mistakes." She giggled again. "Never make love while a roast is in the oven."

He switched off the oven, then turned to tug her into his embrace. "I've got a better lesson," he said huskily. "Never put the roast into the oven until *after* we've made love."

She smiled up at him. "And we both need to learn to cook."

"There's a whole lot more we need to learn than that. And the first thing I want you to learn is very simple."

"What's that?"

"Loving you is easy," he said contentedly. "It's the easiest thing I've ever done in my life."

"Where Love Lives"

Chapter 1

Deputy Virgil Beauregard was having the very devil of a day, and it was only noon. He'd already had to answer a domestic disturbance call that involved a couple he considered friends—although he was rethinking that in light of what Alf had done to Mary Lou's face—and he'd been called to the scene of a messy accident involving a bicyclist from Casper and a driver from Michigan.

It wasn't that these things didn't happen from time to time here in Conard County. They just didn't happen all at once—at least, not usually. He had four hours left on his shift, and already he was wondering what the rest of the day held.

He sure couldn't imagine why a man would hit a woman, and especially not for something as ridiculous as making his eggs too dry. There had to be something else going on in that marriage, Beau thought. Or maybe this had been going on all along, but it was the first time Mary Lou had ever called for help. Either way, he was picking his brain, trying to figure out what he might do about it, beyond arresting Alf.

And he was hoping he could spend the rest of his shift doing nothing but handing out a couple of traffic tickets.

The wish was denied almost as soon as he had it. He was driving along the state highway, just cruising and looking for reckless drivers, when he saw a big, black Kenworth cab and white trailer pulled off to the side of the road.

Slowing down, he pulled off on the shoulder, set his flashers going and got out to investigate.

He walked up to the cab while an occasional car whizzed by on the highway, hitting him with hot eddies of air off the shimmering pavement. The temperature was cruising into the high nineties and he figured the truck had probably overheated on this long, slow grade toward the mountains.

But Beau had learned to be cautious, so as he neared the door of the cab, he pressed the palm and fingers of his hand to the side of the truck, leaving a print that could link this truck to him if something happened. You never knew.

He called out, but no head emerged from the driver's window. The driver must have hitchhiked to town for help. Still, he pulled himself up on the step and looked inside to be sure nobody was in there sick or injured. Empty.

But unlocked. That bothered him. He hesitated a moment, then leaned back and opened the door. Nothing appeared to be out of place. Climbing in, he checked out the sleeper. Nothing. Then he saw the keys in the ignition.

Troubled, he climbed out again and considered the problem. It struck him as highly unlikely that the driver would have left his truck unlocked while he went to town, and he sure wouldn't have left the keys in the ignition.

Maybe he had been taken ill and climbed out in a hurry. Beau looked around, wondering if the guy could have staggered off into the tall grasses beside the road and then collapsed.

He walked back to his Blazer and radioed the dispatcher to tell her what was coming down. "I'm going to be looking around the area to make sure the driver isn't hurt out there somewhere. An extra hand or two would be useful."

"Consider it done," Velma told him.

Taking his shotgun from the dashboard clamp just in case, he carried it with him. You never knew, and the way this day was going, anything could happen.

He found the driver two minutes later, lying in the drainage ditch alongside the road, nearly hidden in the tall grass that grew there.

Damn, he thought, somebody'd sure beaten him up good. Kneeling, he touched the guy's shoulder.

"What happened to you, buddy?" he asked. "Are you awake? Can you hear me?"

The man groaned and started to roll over.

"I don't think you should move," Beau said. "You don't know what might be broken. Can you tell me what happened?"

Another groan. "Couple...guys ran me...off the road. Beat me up."

"I can see the beating up part. Listen, I'm a cop. I'm going to radio for an ambulance."

The guy groaned again, and this time he rolled onto his side. His puffy eyes opened up to narrow slits. "I'm okay."

"You don't know that."

"Yeah...I do. I've been clobbered by half the defensive line of the Dallas Cowboys." He groaned again and sat up. "Bruises. Mild concussion. I'll live."

Beau began to believe him. "When did the Cowboys clobber you?"

A grin stretched the guy's swollen face. "More than once."

"So it wasn't a bar fight."

The man gave a choked laugh and winced, holding his side. "Bruised ribs. Definitely. Nah, no bar fight. I just need some ice and I'll be fine."

Turning his head to one side, he spat blood into the grass.

"Well, come on, then. I'll take you to the hospital. You need to be checked out. And while we're driving, you can tell me what happened." He helped the man to his feet. "How long ago did this happen?"

"Maybe twenty minutes."

"Can you remember what the vehicle looked like?"

The driver closed his eyes for a moment, then sighed. "Concussion," he said. "I can't remember. But it'll come back to me. I swear it'll come back to me."

Beau felt a prickle of apprehension. The guy was well over six feet tall, and built just the way you'd expect a pro football player to be built. He couldn't imagine how a couple of guys had managed to beat him up.

"I imagine the other guys don't look much better," he offered.

The driver sighed again. "I have bum knees. And they had a gun."

Beau picked up his shotgun, then locked up the Kenworth cab. By the time he got to his Blazer with the truck keys, he found the driver sprawled in the back seat, unconscious.

Mild concussion, my aunt Nellie's girdle! Beau kept his flashers on all the way to the hospital.

Carol Tate stood beside a gurney in the emergency room, talking to a six-year-old boy who'd just had a cast put on his arm. It had been a simple fracture of the radius, the result of falling out of a tree, and the boy was already forgetting his discomfort as he admired his cast.

"You'll have to get your mom and dad to sign their names on it," Carol told him.

Timmy seemed to like that idea. Wordlessly, he held his cast out to Carol, who smiled and pulled a pen out of her slacks pocket.

"To Timmy, who's been very brave," she read aloud as she wrote. "Big hugs, Carol." Then she drew a little smiley face that made Timmy grin.

Timmy's mom came back into the cubicle and admired the message Carol had written. "Time to go, sport." She smiled at Carol. "See you in church Sunday, Carol."

"As long as Timmy doesn't fall out of any more trees first."

Timmy's mom frowned at her son. "He's not going to be climbing any more trees, are you, Timmy?"

Timmy shook his head in agreement, but Carol saw a spark of mischief in those young brown eyes. She had a feeling she was going to see this child here several more times before he reached maturity.

She stepped out of the cubicle and considered going to the lounge for a cup of coffee. This was her week to work the day shift, but since she'd just stopped working graveyards two days ago, her body was telling her she ought to be sleeping right now. These rotating shifts were hell, even though she understood the need for them. She was probably the only nurse in the hospital who would have agreed to work graveyard all the time, simply so she could have a regular diurnal rhythm. Most of the other nurses preferred the rotation to the possibility of getting stuck with all evening or midnight shifts, which would keep them away from home in the hours they most wanted to be there. Being single, Carol would have preferred regular hours.

The pneumatic doors opened, and she turned automatically to see what problem was arriving now. She saw Virgil Beauregard. "Hi, Beau. What've you got for us?"

"Guy was beaten up alongside the road. He's been going in and out of consciousness since I found him."

She started toward the door.

"Better get an orderly or two," Beau suggested. "This guy's big."

Carol called two of the orderlies and went out with them to Beau's car. When he'd said big, she'd been expecting someone obese. Instead she found someone who would dwarf most of the human race by virtue of height and muscularity.

"Who *is* this guy?" she asked Beau as the orderlies helped the patient out of the car and lifted him onto a gurney. "Some kind of wrestler?"

"Well, it took me a few minutes to figure it out," the deputy answered. "Seeing as how his face is all swollen. But I finally placed him. His name is Tom McKay. He was a Pro Bowl quarterback maybe five, six years ago. Left the game because his knees went bad."

Carol looked at him. "He's had concussions before."

Beau nodded. "Plenty of 'em."

"Not good."

"No, I don't reckon it is."

"Has he been confused?"

Beau shook his head. "When he's awake, he's real clear on what happened to him, except he can't remember anything about the car the other guys were driving. But I wouldn't say he's confused."

Carol nodded and followed the gurney into the emergency room, wishing they had facilities like a CAT scan or an MRI. They would probably have to transport this guy to a bigger hospital. It was one of the disadvantages of living in a county with only five thousand souls. Any time they had a really serious injury, all they could do was stabilize and transport.

Well, she told herself, it did no good to wish. There were plenty of reasons why she stayed here and worked at this tiny hospital, not the least of them that her entire family lived here—well, except for her sister Janet, who had moved to L.A. with her husband. And besides, Conard County was in her blood. She wouldn't be happy anywhere else.

Tom McKay woke up for good when he was on the X-ray table. Pain tended to have a head-clearing effect on him, and the X-ray technicians kept twisting him into shapes that reminded him just how badly he'd been beaten.

He was used to it, though. You didn't play pro football for eight years without going through this on a regular basis. And you didn't play pro ball if you couldn't ignore pain.

What he didn't like was the way those thugs had handled him. He'd stood up to bigger, tougher guys in his day, but he hadn't had to do it when they were pointing a gun at him.

Then there were his knees. The damn things couldn't be relied on anymore, and on the uneven ground beside the road, they'd become a serious liability, locking up on him or giving way at the worst of moments. He'd managed to land a few blows on the guy who was working him over with the club, figuring they were going to kill him anyway, but mostly he got clobbered. He supposed he was damn lucky they hadn't shot him.

And maybe it was time to start thinking about knee replacement surgery. But then he shook his head. No way was he going to do that to himself.

The techs finally got tired of working him over and sent him on his way. He wound up in a private hospital room with a view of purple mountains in the distance. It gave him plenty of time to think about the woman he'd helped and the men who were after her. And as his head cleared, he got more worried about it. Finally he rang for the nurse.

"Can I see a cop?" he asked when she came into his room.

"Any particular cop?"

"Well, if the one who found me is still hanging around, I'll talk to him, but any cop will do."

She nodded and went out, leaving him to stare at the IV needle in his arm and wonder if hospitals just automatically put everyone who came through their doors on IVs.

Half an hour later not one but two cops came through his door. One of them was a tall, lean guy in his thirties, the other one looked to be about fifty.

"I'm Sheriff Tate," said the older guy. "Nate Tate. This is Deputy Beauregard. He's the one who found you. And by the way, your truck has been towed into town and parked at the truck stop. It'll be safe there."

Tom nodded his thanks to the deputy. "Appreciate it."

Beauregard shrugged. "It's my job. How're you feeling?"

"Like I've been in a fight. But I wanted to talk to you about what happened."

First, of course, they took down the basic stuff, like his name and his address.

"Do you know why these guys beat you up?" Sheriff Tate asked.

"Yeah. Actually I do. Yesterday—at least I think it was yesterday. I didn't lose a day here or anything, did I?"

Beau shook his head. "I picked you up just a couple of hours ago."

"Good. Okay, yesterday I came across a woman in a Mercedes pulled off to the side of the road. She had a flat, it was the middle of nowhere, and I figured I ought to stop and see if she needed help. Turns out she didn't have a spare, so I radioed for a tow truck and waited with her. When the guy arrived, he told her she'd need to buy a new tire, and I kind of picked out of it that she couldn't afford both a tire and a tow. So I paid for it. I mean, what the hell. Then I hopped back in my truck and hit the road."

"A woman in a Mercedes couldn't pay for a tire and a tow?" Beau asked disbelievingly.

"Hey, she wasn't scamming me," Tom said. "Believe me, I could read it on her face. And by the way, she looked as if she'd run into a door in the last week or so. She tried to cover it with makeup, but I could still see the bruise on her cheek."

"Which might have something to do with why she didn't have any money," Nate remarked.

"The thought crossed my mind," Tom agreed.

Nate shook his head. "Gelding would be good for some people."

Beau chuckled, and Tom smiled despite his swollen face.

Nate spoke again. "So you had the feeling she was on the run?"

"Definitely."

"Did you get her name?"

"I never asked."

"And you think this was tied in with the guys who attacked you?"

"No question of it. They come zipping past me in this big pickup—" He broke off and looked at Beau. "Told you I'd remember."

Beau nodded.

"Anyway, they pulled in right in front of me and jammed on the brakes. There was oncoming traffic, so I had to go onto the shoulder to avoid hitting them. They sped up, came around in front of me on the shoulder and stayed there, so I figured I'd stop and have a few words with them."

He shrugged, feeling rueful. "Usually when people get a look at me, they develop a case of caution. Didn't work this time. They had a gun."

"Next time don't stop," Nate suggested.

"Next time I'll just ride right up their tailpipe. I could've gone right over them without doing much except dinging my paint." He shook his head and winced as bruised muscles complained. "Live and learn. I wasn't thinking about hijacking or anything like that, though. My trailer's empty."

Nate nodded.

"Anyway, they wanted to know about the woman I'd helped. I told 'em I didn't know anything about her, that I'd just paid for the tow and tire, but I got the distinct feeling they didn't believe me. I was sure they were going to kill me, but I guess they just wanted to have a little fun. They even wanted to know which direction she was headed, but I claimed amnesia. Damned if I was going to tell those punks anything that might help them find her."

Beau looked at Nate. "Alicia?" he said.

"Maybe."

Tom sat up a little straighter. "Alicia? Who's Alicia?"

"A friend of my daughter's," Nate said. "Her sister-in-law has been looking for her. Apparently Alicia disappeared just before divorce papers were served on her husband. Blond, blue-eyed, five foot ten, looks like a model.''

Tom nodded. "That was probably her. And judging by what I saw, she's got a damn good reason to want to disappear."

Chapter 2

Later that afternoon a doctor stopped by to tell Tom what he already knew. Nothing was broken, and there was no sign of internal injuries, but they wanted to keep him overnight for observation. He could live with that.

"You know," said Dr. Roth as he was getting ready to leave, "the primary reason you have no internal injuries is the great shape you're in. All that muscle is a good protector."

Tom nodded acknowledgment. Keeping in shape while driving a truck wasn't always easy, but long years of participation in sports had taught him that he just didn't feel good when he started to let himself go. Of course, he wasn't at the peak he'd been used to during his ball-playing days, but he was still good enough.

Except for his damn knees. He looked down at the bumps under the sheet and shook his head. Damn things just kept right on betraying him. There was a time when those two goons wouldn't have been able to come anywhere near him.

"Time for more ice, Mr. McKay," said the nurse brightly as she came through the door carrying ice packs. "Twenty minutes on the knees and the cheek. But I guess you know that."

He did. Ice packs were old friends.

"Doctor says we can take you down to the whirlpool this evening if you like."

"I like. I feel as stiff as a rusty hinge."

She nodded. "Hardly surprising."

He was lying there under the ice packs when the door opened again and a different nurse entered. This one was wearing blue scrubs and had a fresh, pretty face. She also had some of the most beautiful red hair he'd ever seen, caught up on the back of her head. And mossy green eyes that made him think of forest depths. He found himself hoping she was a physical therapist. Not that he enjoyed physical therapy, but it sure would be nice to spend some time staring at her.

"Mr. McKay? I'm Carol Tate. I'm the nurse who took care of you in the emergency room earlier."

He nodded. "Tate? Any relation to the sheriff who was in here a little while ago?"

"He's my father." Her smile was a warm and friendly expression that immediately drew him. "How are you feeling?"

"No worse than I've felt before from time to time. I'll be okay."

She nodded. "My dad said he thinks you saw Alicia Dreyfus on the road yesterday. She was my best friend when she lived here. I was just wondering..." She hesitated.

"Pull up a seat," he suggested. This was better than physical therapy; he could look at her without having to endure any added discomfort.

"The woman I saw on the road yesterday was tall, blond and very slender. As your father said, she looked like a model."

"That sounds like Alicia," Carol agreed. "When we graduated from high school, I went off to college and she went off to Minneapolis to become a model."

"Well, this woman could certainly have been a model."

"Dad said she'd been...hurt."

"She looked as if somebody might have hit her in the face."

"God!" Carol jumped up from the chair and walked over to the window, where she folded her arms and stared out at the golden afternoon. "When she got married, I didn't even get an invitation, just an announcement. I felt so hurt. And after that she didn't even write to me anymore. I thought she was just busy with her new life but—'' She shrugged a shoulder. "Abusers do that, you know."

"Do what?"

"Cut their victims off from social support. From their families and friends."

"Well, maybe the woman I ran into wasn't her." It was a slender hope, but it was all he could offer her.

"Maybe." She turned and gave him a forced smile. "Thanks for taking the time to talk to me, Mr. McKay."

"Tom. Please."

"Tom. Is there anything I can get for you? I'm off duty, and I'd be happy to get you a book or something."

"How about a twelve-ounce rib steak?"

She laughed, which was just the reaction he'd been hoping to get. "How do you like it?"

"Rare."

"Consider it done." She glanced at her watch. "I'll be back with it around six. How's that?"

He'd thought she was joking, and now he felt embarrassed. "Hey, I was just kidding. You don't have to do that."

The smile she gave him was almost sad. "You helped Alicia when she needed it. A steak is the least I can do."

After Carol Tate left, Tom wondered if Alicia knew that she had a good friend in this part of the world.

Then he wondered why he was even letting himself ogle Carol Tate. He would be on his way again tomorrow, and that was the way he wanted it. No ties ever again. Besides, nobody wanted a beat-up ex-quarterback. His ex had sure proved that.

Carol sat at the counter in Maude's drinking coffee and waiting for two steak dinners to cook. Maybe she was going off the deep end. She knew better than to have dinner with a guy—even one in a hospital bed—who would be moving on in a day or two. She'd made that mistake once, while she was home for the summer from college and a rodeo rider had taken a fancy to her. In her brilliant nineteen-year-old mind, she had believed he would take her with him when he left. Instead, he'd taken his horse and the gold bracelet she'd given him and disappeared without so much as a "see you around."

But she was older and wiser now, and she really didn't have anything to fear from spending a little time with Tom McKay. Just how involved could she possibly get over a steak with a guy who was hooked up to an IV and whose face was so swollen he was almost unrecognizable?

Besides, she felt she owed him something for helping Alicia out. Between what she'd heard from Melody Dreyfus, Alicia's sister-in-law, and what she'd heard today from Tom, she figured Alicia needed every bit of help and friendship she could get.

"There you go." Maude slapped two white foam dinner boxes in front of her. "Now, where's that thermos?"

Carol passed it to her and waited while Maude filled it with fresh coffee. She could have gotten coffee for them from the urn at the nurses' station, but Maude's coffee was better by a country mile.

"Thanks, Maude." She paid for the dinners, then carried them out to her car.

The August evening was golden and warm, perfect for sitting out on the porch with friends or taking a walk. Well, it would still be perfect after dinner, and with the long summer evenings, it wouldn't be dark until around ten. Plenty of time to do something with her friends or her sisters.

When she entered Tom McKay's room, the first thing she noticed was that he was out of bed, off the IV and sitting by the window. He'd even pulled jeans on under his hospital gown.

And the swelling in his face had improved remarkably. His eyes no longer looked like narrow slits, and his jaw was beginning to reveal strong bone structure.

"You look like a different man," she told him.

"Ice can do wonders. Besides, I think I've got my body trained to handle this."

She smiled at that. "Could be."

She cranked the bedside table down to a more convenient height for him and opened the boxes.

"Man, it smells like heaven!" he said appreciatively.

"Maude does a great job with steaks and fries."

"They wanted to give me a soft diet because the inside of my mouth is all cut up." He shook his head. "Tapioca doesn't cut it for me."

She didn't think it would. He was at least six foot five and probably weighed about 230 or 240. He was a big man, all of it solid, and all that muscle needed sustenance.

"I've driven through this town many times," he remarked. "I think this is the first time I ever stopped here, though."

"You and millions of other people. We're hardly an inkspot on the map."

"That's not necessarily a good thing." He passed on the salt—wisely considering the state of his mouth—and chewed a piece of steak cautiously. "Doesn't feel like anything's loose in there."

"You must have cast-iron jaws."

He laughed at that, and Carol began to relax. They were just two people having a casual meal together, and it didn't mean anything at all that she'd gone home, washed her hair, then dressed in her best Western shirt and jeans.

"I'll tell you one thing," he said. "I'm never going to just drive through this town again. I am very definitely going to stop for one of these steaks."

"I'll tell Maude. She'll like that."

"So what's it like, growing up with a sheriff for your daddy?"

Carol's expression was rueful. "Almost as bad as being the minister's kid. Everyone knows who you are, and every little thing you do gets right back to your dad's ear. And dad didn't tolerate much from us, at least, not outside the bounds of what people consider to be normal hijinks. Everybody in this county expected us to be better behaved than average."

"And were you?"

She shrugged and flashed a grin. "How would I know? None of us ever got in trouble with the law, if that's what you mean. But I did get suspended once for arguing with a teacher."

He laughed. "So you're normal."

"I guess. But this is a small community, Tom. Everyone knows everyone else, and I'm not really sure that it was all that much worse for us, being the sheriff's kids. It was sure better than being the child of a family of known miscreants."

"I suppose you have those around here?"

"Well, of course. Every community does. It's just that here we pretty generally know who the problems are."

"Sounds good to me."

"Where did you grow up?"

"Jacksonville."

"So you're a Florida graduate?"

He nodded.

"A lot of great football players come out of that school."

"A few."

She hesitated, then asked, "Was it hard to give up the game?"

"I didn't really have any choice. Not even surgery could put these knees back to one hundred percent."

"But you must've loved what you were doing."

"I sure did." A reminiscent smile curved his mouth. "It was one hell of an adrenaline rush."

"So what do you do now for adrenaline?"

"Get beat up on the roadside for helping damsels in distress."

He said it wryly, and she laughed, feeling a genuine liking for this man.

"Adrenaline's not all it's cracked up to be," he said more seriously. "It's possible to break the addiction. Would I have liked to play one more season? Sure. But not at the cost of hurting my team. You go into it knowing you have a short career expectancy. I had eight really great years."

"I know how I'd feel if I had to give up nursing."

"I miss it," he admitted.

"So how'd you get into truck driving?"

"I figured it was a great way to see the world."

She sensed there was more to it than that, but she didn't feel she could press any further.

"I was thinking about this friend of yours," he said, clearly changing the subject. "Alicia? Is that her name?"

"Yes."

"Well, would she really be coming back here? Wouldn't her husband know to look for her here?"

"Probably." She looked down at her dinner and shoved a piece of lettuce around in the box. "Apparently he did, if he was following her on the road and ran you down just outside of town."

"So maybe it wouldn't be safe for her to come here?"

She looked at him. "Of course it would! Everyone in this county would protect her. My dad's already got his men out looking for her. If she'd just get here, we'd *all* help her out."

He nodded. "What I'm saying is, maybe that's why she isn't here yet. Maybe she feels it's safer to lay low for a while."

Carol sighed and put her fork down, her appetite completely

gone. "I thought she had everything she ever wanted. A glamorous career, a husband..." Her voice trailed off as sadness welled in her. "Now it sounds like she has nothing at all."

"Except a lot of people who care about her. She'll be just fine, Carol. She has the thing that matters most in this world—friends."

As she drove home a little while later, Carol thought about that. It was true, but she wondered why Tom's voice had been tinged with bitterness when he said it.

Which was a whole lot more wondering than a stranger passing through deserved. And a whole lot more than was wise.

Carol spent the rest of the long summer evening playing badminton in the backyard of her parents' house with one of her younger sisters. But finally Krissie, who was in the eighth grade, needed to get ready for bed. Carol went inside with her and hit the refrigerator for a tall glass of ice water. Her dad found her there a couple of minutes later as she was draining the glass.

"You'll hang around until your mom gets home, won't you?" he asked. Marge Tate was at choir rehearsal. All the Tate women had belonged to the church choir in the past, but now Marge and Patty, the Tates' sixteen-year-old daughter, were the only ones who were still members. Carol and her sister Wendy, who was the flight nurse on the county's emergency response team, had had to give it up because their jobs wouldn't let them go to rehearsals every week. Mary had lost interest since going away to college. Janet had moved to Los Angeles. And Krissie had decreed that it was boring.

Carol felt an unexpected twinge of sadness at the way things changed. The Tates no longer kept the full-size van that had once been necessary to transport the parents and their six daughters on family outings. There were no more family outings that included everyone except at Christmas, when they were all home for the holidays, and then most of them had their own cars.

"Sure, I'll hang around," she told her father. He poured himself a tall glass of iced tea, then sat at the kitchen table. She joined him.

"You're worried about Alicia," he remarked.

She nodded. "The more I hear, the more worried I get."

"I can understand that." He leaned forward, resting his elbows on the table. "It seems like only yesterday she was spending every other weekend here. The two of you would get such fits of the giggles." He smiled reminiscently. "It always made me feel good to hear it."

"I still can't figure out how you managed to stand being the only man in a household full of women."

He chuckled. "I'll let you in on a secret. I *liked* it. A father-daughter relationship is something special, and I was blessed six times over."

"Make that twenty or thirty times over. You were overrun by all our girlfriends, too."

"The house does feel empty sometimes now. Patty and Krissie do their best, but they can't create the same kind of confusion all six of you could."

Carol felt herself smiling, and the smile made her feel better. "She *will* come home, won't she, Dad?"

"Alicia? I sure as hell hope so. She may have left six years ago, but I'd hate to think she doesn't know she still has friends here. Especially in *this* house."

"Melody Dreyfus is almost sure this is where she'll come."

He nodded, turning his glass in aimless circles. "Now, about this Tom McKay."

Carol stiffened. She had a feeling she was about to get a fatherly lecture. "What about him?"

"I hear you had dinner with him at the hospital."

"It was the least I could do to thank him for helping Alicia out."

"I agree. It's just that...tomorrow he's going to get in that truck and drive away for good, Carol."

She knew he was remembering the rodeo rider, too, and her cheeks flamed. "How much trouble can I get into between now and tomorrow, Dad?"

"You tell me."

She couldn't think of a thing to say in response, other than, "I'm older now, Dad."

"Right. And so's he. Older than the rodeo rider, I mean. Look, sweetie, I know eligible men aren't growing on trees around here. You're at an age where finding a mate becomes real important. Maybe you ought to think about taking a job somewhere else. Somewhere bigger."

"What? And never come back here to live again?" Carol shook her head. "I think I'd rather stay single."

He half smiled. "Wait until the old biological clock starts really ticking."

"Well, if it does, I'll think about taking a job in Casper or Cheyenne. But for now, I'm happy right where I am."

He nodded, then looked seriously at her. "We have strong family ties, Carol. But you shouldn't let them get in the way of making your own life."

"I'm not, Dad. I went away for four years to college, remember? I saw the big world. Or at least a little corner of it. I've always been happier here."

"Well, so have I, so I can't really say much, can I?"

They exchanged smiles of understanding. But her dad had a final warning.

"Just watch it with this Tom McKay. Yeah, I know he'll be leaving tomorrow, but watch it anyway. This guy is big league, sweetie. He had the world by a string in his day. Lots of money and lots of female admirers. He could do some damage to the heart of a country girl."

"My heart's not going to get involved." She shook her head and laughed. "Golly, Dad! I can't fall in love overnight."

He tilted his head and said with perfect seriousness, "Wanna bet?"

She didn't think about that again until the following afternoon, when one of the nurses passed a note to her. Her stomach sank as soon as she read it.

"Carol," it said, "I'm sorry I didn't get to say goodbye, but I've got a load to pick up in Miles City. Thanks for the dinner. I hope Alicia turns up soon. Tom."

It wasn't love, she told herself. It couldn't possibly be. She didn't know a thing about this guy. It was just an attraction, and she was just disappointed because it couldn't go any further.

But she had the sneaking suspicion that her father knew her better than she knew herself.

Chapter 3

He shouldn't be doing this.

Tom McKay stood outside Conard County Memorial Hospital, kicking a piece of gravel around the parking lot and telling himself he needed therapy. Four days had passed since he'd checked out of this place. He'd picked up his load in Miles City, Montana, and delivered it to Missoula. Now, with nothing pressing for a week or so, he was back here again, waiting for Carol Tate to finish her shift so he could offer to buy her dinner. Which proved he was crazy.

But he wanted to know the identity of the men who'd beaten him. The more he'd stewed about it on the long drive to Missoula, the angrier he'd grown. He sure as hell didn't want them to get off scot-free because nobody could find them.

It had occurred to him that the easiest way to locate these guys was to locate the missing Alicia. Either she would know who they were, or they would come looking for her. Ergo, the best place to find these scumbags was somewhere in Alicia's vicinity. And the easiest way to find Alicia, he felt, would probably be to hang around with Carol Tate.

But hanging around with Carol Tate could be dangerous. He liked the way she smiled, and he liked the way she worried about her friend. Hell, he even liked the way she'd bought him dinner to thank him for helping Alicia on the road. She was the kind of person anyone would want for a friend.

But he didn't want to get involved with her. Once burned, twice shy, as they said. And it was true. He'd married his high school sweetheart and had believed his future to be a golden one. Well, she'd sure as hell taught him differently.

So if he had one brain cell left that hadn't been concussed into jelly, he ought to climb right back up in his rig and keep going. He ought to write off his assailants for the sake of avoiding problems with Carol.

But he didn't take his own advice. Nope. He kept standing right there, calling himself a fool, until Carol emerged from the building and started walking toward her car.

He recognized her instantly. Her hair flamed in the afternoon sunlight, and she had a graceful, athletic way of moving that a former athlete admired. She was at home in her body the way few people were.

"Carol?" He called out to her and saw her freeze. Pause? No, freeze, he admitted. He had the distinct feeling that she'd been hoping she would never hear his voice again. Why?

It was a question that needed an answer, and it was as good an excuse as any to close the distance between them, his boots scuffing the pavement.

Finally—along about the time he figured she was never going to speak to him again—she turned and smiled. "Tom! How are you doing?"

"Just great."

"You sure look a whole lot better."

"Just a few bruises left is all. Say, I was wondering if you'd heard from Alicia."

Was he mistaken, or did she seem to shrink a little? "Not a word."

"I'm sorry to hear that." He hesitated, then thought, What the hell? "I owe you a dinner. Any chance you could join me at Maude's this evening?"

Once again her hesitation was unmistakable. What in the world had he done? He tried a slightly different tack. "Well, if tonight's not convenient, maybe another night? I figured I'd stay here for a while, get acquainted with the town and wait to see if your friend turns up." Why did he have the feeling he'd said exactly the wrong thing?

"I'm sure Alicia would appreciate your concern."

Ahh. Suddenly he understood, and for some crazy reason, he felt a whole lot better. "Alicia probably doesn't care. I'm more concerned about *you*." Which was partly true, now that he thought about it. He imagined she must be worried sick about her friend.

She smiled faintly. "I'm fine, Tom."

He'd always hated shadowboxing in conversation, and this one seemed to be going the wrong way no matter what he said. "Look. I came back here to take you to dinner. You were nice to me, I want to be nice back. Is that some kind of crime?"

She blinked, as if he had startled her. "What do you mean?"

"I get the feeling that no matter what I say, you're going to take it wrong." He watched with great interest as color rose in her face. It had been a long time since he'd known a woman who could still blush. He kinda liked it.

"I'm sorry," she said finally. "I'm just tired. It was a rough shift."

"Well, that's okay. If you're too tired to have dinner with me, maybe we can do it tomorrow. Or the next day."

"No, no, tonight would be fine." She managed a smile then. "I need to shower and change, though. I smell like the hospital."

"So why don't I meet you at Maude's at six?"

"Great. I'll see you there. And thanks, Tom."

He watched her walk away, feeling at once triumphant and stupid. Common sense said he should have jumped all over her initial rejection and departed before he could get himself into any trouble.

But something else in him was as pleased as punch that he'd stood his ground.

And *that*, he told himself, was why he needed a psychiatrist.

Maude put them in a booth. Carol was uneasily aware that she knew every person in the restaurant, and that every one of them was wondering who the stranger was and what she was doing with him. Gossip would be all over the county by morning, and her dad would undoubtedly hear about it. Oh well. The worst that could happen was that she would get another fatherly lecture.

"So you don't have another load to pick up right away?" she asked Tom.

"Not for a couple of weeks. I take time off like this a few times a year. The road can get to be a drag if you spend too much time on it. Of course, I'm luckier than most. I don't depend on driving to support me."

"Then why do you do it?"

He gave her a smile that didn't quite reach his eyes. "Maybe I'm a gypsy at heart?"

Carol already knew her own weakness for gypsies. Alarm bells sounded deafeningly in her head. "Are you planning to keep on driving?"

He shrugged. "That depends, I guess. I keep thinking that one of these days I'll pull over at a truck stop and feel like I've come home."

Carol didn't quite know what to make of that. Did he mean he intended to settle down eventually? Or did he mean something else entirely? Feeling irritated, though she couldn't really say why, she decided to change the subject.

"Well, you'll probably get bored here, if you stay for a while. There isn't a whole lot to do."

"Meaning?"

"Meaning that you're probably used to a lot more in the way of entertainment. Conard City can only offer you a movie house, a video arcade and a couple of bars."

"Mmm." He sounded noncommittal. "So how do *you* spend your time?"

"With family and friends."

"Well, that's generally how I like to spend my time, too." He smiled. "I've got a few good friends from my football days. They're scattered all over hell and gone, but when I'm passing through, I generally stop to say hi. And I spend a lot of time at home with my family in Jacksonville."

"But you don't have any friends here."

"Not yet." He leaned back a little and looked levelly at her. "Are you trying to get rid of me?"

She blushed again and damned herself for the telltale color. "No. It's just that—well, you must have led a really exciting life. I can't see you enjoying a whole week around here."

He nodded, and his eyes narrowed just a little. "Just goes to show you really don't know me."

"I'm sorry. I'm presuming."

He let it go, turning his attention to the menu. It would be nice, Carol thought, if he weren't so damned handsome. What was it about quarterbacks? Why were they all so good-looking? Her mind riffled through the entire NFL, and she couldn't think of a single homely quarterback.

And they all had beautiful wives. She found herself wondering about that. What if this guy was married and just played around on the road? He had mentioned a family, after all. She looked at his left hand but saw no sign of a ring. Which didn't mean a damn thing.

"I was always a homebody," Tom said after Maude took their orders with her usual aplomb and slapped coffee down in front of them. "I married my high school sweetheart. I was just never all that interested in sowing my wild oats, if you know what I mean."

Her heart nearly stopped. "Are you still married?"

He shook his head. "Nope. Liz didn't like living with a crippled ex-quarterback. It was boring, she said. She always did like the attention, the interviews, that kind of thing. And suddenly she was Mrs. Nobody. I guess it was hard on her."

Carol felt an unwelcome flood of sympathy. "You're not crippled."

"No, of course I'm not. But that's what she said. *Washed up* was the other term she used. Basically, I think *she* had some wild oats to sow. She was almost three years younger than me, and we started dating when she was a sophomore in high school and I was a senior. We got married a week after she graduated. As long as being married to me was full of fun and excitement, I guess she didn't know what she was missing."

"Did you have any children?"

He shook his head. "She was never quite ready to do that. Now I'm glad as hell that we didn't."

"I imagine so."

"It was hard enough losing her, but it would have killed me to have to give up custody of my kids. Anyway, she walked away with a big chunk of change, then married another football player."

"Not one of your friends, I hope."

His eyes lowered to the table, then came slowly back to hers. "Unfortunately."

"That's adding insult to injury!"

"That's what I thought." He gave a crooked smile. "But hell. It happens. They were evidently having an affair even before she threw me out. Like I said, wild oats."

Carol had the worst urge to reach out and touch his hand, but she restrained it. She had to be very careful here, she warned herself, because not only was he a good-looking gypsy, but he'd aroused her sympathy.

"Anyway," he continued, "I'm over it. What's that the sociologists say now? That first marriages are just trial balloons these days?"

"Somehow I don't think it felt like a trial balloon."

"Not really." But he laughed and flashed a devastating grin. "Anyway, that's my sad tale. Don't waste any pity on me, though. Plenty of people have been through worse."

She had always respected that attitude, probably because one of her dad's favorite sayings was "I felt bad because I had no shoes until I met a man with no feet." Nate Tate had been full of those aphorisms and had used them liberally in raising his daughters. "It would make you distrustful, though."

He nodded. "Just a bit. But life does that to everyone."

Worse and worse, Carol thought. Now he was a kindred spirit. But she didn't share her own story of betrayal. Besides, compared to his, hers sounded silly. What had she expected out of that rodeo rider, anyway? From her current vantage, she could only look back at her younger self and shake her head.

Their dinners came, and they ate for a while in silence. But then Carol remembered something he'd said earlier, and uneasiness began to prod her. "So you're just going to hang around waiting for Alicia to show up?"

"Not exactly. I'm thinking about trying to look for her."

Now her alarm bells were clanging wildly. She put her fork down and asked bluntly, "Why?"

"Because I figure she'll probably know who the guys are who beat me up."

She wasn't sure she liked that. There was no doubt in her mind that the man sitting across from her could probably take those men apart with his bare hands. "My dad is looking into it. And he'll certainly ask Alicia about those men—if she ever turns up here."

He nodded. "I imagine so. But *I* want to know who they are. And to be perfectly frank about it, now I'm worried about Alicia. I figured that by the time I got back here, she'd have turned up. Now I'm wondering if those two guys found her after all."

Carol's heart lurched. It was the one possibility she hadn't allowed herself to think about. Denial, pure and simple. She pushed her plate aside, appetite gone.

"Sorry," he said, pushing his own plate aside, too. "I'm not going to kid you, Carol. I've got a selfish motive here. I'm angry as hell, and I want the names of those guys. But the more I think about it, the more worried I become about Alicia. Sure, she's a stranger, but I just—well, it gives me a real burn to think of any man mistreating a woman."

So he was going to be a white knight, Carol thought. He'd come for Alicia. Naturally. Alicia had always been the beautiful one, and back in high school Carol had gotten quite used to being ignored by boys when Alicia was around.

But even as she had the disappointed thought, she realized how ridiculous she was being. The last thing on earth she wanted to do was get involved with a road gypsy, and if the gypsy had his sights set elsewhere, she would be safe, wouldn't she?

She spoke. "My dad has every deputy in the county looking for her, Tom. What more can you do?"

"Look where they might not. I mean, they're probably watching the roads, right? What about other places? Aren't there places around here where she could hide for a while?"

Carol nodded slowly, thinking about it. "Lots of them," she said finally. "There's the old ghost town on Thunder Mountain, the national forest...some old line shacks nobody uses anymore."

"Well, the weather's good, it's warm, and it wouldn't be too hard to go to ground somewhere nobody'd ever think to look."

Carol realized she'd curled her hands tightly around her iced tea glass and now her fingers were aching. "I'm scared," she heard herself admit. "Alicia has to know all she needs to do is call my dad, so why hasn't she?"

"Maybe because she figures after all this time y'all aren't so fond of her anymore. Maybe she realizes you were hurt when she didn't invite you to the wedding."

Carol nodded slowly. "You might be right. If her husband is abusive, he'd certainly foster that idea. But her sister-in-law said she talked about us all the time...."

"But she didn't write. She didn't call. And she didn't invite you to the wedding. It'd be enough to make her doubt that you care."

"Besides," Carol said, her brain slipping into gear again, "abused wives tend to feel responsible for the mess they're in. And most of them tend to feel they deserve it, which leads them to think that no one else cares about them."

"There you go. I'll need your help, though, because I sure don't have any idea where these line shacks you mentioned are, or the ghost town. I imagine I could find the national forest, but that's about it."

"I'll help," Carol decided. "I'll definitely help. There was a line shack not too far from Alicia's house that we used to go to on rainy days when we thought we'd go nuts if we had to hang around at home." She gave him a rueful smile. "I have five sisters. Privacy was hard to come by."

"I've got three brothers. I hear you."

"And we did like to go up to the ghost town when we could get a ride." She was reminiscing now, remembering all the things she and Alicia had liked to do on long summer days.

"I gather her family doesn't live around here anymore?"

"There was just her and her dad. He left after she went to Minneapolis. He got a better job in Texas."

"What's he do?"

"Ranch foreman."

"Maybe she went to Texas."

"It's possible, but I'd be surprised."

"Why?"

"She...well, after her mother died, her dad had some problems with alcohol. He got nasty. My dad wanted to throw him in jail more than once for hitting Alicia."

"But nobody took her away?"

"Alicia always claimed it was an accident, and nobody saw it happen."

"Damn." He shook his head. "She was set up for this, wasn't she?"

Carol looked at him, her heart heavy. "I guess she was."

They both looked up as Maude stopped by their table. She

glared down at them. "Suppose you tell me just what's wrong with my cooking."

Carol felt a smile tug the corner of her mouth. "Nothing, Maude. It's delicious, as always."

Maude snorted. "You're not eating. Now *you* might be able to get away with eating like a bird, Missy Tate, but this man is far too big to settle for half a steak."

"I'm going to finish," Tom promised, pulling his plate back in front of him. "It's one of the best steaks I've ever eaten. We just got busy talking."

"And now it's stone cold." Shaking her head, she pulled the plate from in front of him. "Wasteful, that's what it is. I'll bring you another."

After she stomped away, Tom leaned over the table and asked quietly, "Is she always this way?"

Carol's amusement got the better of her and she laughed. "Always," she said. "You can count on it like the rising of the sun."

Just then a man as big as Tom walked through the door of Maude's. He wore a deputy's uniform, and his inky black hair flowed to his shoulders. He glanced around the room, then strode over to their booth and pulled up a chair.

"Hi, Micah," Carol said. "Tom, this is Micah Parish. Micah, Tom McKay."

Micah shook the man's hand. "I used to watch you play ball," he said. "You had one hell of an arm."

"Thanks."

"Is something wrong?" Carol asked. "Does dad need me?"

"Not a damn thing is wrong," Micah said. He leaned back to let Maude put his usual cup of coffee in front of him, along with a piece of blueberry pie.

"And don't give me no crap about going home to dinner," Maude told him sternly. "There's no law that says a man can't have his dessert first—especially when it's my pie."

Micah thanked her with a grin, and Maude went back to the kitchen. "I still find it hard to believe that woman ever referred to me as 'that damn Cherokee deputy.'"

"So nothing's wrong?" Carol asked again. It was unlike Micah to just pull up a chair and join them without an invitation.

"Not a damn thing," he repeated. "Except that your dad saw you come in here with this gentleman."

"Don't tell me he sent you over here to check on me!"

Micah shook his head and cut a piece of pie with his fork. "Of course not, Carol. You know better than that. Velma sent me."

"Velma?" Velma was the dispatcher.

"Yep. I'm under strict orders to find out if this is a date."

Carol felt a burst of irritation. "What business is it of hers?"

"None, really," Micah replied equably. "Except she says she's never going to have another minute's peace as long as your dad is wondering if it *is* a date. So she ordered me to come find out." He looked from one to the other. "So is it?"

Carol and Tom exchanged glances. She could tell he wanted to laugh out loud, but she had never felt further from laughing in her life. "No, it is not!"

"Good. I'll tell her. She'll tell your dad. And the whole damn county can stop getting kinks in the neck from trying to eavesdrop on your conversation."

Carol glanced around the room and noted how quickly people seemed to become busy with their dinners. They *had* all been trying to eavesdrop. Finally, even *she* couldn't resist the humor of it.

"This is not a date," she said loudly and emphatically. "We're discussing a mutual friend."

For an instant you could have heard a pin drop in the diner. Then a fork clinked against a plate, and conversation resumed.

Micah took his time finishing his pie. "It won't hurt Velma to wait," he said with a twinkle in his eye. "And besides, since this isn't a date, I'm not really intruding."

That was when Carol lost it. She met Tom's grinning gaze and finally burst into laughter.

Living in this county was just too much sometimes. And that was precisely why she would never leave.

Chapter 4

Getting up in the morning hurt. It always did. Tom swung his legs over the side of the bed, trying to ignore the ache in his shoulder from years of abuse, the shriek of his spine from old injuries, and the way his knees were going to scream the minute he tried to stand. It was the price you paid for a career like his, and he didn't regret it.

But he sure as hell missed the game.

Getting up in the morning was like trying to oil the joints on a rusty machine. Everything was stiff, everything protested, but if he made it into a hot shower and moved around for a while, most of it would stop. Except his knees. They hurt more or less all the time.

And except for when they kept him from doing something he wanted to, something he used to be able to do, he didn't much think about it. But there were times, such as when those goons had stopped him, that he really missed the body he had once had.

And yet, inside, he still felt capable of all those things he used to do. Ah, well, it was just the hard brick wall of reality. He'd sure as hell run into that more than once.

After his shower, he walked over to the truck stop for breakfast.

He wasn't yet ready for another round of Maude Bleaker. At least at the truck stop the food came without an attached attitude.

The stroll loosened the last of his aching joints, and he was feeling pretty good by the time he sat at the counter and ordered his usual large breakfast of ham, eggs, grits, toast and coffee.

He asked the counterman if there was some kind of gym in this town where he could work out and was amazed when he was told there was.

"It's not much of a gym by city standards," the counterman warned him. "The Y runs it. You got your basic weight-lifting stuff, a couple of treadmills, and maybe one of them new stair-steppers folks got hot on a while back. This time of day, though, it's probably fairly empty."

He got directions to the Y and after breakfast walked into town to check it out. It occurred to him that if he was going to spend any time around here, he'd better rent a car. Driving his Kenworth around town would be ridiculous. Why did he have a feeling that there wasn't a car rental place around here?

The Y was exactly as the counterman had promised. Adequate, but nothing special. He talked to the woman there and found he would be welcome to come in any time, but mornings after nine were usually the quietest.

"We get a lot of business people who like to come in before they work, so it can be pretty hectic between six and nine. And in the afternoon and evening we have various activities for the kids."

He promised he would see her in the morning, then headed out again. He was supposed to meet Carol when she got off work at three, but until then time hung heavy on his hands. He wasn't used to having nothing to do.

He found himself at the courthouse square, looking across the street at the sheriff's office. Remembering the scene last night at Maude's, he started to grin and decided to go inside. Maybe he could reassure the sheriff that he had no designs on his daughter.

A withered crone of a woman sat at the dispatcher's desk puffing on a filterless cigarette and blowing clouds of smoke.

"You must be Tom McKay," she said before he could speak.

"Yes, I am."

"Velma Jansen." She gave him a nod. "You sure had the sheriff in a tizzy last night. That man's real protective of his girls."

"I gathered. Carol and I were just talking about Alicia."

"Alicia." Velma shook her head. "Now there was one sad story. And apparently it's getting sadder. Poor child."

Nate Tate appeared in the doorway leading to the back of the building. "And you've got to learn to mind your own business, Velma."

She snorted. "You made it my business when you started chewing off my head, boss."

Nate ignored her and looked at Tom. "I'm sorry about that unofficial visit from my deputy last night."

"I thought it was funny. Don't worry about it. Micah Parish was pleasant."

"He probably wanted to do it about as much as he'd want to wrestle a rattlesnake, but dealing with Velma here is worse."

"Good," said Velma, unrepentantly. "Somebody's got to keep you all in line."

Nate continued to ignore her. "What can I do for you?"

"I thought I'd just stop by and let you ask all those questions that are probably running around in your mind."

Nate met his gaze levelly, then nodded. "Come on back. I'd offer coffee, but Velma's brew is undrinkable."

"Then make your own damn coffee!" Velma shouted after them.

Tom didn't know what to make of that exchange until he saw that Nate was grinning. The two of them probably made a habit of this.

Nate sat behind a desk heaped with papers, and Tom took a chair across from him. Nate leaned back, gripping the arms of his chair, and studied him thoughtfully. "What questions do you think are running around in my mind?"

"Whether some gypsy truck driver is going to take advantage of your daughter."

The sheriff nodded slowly. "And?"

"I'm not. I came back here to find Alicia Dreyfus and Carol wants to help me. The last thing I want to do is take advantage of a woman who's ten years my junior."

"And who doesn't have any experience of life in the fast lane."

Tom shrugged one shoulder. "I never lived in the fast lane."

"You expect me to believe that?"

"Believe what you want. But the simple fact is, I never took advantage of my status, my money, or groupies. My mama raised me better than that.''

''What do you want with Alicia?''

''Just to find out the names of those guys who attacked me. It's a personal thing.''

Nate sighed and rubbed his chin. ''Just let the law take care of it, son. If you get involved, you might get into trouble. *I'll* ask Alicia about those men. If I ever find her.''

''I'm sure you will. But I want to know for my own satisfaction. And for my own satisfaction, I want to know Alicia's okay. If those goons were willing to do that to me just because I wouldn't tell them where to find her, then I hate to think what they'd do to her.''

''I've been thinking about that,'' Nate agreed. His gaze was steady as he looked at Tom. ''I can't prevent you from looking, son, but around here the law applies equally. If you've got any notion about doing anything other than finding out the names of those guys, I'll come down on you so hard you won't know what hit you.''

''That's the way it should be. And don't worry about Carol, Sheriff. I like her, and I'm not going to hurt her.''

''That might not be entirely under your control.''

''So let me put it another way—I won't mislead her.''

''I guess I can't ask for any more than that.''

Carol heard about Tom's visit to the sheriff's office just before she got off work that afternoon. Velma, she thought. Velma couldn't keep a secret to save her life and had blabbed all over the place about Tom coming by to reassure the sheriff he had no evil designs on Carol.

Which caused Carol to start a slow burn. She didn't know whether to be angrier at Velma or her dad. All these years she'd appreciated him for being ''hands-off,'' the kind of father who let his children lead a reasonably normal life despite his position in the county. A dad who had let her pick her own friends and learn from her own mistakes.

What had gotten into him? Why was he interfering *now*, when she was no longer a child? Darn it, he hadn't even said much about that stupid rodeo rider except for one brief warning that the guy wasn't the "staying kind."

And this time she was older and had *already* told him she wasn't going to get involved. So what was with him? Why was he embarrassing her like this?

But maybe it was all Velma. Hadn't Micah said so last night? And Micah never lied. So it had to be Velma. But whether it was Velma or her father, the whole damn county was probably chuckling about how protective Nate Tate was being.

And this kind of stuff was apt to guarantee she would never have another date so long as she stayed in this county. The thought turned her anger to gloom, and she began to wonder if she shouldn't take her father's advice and move somewhere else. Somewhere that would put a thousand miles between them—and not because of the dearth of available men in Conard County.

But by the time she walked out the door at the end of her shift, she'd given up on anger and embarrassment and had settled on amusement. It was the only armor that worked in a community this small, because there was absolutely no way you could keep a secret or lead a private life. Sooner or later, everyone knew everything about you.

At home, she showered and changed into jeans and hiking boots, then set out to pick up Tom at his motel, as she had offered to do last night. He was waiting for her out front.

"I appreciate the lift," he said. "It seems I can't rent a car around here."

"No, that's one of the things we don't have here."

"Don't people's cars ever break down?"

"Of course. But the local garages drive their customers around if they need it, and most folks don't. If you live on a ranch, you've probably got more than one vehicle. And if you live in town, you can get everywhere by walking. A car rental business wouldn't last three months."

He nodded. "It's a different way of life here, isn't it?"

Carol thought about the gossip that was probably going around right now. "I guess it is. We're almost like one big, extended family."

"That must be interesting." He was silent for a few minutes. "So where are we starting today?"

"I figured we'd check the ghost town first. I was thinking about

Alicia last night, and I remembered how she used to say the ghost town would be a perfect hiding place. It's so quiet up there you can hear somebody approaching long before they arrive, and some of the buildings are still intact enough to provide reasonable shelter. And almost nobody goes up there except my sister Janet.''

"Why does she go?"

"She's been photographing it ever since she got her first camera. It's really incredible to look at the photos now, because you can see how the weathering and decay are advancing with time. And the play of light and shadow is really dramatic.''

"So if Alicia were up there, Janet might have run into her?''

Carol shook her head. "Janet lives in Los Angeles now.''

"Oh.''

She glanced over at him. "I'm sorry Velma and my dad are hassling you.''

He surprised her with a laugh. "Actually, it was funny last night when Micah joined us. And your dad hasn't bothered me at all.''

"But this morning...'' She trailed off, not knowing exactly what to say or how to say it.

"You heard about me going to the sheriff's office?'' He flashed a smile. "I did that on my own, Carol. I happened to be nearby, and I thought about Micah's visit last night, and I figured we'd all be a whole lot more comfortable if I told your dad I don't have any designs on your virtue.''

"Oh.'' The flutter of disappointment she felt scared her. She absolutely, positively could *not* let herself feel this way. Not if she wanted to avoid trouble. And worse, she felt embarrassed that Tom had deemed it necessary to tell her dad that. God, was there a hole somewhere she could crawl into?

"He has every right to be protective of you, Carol,'' Tom said. "If I were in your dad's shoes, I'd have been feeling uneasy, too. You're a beautiful woman, and I'm just passing through.''

There it was again, that "passing through'' thing. And that was what she had to keep in mind. In a few days, a week at most, he would be gone, carried away on the prairie winds. So it shouldn't give her a glowy feeling that he thought her beautiful. Or, even if it did, she ought to ignore it.

And when had she become a ditherer like this? Stifling a sigh, she turned her Jeep onto the rutted wagon track that led to the abandoned mining town on the slopes of Thunder Mountain.

They had climbed to almost eight thousand feet by the time Carol stopped the car on the edge of the ghost town. The warm summer day had become considerably cooler at this altitude, though the sun still felt hot on her skin.

Weather-silvered shacks leaned at awkward angles near holes in the ground, some of which still had wooden derricks towering over them. Near the mine shafts, huge mounds of slag remained bare and lifeless. There had been some talk of cleaning up the slag, which contained high levels of poisons brought up from deep in the earth, but so far, no money had been found to do so.

And Carol never saw those slag piles without thinking about the men who had moved all that with picks and shovels. It boggled her mind.

Tom turned in a slow circle, taking in the abandoned buildings and the dark depths of the encroaching pine forest. "This place is fantastic," he said. "You can almost feel the hopes and the dreams of the people who built it."

The sentiment surprised her. She hadn't expected it from a former athlete. Of course, her knowledge of jocks was pretty limited. There was no reason to think they couldn't be intelligent or perceptive. She noticed he was limping as he started to walk farther into the town, and she wondered if his knees were stiff after the long ride.

"Man oh man," he said, with all the delight of a boy "I would have loved exploring this place just for the hell of it when I was a kid. Heck, I'm going to enjoy it right now."

"I love it up here," Carol agreed. "It's so peaceful, but there's still so much to look at and wonder about."

He nodded and peered into one of the buildings through a glassless window. "You wonder if whole families lived in these little shacks, or if it was just the miners themselves."

"I don't know. I suppose some of them had families. I always wonder how they got through the winters. It gets pretty inhospitable down below, but up here it must have been really tough at times. If they stayed. I don't know if any of them did."

"Probably. Folks were a lot tougher about things back then. I mean, look at the settlers in the sod huts on the Great Plains. They didn't go back to New York for the winter."

"You're right."

He peered into one of the mine shafts, a big black hole in the ground. "It's starting to fill in."

"Don't get too close to the edge," Carol warned. "The ground isn't stable, and the shoring is getting rotten."

He nodded and stepped back. "How far do some of these shafts run?"

She shrugged. "This whole town is a warren of tunnels." She pointed to the north. "Over there you can even see where some of them have collapsed. There are big, long trenches in the ground."

"Did they ever find much?"

"Some gold and silver, but not enough to turn this place into a thriving town. It was all but played out after about five years."

They spent the next hour exploring the buildings and surrounding area, looking for any sign that someone might have been living here recently. They found nothing.

"Guess we'd better head back," Tom said. "Let me buy you dinner at Maude's."

It was already nearly seven, and it would take a couple of hours to get back to town. "Maude'll be closing up by the time we get back," Carol said. "I'll cook us something."

"You don't have to do that. I can eat at the truck stop."

Carol knew she should have agreed, but some devil made her shake her head and say, "I don't mind. I've got some stuff in the freezer that'll be easy to heat up."

He smiled and nodded. "Thanks."

She wished he wouldn't smile like that. When he did, all her common sense took flight and she started thinking, *If only.*

God, if she didn't watch it, she was going to get herself into serious trouble.

They were walking side by side toward her Jeep when, without warning, the ground gave way beneath Carol. She felt herself beginning to fall, but almost quicker than the eye could see, strong arms reached out and grabbed her.

Tom clutched her to his chest and ran toward the Jeep. Moments later, Carol found her feet on firm ground again, though she could feel the earth trembling, and could hear the shriek of twisting and breaking timber.

Slowly, she turned her head to look at the spot where she had been standing.

There was now a trench six feet deep and nearly twelve feet long where her feet had been moments ago. A shudder passed through her, and she looked up at Tom.

"I don't think this is a safe place to hang around," he said.

Feeling dazed, she nodded and looked again at the trench, thinking about how fast and strong Tom McKay must be to have snatched her away almost before the ground had started to sink. And what if she had been caught in the collapsing earth? She might have been buried alive....

She looked up at him again and saw the way his jaw was clenched, how white his lips had become. "You're hurt!"

He shook his head. "Just my knees. They aren't what they used to be. But don't worry about it. They'll stop screaming at me in a minute."

And then the universe did a strange thing. All of a sudden Carol became acutely aware of how tightly he was holding her to his chest. She was sure he didn't mean anything by it. He was hurting and was probably holding on to her unconsciously as he waited for his knees to settle down.

But, unconscious or not, she felt the hush in the air around them, as if every tree were holding its breath in anticipation. She, too, stopped breathing, in exquisite, agonizing hope. Every cell in her body was suddenly aware of nothing but him, of how strong and hard he felt against her, of how big he was—of how much she hoped he would kiss her. It was as if nothing else in the world existed but this moment and this man.

She closed her eyes, waiting...and then he let go of her.

"We'd better get the hell out of here," he said almost gruffly. "That cave-in has probably destabilized the whole tunnel system."

Reality was like a cold slap in the face. She managed a jerky nod and climbed into her Jeep. He limped his way around to the other side and climbed in beside her.

"I sure as hell hope Alicia isn't hiding out around here," was all he said as she turned the car around and headed for the highway.

She couldn't even manage to say, Me, too. She couldn't manage to say anything at all.

Chapter 5

Carol rented a little house on the edge of town, a small two-bedroom place with wooden floors that sloped with age. It had probably started as one or two rooms, but with the addition of rooms over time it had developed the floor plan known as the "gunshot" because, it was said, if you fired a bullet from the front door, it would pass straight through every doorway in the house.

The front room was her living room. Next came the two bedrooms, and finally the large kitchen, with the bath off of it. Since she lived alone, the floor plan didn't bother her, but having to walk Tom through the entire house to the kitchen made her a little uncomfortable, especially walking him through her bedroom—where, of course, she had forgotten to make her bed this morning. Naturally. The one morning she forgot, she had to bring a stranger through. If he noticed, though, he didn't say anything about it.

She had made some effort to brighten the kitchen with fresh paint, cheerful flowered curtains and pots of herbs on the windowsills. She had found a big round pedestal table at a garage sale and refinished it without removing the deeper gouges, dents and nicks, giving it the feeling of a family heirloom. Maybe someday, she sometimes thought, it would be. The chairs, too, were old and had needed some work to repair broken and loose joints, but they went well with the table.

Tom sat in one, and she was relieved when it didn't creak or groan under his bulk. Apparently she'd done the repairs well.

He stretched his legs out before him and began to rub his right knee.

"Would you like some ice?" she asked.

"If it's not too much trouble, that'd be great."

She had some reusable ice packs in her freezer, left there after she had twisted her ankle last year. She gave them to him, and he held them on his knees.

"Have you thought about knee replacement?" she asked.

"Several times. The problem is, they can't guarantee that I'll feel any better."

"It would probably be more stable."

"Maybe. But if I'm still going to have the swelling and discomfort...I don't know. It's major surgery, and when they told me what they'd have to do—well, I think I'll stick with what I've got as long as I can walk."

"I guess I can understand that." Returning to the freezer, she asked, "You like salad and lasagne?"

"Love them both."

She popped a dish of frozen lasagne in the microwave and started preparing the salad.

"What can I do to help?" he asked.

"Keep the ice on your knees." She tossed a smile over her shoulder. "This'll only take a few minutes."

Twenty minutes later, just as Tom was putting the ice packs back in the freezer, she placed homemade lasagne, Caesar salad and garlic bread on the table.

"Fit for a king," he said with a pleased sigh after he tasted everything.

"Thank you." She hesitated, then asked, "What really made you decide to drive trucks?"

The look he gave her was almost rueful. "Cowardice."

"Cowardice?"

"Running. Same thing. After the divorce, I wanted to get away from everything that reminded me of Liz, so I took to the road."

She felt another surge of sympathy for him. "It's nice if you can get away from it."

He tilted his head inquisitively. "Why do I have the feeling *you* couldn't get away from something similar?"

She felt color stain her cheeks again and hoped he couldn't see it in the reddish sunset light that was pouring through the windows. "I got away," she said finally. "I went back to college."

"But you still had to come back here every summer, right?"

"Right."

He nodded. "Not easy in a town this size. In fact, I figure it's about the same as it was for me. I mean, people I didn't know knew about me and my marriage. Kinda hard to keep secrets when the sports magazines and *First Edition* want to announce it to the world."

"They did that to you?"

"Sure. One of the perks of being a celebrity." His tone was dry, but not at all bitter. "I think I was trying to get away from that as much as I was trying to get away from reminders of Liz. My lawyer tried to get the divorce hearing in camera, arguing that there was no compelling need for the public to know the details, but *First Edition* and a couple of magazines argued against it, and we lost."

"That's awful!"

"Well, I tried everything else I could think of. I offered her a huge settlement, but she wouldn't take it. Apparently she felt she could get more by going to trial."

"Did she?"

He shook his head. "The judge felt she was at a disadvantage, since I'd married her right out of high school so she didn't have any work qualifications or experience, but he lost some of his sympathy when the details of her affairs came out. So she didn't get the alimony she wanted, just the community property. Which was fine by me. The thing is, if she'd gotten alimony, I'd probably have had to take some job I didn't want in order to be able to meet it."

"Why?"

"They have this thing called 'imputed income' in Florida. It doesn't matter what you're *actually* making. If the court thinks you ought to be making more, that's the amount they use to calculate the alimony."

"Ouch!"

"Well, it's a way to keep people from quitting their jobs so they don't have to pay. I understand that, but if they'd set alimony based on what I could make as a network broadcaster, then I'd have had to take the job, even though I really didn't want it."

"Really?"

He shrugged. "Cowardice again. Standing there watching a game I couldn't play anymore because some defensive lineman clobbered me from the side and blew out my knees was a little more than I could handle right then, on top of everything else. It wouldn't bother me now, but at the time I wanted to get away from football as much as I wanted to get away from Liz."

He tilted his head again, then smiled. "In fact, I guess I was running from a whole bunch of stuff."

"Maybe you just needed some peace, quiet and privacy to assimilate everything. It was a real one-two punch, wasn't it?"

"It felt like it. So I crawled into the cave of my Kenworth cab and licked my wounds for a few years." He shook his head and laughed ruefully. "At first I just wanted to be left alone. Then I discovered I loved it. Now...now I don't know anymore. It's beginning to feel aimless. I guess I need to set some goals."

Carol could understand that. You didn't get to be a pro football player without a lot of drive and determination in addition to talent. That kind of nature wouldn't be happy for long without something to work for.

"So," he said, "what's *your* deep, dark secret?"

She felt her cheeks flame again and looked down at her plate. What the hell? she decided finally. He'd told her plenty. She ought to reciprocate. And it didn't matter what he thought of her, anyway, since he would be back on the road in a few days. "An old country-and-western song. Teenage girl and unscrupulous rodeo rider just passing through town."

He put down his fork and reached across the table, touching the back of her hand with his fingertips. "I'm sorry. That must have hurt like hell."

"At the time. Now I'm just embarrassed I could have been so stupid. That I could have let myself be used like that."

His fingertips stroked the back of her hand gently. "My pappy always says the only fool is one who doesn't learn from his mistakes."

"So does *my* dad." Feeling inexplicably better, she lifted her gaze and smiled at him—and felt the earth stand still. Every cell in her brain stuttered to a halt, locked on one realization: he was gorgeous, absolutely gorgeous, and she wanted him even more than she'd wanted that rodeo rider six years ago.

Something hot flickered in his gaze, something dangerous. She felt the heat wash over her until every cell in her body seemed to glow.

All of a sudden he jerked his hand back, as if touching her had scalded him, and looked down at his plate.

"Really great dinner," he said again, his voice sounding thick. "You're a wonderful cook."

"Thanks." She had to force the word through a throat suddenly locked with disappointment.

He's just passing through, she reminded herself. They both knew that, and she ought to be grateful that he didn't want to take advantage of her. Yes, gratitude, that was what she ought to feel.

So why was it that the only thing she did feel was an ache for what could never be?

Tom carefully avoided making plans to meet Carol the next afternoon. It wasn't that he didn't want to find Alicia—hell, he had a burning in his gut to find out the names of his assailants and see them put behind bars—but he was afraid of Carol Tate. Afraid *of* her and afraid *for* her.

He had insisted on walking back to the motel, over her objections about his knees, because he needed to get away from her. She was clouding his judgment more than any woman he'd ever known. He hardly knew her, but he was ready to throw over all his resolutions about never becoming involved again.

And that was a bad thing, because he couldn't make her the kinds of promises a woman like her had every right to expect. He couldn't promise forever. He would never be able to promise that again, because the one time he had, forever had turned out to be just a few years long and had been thrown back in his face in the most vitriolic way possible.

So he wasn't a believer in forever anymore. And at this point, he didn't even think he could promise next week.

When he got back to the motel, he filled an ice bucket at the machine, then wrapped the ice in towels and put it on his knees.

If he wasn't careful, he was apt to find himself unable to walk at all tomorrow.

Which, as problems in life went, was a relatively minor one, but the only one he could do something about right now.

He lay back on the bed, with the ice on his knees, and stared up at the ceiling. The plaster was cracked in some interesting patterns, so he played mind games, trying to see various states or countries in the outlines. Unfortunately, the universe had played a joke on him, and the outline he identified most frequently resembled Carol Tate's profile.

Damn, he thought, giving in, she had the most beautiful red hair. And those beautiful eyes, that looked at once kind and peaceful. He could easily imagine drowning in those eyes.

As for the rest of her...well, nature had blessed Carol with exactly the kind of body that most attracted him, sweetly curved but not too voluptuous. She was the kind of woman he could fantasize about for years.

And fantasize was all he was going to permit himself to do, because he didn't want to hurt her. She wasn't the kind of woman who could have a fling unscathed, and he wasn't the kind of guy who liked flings, anyway.

But he could sure as hell think about her, and that was what he did while the ice chilled his knees and thoughts of Carol inflamed the rest of him.

It was a shame, he found himself thinking, that he hadn't met her before Liz. He had the feeling that no matter how disenchanted she might become, Carol Tate was not the kind of woman who would cheat on a man.

But what did he know? He never would have believed that about Liz, either, until she rubbed his face in it.

Reminding himself of that fact, he tossed the ice into the bathtub, hung the towels to dry, wrapped himself around the poor comfort of a pillow and drifted off into sleep.

Carol followed him even there.

Carol's "weekend" occurred in the middle of the week this time, and she woke up on her first day off determined to make the most of it. The memory of Tom McKay sat at the back of her mind like an almost-toothache, not painful yet, but twinging from time to time in warning.

She was lucky, she told herself. The man hadn't taken advantage of her. In fact, he'd had the common decency to disappear before she could get herself into trouble. He was a real gentleman.

She called her sister and mother, and offered to take them shopping. Krissie, who was still too young to have a summer job, leapt at the opportunity to do something different.

Their mother, Marge Tate, declined the invitation, saying she had to get ready for the Sheriff's Auxiliary tea that afternoon. The wives of the Conard County deputies were working on a fund-raiser for the Police Athletic League. "We need new basketball hoops," Marge told her daughter. "Heaven knows how these kids do it, but even the ones that are made with chain-link baskets don't last a whole season."

"I think it's all that hanging they do from the hoops, Mom."

"Could be. The soccer balls are also worn out, the backstop at the baseball field is full of holes...." She trailed off and laughed. "Listen to me! You'd think I paid for them myself!"

"Well, count me in for a donation. Remind me to write you a check—but not until we get back from shopping. I'll have to see what I have left after Krissie buys everything in the store."

"Don't spoil her, now!"

"Of course not. But I remember how important clothes were when I was her age."

"Buy *yourself* something, dear. Something pretty. You've earned it."

But what was the point? Carol wondered. Around here there was no place to dress up for and no reason to most of the time. Krissie had her friends in school to impress, but Carol had no one, and the contents of her closet were more than adequate for church and the occasional date.

Freitag's Mercantile had a department that catered to high school girls, with clothes that would probably be out of date by that age-group in California but were considered the height of fashion here. Krissie surprised her, though—and relieved her—by not wanting extremely short skirts.

"Are you kidding?" Krissie said as she looked through the racks. "The boys already gawk enough. Besides, jeans are more comfortable."

In the end she bought a demure dress that she could wear to church and a pair of pumps with one-inch heels.

My sister, Carol found herself thinking, *is more sensible than I am.*

It was Carol who, when they passed by a small boutique on their way to get ice cream, fell in love with the dress in the window. She halted and stood staring at it. It was a sea-green voile with a subdued dusty-rose flower print, and a short sea-green matching jacket.

"Ooh, that's pretty," Krissie said, looking over her shoulder. "You'd look wonderful in that."

A familiar voice spoke from behind them. "Yes, she would."

Carol whirled around and found Tom McKay standing at the curb. He was wearing jeans, boots and a white Western shirt, and she felt her heart leap at the mere sight of him.

"You *would* look wonderful in that dress," he said again.

"So buy it," Krissie said to Carol. Then she turned to Tom. "Hi. I'm Krissie Tate, Carol's sister."

"Tom McKay."

"I heard about you," Krissie said with the ingenuousness of her age.

"Everybody in town seems to have heard about me."

"Well, sure," Krissie said. "You're a famous football player. The guys are talking about you all the time. They kind of wish you'd come to football practice some afternoon before you leave. They start practice three weeks before school opens," she added, in case he didn't know that.

"So they're already practicing."

She nodded. "They do it every morning at ten, if you want to drop by."

"Maybe I will."

Krissie turned back to Carol. "So go in and try the dress on."

It *did* seem to have her name on it, Carol admitted as she dragged her gaze away from Tom and back to the dress.

"Go on," Tom said.

And going into the store would be easier than standing out here talking to Tom any longer, she realized. He made her want things she couldn't have.

"Okay." She ducked into the store's cool interior with relief and hardly noticed that Krissie didn't follow her.

Krissie perched on the bench in front of the drugstore next door and looked up at Tom. "I bet Wanda—she's the woman who owns the store—put that dress in the window because she knew one of us would see it."

"One of you?"

"One of us Tate women with red hair," Krissie elaborated. "Mom says Wanda buys with certain customers in mind, and she knows their tastes. Nothing she puts in the window ever stays there long."

Tom nodded and wished he could see Carol in that dress. Instead, all he could do was watch as a woman removed it from the mannequin in the window and carried it back into the dark depths of the store.

Krissie spoke. "Do you like my sister?"

Tom felt a jolt of surprise, quickly followed by a nervousness he hadn't felt since the last time he faced a really big game. Buying time, he lowered himself to the bench beside Krissie.

"Do you?" she asked again, with childlike persistence.

"Sure," he said finally, hoping he sounded offhand. "She's a nice lady."

"I don't mean like *that,*" Krissie said.

Of course she didn't. Tom focused his gaze on a woman across the street who was trying to encourage two toddlers to get into a car. When Krissie kept staring at him, waiting, he fell back on the lame, "Your sister and I are just friends."

"Mmm." Krissie, still caught between childhood and adulthood, began to swing her legs. "Dad keeps telling her she needs to move to the city so she can meet a nice man."

Tom didn't know why, but he didn't like that idea. "Not very many eligible men around here, huh?"

Krissie grimaced. "Not when you get to be Carol's age. In high school, yeah, there are lots of guys. Some of them are even okay. But by the time they're twenty-five, most of them are married—if they haven't moved away."

"And so are most of the girls, then," he suggested, finding himself somehow fascinated by this conversation.

"Yeah. Carol dated Dr. Adam for a while, but it didn't work out, and now he's hanging around with Alicia's sister-in-law."

"I gather you want to see Carol married."

Krissie shrugged. "What I want is to see her *loved*. Nobody ever loved her that way, you know?"

He nodded slowly, thinking that there was wisdom in this child-woman.

"Anyway," Krissie continued, "most of the good guys leave town. Not enough opportunity here, Dad says. And most of the girls stay, because this is home. I'm going to leave, though."

"You are?"

"Sure." She waved a hand and grinned at him. "I want adventure, you know? I can always come back here if I want, but I want to see things and do things I could never do here. Janet went to school in California. I think I'll do that, too."

"How many of you are there?"

"Us Tate kids, you mean? There are six girls, and we have a brother, too. He's in the SEALs."

"So he left for adventure, too."

Krissie shook her head. "He didn't grow up here."

Tom wanted to ask about that, but didn't feel he ought to pry.

"He was adopted," Krissie continued. "Everybody knows the story. He was born before Mom and Dad were married. Dad was in Vietnam—he was in the Special Forces—and back then girls didn't keep babies out of wedlock, and besides, Mom thought Dad was dead. Anyway, a few years ago Seth suddenly turned up, looking for his birth parents." She shook her head. "Boy, did that cause an uproar for a while. Dad moved out and would hardly talk to Mom until he got used to the idea."

"You mean he didn't know about your brother?"

Krissie shook her head. "Mom never told him. There was nothing he could do about Seth at that point, and she thought it would only hurt him."

"Man!" Tom thought about what a hoopla that must have been.

"It's okay now, though," Krissie assured him. "Everything worked out."

"That's good."

"They're really in love, you know," Krissie said. "My mom and dad, I mean. I want the same thing someday. And that's what Carol deserves."

"She certainly does." Hell, it was the kind of thing he wanted for himself, a relationship that could stand up to anything, a love that endured no matter what.

Not that he believed in that anymore, he reminded himself. He'd learned about reality the hard way.

Just then Carol walked out of the boutique barefoot, wearing the new voile dress and jacket.

"What do you think?" she asked brightly, looking at Krissie. "Do I buy it?"

Tom rose instantly to his feet, ignoring the sudden stab of pain in his knees. "Buy it," he said huskily. "Buy it and wear it tonight."

She looked at him, her expression uncertain. "Tonight?" she asked hesitantly.

"When I take you out to dinner," he answered. "At the fanciest restaurant in this entire state."

Chapter 6

She never should have accepted the invitation, Carol thought as she waited nervously for Tom. *Never.* What had happened to all her common sense?

Why had she ever stepped out of that store to ask Krissie what she thought of the dress? *Because you wanted to see Tom's reaction,* answered some honest little corner of her mind. That scared her to death.

Damn, she was a fool. She hadn't even asked *where* they were going to dinner. It was almost as if she'd lost the will to stand up for herself.

She kept waiting for the phone to ring. Krissie surely would have spilled the news to everyone in the family by now, and she kept waiting for her mother to call and caution her, or her father to call and remind her that Tom was just passing through.

But nobody called, and at four-thirty Tom picked her up in his big, shiny black Kenworth and drove her to the airport.

The airport? She looked at him. "What are we doing here?"

"I chartered a plane," he answered. "We're flying to Denver for dinner."

"Denver? I thought you said we were going somewhere around here."

"I said in *the state.*" He flashed her a grin. "I changed my mind. Denver has more to choose from."

Flying to Denver. She didn't know whether to be wowed or terrified. The people she knew—with the exception of Jeff Cumberland, who owned his own plane—didn't just fly to Denver for dinner. The people she knew couldn't afford this kind of extravagance.

But apparently Tom McKay could, which raised questions about why he was doing this. Was he just hoping to dazzle her enough to seduce her?

The thought should have appalled her, but instead it caused a warm tingle deep inside her. Nobody had ever wanted to seduce her badly enough to try to dazzle her. The rodeo rider had simply taken advantage of her youth and never spent a dime on her. Chartering a plane was in a whole different league.

She decided she could handle it. She certainly didn't *owe* him anything for taking it upon himself to go to these lengths. And the word *no* was very much in her vocabulary these days.

So, she decided firmly, she would have a fun evening, stand her ground if he made a pass at her and come home no worse for the wear. It wasn't an impossible situation.

The noise of the small twin-engine plane made conversation difficult, which was just as well, because Fred Hollister was flying the thing, and Fred was one of the biggest gossips in the county, second only to Velma Jansen. The tale of this trip was going to be all over the place by tomorrow morning, and Carol didn't want to add to it by providing any additional fodder.

They caught a cab at the Denver airport, and it was while they were driving into town that Carol realized Tom looked almost angry.

"Is something wrong?" she asked him.

He shook his head.

"You look angry."

He finally turned toward her. "I'm not angry at *you.* Really."

She hesitated, wondering whether to press him further, then deciding to change the subject. "Do you do this kind of thing often?"

"No. This is the first time."

"Well, if you're worried about the cost..." She didn't quite know how to end that sentence. If he was worried about the cost, he shouldn't have done this. *She* certainly hadn't *asked* for it.

"Money's the last thing I'm worried about." After a moment, he smiled. "I'm sorry. I'm being a bear. I'm having mixed feelings about this."

"Really?"

"Yeah." He gave a quiet laugh. "I just wanted to take you out to dinner someplace, where we wouldn't be bothered by a deputy."

Color stained her cheeks. "You didn't have to..."

"That's the other thing. I didn't *have* to. I *wanted* to." He sounded as if that didn't please him.

Well, why should it? Carol wondered. He had as much reason not to want to get involved as she did, maybe more. The understanding relaxed her, and suddenly she felt like smiling again.

"Hey," she said, "let's just enjoy dinner. No complications. Neither of us wants any of those, so we'll just laugh, talk, eat and go home, okay?"

He looked at her, and his face slowly relaxed. "Yeah," he said, "we'll just have a good time."

They dined at a Japanese restaurant, where they ate kobe steak and sushi. Afterward he asked if she wanted to go dancing or if she would prefer to do something else.

She should have suggested something else. Miniature golf, a movie—anything but dancing. "Your knees," she began, trying to find any excuse she could to avoid doing what she most wanted to do, which was dance with him.

"They're pretty good today, and a little dancing won't kill them."

Then she had to hope he took her to some wild place where people danced without touching. Instead he took her to a club with low lighting and soft, easy music. His knees, she reminded herself. He couldn't dance at one of those wild places without hurting his knees.

It was a great excuse until he took her into his arms. Then there were no excuses left at all. She melted. In an instant she was leaning against him, as soft and yielding as she had ever in her life felt.

Her last resistance died; all her fears and concerns evaporated as if they had no substance at all. All that existed in the world was the man who held her.

He drew her a little closer, and she went willingly, feeling as if some long aching need was filled by the feel of his strength against her. Gently they swayed together as the music wove a seductive spell around them and time slipped away.

She could have stayed there forever.

"We need to go," Tom murmured.

Feeling almost dazed, as if she were waking from sleep, she opened her eyes and tilted her head back to look at him.

"It's nearly midnight," he said. "The plane's waiting for us, and I need to get you home."

She nodded, even though she wanted to stay right where she was. He let go of her, stepping back and taking her hand. Neither of them said anything as he led her out of the club.

This time in the taxi, though, this time they didn't sit as far apart as they could get. This time Tom slipped his arm around her shoulders and drew her close, so that her head rested on his chest.

She felt the lightest brush against the top of her head and wondered if he had kissed her. She hoped he had, feared he had, and closed her eyes against the warring emotions within her. She wanted him. Oh, yes, she wanted him. But she feared what that wanting could do to her.

He was leaving, she reminded herself. In a day, maybe two, he would be gone, and she would never see him again. But instead of chilling her yearning, that only seemed to make it grow. She wanted to seize the moment and damn the consequences, to taste every pleasure and joy he could give her for however long he was willing to give them. Right now, the next few hours seemed far more important than the rest of her life.

But opportunity didn't offer itself. They reached the airport and flew silently home. The distance was between them once again.

Just as well, she told herself. Just as well.

He drove her home from the airport and walked her to her door. It was nearly two now, and Conard City was quiet, the cool night air punctuated only by the occasional whine of a vehicle on the state highway and crickets chirping their happy songs.

At the door she faced him, feeling wistful and sad. "I had a wonderful time," she said. "Thank you very much."

"It was fun, wasn't it?" he agreed. He stood looking at her, and when his gaze dropped to her mouth, she felt every cell in her body fill with anticipation and hope. Just a kiss, she told herself. Just one kiss. Surely a kiss wouldn't hurt?

But he didn't kiss her. He gave her a crooked smile instead. "Good night, Carol. Thank you for a great evening."

He turned and walked back to his truck, which throbbed with life, and climbed in. She closed the door so she didn't have to watch him leave.

When she heard the deep growl of his engine roar away, she gave in to sudden, unexpected tears that seemed to come from some place deep in her soul.

The shriek of the telephone woke Carol in the morning. She reached for it groggily and heard her mother's voice.

"What's this I hear about you flying to Denver last night with Tom McKay? And I heard his truck was parked out in front of your house at two this morning."

Carol stifled a groan. "Nothing happened, Mom. We flew to Denver, had dinner, danced, he brought me home, said good-night at the door, and that was the end of it."

Marge Tate was silent for a moment. "You're sure?"

"I was there, Mom. I know what happened. He didn't even try to kiss me."

"Well, I certainly can't understand that," Marge said, sounding indignant. "Any man would want to kiss you!"

Now Carol had to stifle a laugh. "It's okay, Mom. Neither one of us wants to get involved, so we're keeping it light."

"Flying a woman all the way to Denver for dinner doesn't sound light to me."

It didn't sound light to Carol, either, but that was the only way she could allow herself to take it. Anything else would be dangerous to her peace of mind—and her heart. Which, now that she thought about it, was aching this morning because he *hadn't* kissed her.

There was nothing like a man to make a woman dither like an idiot, she thought sourly. Yes, no, yes, no... There was no way to make up your mind about anything when your feelings started to get all balled up in a jumble.

"In fact," Marge said, "flying a woman to Denver for dinner sounds like a setup for seduction."

I wish, Carol thought. "Well, if that was his plan, he sure didn't carry it out, Mom. Actually, I think he just wanted to say thank-you because I cooked him dinner the other night."

"That was a very extravagant thank-you." Marge sighed. "Well, I suppose he moves in very different circles, and he probably has a lot of money. I hear quarterbacks make millions."

"So maybe for him it wasn't extravagant at all."

"Maybe." Marge paused. "I just don't want you to get hurt, Carol."

"I know. And I won't, Mom. I'm a big girl now."

But after she hung up the phone, she lay staring at the ceiling, dealing with the fact that even big girls could get hurt. In fact, ridiculously enough, they could get hurt by nothing at all.

Because Tom had done nothing. And that hurt very badly indeed.

Never had a day stretched so long and endlessly before Carol as this one did. Usually she loved her days off, time when she could catch up on necessary tasks and spend a little time doing only what she wanted to. Today, however, the hours looked empty.

But that was only because she had planned to spend the time looking for Alicia with Tom, she told herself. And she could still look for Alicia without him. The thought galvanized her. Rather than sit around and mope about what couldn't be, she would look for her friend. Tom had been right; Alicia might be hiding where no one could possibly think of looking for her, and if she didn't have any money, as Melody Dreyfus had said, then she couldn't very well afford to stay in motels.

Remembering the line shack where she and Alicia had often spent long summer afternoons as teens, dreaming of boys and babies and prom dresses, Carol dressed swiftly in jeans and boots. Just because Tom had given up looking, that didn't mean *she* had to.

And what was with Tom, anyway? He'd been so hot to trot on this, and then he seemed to have forgotten the entire matter.

Wondering if he was some kind of flake, she stepped out her front door, only to see Tom limping up her narrow front walk.

"Mornin'," he called.

Carol froze, overwhelmed by a mixture of feelings. She wanted to see him, she didn't want to see him, she was excited, and she was scared. He had too much of an impact on her. Entirely too much for her peace of mind.

"Good morning," she managed to reply, sounding as croaky as an old bullfrog.

"Are we still going to look for Alicia today?" he asked.

"I thought you'd forgotten all about it."

He shook his head. "Yesterday I *couldn't* look for her. My knees were killing me most of the day."

She remembered how they'd hurt after he'd yanked her out of the mine shaft cave-in. "How do they feel today?"

"Good as new." He laughed ruefully. "Well, as good as they can. So, are we still looking for her?"

"I was about to check out the line shack."

"Your steed or mine?"

"Mine. I don't know that you'd want to drive your truck up that old wagon track."

As she drove them out of town, Carol decided that Tom *was* a flake. What else could he be? He'd been wavering since he arrived, wanting one thing and doing another. If a girl was paranoid, she might get the idea he could take her only in small doses.

"This is a wild-goose chase," Tom said when they were nearing the shack.

"Probably."

"Like looking for a needle in a haystack."

"Yes."

"I've had better ideas in my life."

"I'm sure." She looked at him. "Why are you so down today?"

He shrugged. "Just colliding with reality. I do that every now and again. The simple fact is, there's no reason to think we're going to find this woman until she wants to be found. And looking for her was just an excuse to be with you."

Her heart skipped a beat, maybe two. Her hands tightened on the steering wheel until her knuckles were white.

"Admittedly," he continued, "I had myself pretty well fooled. But the straight up truth is, I came back here because I wanted to see *you.*"

She caught her breath. "And?"

"That scares me to death."

She glanced at him and found his expression almost grim. "Me, too."

"I figured. How much farther is this shack?"

"Maybe half a mile."

They jolted up the side of a hill on a pine-shaded wagon track that probably hadn't been used more than a couple of times since she and Alicia last had come out here to share their deepest dreams.

What, Carol wondered, was she doing in the middle of nowhere with a man she hardly knew? She ought to turn around and head back for safety right this instant.

But she kept going and finally brought them to a jolting halt about a hundred feet from the weathered shack.

"This seems like an odd place for a line shack," Tom remarked. "It doesn't look like very good ranch land to me. Too many trees."

"Right here, maybe," Carol agreed, "but there's water near the shack. I think it was fenced to protect a water supply."

He climbed out of the car and stood looking around at the sun-light-dappled clearing. "It sure is pretty up here."

"I used to dream about building a house up here," she admitted. She turned and pointed to the east. "Look at that view. It's almost like an eagle's eyrie up here."

"Why don't you build a house here?"

"Because when I think about having to drive to town in the winter, it doesn't sound so good. Snowfall up here can be nearly two hundred inches in the winter."

"That's a lot of snow." He turned slowly and suddenly pointed. "Someone's been up here recently. Look at those wheel ruts."

She walked over and looked at the tire treads in a patch of damp ground. "Those look fresh." Excitement began to grow in her.

"Since the last rain." Grimacing, he squatted down and looked more closely at them. "They wouldn't be this clear if they'd been rained on since. I'm no expert, though. I couldn't tell you what kind of vehicle made them."

"Let's check the shack."

She almost offered a hand to help him up but decided against it. If he didn't ask, he didn't want it. But she did look away, not wanting to see how much it hurt him to straighten.

Together they walked over to the shack and opened the creaky plank door. The interior was shadowed, cooler than the air outside. They left the door open to let in light and waited while their eyes adjusted to the dimness.

"Someone's been here recently," Carol remarked.

"How do you know?"

"No spider webs. And look at the woodstove. There's no dust on it."

"You're right. But it could have been anybody, I suppose, and there's no sign that they intend to come back."

Carol had to agree. Someone who was planning to stay here would certainly have left something behind, even if it was only a can of food, or a saucepan to heat it in.

"Wild-goose chase," Tom said again. "Definitely one of my more harebrained ideas."

Which reminded Carol of what he had said about coming back here to see *her*. The air was suddenly too thick to breathe. They were out here, miles from anyone else, in this line shack that had listened to some of her dearest dreams, dreams that had never seemed so far away or so close as they did right this instant.

Her heart began a slow, heavy beating, and she found herself staring fixedly at the floor, afraid that if she looked at him he would read what must surely be in her eyes. She had *some* pride, after all, and if she salvaged nothing else from her acquaintance with Tom McKay, she could at least come away with her pride intact. After what had happened with the rodeo rider—whose name she had banished from her thoughts—she was determined never to swallow her pride again.

"We might as well go," Tom said. "There's nothing here."

She turned to head for the door and bumped right into him as he pivoted. Instinctively, they both reached out to steady themselves, and an instant later they were in one another's arms.

Tom swore. He grimaced as if he were in severe pain. Carol, forgetting everything else in her concern for him, opened her mouth to ask if he was okay. Before a sound could escape her, his mouth swooped to take hers in a devouring, hungry kiss.

He wants me! The realization resounded in Carol's mind as her senses gave in to the swamping wave of desire that filled her. All the aching, yearning wistfulness of the past few days coalesced into a heat that consumed her. *I want him.* And not one other thing mattered.

Reticence, hesitation, fear—all those things vanished. She kissed him back with as much hunger as he kissed her, their tongues dueling in a dance as old as the planet. The ache that filled Carol now wasn't wistful. No, it was heavier, thicker, muffling reason with its demand for culmination.

She ached for him more than she had believed it possible to ache. When his hands slipped down her back and cupped her bottom, lifting her against him, she responded by wrapping her legs around his hips, opening herself to him, drawing him closer still to that aching, throbbing place where she most needed him.

He groaned something, but she could hardly hear him over the drumbeat of her own blood. She felt her back press against something hard—a wall?—then he leaned into her, locking his hips to hers in mating rhythm.

It felt so good! Again and again he thrust against her, rubbing in a way that deepened the ache between her thighs. Never in her life had she done something as wanton as this, and right now she didn't care, if only he would never stop.

"Carol..." He groaned her name, and exultation filled her, even as the spear of desire lifted her higher and higher. She was blind with the need for him, driven by a hunger that left her mindless.

Desperate. She was desperate for him, and in some corner of her mind she realized that she was desperate *only* for *him*. She would have clung to no other man the way she was clinging to him. She would have given no other man what she was giving him.

The throbbing within her peaked, shooting her out over the edge of the precipice in a blaze of sensation. She felt him jerk, then shudder, his cry joining hers.

Then, slowly, she drifted down.

Back to reality.

Chapter 7

Tom McKay was ashamed of himself. It wasn't a feeling he enjoyed, and it was one he'd always made a point of trying to avoid. But this time he had failed himself, and he was feeling as ashamed as a man could feel.

What had happened between him and Carol at the line shack wasn't something he could feel any other way about, and apparently she felt as humiliated as he did. They hardly spoke a word as she drove him back to the motel and dropped him off.

He watched her drive away, trying to figure out what he could possibly say or do that would at least make *her* feel better. Nothing, of course, was going to make *him* feel any better about acting like an animal in rut.

In his entire life, he had never treated a woman that way. He had never taken sexual pleasure without kindness and caring. He had never allowed himself to be overwhelmed by his urges.

Carol, he thought, must be feeling used. The fact that she had apparently been as hungry as he didn't excuse the way he had treated her. Nor did it excuse the fact that he had taken advantage of her. She was ten years younger than he, and for all the talk of this rodeo rider in her past, he sensed that she was basically sexually inexperienced. She hadn't known how to handle the urges that had overwhelmed them. If she had, he had not a single doubt that she would have told him where to stuff it.

He had no such excuse. He'd lost his head, and while that might be excusable in a sixteen-year-old boy, it wasn't excusable in a thirty-five-year-old man.

Frankly, he felt ashamed enough to want to crawl into a hole and hide.

Hell.

He spent the rest of the day walking. Not until the sun was setting did he emerge from his gloom enough to notice that it was late, his knees hurt like hell, and it was getting chilly. He made his way back to the motel to get a jacket and wondered what he could possibly do to make this up to Carol.

Carol hid in her house for the rest of the day. She went on a cleaning binge that left every square inch of the place spotless, but even physical fatigue couldn't drown her sense of horror over her behavior.

She had been *wanton*. Tom must think the most horrible things about her now, and that hurt. She didn't want him to think poorly of her, but she couldn't imagine what she might do to cure the tattered impression he must have of her.

God, she had been *easy*. She'd acted like an animal in heat. Why wouldn't he take advantage of it? Men had strong drives. She'd been warned about them since puberty. They had strong drives and were apt to take whatever was offered and not think another thing about it.

And she *had* offered. Closing her eyes and remembering, she could feel her cheeks burn—and feel herself throb. She wanted him again, and that only increased her sense of humiliation.

As for all her resolutions about not getting involved with a man who was just passing through, they had blown away in the wind. She admitted it to herself with a soul-deep ache of yearning and loss. She was well and truly involved now. If he never touched her again, she could survive, but she wasn't at all sure she could survive if she never saw Tom McKay again.

Because somehow he had touched her heart.

Oh, Lord, would she never learn?

Finally, as night settled over the world, she gave in to the tears and cried as if her heart were breaking.

Which it was.

After he got a jacket, Tom started walking again. Up one street and down another, he paced off most of Conard City while the stars wheeled overhead.

What, he asked himself, was really the problem here? He was going to get into his truck tomorrow morning and leave forever, wasn't he? He never had to face Carol again. He could wire her flowers from some town along the road, include a heartfelt apology, and continue his life sadder but wiser.

He had long since forgotten his urge to find Alicia. He even admitted that he hadn't come back here for Alicia but for Carol. And what did that say about him? He knew he couldn't offer permanence and all the other things a woman like Carol deserved. So why hadn't he just stayed away?

Why didn't he just get into his truck right now and hit the road, before he could do any more damage to himself or her? He was broken in ways that made him a bad choice for any woman's affections, and he knew it. He was hobbled by bad knees, and even more so by a battered heart. Carol deserved somebody who could offer her all those things he didn't believe in anymore, somebody who could offer himself whole and unscarred.

He couldn't do that.

But one thing he knew for sure, he would never forgive himself if he took the coward's way out of this. He couldn't just wire her flowers and an apology. She deserved better than that. And he was a better man than that.

Nor could he do to her what that rodeo rider had done and leave town without saying goodbye. No way.

So he turned himself around and headed for her house. He owed her an apology, and he owed her an opportunity to tell him just what a scumbag he was. He owed her that much respect.

When he reached her house, he stood on the sidewalk in the moonlight and considered what he was about to say. No easy words came to mind. There was no easy, coherent way to apologize for acting like an animal. No excuse for taking advantage of a woman.

And that was what he had to tell her. But he was amazingly reluctant to do so. It wasn't that he had a problem with apologizing. He had never minded admitting his errors when he felt he was wrong.

But this time he felt as if the words were going to stick in his mouth. And, like a coward, he wished she were asleep. But she wasn't. He could tell from all the light pouring out her windows that she was probably in the kitchen, and probably just as sleepless as he. Why shouldn't she be? He'd hurt her in a way no one should hurt another human being.

God, he hated himself.

At last, deciding that things couldn't get any worse, and that at least if she dumped vitriol on his head he would feel he'd gotten his just deserts, he walked up to the door and knocked.

No one answered. After a couple of minutes he knocked again, louder. Half a minute later, he saw the curtains twitch in the window beside the door. Then the door opened.

Carol's eyes were puffy, and his heart squeezed. She had probably been crying, and he was probably the cause of it. If he could have booted his own butt right then, he would have done it.

"I'm sorry," he said. "I am really, truly sorry."

She looked mutely at him, and after a moment stepped back to invite him in. He didn't really want to go inside; it was dangerous territory in there, mainly because he was no longer sure he could trust himself, and he was feeling an overwhelming urge to sweep her up in his arms and hug her until she no longer felt like weeping.

But if he stood out here and things got emotional, half the town was apt to hear them. So he stepped inside and let her close the door behind him.

"I was...making tea," she said. "Want some?"

Why not? he thought, following her back to the kitchen. She waved him to a chair at the table and got out another cup and tea bag. When she had filled both cups with boiling water, she sat across from him.

But she didn't look at him, he noticed, and his heart squeezed again. God, he had never wanted to hurt her like this, and he couldn't stand the thought that he had.

"I'm sorry," he said again. "The way I treated you up at the line shack was—well, it was inexcusable. I had absolutely no business coming on to you that way. I'd like to say I don't know what came over me, but the simple fact is, I do. I want you more than any woman I've ever known, and I lost my head."

Her head lifted a little at that, and he felt a stirring of hope, which died when she didn't meet his gaze. She didn't want to even look at him. Why should she?

But then she said something that rocked him to the soles of his boots.

"You must..." Her voice sounded strangled. She trailed off, then tried again. "You must think I'm so...cheap."

Cheap? The word struck him like a lightning bolt. Is that what he'd made her feel? That he considered her cheap? Oh, God! "Carol, no! I don't think you're cheap. How could I possibly think that?"

"Because...because of the way I...acted."

Flummoxed, he stared at her, trying to find some way to reassure her. Only one thing occurred to him. "I seem to remember we both were...acting the same way. I don't consider myself cheap, so why should I think *you* are?"

Her head lifted a little higher, and she darted a quick look at him.

"I think I deserve to be horsewhipped," he continued. "I showed very poor self-control. But given that I initiated the entire event, that I...touched you the way I did, what happened was...inevitable. Once I set that ball rolling...well, I don't hold you responsible."

"You don't think *I* should have had any self-control?"

He didn't like the way that sounded. "I didn't mean that. But I was the one who initiated it, when I certainly should have known better."

She shook her head and gave him a weary smile. "You can't have it both ways, Tom. Either we were *both* responsible for losing our heads, or neither of us was responsible. But it took two of us to...make that happen."

He acknowledged the justice of what she said, but it didn't make him feel any better. "Would you have grabbed me the way I grabbed you? I somehow doubt it."

She looked down at her teacup. "I was thinking about it," she said in a hushed voice.

"But you didn't actually *do* it. I should have had at least as much self-control."

She sighed, taking her tea bag out of the water and setting it on a saucer in the middle of the table. He followed suit.

"What's the point?" she asked finally. "We both got carried away, and we both wish we hadn't. End of discussion."

He was surprised by how much that hurt. He didn't want her to regret getting "carried away" with him. Not ever. Maybe apologizing for what he'd done had been exactly the wrong tack to take.

Stymied, he tried to read some answers in the depths of his tea cup. Of course there was nothing there.

"Look," he said finally, looking straight at her, "maybe I need to make something clear here. I'm ashamed of the way I acted. I think I acted like a stupid sixteen-year-old, and it embarrasses me. But if you think I *regret* what happened, you're far and away mistaken."

Her face reflected confusion. "You don't?"

"Of course I don't! And quite frankly, Carol, if things weren't so messed up between us right now, if I weren't going to have to go on the road again in three days, I'd try my damnedest to make love to you again for real, right now."

She caught her breath.

"See?" he said. "I'm not good for you. I don't want to be another rodeo rider in your life. How are you going to feel every time I get into that truck and drive away? Are you going to wonder if I'll ever come back?"

"Every time?"

He threw up a hand. "Every time. And why wouldn't you, after what that son of a bitch did to you? I can tell you I'll be back, but are you going to believe it? How could you?"

"I thought you didn't want to get involved?"

"I didn't! But I sure as hell did." He swore and looked away.

"The simple truth is, if I was sure it wouldn't be bad for you, I'd keep coming back. But what kind of life would that be, waiting for me to turn up on my next run? It wouldn't be fair to you at all."

When she didn't answer him, he felt his heart plummet. She didn't feel the way he did, he realized. How could she? What he was offering was no life at all for a woman.

"Besides," he said finally, "you said you didn't want to get tangled up with another guy who was just passing through. Passing through seems to be all I'm able to do anymore."

"It's already too late," she said weakly.

He looked at her then. "What? What's too late?"

A tear trickled down her cheek. "I already seem to be tangled up."

Now he'd really done it, he realized. He thought he'd been the only one who had an emotional stake in this. He'd thought she was just embarrassed by what had happened between them. Never had he dreamed that she actually *cared* about him.

It was definitely time to go, he decided. He had to get out of here before either of them got hurt any worse. He needed to make a clean break for both their sakes.

He shoved his chair back from the table, intending to walk out of this house—and out of Carol's life—forever, before anything got any messier.

But apparently his body had a mind of its own. Instead of striding toward the door, he rounded the table and stood over her.

"Carol?"

She looked up at him, and the tearful yearning in her gaze seemed to answer the aching pain in his heart. One look into her misty green eyes and he was over the edge.

Bending, he kissed her gently on the mouth. He felt her moment of hesitation, but before he could turn it into a rejection and walk away, he felt the tremulous response of her lips. Man, how he wanted this woman!

A little gasp escaped her; then she pressed her mouth to his, deepening their kiss. Triumph, relief and desire crashed in his head, driving away all his other concerns.

She wanted him! After all this, she still wanted him. He felt blessed in a way he had never before known, as if she had some-how elevated him above all other men, transporting him to a pin-nacle he was sure he didn't deserve.

He heard her chair scrape back on the linoleum, but he didn't know who pushed it back. Nor did he know whether he drew her to her feet or whether she rose all on her own. All he knew was that she was suddenly filling his arms and filling his heart.

God, it felt so good to hold her and feel her arms around him. He had forgotten the soul-deep satisfaction that could come from being held by someone you love. He had forgotten that sometimes a hug could be all that mattered in the world.

But not for long. When he felt her hands run over his back, stroking muscles that hadn't been stroked in years, and felt her press even closer to him, need overwhelmed him. He needed this woman as he had needed no other.

Galvanized, he swept her up into his arms and looked down into her hazy eyes. "Say no now," he said thickly. "Say it now."

"I can't...." Her voice trailed off as she reached up to touch his cheek in a gentle caress. "Oh, Tom, I can't."

No words had ever made him happier. Casting aside caution, he carried her toward her bedroom, bent on only one thing: making love to Carol Tate until they both hummed with repletion.

He set her on her feet beside the bed, and he never had any idea whose hands removed whose clothes. It didn't really matter, except that her eagerness made him feel more wanted than he had ever before felt. His wife had always been a shy, hesitant lover—which was part of the reason he had been so stunned to learn she was having affairs.

But there was nothing shy or hesitant about Carol. She might be largely inexperienced, but whatever experiences she'd known hadn't made her tentative or shy.

And he liked that. He loved feeling as if she were meeting him as an equal, demanding as much as she gave. Her eagerness made him feel more certain of himself, her openness and honesty made it easy to know how to please her.

At last they tumbled naked together on the bed, mouths and hands straining for one another, bodies seeking completion impa-tiently.

Not like this, he thought suddenly. Not like a rutting animal again. Gathering the shreds of his self-control, he tore his mouth from hers and buried his face in the warm, sweet hollow of her throat.

She stilled, breathing as raggedly as he, and he felt her fingers twine into his hair.

"We've got all night," he said hoarsely. "Let's take all night. I want to make slow love to you. I want to learn every part of you...."

She released a shuddering breath, and he felt her body soften as she let go of the driving tension. "Yes," she whispered. "All night. Forever."

Pushing himself up on one elbow, he looked down at her and thought how exquisite she was. The lights were still on, and there were no shadows to hide anything. "You're perfect," he whispered. "Absolutely perfect."

He loved it when she blushed, and she blushed under his gaze. But it was true. There wasn't a single little thing he would change about her, not the small freckles on her arms, or the small mole on her left breast. Giving himself the luxury of enjoying her, he ran a hand over her slowly, petting her, learning the unencumbered feel of her every hill and hollow.

He could see the pulsebeat in her throat, and he found himself watching it, noting how it speeded up when he touched her breasts. Noting how she gasped when he gave her pleasure.

She didn't lie still for long, though. Finally, as if impatient with his worship, she pushed him back on the mattress and rose over him, taking her turn to learn him.

There were scars, and for her sake he wished them away, but she surprised him by kissing each and every one as she found it, from the cleat mark in his side to the small marks on his knees from arthroscopic surgery. Her hands kneaded him as they moved over him, relaxing aching muscles even as they heightened his desire for her.

Then she teased him with her tongue, running it around his ear and down his neck, making him shudder with longing. She found his small nipples and licked him there, tightening the violent coil of desire in him until he thought he would explode. When she wandered lower, he stopped her, uncertain of his control.

Side by side they lay for a few minutes, allowing their desire to ease just a little, playing it out for every moment they could squeeze from it. But then he took her lead and began to tease her with his tongue, first in the hollow of her throat, until she arched, and finally finding her breast.

And once there, he gave in to a need of his own, sucking with a rhythmic pulse that mimicked the throbbing of his own body. She began to whimper softly, her hips moving in time to his mouth, and he could feel the need growing in her as surely as it was growing in him.

When a deep groan escaped her, he offered her more. His hand slipped downward, finding her dewy petals. He stroked her wetness gently with his fingers, goading her even higher but taking care not to carry her over the edge. No, he wanted them to do that together.

Her fingers clutched at his shoulders, her nails digging into him, and he heard her beg, "Tom, please...please..."

Rising over her, he settled between her parted thighs. Even as he reached for her, he felt her rise toward him, and in a single instant they became one.

Exquisite. Perfect. The words rolled around in his head as he looked into Carol's eyes, suspended between one instant and the next, and read his own wonder in her gaze.

In that instant, something inside him shifted irrevocably. He knew he was never going to be the same again. But he didn't have time to think about it just then, because her body was arching against his, demanding more from him.

He was only too happy to comply. With long, deep strokes, he carried them away once again.

When he awoke in the morning, the first thing Tom noticed was that Carol wasn't beside him. The next thing he noticed was that she was singing somewhere in the house. The sound brought a smile to his face, and he stretched luxuriously as he listened to her lovely soprano.

"Greensleeves was all my joy
Greensleeves was my delight
Greensleeves was my heart of gold
And who but my lady Greensleeves."

Still smiling, Tom climbed out of bed and pulled on jeans. Then he padded barefoot into the kitchen, where he found Carol wearing shorts and a T-shirt, and rolling out dough. She looked over her shoulder when he entered the room and smiled. And blushed brightly.

"Don't stop singing on my account," he said. Coming up behind her, he slipped his arms around her waist and nuzzled her neck.

"How are your knees this morning?" she asked.

"Knees? What knees? Can a man walking on clouds even feel his knees?"

A soft laugh escaped her, and she turned within the circle of his arms, smiling shyly up at him. "I'm making biscuits for breakfast. I hope you like them."

"I'm a good Southern boy. Of course I like biscuits. And nobody has made them for me fresh for breakfast since my mother."

He kissed her soundly. He would have carried her off to bed again, but she protested that the biscuits would be ruined, so he settled at the table with a cup of coffee and watched her bustle about, humming softly.

"You have a beautiful voice," he told her.

"Thank you. I used to sing in the church choir, but my current schedule doesn't allow it." She popped a sheet of biscuits into the oven and turned her attention to making eggs.

He could get used to this, Tom thought. He could very easily get used to waking up to the sound of Carol's singing in the morning. But if he wanted to get used to that, he had to offer something in return.

The thought darkened his mood. When Carol placed a cup of coffee in front of him, he found himself staring into it and trying to envision how he, with all his hang-ups, could try to cobble together something that would be worth enough that she would be willing to waste her life on him.

The question rocked him to his core. How could he be thinking in terms of lifetimes? Hadn't he sworn off forever?

But forever was exactly what he wanted, he realized with trepidation. For the first time since his marriage, he found himself wanting to take that risk again. Oh, man. The idea chilled him.

They ate breakfast in silence as he waged an inner war with himself. He grew aware that Carol was looking at him uncertainly, as if she were aware of his struggle and his unhappy mood, and didn't know what to make of them.

But he wasn't ready to talk about his turmoil. Not yet. He had to come to some conclusion in his own mind before he said anything at all.

After breakfast, he insisted on washing the dishes. She excused herself to go take a shower, as she had to go in to work at three.

He found himself looking at the clock, counting the hours. It was nearly noon already, and in less than three hours she would walk out of this house to go to work. The question was whether he was going to be here when she came back tonight, or whether he was going to climb into his truck and leave...forever.

That was the real question, he realized. What he had to offer and whether she would want it were irrelevant next to the basic question: was he going to stay or was he going to go?

Closing his eyes, he stood at the sink and thought about it. Staying terrified him. Of that there was no doubt. But for the first time in his life, leaving terrified him even more.

Because suddenly he was no longer able to imagine a life without Carol Tate.

His eyes snapped open. Grabbing a towel, he dried his hands and went to find her. She was in the shower, but that didn't stop him. Very little had ever stopped him once his mind was made up.

Walking into the steamy bathroom, he closed the door behind him and watched her shadowy shape moving behind the translucent shower curtain.

"Carol?"

The curtain twitched back a couple of inches, and she looked out at him. Shampoo foam covered her hair, darkened with water, and dewy drops of moisture gave her skin the fresh look of flower petals in the morning.

"Is something wrong?" she asked.

"I guess that's up to you."

"Me?"

"Well, yeah." He shifted to his other foot, feeling as awkward as he'd ever felt in his life. "Wanna marry me?"

Her eyes grew so huge that they seemed to fill her face. "Are you feeling okay?"

"Not yet. I kinda need an answer to feel better. Preferably a positive one, because I think a negative one is going to make me feel worse."

"How can you ask me this when I'm standing in the shower?"

He shrugged and felt an errant smile tug at the corner of his mouth as he realized she wasn't saying no and wasn't telling him to get lost. "'Cause I can't wait?"

"Tom!" But suddenly she was laughing. She closed the shower curtain. "At least let me rinse off!"

"Can't you give me a hint?" he asked. "I mean, something like should I just get the hell out of here now?"

The curtain snapped open, and she stuck her head out again. "Don't you dare go anywhere!"

"Okay," he said meekly enough, feeling considerably better. In fact, he almost felt as if he were flying. "I know I haven't got a whole lot to offer," he continued, addressing the closed shower curtain. "But I figure I can find something to do besides drive a truck, if you want. Sell insurance. Buy a ranch. It's not like I don't have enough money to last me the rest of my life, as long as I'm careful. I'm sure I can find something that'll keep me underfoot—if that's what you want. Of course, maybe you'd rather I just take to the road and keep out of your hair most of the time...."

She stuck her head out. "Don't even consider it. If you want to drive, that's fine by me, but if you'd like something more settled, that's fine by me, too. In fact, I'd prefer it."

That was when he was sure she was going to say yes. "Well, if we have kids, it'd be better if I was around most of the time, wouldn't it?"

"Kids?" Her expression became soft, and a dewy smile spread across her face. "Really? Truly?"

"Of course. I've always wanted children. Don't you?"

She pulled the shower curtain back and stepped, dripping wet, out of the tub. The next thing he knew, his arms were full of naked, wet woman. And nothing in his life had ever felt better.

She turned her face up. "Why, Tom? Please tell me why."

He knew what she wanted, and for the first time in the longest time, he said the words with heartfelt sincerity. "I love you, Carol. I love you with my whole heart. And I want to stay in Conard County with you."

"Why?"

He smiled. "Because this is where love lives. So will you marry me?"

"Yes. Oh, yes!"

And suddenly forever looked like the easiest thing in the world.

"You Loving Me"
Chapter 1

Beau Beauregard was looking less kindly at strangers these days, after what had happened to Tom McKay. Maybe he was being paranoid, but it was wise to be concerned when a man as powerful as Harold Dreyfus was willing to hire thugs to hunt down his wife. So far Alicia Dreyfus hadn't turned up anywhere—nor had the thugs who'd beaten Tom McKay—but now there was a new stranger to be concerned about.

The stranger had walked into Mahoney's not five minutes ago and was eating a sandwich at the bar two seats down from where Beau was eating his own lunch.

Beau might have ignored him, except the guy was asking Mahoney about places he could stay other than the Lazy Rest Motel. That seemed to indicate the stranger was planning on sticking around...and that made Beau interested.

He spoke. "There's a schoolteacher who lets rooms," he offered.

The man looked at him, taking in his deputy's uniform, and nodded. "Thanks. Where would I find the place?"

"Up Front Street, east," said Mahoney as he polished a glass. "She's got a sign out front."

Beau wished Mahoney were less helpful. He'd wanted to ask a few more questions before revealing that information. "You staying in town for long?" he asked the stranger.

"A week, maybe. Maybe longer. I hate motels."

Beau nodded. "You a salesman?"

The stranger shook his head. "Nope. I'm doing research for a book on small Western towns."

Well, it was possible, Beau thought. He made a mental note to check the guy out. Offering his hand, he said, "I'm Virgil Beauregard. My friends call me Beau."

"Pleased to meet you. I'm Vic Towers."

Mahoney and Vic shook hands. "You gonna say good things about us?" Mahoney wanted to know.

"Sure," said Vic. "People in this country have a nostalgic idea of what small-town life is like. I'm not going to disappoint them."

Mahoney chuckled, and Beau smiled.

"But that's part of the reason I'd rather stay in a rooming house," Vic said. "I'll get a better feel for what life is like here if I live on a residential street."

Mahoney spoke. "Well, Hope Litton has a house in a good neighborhood. If you stay with her, you'll see just what it's like around here."

"Good. That's what I'm looking for."

And maybe that *was* all he was looking for, Beau thought as he returned to his sandwich. People had come to Conard County for a lot stranger reasons.

Hope Litton was sitting on her front porch sipping iced tea when the car pulled up out front. She was hot and tired from a full day of housecleaning—her annual get-ready-to-go-back-to-school ritual. From experience she knew that once the school year got under way, major cleaning would wait until Christmas break.

So she had cleaned the closets, cleaned the basement, cleaned the garage, stripped the wax off the wood floors and applied a fresh layer, and even washed the heavy drapes in the living room. The house smelled fresh, scented with pine and disinfectants, and every surface gleamed. She felt good but exhausted.

A man climbed out of the car and looked up and down the street. He was a tall man, handsome in a rough-hewn sort of way, with a sturdy build that looked as solid as rock and a healthy summer tan. Very good-looking, Hope thought.

And that made her immediately aware of what she looked like in her stained white shorts and dusty T-shirt, with a bandanna covering her hair. Like something that had just crawled through a dirty tunnel, she thought with amusement. Oh, well!

"Miss Litton?" the man called from the curb.

Oh, great, he was here to see her. "Yes?"

"I'm Vic Towers." He started up the walk toward her. "Deputy Beauregard said you have rooms to let."

"Yes, I do," she said readily, wishing like mad she had showered before she came out here for her break...especially when his eyes wandered over her, taking in every detail. "I'm a mess because I've just been cleaning," she said apologetically. "Believe me, the rooms are spotless."

A smile spread across his rugged face and lit the depths of his incredibly blue eyes. "There's nothing wrong with the way you look. Anyway, I was wondering if you'd be willing to rent me a room for a week or two."

She was disappointed. Finding long-term renters was always a problem, and invariably when someone moved out she had a major cleaning chore ahead of her. On the other hand, if she refused short-term tenants like this one, she would hardly ever rent anything, except the one room taken by an elderly teacher.

"No problem," she said with a bright smile. "There is a cleaning deposit, though, for people who rent for less than six months."

"Fine by me."

"Well, come in and I'll show you the room. I'm afraid I don't offer meals. With a full-time job, I just can't do that."

"That's okay." He mounted the steps until he stood beside her. "Mahoney's makes a good sandwich, I just discovered."

"And the City Diner is wonderful if you're not worried about cholesterol."

He laughed and patted his flat belly. "Maybe someday. Right now, I'm all in favor of flavor."

"You and Maude will get along great."

"Maude?"

"She owns the City Diner."

He followed her inside and looked around at the large foyer with the stairs rising to the right. Everything gleamed with polish and wax. "Very nice," he said appreciatively.

"I grew up in this house," Hope said. "It's old, and it takes constant repairs, but I'd never give it up."

"I can see why. They don't build them like this anymore."

"No." But the age of the house and the cost of its upkeep were the primary reasons why she had to take roomers. She pointed out the living room on the right, the arched entryway near the foot of the stairs. "My guests are always welcome to use the living room. There's a TV in there, and plenty of comfortable chairs."

He nodded.

She led the way upstairs. "I have one other roomer right now, an elderly schoolteacher, Miss Muffet."

"Really?" His sparkling blue eyes looked over at her as they climbed. "Miss Muffet?"

"Honestly." Hope smiled. "The kids love it."

"I bet."

"Anyway, she goes to bed around ten, so we try to keep quiet after that."

"No problem. I'm a quiet kind of guy. I don't like loud music, and my favorite pastime is reading."

"What do you do?"

"I'm a writer. I'm researching a book on small Western towns."

"Well, you've come to the right place. We're small, all right." She pointed out Miss Muffet's room, then led him around a corner in the hallway. "I have two vacant rooms, so you can pick whichever you like best."

He chose the one with the view of the street out front, probably because it had a bed with no footboard to bang his feet on. He was tall enough that that was probably a consideration, she thought.

"One question," he said. "Is it a problem if I use the phone line to go on the Internet?"

Hope shook her head. "I don't think so. Miss Muffet doesn't make too many phone calls, and I have a separate phone line for myself downstairs."

"Great."

Back downstairs, he paid her in cash for the first week's rent and the cleaning deposit. She didn't know anyone who carried that kind of cash on them, but decided he was probably doing so because he was traveling. She gave him a receipt, and a minute later he was moving into his room.

Vic didn't have much to move. A suitcase full of clothes and his laptop computer were all he had brought with him, because he preferred traveling light. In his business, he had to be prepared to leave on a minute's notice.

And that, he thought as he hung his clothes in the large walk-in closet, was a situation he was getting heartily tired of. When he'd retired on disability from the Minneapolis police force two years ago, becoming a private investigator had seemed like a logical next step. Instead, he was discovering that it was more boring by far than police work, and a whole lot more rootless. Chasing down runaway spouses and staking out cheating husbands was not his idea of fun, especially when they insisted on running away to strange places.

Take his current case, for instance. Why in hell would anyone want to run away to this tiny little burg? Alicia Dreyfus must be out of her mind. He was willing to bet they rolled up the sidewalks at six.

Given the smallness of the town, he had felt it would be wiser to use a cover story. In a larger city he could have asked questions openly, but in a place this size, if the locals decided they didn't want to talk, everybody would clam up in no time flat.

He hung his last shirt in the closet, then reached for the phone, punching in his credit card number, followed by Harold Dreyfus's private number.

"It's Towers," he told the answering machine. "I'm in place. I'll keep you posted." He hung up, glad Dreyfus hadn't answered the phone. The man wanted to control every detail, a serious personality flaw as far as Vic was concerned. Dreyfus didn't know anything about investigating but Vic did—which meant, to Vic's way of thinking, that Dreyfus should just leave him alone and let him do his job as he saw fit.

He walked over to one of the windows and pulled the sheers back to look down on the street. Now that he'd given himself a cover story, he had to find a way to make asking questions about

Alicia Dreyfus look innocent. Somehow he had the feeling that this was not going to be a piece of cake.

Some assignments were. Some of them were almost too easy to be believed, like the guy who was suing his wife for alimony, claiming he couldn't work. It had taken Vic all of two hours to get pictures of the guy walking into his place of employment and to find out how much the guy was making. Piece of cake.

But Alicia Dreyfus had grown up in this town, and there was no reason to think most of the people here wouldn't feel protective about her if a stranger started asking pointed questions. Somehow he had to get around the small-town mentality. Somehow he had to make the locals think he was on their side.

Sighing, he let the curtain fall back into place and went to get the file from his suitcase. Refreshing his memory never hurt.

Alicia Dreyfus, age twenty-four, was as knock-down gorgeous as a model ought to be. Although for his money, Hope Litton was a lot more attractive, with her wide gray eyes and pleasantly rounded figure, even with her face smudged and her hair hidden under a bandanna. Of course, he just didn't understand the current fascination with ultrathin. He didn't want to feel bones when he hugged a woman.

Shaking himself, he forced his attention back to the file. Alicia had filed for divorce, then disappeared the day before the papers were served on her husband. She had taken one of his cars with her, a rather expensive Mercedes, and some family jewelry. Reason enough for Harold to want to find her, he figured...although, in his opinion, when a woman took off like that, a smart man let her go.

But Harold, he found himself thinking, wasn't the type to let anything or anyone go easily. Besides, the guy claimed he was heartbroken and just wanted a chance to talk his wife into coming back.

Possible, Vic supposed. He hadn't felt that way when his own wife had left him. She'd declared she couldn't handle the fear and anxiety about his job as a cop anymore and had to get out. He'd let her go without an argument, even though she was pregnant. Not because he hadn't loved her, but because he *had*. Sometimes you had to put yourself second, and Julia had been on the edge of a nervous breakdown.

And that had been his fault, he admitted readily. She'd been telling him for years that she couldn't handle the stress of his job, the hours and the worry about him. He'd kept soothing her and refusing to face the obvious: that his job as a police officer was killing *her.*

And finally it had. Two weeks after they separated, he had been shot, and the news had caused her to have a miscarriage that had killed both her and the baby.

All he could do now was wish he'd had the sense to let Julia go sooner. Or to take care of her needs before his own.

Dreyfus apparently didn't see things that way, and he had the money to chase his belongings, including his wife.

And Vic Towers did this for a living. Sometimes he thought he seriously needed to get his head examined.

Back to the file, he told himself. Concentrate on the case, not the curiosities of human nature.

Alicia had lived here in Conard County until she was eighteen. Her only living relative, her father, had moved away about the same time, and no one knew where he was now. But Alicia apparently had friends here, and Dreyfus had supplied him with a list of names.

The sheriff, Nate Tate.

Tate's daughters, Carol and Patty.

Great. How about somebody who wouldn't be all over him like white on rice if he asked a few questions? Someone he could safely cozy up to?

He scanned further down the list, saw there was a preacher named Fromberg...also a bad choice to question. A couple of other friends from high school who might or might not still live here, and...

...and Hope Litton. She had apparently been a favorite teacher of Alicia's.

Things were brightening, he decided. Living here, he could get to know Hope and probably encourage her to do a little gossiping.

Cozying up to the schoolmarm would be a pleasant task indeed.

While Vic Towers moved into his room, Hope retreated to her own bed-sitting room at the back of the first floor and took a shower. She'd only met one other published writer in her life—Mandy Laird, who wrote science fiction and fantasy—and she found herself hoping she would get a chance to talk to Vic Towers about what he did. It would give her some interesting information, and maybe some anecdotes, for her high school English and writing classes. Maybe, if he stayed for an extra week or so, she could even persuade him to talk to some of her classes.

And, she admitted honestly as the shower spray rinsed the shampoo from her hair, she would like to get a chance to know him better. She, like so many young women in this county, was suffering from a dearth of eligible men. At least, eligible men she hadn't already discovered weren't right for her. And now that she was in her thirties, any eligible men at all were few and far between.

Of course, she reminded herself, she knew nothing about Vic Towers. He might be married, and he was certainly only just passing through. It would be best to keep a safe distance.

Nevertheless, as she toweled dry, she found herself turning in front of the mirror, inspecting herself. No sags or bags yet, which was pretty good, considering she could afford to lose fifteen pounds. Her face showed some of the thin lines that were common to her age, just soft little creases around her mouth and eyes, nothing really noticeable yet. Her eyes were still clear and wide, and her smile revealed even, white teeth.

Not bad, she assured herself. Not great, not beautiful, but adequate.

Feeling a little more confident, she used the blow-dryer on her shoulder-length black hair, then dressed in gray cotton slacks and a pink shell.

Suddenly embarrassed by her uncharacteristic moment of vanity, she slipped her feet into canvas shoes, then went to the dining room, where she had her lesson preparation materials laid out. School started next week, and she rarely used the same lesson plans each year, because each year she discovered better ways of doing things—within the limits of the syllabus, of course.

This year, for example, instead of having her creative writing students keep a journal in the traditional way, she was going to ask them to record just one incident every day. Then, at the end of each week, she was going to have them choose one incident from the week and turn it into a four- or five-page story. She hoped that by doing this she could break through the "just record" mentality so many of the students had and get them to explore the possibilities which were at the heart of creative writing. "Don't tell it the way it *was*," she was going to say to them. "Tell it the way it *could* be."

But that meant coming up with an example of her own to show them what she was after. And the arrival of Vic Towers had provided just the possibility she needed. Pen in hand, she began to write a fictional story about her new roomer.

Absorbed, she lost track of time. The sun coming in the west window sank lower, casting a golden light over the mahogany table and sideboard. Her stomach rumbled noisily, distracting her from her writing.

"I heard that," said a familiar male voice from the doorway.

She looked up and found Vic Towers standing there, looking amused. Her cheeks heated. "Sorry," she said.

He shrugged a shoulder. "It's not like you can help it. I was just on my way to hunt up dinner. Care to join me? I'd like to question you about the town."

It sounded innocent enough, and safe enough, plus it would give her an opportunity to learn more about him. She accepted the invitation gladly.

"I'd love to. Just let me get a sweater. The evenings are getting cool."

"Sure. I'll wait out front."

A moment later, with her sweater over her arm, she joined him. "Shall I drive?" he asked.

"It's only a few blocks to Maude's, if you don't mind walking."

"Sounds good. It's a beautiful evening."

It was a perfect evening, Hope thought as they strolled down the sidewalk. The sun was still warm, though it would sink soon behind the western mountains, a cool breeze rustled the leaves in the stately old trees that lined the street, and the town was quieting down for dinner. They skirted a child's scooter and a couple of trucks, and from the open windows of a house they could hear children's laughter.

"So," Vic said, "am I right? The sidewalks roll up at six here?"

"Pretty much." Amused, she glanced at him. "Where are you from?"

"Saint Paul."

"Well, you'll probably experience some culture shock here. About the only things open after six most of the time are the movie theater, the truck stop and a couple of bars. Oh, and Maude's. She doesn't stop serving until ten."

"So what happens if somebody needs a quart of milk at eleven o'clock at night?"

"The truck stop has a convenience store. Oh, and the supermarket is open most nights until nine."

"Life in the fast lane."

She laughed. "You know, it's not that difficult to deal with when you're used to it. If you're not in the habit of running out in the middle of the night for milk, you don't miss it."

"Well, I'm certainly going to have to make some adjustments. I'm one of those people who does things when they occur to me. Breakfast at 4:00 a.m. A movie at midnight."

"You don't keep regular hours?" She thought he hesitated, then decided there would have been no reason for him to.

"I just keep my own hours. I might work for twelve or fourteen hours at a stretch, suddenly realize I'm hungry, and be looking for a diner in the wee hours."

"That's not going to work too well here. Well, if you get the gobbles at 3:00 a.m., help yourself to whatever's in the fridge. You can always replace it when you have the chance."

"Thank you." He looked at her, his blue eyes smiling. "That's very generous of you."

"I don't want to find you dead of starvation at the foot of the stairs some morning."

They were approaching the town center now, and Hope pointed out things as they passed, the library, the courthouse, the sheriff's office, city hall, the offices of the *Conard County Times*. Then they turned down First Street toward Maude's, passing shops that were closed for the night.

"You could probably learn a lot from back issues of the paper," she suggested to him. "They'll certainly tell you how very little happens around here."

"I'll check it out."

There were a half-dozen cars parked in front of Maude's diner, and when they stepped inside, they found the place fairly crowded. As they made their way to a booth in the back, Hope waved and nodded to people.

Maude, in her usual style, didn't lose any time in coming over to check out the stranger.

"Heard you're writing a book," she said as she slapped menus in front of the two of them.

Vic looked startled, but nodded. "Yes, I am."

"About small towns, is what I hear."

Vic nodded again.

"Well, just you be careful what you say about this here town. This is a nice place, with lots of good folks."

And that, Hope thought, must be the most generous statement Maude had ever made.

"I wasn't planning to say anything bad at all," Vic assured Maude. "I'm here trying to capture all those things that make people wish they lived in towns like this."

Maude looked satisfied but didn't say so. "The steaks are extra good tonight. Just got a fresh shipment of vegetables, so the salad's a good choice. Coffee?"

"Yes, please," Vic said. "Black."

"I'd rather have a glass of club soda, Maude," Hope said.

Maude astonished her with a smile. "Keep it on hand just for you, Miss Hope." Then she turned and stalked away.

"What a character!" Vic said, the corners of his mouth twitching with laughter.

"You never have to wonder what she thinks."

"I guess not."

"So you're really only going to say good things about us?"

"That's the plan."

But his eyes slid away as he spoke, and Hope felt a twinge of uneasiness. Was he lying? But why on earth would he do that?

Deciding that something must have just caught his eye as he was speaking, because now he was looking straight at her and smiling, she let her questions go.

"How's the local library?" he asked her. "Lots of information on local history and prominent people?"

"Oh, there's a wonderful collection there," Hope assured him. "Talk to Emma Dalton, the librarian. Her family was one of the first to settle in this area, and her father was a judge. She's got a whole room full of interesting things. Photos, memorabilia, papers... She's talking about writing a history of the county. I'll bet there's nothing she doesn't know."

"Good! Then I'll put her on my list for first thing tomorrow. What time does the library open?"

"Ten."

"After that, would there be any chance you could show me around the area, point out the best stuff?"

Hope hesitated. She supposed she could spare the time from her planning, but...she wasn't sure she wanted to spend all that much time with this man. She felt his attraction like a magnetic pull, and the last time she had felt that way about a man, she'd gotten into some very serious emotional trouble.

But Vic was only going to be here a week or so, she told herself. How much could happen in a week?

"I'm sorry," he said. "That was an imposition."

"No, no, it's all right. It's just that I'm preparing for the new school year, but I'm sure I can take a few hours away without any problem."

"You're sure? Because I really don't want to cause you any trouble."

She shook her head and felt herself smiling. He was such a *nice* man. "I'd enjoy it, actually. Tomorrow afternoon?"

Only later did she wonder if she'd let her common sense be overruled by a pair of sparkling blue eyes.

Chapter 2

He was the lowest of pond scum.

The uncomfortable thought followed Vic as he drove to the library the following morning, and he couldn't shake it off. It wasn't that he believed his job was scummy, or that looking for Alicia Dreyfus was a bad thing. After all, the woman seemed to have disappeared from the face of the earth, and Dreyfus seemed to be genuinely worried about that.

But he sure as hell hated lying to Hope.

He told himself it didn't matter, that in a week or so he would be gone and she would probably never even know that he'd lied. The rationalization didn't make him feel any better. Hope deserved honesty, and he wasn't giving it to her.

Ergo, he was the lowest of pond scum.

He was feeling like a black thundercloud on a bad day by the time he walked into the library. The building was typical of the libraries philanthropist Andrew Carnegie had built in small towns all over the U.S. decades ago, and had that particular aroma of books, wood and people that was peculiar to old libraries.

The desk faced the front door, and behind it stood a beautiful woman with flaming hair. She was talking to an elderly lady, laughing quietly. Vic waited his turn patiently.

Finally, she looked at him. "May I help you?"

"My name's Vic Towers, and I'm looking for Emma Dalton. Hope Litton said she could help me with research."

"I'm Emma Dalton." Her smile widened. "What kind of research?"

"I'm doing a book on small Western towns, and Hope says you have lots of historical information."

"I certainly do. Come on upstairs and let me show you my trove."

She had quite a trove, and under other circumstances he would have been delighted to spend days going through all the fascinating artifacts, news clippings and photographs. He was on business, though, and this visit was primarily to establish his cover. Once he had learned that nothing in the room related to Alicia Dreyfus or her family, he spent his time garnering stories he could discuss with Hope that afternoon.

All so he could convince her that he was on the up-and-up.

He wondered if this would trouble him less if he'd ever worked undercover as a cop, then decided it didn't matter. Lying to criminals was a far cry from lying to a very nice schoolteacher.

Finally he felt he'd spent enough time and gathered enough information to make his role believable. On his way out, he complimented Emma Dalton on her collection.

"I'm thinking about putting it all in a book," she told him. "I don't imagine it would have much of a market outside the county, but at least it would be safely preserved, especially the oral history I learned while I was growing up."

"That's a great idea," he said, hoping she didn't want to discuss the details of publishing, because he didn't know a damn thing about the subject.

"I thought I'd be better off going to a small regional publisher, rather than one of the big houses."

"Probably." At least it sounded reasonable to him. He eased toward the door, not wanting to get into this any further.

"I checked *Books in Print*," she said, "but I'm afraid I didn't find any of your previous titles. Do you write under a different name?"

Hell! He paused, summoning a smile. "First book," he said, hoping she would leave it there.

She didn't. "Do you have a contract?"

"Umm, yeah. With Hargrove." He took another step toward the door. "Thanks, Mrs. Dalton. I'll probably be back to spend more time with your collection, but I have an appointment now."

"Come back anytime." She smiled. "And everyone calls me Emma, or Miss Emma. Whichever you prefer."

"Great. Just call me Vic. See you soon."

He escaped into the sunlight of the warm August day feeling as if he'd just received a reprieve. He had a feeling that if he'd really been writing his first book, and really had a contract for it, he would have been willing to stand around and shoot the breeze with her all about it. Hell, he probably would have done a little bragging.

He hoped Miss Emma just thought he was modest and shy but he had the uneasy feeling that all he'd done with his library visit was raise more questions.

Next time, he promised himself, he was going to come up with a better cover story. But how was he to guess the librarian would start asking questions?

Feeling grumpy and disgusted with himself, he climbed into his car and drove back to Hope Litton's house. Unfortunately, it was just now occurring to him that Hope, being an English teacher, was apt to be every bit as interested in his "writing" as Miss Emma. Maybe more so.

And he'd just signed on to spend the entire afternoon with her. Worse, he hadn't yet come up with a plausible reason to discuss Alicia with her.

Oh hell!

Hope spent most of the morning working on her lesson plans, including her fictional story about the arrival of Vic Towers at her rooming house. By the time she stopped, she had turned Vic from an attractive man writing about small towns into a dangerous, mysterious figure with a threatening secret agenda. It was a tale, she thought, that ought to impress upon her students what imagination could do with the ordinary.

She considered sharing it with him, sure it would make him laugh, then decided not to. He was an author, after all, and probably wouldn't be impressed with her efforts. Besides, he might feel she was imposing on him.

Anyway, she reminded herself, the story was intended only to be instructional for her students. She slipped it into a manila folder on the dining room table, then decided to pack a picnic lunch for her outing with Vic.

She had a couple of crispy fried chicken breasts left from Sunday dinner, which she had shared with Miss Muffet, and it wasn't any trouble to throw together a green salad and wrap up a couple of pieces of buttered homemade bread.

Then she hunted up the picnic cooler in the garage and wiped it down. The reusable ice packs were still in the freezer, so she could keep the food chilled without any trouble.

It was only as she was standing in her bathroom, freshening up and changing into clean shorts and a shell, that she realized she was going to more trouble than she should. This wasn't a date, after all.

The thought caused her a quiver of uneasiness, and she stopped brushing her hair to stare at her reflection in the mirror.

Hadn't she learned anything in thirty-two years? She was acting like a desperate old maid who'd spied a man on the horizon and was going to hunt him down. Good heavens, she didn't even know if he was married! Or whether she really liked him. Or if he was even remotely interested in *her*. This was ridiculous.

Besides, he would be gone in a week. *That* was the thing she needed to remember here. The minute she let herself lose sight of that fact, she was going to be in deep trouble. She knew all about men moving on. Too many of them did it sooner or later, including her ex-husband, who had decided that he couldn't really handle being tied down. Hank had drifted off to Montana and then to Texas, and finally she had divorced him.

So she knew better. In fact, she had vowed that she was never again going to get interested in a man who didn't have a strong reason to stay put. Somebody whose job would keep his feet nailed right where he was.

Vic Towers didn't fit that profile.

Shaking her head at herself, and firming up her resolve, she finished brushing her hair, then went to the front of the house.

Vic was waiting for her in the living room. He rose to his feet and smiled as soon as he saw her.

"How was the library?" she asked him.

"Miss Emma has a wonderful collection. I could get lost in there."

Hope nodded, pleased that he felt the same way about it that she did. "I love to go there on a rainy Saturday afternoon and just look through things. It's amazing what she and her family have collected."

"Well, I intend to go back, that's for sure. Are you ready?"

She hesitated, thinking about the lunch, half deciding not to pack the cooler. But she had another thought. "Have you eaten?"

"I thought I'd buy you lunch somewhere. To say thanks for helping me."

She shook her head, deciding it was safe. "I've got some stuff I can throw in a cooler. More convenient, if you don't mind picnics."

His smile deepened, reaching his amazing blue eyes. "Sounds good to me."

She packed the cooler, and he carried it out to his car, while she got a blanket for them to sit on. Then they were off, heading for the countryside.

"I hope you don't mind driving the back roads," he said, "but I've got a feeling the character of Conard City has a lot to do with the character of Conard County."

She nodded, pleased by his perception. "Basically, the town exists because of the ranches."

"That's what I thought."

"That's also one of the reasons we stay so small. There's no other industry in the area, so we grow only as big as we need to in order to provide services to the ranches and to the people who serve the ranches." She laughed. "That was a terrible sentence."

"That's okay, teach. I followed it." He flashed her a grin. "I imagine a lot of young people leave?"

"Oh, yes. It's sad, really, but I can understand it. There aren't a whole lot of opportunities here."

"But you stayed."

"Yes, I did. But if I hadn't been able to get a teaching position, I wouldn't have been able to."

"That's the downside of small towns."

"It certainly is."

"So what do young people do when they leave?"

"Go to college, find better-paying jobs in the cities, jobs with opportunity for advancement. Out of our graduating class last year, we had two students take manager-trainee positions with a convenience store chain and a few got jobs in industry. Most of the kids who leave go to college, though.''

''That's good. So, have you generated any famous people from here?''

''Well, not lately. No movie stars, no famous authors...well, actually, we do have a famous author living here, but she didn't grow up here.''

''Who's that?''

''Mandy Laird. She and her husband have a sheep ranch, and she writes fantasy novels.''

''Neat. Anybody else?''

Hope suddenly had the feeling he was looking for a specific name, but she couldn't imagine who, or why. Then she decided she was being entirely too suspicious about a casual conversation. ''Not really, unless you count Tom McKay.''

''Tom McKay? The Pro Bowl quarterback?''

Count on a man to recognize a football player, she thought with amusement. ''The same. He just got engaged to one of the sheriff's daughters, Carol. Apparently he's decided to settle here.''

''Wow! Whatever got him here in the first place?''

''An accident.'' She hesitated, then decided there couldn't be any reason not to tell him. ''He's a truck driver these days.''

''What a change from football!'' He shook his head. ''Wonder why the hell he's doing that. Never mind. What'd he do? Run off the road?''

''Actually, two guys stopped him and beat him up. He wound up in the hospital here, and that's where he met Carol.''

He gave a low whistle. ''Why would anyone want to do that?''

''Well...'' Again she hesitated, feeling almost as if she were going to betray a confidence, then realizing that was silly. *Everybody* in the county knew the story. ''He stopped to help a woman whose car broke down by the side of the road. Apparently her husband hired some guys to find her, and they heard about him helping her, so they stopped him to ask where she was. When he told them he didn't know—or wouldn't tell, I don't know which—they beat him up pretty badly.''

''Damn!'' He shook his head. ''What kind of guy would hire creeps like that to find his wife?''

''Good question.'' She sighed. ''I don't know. Maybe he didn't know what kind of men he was hiring.''

"It's possible, I guess." He shook his head. "I hope the woman got away."

"No one knows."

They drove up and down the back roads, giving Vic a feel for the great distances in the county and the surprising size of the ranches. Around midafternoon, they found a shady spot beside the road near a summer-tired brook that was little more than a trickle between banks carved deep by spring runoff.

It was a perfect afternoon, Hope thought. The warm breeze ruffled the cottonwood leaves overhead, and the only sound other than the breeze was the buzzing of insects in the tall grass. They could see the mountains to the west, a dark, jagged wall against a blue sky that went on forever.

"Damn, those bugs are noisy," Vic said, laughing.

"City boy," she teased.

"Not exactly. Yeah, I spend most of my time in Saint Paul, but I get out into the woods, too. I love to go fishing on the northern lakes. You know, everything is so much greener there than it is here."

"You've got a lot more water."

"Also more trees. You don't see this far anywhere there." He opened an arm, indicating the horizon. "You can almost see the curvature of the earth."

"Do you have to travel a lot to research?"

"For this book, yeah." He shrugged a shoulder. "Actually, this is my first book."

"Really? Wow, you must be so excited!"

He gave an embarrassed smile. "Yeah. I'll be more excited when I'm done."

She laughed, thinking she understood. "What did you do before?"

"I was a cop."

She thought she should have been more surprised by that information than she was, but somehow it was as if she had already known. "Why'd you decide to change careers?"

"It wasn't a decision, exactly. I got shot and had to retire on a disability."

Her heart squeezed. "I'm sorry, Vic. But you look fine now."

"I am, pretty much, but I'm nearly blind in one eye, so..." He shrugged.

"I'm so sorry." She had the worst urge to reach out and touch him, but she restrained it. She didn't know him well enough to do any such thing. "You...got shot in the head?"

He nodded. "Funny, really, when you think about it."

"Funny? What could possibly be funny about it?"

"Just that it's so weird. I was wrestling with this perp who had a .22 pistol. Hardly a pop gun, which is why I'm here to tell about it. Anyway, I was shouting at him to drop the gun when he fired it. Bullet went right through the roof of my mouth and damaged the optic nerve to one eye. Didn't do any other real damage though. But I keep wondering whether if I hadn't been shouting the bullet would have been deflected by my teeth."

She didn't know what to say to that. "Maybe it would have been worse?"

"I suppose it's possible." He shrugged and flashed her a smile. "I was damn lucky. I'm not complaining."

She hesitated, biting her lip, then decided to test the waters anyway, because if she didn't, she was going to go crazy wondering. "I imagine your wife is glad you're not a cop anymore."

He looked away, staring toward the mountains, and it was a long time before he answered. "She's dead," he said, and not one word more about it.

And Hope, instead of feeling glad at the news that he wasn't married, felt like an absolute heel for even bringing the subject up.

Turkey! she thought angrily. *I'm an absolute turkey.* She wasn't interested in this guy. She had no business being interested in him. She shouldn't have let her curiosity get the better of her, and now that she had, she could only apologize. "I'm sorry, Vic."

He didn't say anything for a minute, but finally he looked at her again. He smiled, but it was a sadder expression than before. "What say we eat? I'm starved."

That night, after she went to bed, Hope lay awake for a long time, thinking over the day, mostly about Vic. She honestly regretted asking about his wife, primarily because it had saddened him. But she regretted it, too, because now she knew for sure he wasn't married.

So she tried to tell herself that he must have a girlfriend back in Saint Paul, somebody to whom he was committed. Because she didn't dare allow the possibility that she might become involved with him.

Facing the fear of being hurt again brought her around to thinking about her marriage and how much it had cost her. Hank Litton had been an attractive rogue of a man, just the kind to make a young woman's heart beat faster. She had met him the first year she was teaching, and had been head over heels in no time at all.

And at first it had been wonderful. Like any young couple in love, they'd shared magical times, lots of laughter, and occasional fears and tears. But after about a year, Hank had started to get restless.

At first it had made her uneasy, and she had redoubled her efforts to please him. But that had only seemed to make him more restless. Then she had tried reverse psychology, making herself remote, and for a little while he had become more interested.

Then one morning she had opened her eyes to find him gone. A note was waiting for her on the refrigerator, and she would never forget its brief, heart-crushing message: *Gone to take a job in Montana. See you around.*

He came home once after that, six months later, when winter was deep on the ground and the work was scarce. But as soon as spring began to unfurl, he was gone again, and this time he stayed in Texas for good. She spent more than a year of her life waiting for him to come back, but finally she couldn't delude herself any longer. She divorced him.

It was another year after that before she stopped thinking of him first thing every morning and last thing every night. In all, he'd stolen three years of her life and in exchange had given her a handful of good memories and a truckload of bad ones.

She'd been angry for a while, until she realized it was affecting her teaching. Finally she had settled into quiet sorrow, a sorrow that had eventually faded and left her free.

Free of everything except a strong wariness when it came to men.

She would do well to remember that wariness now, she told herself. The wisest thing she could do was avoid a man like Vic Towers, a man who was just blowing through her life.

Because never again was she going to let anyone put her through what Hank had put her through.

Chapter 3

Vic didn't see Hope before he left the house the next morning, and he was relieved. Something had happened during their picnic yesterday, something that had melded his deceit into his real life in the most uncomfortable way, and he was feeling guilty as hell.

Besides, he needed to call Dreyfus and report in, and he didn't want to do it from the house, where he might be overheard.

Talk about feeling like a sleazoid.

He felt as if he ought to put on an overcoat and a black hat and skulk down the sunlit streets. Instead he was driving along like any other person with a right to be out on a beautiful day.

And he was getting melodramatic. Hell, he'd always had a melodramatic streak. Maybe he *should* have been a writer. How many nights had he whiled away a boring patrol by making up stories in his head, by imagining himself as being on an important mission to save the sleeping citizens of Saint Paul?

But that was all this was, he told himself. Melodrama. He was here doing a job, and he was doing it the only way possible, and he needed to focus on that, not whether a schoolteacher with soft eyes might get angry if she found out he'd lied to her. In the long run, it didn't matter.

He found a pay phone down near the railroad tracks, where

there was nobody around to hear him, and put in his call to Dreyfus. Unfortunately, he didn't get the machine this time.

"Where the hell have you been, Towers?" Dreyfus demanded.

"Here, doing what you're paying me for."

"What did you find out?"

"Not a damned thing."

Dreyfus swore. "At five hundred dollars a day plus expenses..."

"I'm cheap," Vic said flatly. "You got a volume discount. My usual rate is a hundred bucks an hour. Look, this is a small town. I can't just barge around asking questions. People would get suspicious and clam up. I'm working on it."

"Working on what?"

"Getting some of them to trust me enough to talk to me. It'll take time, Dreyfus...unless she just happens to walk down the street when I'm standing there."

Dreyfus muttered something that he couldn't hear because a truck chose that moment to roar by. Probably just as well, Vic thought.

"Look," Dreyfus said, "I'm really, *really* worried about her. The longer she's gone, the more concerned I am that something bad has happened to her."

"I understand." Vic felt a twinge of sympathy for the poor guy. This was something he could relate to, and it made him feel a whole lot better about what he was doing. Hell, if *his* wife had disappeared, even after she had left him, he would have moved heaven and earth to find her. He could understand Dreyfus wanting to do the same. "Listen, I think my cover story is pretty well in place now, and I can start asking questions without drawing a lot of suspicion."

"Good! Although why anyone in that town should want to get suspicious because a man is looking for his wife—well, maybe I can understand it. She said some terrible, untrue things about me in the divorce filing. If she tells people there the same lies, they'll probably never tell anyone where she is."

Something about that bothered Vic, and he thought about it after he hung up the phone. Alicia had said terrible things about Harold, terrible *untrue* things, but he still wanted to find her? Why didn't she just stand up in open court, tell her lies and collect a piece of the Dreyfus fortune for her trouble?

Maybe because she really was hurt or dead. Maybe somebody had kidnaped her. In which case, Harold had sent him on the biggest wild-goose chase of all time.

But Dreyfus was convinced she had come here...or so he had initially said. Now he was worried she was hurt. Hmm.

Things weren't adding up here.

But maybe, the longer she was gone, the less Dreyfus believed she had just flown off in a tizzy and the more he began to wonder if someone had killed her.

Yeah, that might explain it.

He climbed back into his car, started the engine and headed back for the sheriff's office. Genius that he was, he'd figured out a way to lead into questioning the sheriff about Alicia Dreyfus...if his ruse worked.

The sheriff's office was quiet. The woman at the dispatcher's desk, a withered crone who was smoking up a storm, waved him to just walk back to Nathan Tate's office.

Tate was sitting at his desk, working his way through a stack of papers, when Vic rapped on the door frame. He looked up immediately. "What can I do for you?"

"Sheriff, I'm Vic Towers. I'm writing a book about small Western towns."

Nate nodded. "Deputy Beauregard mentioned you."

"He was nice enough to direct me to Hope Litton's rooming house. Anyway, I was wondering if I could talk to you about crime here."

Nate cocked his head. "Sure. Come on in and take a seat. Want some coffee?"

"No thanks."

"Wise decision. I swear Velma ruins it on purpose. What do you want to know about crime here?"

"Do you have a lot of it? Serious crime, minor crime...you see, people have an idyllic notion of small towns. I'm just wondering whether it really is idyllic here."

The sheriff smiled at that. "Most folks would tell you it is. Boring, but idyllic. Oh, we've got the usual penny-ante stuff any town has. Shoplifting, burglary, domestic violence. And on Friday and Saturday nights we have to break up a lot of drunken fights. Most of our really big problems come from outsiders."

"Such as?"

"Oh, we had some kind of devil cult here a few years ago. They were mutilating cattle and tried to kill one of our residents. Then there was some California company that decided we'd be a great place to dump toxic waste."

"All the problems of the twentieth century, hmm?"

"You could say that. We just don't have as many of them."

Vic had pulled out a pad as soon as he sat down, and now he scribbled a few things on it, as if he cared. "No murder?"

"Occasionally. Like anyplace else, sometimes people grab a gun too quickly. We had three murders just last fall, but that was linked to a cattle rustling operation."

"So there are still rustlers?"

Nate nodded. "You bet. These days they load the cattle onto trucks and get 'em out of here lickety-split."

"But you caught them?"

"Hell, yeah. We may be small, but our cops are as good as any. Hell, our chief investigator, Gage Dalton, used to work for the DEA."

"The DEA? Do you have a drug problem here?"

Nate sighed and leaned back in his chair. "From time to time folks get ahold of marijuana, but so far we don't have any hard drugs. Least, not that I know of. I'm keeping my fingers crossed."

"I heard something about a trucker being beaten up on the highway a couple of weeks ago."

Nate nodded. "Outsiders again."

"Are you really sure of that?"

"Given what they were after, it *couldn't* have been anyone from around here."

"What *were* they after?"

"They were looking for somebody. Not important."

Two things struck Vic just then. The first was that Nate was reluctant to tell him about the incident. The second was that...nah. He didn't see why Harold Dreyfus should have anything to do with the guys who beat up the trucker. If he had, why would he have hired Vic? It seemed like overkill to already have two guys looking for the woman, then hire a private detective on top of it. No, those guys couldn't have anything to do with Dreyfus. A man who was as worried about his wife as Dreyfus would hardly send a couple of thugs after her.

Trying to bring the conversation around to the subject he was here for, he asked, "Do you ever have missing persons? Kidnaped children? Things like that?"

"Every now and again some kid will disappear from home, but they almost always turn out to be runaways. We did have one case where a child was kidnaped, molested and killed. But only one. Generally speaking, this is a pretty safe place to live."

"It sounds like it." And he wasn't going to get anywhere on the subject of Alicia without just coming right out and asking about her. He was half tempted to do so, but that would blow his cover, and Nate Tate was apparently a friend of hers. If folks around here were trying to hide Alicia from her husband, he would be putting his foot into it big time.

Scratching another idea that hadn't worked, he chatted with the sheriff a little longer, then headed back out into the sunshine and took a seat on a park bench in the courthouse square.

Clearly, he told himself, this whole plan wasn't working very well. Dreyfus had felt Alicia might be hiding here. Why would Alicia want to hide? But even if she did, his cover story wasn't going to get him any closer to the truth if he couldn't even mention the woman's name.

He'd accepted this job thinking it would be a routine assignment. His first inkling that it wouldn't be had come when he'd seen the size of this two-bit burg. He'd instantly realized that he was going to have to use subterfuge to get any information out of the locals.

Instant change of parameters. Instant headache.

Well, he might as well go back to his room and use his computer to find out if Alicia had gotten a speeding ticket or anything in the last couple of days. Damn, he wished she would use a credit card. That would make life a whole lot easier.

Except that, according to Dreyfus, she didn't have any cards. What did she need them for, when she always had enough cash? Dreyfus wanted to know. Any major purchases could be put on his department store accounts, and everything else he handled himself.

Except that seemed strange to him now, Vic thought. Initially he'd shrugged it off. What did he know about how the very wealthy chose to live anyway?

But as he sat there watching people walk by, he found himself wondering what Alicia was supposed to do without credit cards if she ever wanted to travel. And what if she wanted something from a store where Harold didn't have an account, and didn't happen to have the cash on her? She didn't even have a checking account.

Weirder and weirder.

The more he thought about it, the more it sounded like Harold Dreyfus hadn't trusted his wife. No checking account, no credit cards. Maybe he was just an eccentric millionaire who was afraid everybody was after his money. Or maybe it was something more sinister.

Feeling as if he'd just swallowed something very unpleasant, Vic went back to the rooming house. Hope was in the dining room, working on her lesson plans. She looked up and smiled as he passed by the door, but she didn't invite him into a conversation. Just as well. He was having trouble meeting her eyes today.

Up in his room, he hooked his computer to the telephone line and began to hunt around for any whisper of the presence of Alicia Dreyfus née Barstow. She hadn't gotten a telephone, at least, not in her own name. She hadn't gotten a traffic ticket. All he could find was an outstanding warrant in Minneapolis for car theft.

That was another thing that bothered him. Dreyfus insisted he'd filed the car theft complaint only as a way to get the police to help him look for Alicia. Maybe. Vic had accepted it without question at first. But now...

Now he was faced with Harold's controlling behavior and a whole bunch of things that simply didn't add up. Curious, he checked hospital records in the Minneapolis vicinity to see if Alicia had ever been seen at an emergency room.

Nothing. Vic felt an easing of his tension. For a minute there he'd been worried that Harold beat his wife.

Feeling utterly frustrated, he went downstairs and found Hope just wrapping up her work for the morning. "Can I ask you a question?"

She looked up with a smile. "Sure."

"This trucker who got beat up. Nate Tate says the guys were looking for someone. Do you know the story behind that?" He thought she looked at him oddly.

"Why? Do you want to use it in your book?"

"Just curious. It seems like such a strange thing."

"Well..." He could see her hesitate. "I really don't know anything about it."

"Okay. Just wondering." Another dead end. Although if she knew anything about it, why would she hesitate to tell him? Unless she was suspicious of *him* for some reason. The sour feeling in his stomach grew.

"There's some lemonade in the fridge," she offered. "Help yourself."

"Thanks, I will."

Change of subject. He'd been a cop long enough to know when someone was trying to divert the conversation. He walked past her into the kitchen, where he hunted up a tall glass and poured himself some lemonade.

"Thanks," he said as he walked past her again on his way to the front porch.

She appeared to be absorbed in the papers in front of her and murmured a distracted, "You're welcome."

Sitting in a shady spot on the front steps, he sipped the lemonade and mulled things over.

First question: why should Hope be suspicious of him?

Second question: why were both she and Nate Tate reluctant to discuss the trucker's mugging?

Third question: what the hell more could he do about finding Alicia Dreyfus, short of coming right out and questioning people about her?

And the final question: why did it make him feel so awful that Hope was suspicious of him? She had every right to be. Besides, he didn't really give a damn what she thought of him, did he?

A few minutes later he heard the screen door creak open. Looking back, he saw Hope. She smiled and came to sit beside him on the step.

"I'm sorry," she said.

"For what?"

"For not answering your question about the mugging. Everybody is feeling a little paranoid around here lately."

"Why's that?"

She sighed and rested her elbows on her knees. Very pretty knees, he noticed. Nicely soft and rounded. Very pretty legs, come to that. He dragged his gaze away, feeling guilty for noticing.

"Well, it's a long story," she said finally. "There's a woman who used to live here who's missing."

He felt his heart slam. "Missing?"

"Yes. Apparently she left her husband a few weeks ago and hasn't been seen since."

Bonanza. At last, the subject he most wanted to talk about. So why did he feel like an absolute scumbag? "That's...worrisome," he said finally.

"To say the least." She propped her chin in her hands. "Nobody really knows what happened. The first we heard she was missing was when her sister-in-law showed up looking for her."

"Uh-oh."

She gave him a worried smile. "Exactly. Then, when Tom McKay got beaten up...well, everybody's on edge now."

"I can see that. Did you know the woman who is missing?"

She nodded. "She was my student. After her mother died, she had a really rough time of it. We suspected her father was beating her, but she would never admit it. Then, after she graduated, she went to Minneapolis and became a model. We were all so happy for her. Now this. I don't mind telling you, I'm worried sick. So many bad things can happen to people."

"Especially to women," he agreed.

She shrugged a shoulder. "It seems that way."

"But nobody's seen or heard from her?"

"No." She sighed and straightened. "Anyway, we're all a little suspicious right now. Which isn't the way we usually are with strangers, Vic. The folks here are generally very warm and welcoming to new people. I hope you don't get the wrong impression."

"It's okay. I understand. I'd be suspicious, too."

Her smile was warm. "Thanks."

She started to rise, but he spoke, stalling her. "Say, can I buy you dinner tonight?"

For an instant he thought she looked like a frightened doe, ready to bolt. He offered the only reassurance he could.

"No evil designs, I promise. I just want to share dinner with a friendly face."

She relaxed. "Okay. Sounds good. What time?"

"Say around six?"

"Great. And thanks. Now I need to get back to my work."

He watched her disappear inside, thinking she had one of the most enticing posteriors he'd seen in a while. With effort, he corralled his thoughts from the dangerous byways.

What the hell was he doing, anyway? he suddenly asked himself. He had just found out what he needed to know from Hope. He really didn't have to cozy up to her any more than he already had.

Sure you do, said the little voice in his head. *How else will you learn about it if Hope hears something more?* As excuses went, it was lousy, but he was desperately looking for excuses.

Any excuse would do.

Chapter 4

As she was dressing for dinner that evening, Hope came across a picture of Hank in her dresser drawer. She'd forgotten she'd tucked it in there under the fancy lingerie she hadn't worn since Hank left.

Finding it was like a kick in the gut. She held the framed photo in her hands and forced herself to stare at it, to feel the remembered pain and the self-disgust that went with it. Then, angry with herself, she dumped the photo and all the lingerie into the wastebasket beside the bed.

What was she thinking of, getting out her sexy lingerie to go to dinner with a man who would be leaving town in a few days? What kind of crazy thoughts was she having?

Grabbing the plastic liner from the wastebasket, she tied it off and set it by the door to carry out to the trash can. Never again was she going to wear sexy things for a man. Never. And never again was she going to even consider putting on the things she had once worn for Hank. She should have gotten them out of her life a long time ago.

Well, today was as good a day as any. And when she thought about it, she was actually glad she'd come across Hank's picture.

It was an excellent reminder of why she wasn't going to lower her guard with Vic Towers, or with any other man, for that matter.

And she apparently needed that reminder. Why else would she have been looking through her drawer for something black, lacy and sexy?

She shook her head at her own folly and settled on plain white tricot. This was just dinner with a friend, she reminded herself. And that was *all* it was going to be.

Dressed in a simple shirtwaist that she wore to work and low-heeled pumps, she went to meet Vic in the foyer. He was wearing an open-throated sport shirt and gray slacks, and while she had always in the past preferred men in jeans, she found herself thinking that he looked almost good enough to eat.

The thought made her blush, then smile with amusement at herself. Talk about reverting to sixteen!

"I figured, as part of my research, I ought to check out the better dining opportunities in the area."

"What better dining opportunities?"

He grinned. "I hear there's a great restaurant in the middle of nowhere."

"About a hundred miles from here!"

He laughed. "We'll be there by eight. Home by midnight. Come on, it'll make a great story for my book."

A chef who had worked in some of the world's great restaurants had decided to retire at fifty and pursue his dream of having a ranch. Apparently retirement hadn't fully satisfied him, so on a corner of his property he'd built a small restaurant that served fine cuisine in a rustic decor.

The restaurant was seldom empty, and on weekends it was packed. The chef ruled with an iron hand, and his wife acted as hostess, greeting everyone personally and stopping by each table near the end of the meal to make sure the guests were happy with both the service and the food.

Hope had only been there twice before, both times with a group of teachers. She thought of this place as an unexpected jewel discovered in the middle of nowhere. From the outside—rustic, with an unpaved parking lot and a weathered sign—one would never expect the quality and charm within. Word of mouth alone kept the place thriving.

"This is quite some menu," Vic remarked. They were seated

at a table beside a window, with a view of the approaching sunset over the distant mountains. "As good as any I've seen anywhere."

"Do you travel a lot?"

"I get around some."

"It must be nice to have a job that lets you travel."

He opened his mouth, then apparently thought better of what he'd been about to say. "I've enjoyed a few trips."

Hope let it go, deciding not to wonder what he had chosen not to say. She was just going to enjoy the evening, an excellent dinner in the company of an attractive man who was gathering stories for a book.

"Well," she said after a moment, "your readers are bound to think twice about the joys of small-town life if they start thinking about driving a hundred miles for food that's better than diner fare."

He chuckled. "Probably. It certainly gives a city dweller pause."

"It's actually not so unusual in the western states. People who live in small towns get used to driving to the larger cities for things they want. An awful lot of people who live in Conard County drive to Laramie or Casper once a month to shop."

"You get used to the distances."

"Exactly."

"Well, living in the Twin Cities area, there isn't much I have to drive very far for. This is kind of fun, actually."

Hope put her menu down. "I have a college friend who took a teaching job in Key West. She says that every couple of weeks she drives up US-1 to Miami to go mall crawling. It's over a hundred miles."

"Malls. The homogenization of America." He grimaced. "You can't even tell what part of the country you're in anymore, once you go into a mall."

The waitress took their orders. Hope asked for a cocktail, but she noticed that Vic stuck with water and coffee.

"I used to be a cop," he said when she mentioned it. "There's no way I'm going to have even one drink and drive. I saw too much of what happens when people make that mistake."

They chatted more about Conard City and Conard County. Hope relaxed comfortably into the feeling that he was picking her brains about her hometown, and was more than happy to tell him whatever she could. She even imagined what a thrill it would be to be mentioned in the book's acknowledgments.

But somehow the subject came back around to Alicia Dreyfus. By then they were finishing up their meals and in a truly companionable mood. Hope was beginning to feel as if she'd known Vic all her life.

"I'm so worried about her," Hope admitted when Vic mentioned Alicia. "If she really was running away from her husband and coming here, why hasn't someone heard from her?"

"Good question. But maybe she took off for the Bahamas or something."

Hope thought about that for a minute. "It's possible, I guess."

"How well did you know her?"

"As well as a teacher can know a student. She used to hang around after school and help me with things. She certainly didn't want to go home." She shook her head. "I think I told you, her father was abusive."

He nodded, encouraging her to continue.

"One of the worst things about being abused by a parent, apart from the abuse itself, is that it sets up a child to get into abusive relationships later. If your parents knock you around, how are you supposed to realize that it's wrong when your husband knocks you around?"

His hand stilled, the fork halfway to his mouth. It seemed to Hope that his eyes grew opaque. "She was abused by her husband?"

"Apparently. That's what her sister-in-law suspects, I hear."

He put his fork down. "Sometimes people make those accusations to get a better position in a divorce."

Hope shook her head vehemently. "Alicia's not the type to do that. She'd come to school with bruises all over her and deny that her father ever hit her. She'd make up stories about how she fell down or got thrown by a horse. We all knew she was lying about it, but we couldn't prove it."

"But if she lied then..."

Hope shook her head again. "You don't understand. She lied partly to protect her father and partly because she was ashamed of the way she was being treated. Victims of abuse feel *ashamed*, Vic. She'd hardly turn around now and tell lies about being abused. It just doesn't fit."

"Maybe not." He looked down at his plate and pushed it to one side. "I'm stuffed."

They passed on dessert and by ten o'clock were driving home. Vic had fallen silent except for the most casual of conversation, and Hope was beginning to wonder what she'd said or done wrong.

Finally, though, as they were driving toward a star-studded sky, he spoke. "My wife felt abused."

Hope felt a jolt of shock. She turned quickly to look at him. "You didn't..."

He shook his head. "No. I wasn't abusive in the traditional sense. But in a way, I guess I was. She hated my job. It terrified her. She was scared to death that I was going to get myself killed."

"She should have expected that when she married a police officer."

"Thinking about it and actually living it are two different things."

"Maybe."

"No, really, they are. People can accept things intellectually, then discover later that they really can't handle them in real life. Besides, fear wears on you over time. Eventually it just wears you out. I should have paid attention, but I didn't. I had an attitude. You know the one. 'Well, she knew I was a cop when she married me....' That one."

"But that's not unreasonable, is it? You're a fool if you marry someone you want to change."

"I don't think she wanted me to change at first. But it was eating her alive, I guess. We bopped along pretty good until she got pregnant. Then it got to be too much for her. She couldn't stand my hours, couldn't stand never knowing when I'd be there, or whether I'd even come home...and I didn't listen, so she threw me out. She said she'd rather just get it over with."

"I'm sorry." She wanted to reach out and touch him, but stopped herself. She didn't know him well enough.

"My fault. Anyway, I figured it was her choice. She wanted out, she had a right to get out. Never occurred to me to quit my job and find something else."

"You must have loved being a cop."

He nodded. "More than her, I guess. Which is another kind of abuse, whether we want to admit it or not. When you love someone, you shouldn't put anything else first. Not your job, not your hobby, not money. Nothing. The people you love have a right to come first. But I put her second. And finally it killed her.''

Hope's heart skipped a beat. ''How?''

When she got the news I'd been shot, she had a miscarriage. She and the baby both died.''

She didn't know what she could possibly say. ''I'm so sorry....''

''It was my fault. There's nobody to blame but me. I should've listened to her, Hope. I should have believed her when she said my job was killing her.''

''People say things like that all the time, Vic. They exaggerate. They don't really mean it. There's no way you could have known what would happen. And while a lot of cops do get shot or killed, an awful lot more never get hurt at all. There are some things you just can't anticipate.''

''My wife anticipated it.''

''No, she worried about it. There's a difference. Some people eat themselves alive with worry about things that might happen and never do. Some people don't worry until those things happen.''

''What kind are you?''

Hope gave it some thought. ''I don't seem to spend a whole lot of time worrying about things that might never happen.''

''Me neither. But it's kind of irrelevant. She worried about it, it happened, and when it happened the shock killed her and the baby.''

''Are you absolutely certain something else wasn't going on? I mean, lots of women lose husbands without losing their babies. And you weren't even killed.''

He shrugged a shoulder. ''Maybe.''

But he was blaming himself and would probably always blame himself, she thought. Maybe he should have taken his wife's fears more into consideration, or maybe not. Either way, she didn't see how he could be responsible for the outcome. Speaking hesitantly, afraid of how he might take her words, she suggested, ''You know, your wife left you before you were shot. She didn't love you enough to stay. She loved security more.''

He nodded slowly.

''And if she'd already given you up, why would the shock of you being shot be so devastating?''

"Maybe because she thought if she left me she could convince me to quit the force and then she could take me back."

Hope hadn't thought of that. And there wasn't a damn thing she could say.

Catching her by surprise, he reached out and took her hand, squeezing gently. "You're a very nice lady, Hope."

"Thank you."

The atmosphere in the car underwent a subtle shift, one that left Hope filled with anticipation. She was acutely aware of the warm roughness of his palm against hers, of him as he sat beside her. It would be easy, so easy, to lean over and rest her head on his shoulder. And if she did that, he might put his arm around her and hold her all the way home.

But it was a risk she couldn't take. Too much more was involved than a simple hug. She wasn't built for affairs.

But right now, she was awfully tempted to try one.

It had been so very long since a man had held her that it was almost as if her back ached to feel arms around it, arms that held her snugly. From the distant past she remembered how good it felt to have another person's skin against hers, that delightful roughness of a man's cheek brushing hers. Was it too much to want that just once in her life again?

She tried to think of something else, but her body had already responded to the mental images and was feeling heavy and languorous. Her heart speeded up, and butterflies of the most delicious kind fluttered in her stomach.

And all because a man had reached for her hand. She had mistakenly thought that she'd left these feelings somewhere in the past.

"Have you ever been married?" Vic asked.

"Once, a long time ago."

"What happened?"

She sighed, feeling her anticipation ebb. Thinking about Hank always brought her brutally back to reality. "He was a drifter. He drifted away in stages. First to Wyoming, but he came back in the winter when he was out of work. Then he drifted to Texas and never came back at all."

"I'm sorry."

"I should have known better. Very few cowboys are the staying kind."

"But you are?"

"You bet. I'm a teacher. I wasn't going to give up everything I worked for to knock around the country following a cowboy. So maybe I didn't love him enough."

"Maybe falling in love and being in love are two different things."

"Maybe. I don't know. If he had gone somewhere and stayed...and asked me to come with him, I might have done it. But when he went to Texas, he didn't ask. He just left, and I never heard from him again."

"Not a very reliable sort of guy."

"No." She sighed, and realized that it didn't hurt quite so much anymore. "I think my pride was wounded more than anything."

"In the long run that's usually what hurts longest."

A little laugh escaped her. "You're probably right. I felt so rejected."

"I wouldn't be sure he was rejecting *you*. It sounds more like he was rejecting a life-style."

"Probably. I'm a picket fences kind of gal. I was also very young when I met him. Darned if I know why women are so attracted to rogues and rebels. He was dashing, exciting, endlessly fascinating—until I had to live with him. I was even stupid enough to think that if I got pregnant he'd settle down. Thank goodness I didn't. It would be so hard on a child to have a father just ride off into the sunset."

He nodded agreement and squeezed her hand gently. "I keep telling myself that life always works out for the best."

"It's a good philosophy to hang on to."

"Hard to believe sometimes, though."

They both laughed, and a companionable silence fell.

It was nearly midnight when they pulled into the driveway. Vic came around to help Hope out of the car. Together they entered the house, then stood in the darkened foyer.

Vic spoke. "I had a lot of fun, Hope."

"Me too. Thank you for a wonderful dinner." She stood waiting, reluctant to have the evening end, reluctant to turn and walk away from him, feeling as if she were standing on the cusp of something very important. As if a wrong move right now would shatter an endless stream of wonderful possibilities. She found herself holding her breath and hoping for things she was afraid to even imagine.

"It feels awkward saying good-night here," Vic remarked quietly. "I feel like I should walk you right to your door. This doesn't count."

What he was saying made a kind of sense to her. Slowly she turned and walked down the hall to her bedroom door. He followed, his footsteps quiet on the threadbare rug.

At her door, she faced him again, her heart hammering. She opened her mouth to say good-night, but the words never emerged.

"Oh, hell," he said, and the next thing she knew, she was wrapped in his arms and his mouth was questing gently against hers.

Shock held her still for an instant, but then came a flood of incredible joy. She had forgotten how good it could feel to be held by a man. Or maybe it had never felt this good. All she knew was that it felt exquisite to be pressed to his strength, to feel his angles and planes pressed against her curves.

And his mouth... His kiss was gentle, not at all forceful, as if he were asking something of her, not demanding it. She was sure she had never been kissed like this before, not ever, and it had the most curious effect on her, making everything inside her soften and still into a warm, expectant hush.

She leaned into him, forgetting everything except that she wanted more.

He felt the softening come over her, felt the unmistakable invitation. He would have been less than a man if he hadn't felt a surging response of recognition in his own body. He would have been less than a man if he hadn't wanted to accept her invitation.

And he did want her. He wanted her until he ached with it. Desperately he reached for his common sense, trying to remind himself of all the reasons this would be a major mistake.

He was leaving in a few days. He'd been less than truthful about himself to her. She wouldn't want to leave this area and the house she had grown up in, and he couldn't come here, because there would be no work. And mostly, he was scared to death to care about a woman again because he had been so badly hurt by Julia's defection and death.

He couldn't risk dreaming those dreams again, and he wasn't

the kind of man who would take advantage of a woman like Hope for a one-night stand.

There were a lot of good reasons to end the embrace right there and then.

And not one of them seemed to matter against the feeling of Hope in his arms, Hope warm and willing.

Hope. She seemed like the answer to every objection he raised. He was lost.

Chapter 5

V ic lifted his mouth from Hope's, making one last effort to save them both. It was a monumental effort of will, and he felt as if he would die if he let go of her. "Tell me to go," he whispered.

There was very little light in the hallway, and he could just make out the gleam of her eyes as she looked up at him. He heard her catch her breath, then heard her whisper, "I can't...."

He gave up the battle. In some corner of his mind he knew he was making a mess of things, but right now that didn't matter. He would deal with the mess later. Right now all that mattered was that he make love to Hope. It would have been easier to cut his own throat than to stop now.

He fumbled with one hand until he found the doorknob. He twisted it and pushed the door open. The light from the late-rising moon was pouring through one of the windows, spilling a silvery glow over everything. Magic. The night was magic, and it was filling his blood, intoxicating him.

Bending, he slipped an arm behind her knees and lifted her high against him, carrying her across the threshold. He felt like a conquering hero of old, and Hope felt like a blessing in his arms.

Beside the bed, he set her carefully on her feet. He turned away just long enough to close the door, to shut out the rest of the world;

then he gathered her into his arms again and kissed her with all the need and desperation of a man who was dying of thirst.

She welcomed him, wrapping her arms around his neck and drawing him closer. With her embrace she made him feel that nothing could ever hurt him again, as if she had cast a spell of protection around him. He wanted to sink into that spell, to lose himself in her and never emerge again.

His hands swept down her back, feeling the gentle curves and the quiet strength of her body. She made a little murmur against his mouth, encouraging him, and delight exploded in his head. She was his!

Filled with hunger, he slipped his hand between them and found her breast. It fitted his hand perfectly, round and firm, and he felt an ache of desire spear through him as he held her. She shivered against him, and her hands tightened on his shoulders, clinging. Pain-pleasure coursed through him, and he squeezed her breast, trying to give her the same feelings she was giving him.

A moan escaped her, and he felt her nipple harden against his palm. Electric shocks of delight exploded within him and settled in his groin, a demanding throb.

She arched against him, twisting like a cat, rubbing her belly against his. He growled with pleasure deep in his throat and fumbled at the buttons of her dress, needing to feel her skin as much as he had ever needed to feel anything.

She gasped for air as the buttons fell open and his warm, rough palm touched her smooth skin. Leaning back as far as she could, she gave him access to her, to any part of her, knowing only that she would probably die if he didn't make love to her.

Her dress slipped off her shoulders, a cool caress against her fevered skin. Every cell seemed to have become hypersensitive, and she found she was even aware of the brush of his breath and the movement of the air in the room. And everything, everything, seemed to add to the heavy heat growing in her center.

She clung to his shoulders, fearing her legs would give out, but he encouraged her to let go and steadied her as he stripped the dress away. Then, as if sensing she needed the closeness, he hugged her tightly. The brush of the fabric of his garments against her skin was yet another erotic sensation, making her feel delightfully wanton to be wearing nothing but her undergarments while he was still fully clothed.

He kissed her again, this time his tongue spearing deeply into her, a promise of things to come. She responded in kind, her tongue joining the teasing, suggestive play, and almost before she realized it was happening, her bra was gone.

She felt a brief moment of embarrassment—she wasn't used to being naked with a man, and certainly not with this man—but before the feeling could grow disturbing, his mouth closed over her breast, his tongue lapping at her nipple. Desire shot through her, filling every part of her with languid heat, and all that kept her from collapsing was his arm around her.

He sucked gently at first, drawing her deeper and deeper into the web he was weaving around her. Then, gently, he nipped at her, causing pleasure to arc from her breast to her womb. She was making soft little murmurs, lost in the moment, totally absorbed by his magic.

He moved to her other breast, making it ache, too, making her feel cherished and loved as never before. Her hips began a rhythmic movement against him, helpless to stop.

Then gently, carefully, he laid her on the bed.

He stood over her and in the moonlight stripped away his clothes until he stood naked, reminding her of a silvered warrior. She looked at him, needing him, but wanting to admire him, for he was a beautiful man.

But finally she lifted her arms, needing him with her more, and he lay beside her, pulling her close so that they met face-to-face, breast-to-breast, hip-to-hip. Then he cupped her face gently and stole her soul with a kiss.

The moment bloomed until her body felt filled with light and heat. He trailed kisses over her entire body, as if afraid he might miss a single inch of her. Over her shoulders, with gentle licks of his tongue to make her shiver, over her breasts, her belly, her thighs, and even on the delicate arches of her feet, after he tugged off her shoes.

Then, with gentle hands, he pulled her panties away, leaving nothing at all between them. He turned her over and sprinkled kisses over her shoulders, down the soft indentation of her spine and across her rump. She shivered delightedly. Down her thighs, to the backs of her knees where he discovered she was exquisitely sensitive, and there he stayed until she felt she could bear no more.

Turning over, she pushed him onto his back and explored him

with her hands and mouth just as he had explored her. Moonlight
let her see, but her hands and her mouth wanted to know him just
as well. She passed her palms over her his chest, feeling muscled
strength, then followed with her mouth, discovering finally that his
small nipples were every bit as sensitive as her own.

Down she moved, admiring the ripples in his belly, loving the
way her gentle touches and kisses made his breath catch. Lower,
to his thighs, avoiding the most sensitive part of him, saving that
for later. His legs were strong and straight, and she almost got lost
in the wonderful feeling as she rubbed her palms up and down
them.

But he grew impatient. With a soft laugh, he caught her hand
and brought it to his manhood.

She drew a sharp breath of delight and learned him there, his
silky textures and iron strength. She loved the feeling of power it
gave her to cup him, to make him moan, to cause him to writhe.
Exultation filled her, unlike anything she had ever known.

He retaliated, slipping his hand between her legs and parting
her silky folds with his fingers. She gasped and threw her head
back, instantly impaled on a shaft of need so strong it drove every
other thought from her head.

He stroked her gently, expertly, seizing back the power he had
given her only moments before, taking control until she was lying
helplessly under his ministrations, more open, more vulnerable and
more alive than she had ever been.

His fingers taunted and teased, lifting her higher and higher. She
hardly knew she moaned, or that her hips lifted from the bed again
and again. But finally, hanging on the edge of the precipice, ready
to explode, she needed so much more.

She reached for him, and he came to her, sliding into her as
easily as if she had been made for him. A long sigh of deep
satisfaction escaped her, and for long moments they held still,
savoring the exquisite moment, looking down into one another's
eyes in the moonlight.

But as perfect as it was right then, it could grow more perfect
yet. He began to move, and Hope felt herself being lifted higher
and higher to a place she had nearly forgotten.

Her breath came in short gasps. His own breathing was ragged.
She opened her eyes, not wanting to miss any part of these moments, and saw his face twisted as if he were in mortal pain. In

the last moments before completion flung her to the stars, she felt an ineffable tenderness for him.

And then the night exploded in a shower of stars, and a deep groan was ripped from her as satisfaction took her. Moments later, he joined her.

They lay together afterward, twined in one another's arms, cooling down, coming back from the faraway place they had visited. Vic got up, opened the window a crack to let the cool night breeze waft over them, then climbed back into the bed beside her. He gathered her close, as if he couldn't bear to let go.

A long time later he spoke. "Thank you."

She stirred against his shoulder and nuzzled him, smiling to herself. "Thank *you.*"

His arms tightened in a quick hug. "I hope Miss Muffet didn't hear."

"Her room's at the other end of the house, and she's partially deaf besides. As long as she doesn't have her hearing aid in, she wouldn't have heard us if we'd howled."

He laughed and rolled her over, propping himself on his elbows above her. "You're wonderful, Hope. Fabulous. Fantastic. Incredible."

She felt her cheeks warm a little. "I'm just me."

"Well, 'you' is pretty damn incredible."

He dropped a kiss on her mouth. "I'm also hungry. I kind of lost my appetite at dinner."

"I noticed."

"Well, can we raid the fridge? I figure a nice midnight snack followed by another round of devouring you would make this a perfect night."

A delighted little laugh escaped her. "Sure. Let's go."

"In a minute. First, I want to do this...." He dropped a kiss behind her ear. "And this..." A kiss fell on her shoulder. "And this..." A kiss found the hollow of her throat.

"You keep that up and you won't be eating for a while," she said raggedly.

He laughed again, and she realized just how very much she loved that sound. He should always laugh. Always.

He pulled on his jeans, and she put on a frilly cotton nightie dotted with rosebuds. They crept down the hall together, whispering and trying not to laugh, as if they feared they would be discovered.

Once in the kitchen, Hope closed the kitchen door and flipped on the light. Her breath caught in her throat, because Vic was even more magnificent in the harsh light than he had been when silvered by the moon.

He apparently enjoyed the view of her, too, because his gaze swept over her from head to foot; then he smiled appreciatively. "You're so pretty," he said.

She felt herself flushing and hurried to the refrigerator to cover her embarrassment. "Ham-and-Swiss sandwiches?" she asked, looking in the fridge. "Or maybe I've got some sliced turkey in here...."

"Ham and Swiss sounds great."

He helped make the sandwiches, piling his thick with ham and a generous amount of mustard. They sat together at the table and talked aimlessly.

"When I was a kid," Vic said, "I used to think the best part about being an adult would be raiding the refrigerator in the middle of the night. I was right."

She laughed. "The *best* part?"

"Well, the best part because I'm doing it with you."

Pleasure warmed her all over, and she found herself sinking into his gaze. He broke the spell by taking another bite.

"Eat first," he said, as if reminding himself. "We need to keep our strength up."

"For what?"

He gave her a playful leer. "What do you think?"

She laughed again and found herself thinking that it had been a very long time since she'd had this much fun with a man. Not since she and Hank had dated, in fact.

Once they had married, there had been very little fun. The thought saddened her in some ineffable way, and she lost her appetite. What was she doing? Heading for more heartbreak? Nothing was ever as good as it seemed once you had it, she reminded herself. She had thought Hank was perfect until the week after the wedding, when he'd gone out with his buddies and gotten rip-roaring drunk. He'd been arrested, and she'd spent six months paying off the damage he'd done to the roadhouse where he'd gotten into a brawl. Had that stopped him from going out and getting drunk with his buddies when he got a paycheck? No. Every other week, when he got paid, he left her sitting at home worrying about what kind of trouble he was going to get into.

"What's wrong?" Vic asked. "I can see unhappy thoughts flitting across your face."

"I was thinking about my ex-husband."

"Not good." He put his sandwich down and reached for her hand, squeezing it. "Honey, the past is not necessarily a predictor of the future."

What future? she wondered. There was no future in this. On the other hand, there *was* tonight, and there might never be another night like it in her life. Was she going to waste it on vain regrets?

He leaned over and kissed her, his breath scented with ham and milk. The touch, light though it was, softened her and weakened her, and started to push the memories of Hank away.

"I could sit here and think about my wife, too," he said as he drew back. "I could think about all the mistakes I made and beat myself up over them, but nothing would change. All I can do is try not to repeat my mistakes."

She nodded, acknowledging the wisdom of what he said, but also acknowledging that she was dangerously close to repeating her mistake by getting involved with a man who wasn't going to stay.

If she had an ounce of wisdom, she would put an end to it right now. But she couldn't. There was no way she could end this night any earlier than she absolutely had to.

She was certainly old enough to know that everything in life had a price, and she told herself now that she was willing to pay the price. What she absolutely couldn't bear to do was miss this experience.

After they finished eating, they cleaned up, then tiptoed down the hall to her bedroom. As soon as the door was closed behind them, Vic drew her to him and kissed her deeply.

The moon was higher now, and the light no longer poured through the window. The dimness made a private cocoon around them, closing out everything else.

Hope caught her breath as he lifted her gown over her head and tossed it away. His pants sailed across the room a moment later.

Then he drew her over to the edge of the bed, where he sat, tugging her gently until she stood between his legs.

"Let me admire you," he said.

She thought he wanted to just look at her, but when his hands started to brush over her as lightly as butterfly wings, she understood that he meant so much more.

"You're beautiful," he murmured huskily. "Perfect."

"I need to lose weight."

He shook his head. "Don't ever let me hear you say that. I wouldn't change a hair on your head."

He stroked her from her shoulders down to her wrists, and she felt her nipples pucker in response to the gentle caress. His fingertips slipped lightly over her collarbone, then down between her breasts, causing a delightful shiver to run through her.

His fingers ran across her stomach, causing her to shiver again, then lower, down the outsides of her legs, and back up along the insides. She found herself holding her breath in anticipation as her breasts ached for his touch, as she longed to feel his hand between her legs.

But he teased her, coming close, then slipping gently away, like a promise awaiting fulfillment. Her heart was beating heavily, and the languorous weight of desire filled her.

She wanted—oh, how she wanted—his kisses, his touches, his manhood deep within her. Her body was alight with longing and need, and the pulsing deep within her echoed the drumbeat of her heart.

Her legs were getting weaker by the moment, and finally she reached out to steady herself against his shoulders. As she did so, her breasts came near his face, and he rewarded her by taking her nipple into his mouth and sucking strongly.

A soft cry escaped her, and her head fell backward as she gave herself up to the wonder of Vic's loving. Each movement of his mouth caused an aching throb of desire to ripple through her to her womanhood. Each movement of his mouth was counterpointed by a gentle movement of her hips as her body begged for deeper, more intimate touches. She was completely his, and nothing else mattered. She felt as if she could spend the rest of her life exactly like this, hovering on the cusp of a need as old as the stars.

His mouth moved to her other breast, stoking the fires within her, drawing helpless murmurs from her. Then, taking her utterly by surprise, he slipped off the bed and sat on his heels before her. Her eyes flew open as she felt his fingertips gently parting her;

then a gasp escaped her as she felt his lips and tongue kiss her in her most private place.

The shock of passion that ripped through her nearly caused her to collapse, but his hands on her hips held her where she was, imprisoning her and supporting her all at once.

She had never imagined such sensations as she was feeling now. Everything fell away except this moment, this need, these touches. Nothing else existed in the entire universe but Vic and what he was doing to her.

His tongue drove her like a lash, sweeping her higher and higher, holding her in a spell she could not break. Mindless now, she went where he took her, feeling the edge of the precipice coming ever closer. She held nothing back. She could hold nothing back.

Satisfaction ripped through her suddenly, almost violently, tearing a cry from her throat. Then, before she could even begin the fall back to earth, he tugged her down onto the bed and entered her, lifting her once again on a journey she wouldn't have believed possible.

It was better this time. It was as if every cell in her body had become attuned to him, to his movements, as if having once learned the way, she could now follow it with greater ease.

She ached and felt full and satisfied all at once. It was as if her earlier peak made it possible to climb to an even higher one now. As if having been satisfied only made her need satisfaction more.

He seemed to be in no hurry, giving them every opportunity to savor each sensation of their union as if it were the ultimate moment.

Pinwheels seemed to explode behind her eyelids, then her body rippled into a series of contractions that carried her over the edge and flung her out beyond the stars.

This time she was so far gone that she hardly knew when he found his own pleasure. And the magic of it touched her soul.

Chapter 6

When Hope awoke in the morning, Vic was gone. She felt an instant ache of disappointment, then realized he had probably slipped away early so that Miss Muffet wouldn't see him coming up from her room. The consideration touched her.

She showered and dressed, her body aching in the most delicious way. Every movement reminded her of last night and all that had happened, bringing a silly smile to her face.

She paid extra attention to her makeup and hair this morning, wanting to look her best, then made a light breakfast of oatmeal.

She kept waiting for Vic to come down and say good morning, but he didn't. He was probably exhausted from last night. They hadn't gotten much sleep, but Hope didn't feel the lack of it this morning. She felt too good.

She settled at the dining room table to work on her lesson plans and to make out a budget for the little extras she wanted for her classroom. Like many teachers, she used her own money to augment the materials provided by the district. She didn't mind it, though. It was always fun to discover materials and ideas that she thought would awaken some interest or excitement in her classes.

At ten o'clock Miss Muffet came downstairs and announced she was going to Casper with some of the other teachers. She invited Hope along, but Hope declined. She really wanted to see Vic.

The house remained quiet until nearly noon, when she could hear Vic walking around upstairs. Excitement filled her, and she waited impatiently for him to come down. Minutes began to tick by even more slowly, and finally she thought up an excuse to go upstairs herself.

She told herself it was silly, that she shouldn't be acting this way, but as the minutes passed, she grew more and more worried that he didn't come down to say hi. Maybe he was disgusted with her, at how easily and quickly she'd given herself to him. Men had a double standard about things like that, she knew. And if *he* did, she was going to punch him in the jaw.

But maybe he thought she was still sleeping. It was possible, considering she hadn't fallen asleep until the sun was rising. In either case, she grabbed the towels Miss Muffet had left on the dryer, and carried them upstairs.

Vic's door was open, and she could hear him talking as she approached. Making a phone call. Maybe he was talking to his publisher? She stopped in Miss Muffet's room to leave the towels on her bed, then continued down the hall to Vic's room, a smile on her face.

The smile died as she reached his door and saw him on the phone. His back was to the door, and he didn't know she was there as he said, "Look, Dreyfus, how many times do I have to tell you? Nobody here knows where Alicia is!"

Hope stood frozen in horror, something inside her breaking with a snap that left her feeling wounded to her very core.

He turned then, and saw her. His mouth opened, a crease appeared between his brows, and he reached out a hand to her.

She couldn't stand it. She couldn't stand to hear any more of his lies and excuses. Turning, she fled.

And all she knew was that it hadn't hurt this much when Hank had gone to Texas. She hadn't felt this betrayed.

She never wanted to set eyes on Vic Towers again.

When Hope turned and ran, Vic swore savagely, forgetting he still had the phone to his ear. Dreyfus heard him and started shouting.

"Don't you talk to me that way, you son of a bitch! I'll have your investigator's license for this! You're not doing the job I paid you for."

"I'm doing exactly what you paid me for," Vic said, holding on to his temper with difficulty. "And I can tell you right now, your wife is *not* here. No one here has seen her. She's dropped off the face of the earth."

"There's no place else she would go. She doesn't have any money."

Vic felt his loathing of Harold Dreyfus grow by leaps and bounds. "That's another thing, Dreyfus. Why doesn't she have any money? Or any credit cards?"

"She didn't need them! I told you."

"Either you're a tightwad or you wanted her on a short leash. Either way, I'm not surprised she ran."

Then, before Dreyfus could do more than splutter, Vic hung up the phone.

Hope! What the hell was he going to do about Hope? He hadn't meant for her to learn the truth this way. After last night, he felt he owed her the truth, and he had planned to tell her first thing when he saw her. Now she would never believe that he had been about to be honest.

God, she would probably never want to set eyes on him again.

He searched the house for her, but it looked as if she had run off somewhere. The thought made him feel sick. This was *her* house, and she shouldn't have to run away from it because of him.

He had to move out, he realized. He couldn't stay here if she felt she couldn't be in her own house. He would move into that motel on the other side of town and leave a note of explanation for her.

God, he was a screwup! He should never, ever have made love to Hope without telling her the truth first. Never. But he should have listened to his wife's complaints more closely, and he hadn't done that, either.

Hell. This was the second time he'd messed up a woman. He'd better get out of here before he did any more damage.

He packed quickly, cramming things into his suitcase without regard to whether they were folded properly. He couldn't do this to another woman. He just couldn't. His guilt over Julia was enough to last him a lifetime.

He stepped out onto the front porch with his laptop and his suitcase, and discovered that Hope was sitting on the porch swing, one leg tucked beneath her. She was staring aimlessly in front of her and didn't even turn when the screen door slapped closed.

He set his bags down and looked at her, hoping like mad that she would look at him. She didn't.

He cleared his throat finally. "I'm leaving." The words almost wouldn't pass his throat.

"I'll give you your deposit back." Cool words, spoken with utter indifference.

"No. I don't want it. That was part of the deal."

"Fine."

No it is not *fine!* In a burst of frustration, he wanted to shout the words, but he restrained himself. He had to explain to her, to try to make her understand that he hadn't intended to hurt her, but, man, it was going to be difficult when she was sitting there looking as stony as the Sphinx.

"I'm sorry," he tried.

She didn't reply.

"I never wanted to hurt you."

"Who does?"

The words cut him to the quick. She was right; people rarely intended the hurt they caused, but they hurt others anyway. It was a lousy excuse.

"Look," he said finally. "I really *am* sorry. I'm a private detective. I came here under cover to try to find a man's missing wife. I never intended to get involved with anyone, and I sure as hell never intended to hurt anyone."

She looked at him then, her eyes tear-reddened. "How can you say that, Vic? You came into this town and took advantage of a lot of people with that bull about writing a book! What makes you think you have the right to do something like that?"

"It's my *job*."

"Well, your job sucks! Do you even think about what might happen if you find Alicia? Are you even a little concerned that her husband beats her?"

"I have no proof of that, and neither do you."

"Harold Dreyfus's own sister says he beats Alicia!"

"A lot of women make claims like that when they want a divorce. Without proof—"

"Would bruises be proof? Melody saw them!"

"If that's true, Alicia can get a restraining order."

"A restraining order! How much good do you think that would be against two thugs who beat up a total stranger just because he helped her out when she had a flat tire?"

"Don't get a couple of jerks mixed up with her husband."

Hope shook her head violently. "You just don't get it, do you? Well, go ahead, justify your paycheck any way you want. But take your lying face out of my sight!"

This apology was not going the way he had wanted it to. Worse, it was his fault it wasn't. They simply weren't going to see eye to eye on the Alicia thing, and it didn't make him any more comfortable to be feeling that Hope was probably right about the situation.

Nor could he think of anything to say, because the heart of the problem wasn't about Alicia, it was about the fact that he'd lied to her. They both knew it. And there was no damn way he could fix that now.

He picked up his bags again. "I'm sorry, Hope. I was going to tell you the truth."

She didn't answer.

He walked down the steps toward his car and wondered how it was that life could change so fast from heaven to hell.

Hope watched him walk away with dry eyes that belied the awful pain in her heart. Once again a man had betrayed her. She tried to tell herself that this was different from Hank, that Hank had made vows and broken them, but it didn't feel any different. Vic hadn't told her the truth about himself. While she might have been able to forgive him that because he was doing his job, she couldn't escape the feeling he had been using her. If she hadn't known Alicia at all, she might have felt very different. But she *did* know Alicia, and he knew it, and he had gotten close to her in order to question her. Of that she had not the least doubt.

And that was what really hurt. Not so much that he hadn't been fully truthful about himself—even in her current state, she was reasonable enough to see why he had thought the deception necessary. And as fast as things had happened between them—well, they really hadn't gotten to the point of soul-baring truths, and she was as much to blame for that as he. Things between them had happened too quickly.

But she couldn't stand the feeling that he'd been using her. That hurt beyond bearing. The questions he had asked, which had seemed so casual at the time, loomed large before her now, a reminder that there had been nothing at all casual about them. He probably never would have even taken her out for dinner that first time if she hadn't been acquainted with Alicia.

And that was what she wasn't going to be able to forgive him for. She sat on the swing for a long time after he left, staring blindly across the street and wondering why she was always foolish enough to get involved with the wrong men. It wasn't really their fault, she thought. It was *hers*. She tended to throw her heart away far too quickly and had no one but herself to blame when she discovered what they were really like.

Apparently she hadn't learned her lesson from Hank, because here she'd gone and done it again. She'd known the man less than a week, but she'd climbed into bed with him, thrown caution to the wind...and now she was paying the price.

Nope, nobody to blame but herself. That didn't mean that she didn't want to spit in Vic's eye, but she had to accept her own share of the blame. If she'd been as cautious as she should have been at her age, she would never have let the man get so close.

She muttered a dirty word that she never used, then felt better somehow for having said something so shocking. Then, angry at herself, she got up and went back into the house to call Sheriff Tate. She couldn't undo what Vic Towers had done to her, but she could certainly make sure he didn't do it to someone else.

The sheriff's gravelly voice rumbled reassuringly in her ear. It suddenly struck her that Nate Tate had been sheriff in this county for most of her life—and that the sound of his voice made her feel as safe as her father's once had.

"Hi, Hope," he said warmly. She found herself missing the way he had once called her sweetie and petunia. Since she'd become a teacher, though, he always addressed her formally, as Hope or Miss Litton. It was old-fashioned, but Nate was old-fashioned in a lot of ways. "How are you doing?"

"I'm...fine," she managed to lie. "Listen, I thought you should know, that writer who's wandering around town? Vic Towers?"

"What about him?"

"He's a private investigator working for Harold Dreyfus."

Nate swore. "I had a feeling about that guy. He was too damn interested in crime around here. Did he tell you who he was?"

"No. I overheard him on the phone. I don't suppose there's anything you can do about him."

He sighed. "Not a damn thing as long as he doesn't break any laws. He's allowed to poke around and ask questions. Anybody can."

"But he's probably not licensed in Wyoming."

"All that means is that he can't set up shop here and get folks to hire him. But he can walk around asking questions."

Hope felt a burst of disappointment that shocked her. She hadn't realized that she was hoping Nate could make Vic leave town, and that struck her as incredibly petty. All that mattered was that people know the truth so they could decide whether they wanted to talk to him or not. Anything more than that was unnecessary...and vengeful on her part.

And Nate, ever more perceptive than one expected, said gently, "Did he hurt you, Hope?"

Her sense of humiliation wouldn't let her tell the whole truth. "I just don't like being lied to, Nate."

"Nobody does. Well, I reckon it's time I had a word with Towers. Maybe set him straight on this Alicia thing."

"I'd appreciate it. I'm scared to death that Alicia will wind up falling back into her husband's clutches."

"We're all worried about that, Hope. Maybe a word in this guy's ear will...uh...send a message."

And with that she had to be content. What more could she possibly do? Telling herself to pretend that last night had never happened, she went to the kitchen to make a late lunch for herself and try to convince herself that Vic Towers hadn't walked into her life and turned it on end.

After all, she rationalized, what difference did one night make in the scheme of things? It was hardly a ripple on the surface of her life. In a few days it would fade completely away, and in a year she would probably remember it with amusement at her own foolishness.

It was *no big deal.* She almost convinced herself of that, thinking how much worse it all could have been if she hadn't learned the truth so quickly.

Then she sat down and had a good cry, because it didn't matter how much worse it could have been, it only mattered how bad it was. And it hurt every bit as badly as Hank's leaving.

Before he checked in to the Lazy Rest Motel—well, actually right after he pulled into the parking lot, looked the place over and decided he would rather walk to Laramie—Vic headed for the sheriff's office. The cat was out of the bag, and he'd better mend some fences quickly.

But more importantly, he had to find out what the truth was about Alicia Dreyfus. He'd been having serious qualms about this situation from the start, but he'd been trying to ignore them, because of his duty to his client. He'd agreed to find Alicia Dreyfus; he hadn't agreed to judge the situation or the parties to it.

Unfortunately, his ethics weren't as simple as all that. What he owed to Harold Dreyfus, as his client, was getting seriously muddied by his growing suspicion that this wasn't a typical damn-your-eyes divorce case. He owed it to himself to be sure he wasn't putting a woman in a situation that would seriously jeopardize her.

So he pulled out of the Lazy Rest parking lot and drove back to the sheriff's office.

He wasn't surprised to receive a cool reception when he stepped into the building. He had figured that Hope would call the sheriff and let him know what she'd learned. This was a small town, after all, and this was the kind of thing he'd expected—and the very reason he'd concealed his true identity.

The dispatcher blew a cloud of smoke in his direction and jerked her head to the back when he asked for Nate Tate. Not even a hello-may-I-help-you. Apparently his stock around here was so low he could probably single-handedly pull down the Dow-Jones.

He walked back to the sheriff's office and got a cool look from Nate and a short nod toward a seat. He sat. Tate didn't say a word, just regarded him steadily.

"I guess Hope called you," Vic said.

Nate gave a nod.

"Well, she didn't tell you the whole story."

Nate's reply was unyielding. "Why not?"

"Because she wouldn't let *me* tell *her* the whole story."

"And?"

Vic sighed. This wasn't going to be easy. Though, to be honest, he wouldn't have made it easy for Nate if their positions had been reversed.

"Okay," he said. "I'm a private investigator hired by Harold Dreyfus to find his missing wife Alicia."

"Did it ever occur to you that she might *want* to be missing?"

"Sure." He shrugged. "People are generally missing because they want to be—unless they've been killed. Which was what Dreyfus told me was his primary concern about Alicia."

Nate snorted. "Yeah. So he filed a stolen car report against her."

"It's one way to get the cops to look when a spouse turns up missing and a divorce has been filed."

Nate's eyes narrowed, then he nodded. "Okay, I can see how you might think that."

"So I came here because Dreyfus felt that if Alicia had just run away, she would probably come to her hometown. I decided to do it under cover, because I figured you'd all clam up otherwise."

Nate waited, saying nothing.

"But basically, I'm just a P.I. hired to find a missing wife. It's the kind of thing I do all the time. I'd rather be a cop, but I'm blind in one eye, so...I look for missing spouses, hidden assets and love nests."

Nate nodded again. "I'm not faulting you for what you do for a living."

"Really? You could've fooled me."

"No. I'm faulting you for lying about it. Mostly I'm faulting you for lying to Hope Litton."

Vic sighed. "I know. I know. But I didn't expect to get involved with her. She was just the lady who owned the rooming house where I was staying for a week."

"At some point or other you knew it was going further than that."

Vic couldn't answer that, because it was true. He felt a serious rush of distaste for himself when he remembered how he had planned to "cozy up" to the schoolmarm. He wanted to kick his own butt.

"You used to be a cop?" Nate asked now.

"Yeah."

"What happened to your eye?"

"I took a .22 in the head."

Nate rubbed his chin and swivelled his chair so that he looked out the window at the courthouse square. When he spoke, his words were almost tentative. "Being blind in one eye wouldn't be a problem on the force here. 'Course, the pay's not all that great...."

Vic could hardly believe his ears. After all this, the sheriff was offering him a job? He wanted to jump all over it. But unfortunately... "I have a job to complete first," he told Nate. "I need to talk with Melody Dreyfus. Then I'll close out my case and give serious consideration to what you said."

Nate turned back and gave him a level look. "You do that, son. Some jobs are a hell of a lot easier on a man's conscience than others." He scribbled a phone number on a piece of paper and passed it to Vic. "You can reach Melody at this number. And no crap about writing a book."

"I'm past that, sheriff. Permanently."

A smile lifted the corners of Nate's mouth. "I had a feeling you were, son. I had a feeling."

Feeling more hopeful than he had a right to, considering he was a slimeball, Vic hunted up a pay phone and called Melody Dreyfus. "I'm a private investigator your brother hired to find his wife," he explained immediately.

Her voice was chilly. "I don't know where she is."

"I realize that."

"Then why are you calling me?"

"Because I want a reason to drop this case immediately."

"Why?"

He sighed and damned his professional ethics. "Because I'm beginning to think your brother is a snake, Ms. Dreyfus, and I don't think he told me the whole story."

"Harold never tells anybody the whole story." She hesitated, then said, "What do you want to know?"

"Everything."

And that was exactly what she told him.

Chapter 7

The evening was warm and still, dusky with twilight. Hope sat on her front porch swing, watching as the street quieted down for the night. Children disappeared indoors, the faint sounds of television programs could be heard through open windows, along with an occasional laugh.

Ordinarily she felt very much at home on this street. She had lived most of her life right here; she knew her all her neighbors, and sitting on her front porch swing had never made her feel anything except good.

Until tonight. Tonight she felt as if she were an outsider eavesdropping on things she could never know and never have. Instead of smiling when she heard the mothers call their children, she felt wistful. And listening to laughter wafting out the windows made her feel more melancholy than happy.

Apparently her house would never be filled with that laughter, and she would never be a mother calling out the door for her children to come in for dinner or bed. She was going to wind up like Miss Muffet.

Not that Miss Muffet seemed unhappy with her life. Quite the contrary. But Hope knew herself better than to believe she would ever be happy without children. But having children required having a father for them, and so far her track record with men was abysmal. She just kept right on picking the clunkers.

Of course, she told herself, this was just a generalized pity party brought on by her experience with Vic. She'd been pretty much content before he showed up, and she would be pretty much content again one of these days, when the sense of betrayal faded a little more. Time healed all wounds, even the ones left by lying scallywags.

She sat there swinging until the last of the twilight faded from the street and the only light left came from the streetlamps and from the windows of the houses...and one by one those were winking out.

Then a car pulled up in front and parked at the curb. For an instant she wondered who it could be, then felt her heart lurch as she recognized Vic. What was he doing here?

He climbed out of the car and stood on the sidewalk for a minute or so, staring up at her on the porch. She didn't say anything, just sat frozen on the swing, wondering if she should run, or tell him to get lost. Wondering if she could even make herself move or speak. Because her heart seemed to have stopped and was locked like a huge lump in her throat.

Finally he moved. He strode up the walk and climbed the porch steps like a man with a purpose. He stopped right in front of her, looking down at her, his face unreadable in the dimness. Then he put his hands on his hips and sighed.

Hope heard herself draw a shaky breath, then felt every muscle in her body tense for flight. Whatever he had to say, she didn't want to hear it. She didn't want to hear any excuses for the way he had betrayed her. And she didn't want to be reminded of how stupidly she had given herself to him.

"I was on my way back to Minneapolis," he said.

Her heart sank, and something akin to grief began to well in her. He was giving up this easily? Of course he was. She meant nothing at all to him. She knew that, so why did the feeling shock her?

"Anyway, it occurred to me..." He hesitated. "It occurred to me that I paid for this damn room through the end of the week, so I'm moving back in."

She didn't say a word—actually, she couldn't think of a word to say. This was insane.

After a moment he shrugged visibly, then went to the car to get his suitcase and laptop. Without a word, he walked past her into the house. Through the screen door, she could hear him climb the stairs.

This was nuts! It took a moment for her shock to wear off, but when it did, she became furious. What did he think he was doing? He'd lied to her, taking advantage of her so he could find out about Alicia, and now he had the nerve to come back here and pretend she still owed him the rest of the week? Besides, he'd moved out just that morning. He'd said he was leaving. She had every right to rent the place to someone else.

Except that there was no one else to rent it to. Nor was there likely to be.

But she was still angry anyway. How dare he! Jumping to her feet, she went after him to tell him to take his butt back to Minneapolis. Heck, she had offered to give his deposit back....

She stormed up the stairs and down the hall to his room, expecting to find the door closed, expecting to find him unwilling to even talk to her. What she didn't expect to find was him sitting on the edge of the bed waiting for her.

She drew up short on the threshold and glared at him. "You can't just move back in like this. You moved out this morning!"

"This afternoon, actually. Precisely ten hours ago. And I'm back. I gather you haven't already rented the room to someone else."

She couldn't bring herself to lie. "Well, no. But I will. And I can do it a whole lot faster if you're not here."

"I imagine so. But I'm staying right here until the week is up...or until you listen to me."

"Why should I listen to you? So you can tell me a whole bunch of new lies?"

"I swear on a stack of Bibles I'm not going to lie to you. So would you please just sit down for a minute and listen to me?"

Not in here, she thought, feeling suddenly desperate. Not in his room. "Downstairs," she said. "You come downstairs."

"All right."

At least the living room was *her* territory, familiar and safe. She would be able to handle him better there.

He followed her down the stairs, his eyes on her. His watching her made her feel awkward, as if she had two left feet, and she half expected to trip. She was grateful when she made it safely to the foot of the stairs.

In the living room, she perched on the edge of a straight-backed chair and waited for him to speak.

Vic shoved his hands into his pockets, looked at her closed expression, then started to pace.

"I was leaving," he said. "Heading back to Minneapolis to tell Harold Dreyfus to stuff it."

"Why'd you change your mind? About Dreyfus." She absolutely, positively was not going to give him the satisfaction of asking why he'd come back here.

"I'd been getting an uneasy feeling about this whole job for some time. There aren't many men who won't let their wives have access to money or credit cards, and the ones who are like that are very often abusive."

"Well, hear, hear," she said sarcastically.

"All right." He spread his hands and looked at her. "I admit I was trying to ignore the obvious. Dreyfus had me snowed. He really seemed concerned about Alicia's safety."

"What changed your mind about that?"

"You. And Melody. I talked to her this afternoon. She didn't see a lot, but she saw enough, and what she saw... Well, it sounds like Dreyfus was beating up his wife."

"I *told* you that, but you wouldn't listen. You said women make claims like that all the time."

"That's right. And I had a duty to my client to do what he paid me to do, which was locate his wife. Plus, I figured if he really was whaling on her, she'd tell me herself if I ever found her. And if that was the case, I was going to see to it that she filed charges against the SOB."

"So what's changed now?"

He sighed and ran his fingers through his hair. "I had kind of an epiphany this afternoon. I got to thinking about what I was doing. And I didn't like what I saw in myself. Here I was, making rationalizations about finding a woman who was apparently getting beaten by her husband. I was making excuses for what I was doing, and I was lying to other people about it, and..." He shrugged and looked away. "I didn't like what I saw."

She nodded agreement.

"I talked to Melody, and things suddenly got very clear. Dreyfus was probably beating Alicia, but he was also being cruel to his sister. Did you know she doesn't even want him to know where she is because she's afraid he'll come after her?''

"No, I didn't know that. If I had, I certainly would never have mentioned her to you or anyone else.''

"Well, it's true. She told me herself. She's not afraid he'll beat her up—apparently he's never hit her—but he has lots of other ways to control her. I sat there listening to her, and I figured that even if this guy never once hit her, he'd still abused her—and he was apparently using the same techniques on Alicia. Total financial control, verbal abuse...that kind of stuff is every bit as bad as beating someone.''

"It can be, psychologically.''

He nodded and looked at her. "So I had this great moment of understanding. Everything I'd seen myself from Harold, everything I'd heard...and me being the guy's front man, accomplishing his purposes and rationalizing what I was doing. Hell, it wasn't *my* problem, right? I was hired to do a job, a perfectly legal job. The consequences didn't matter.''

In spite of herself, Hope was beginning to feel sympathy for him. It was easy to concentrate on what you were doing and forget the larger picture. People did it all the time.

"Well,'' he continued, "the consequences *do* matter. I got in my car and was heading back to Minneapolis to tell Harold Dreyfus what I thought of him, figuring the absolute worst case was that he'd hire somebody else to do his dirty work...which wouldn't be easy, since I'd kind of dirtied the nest in Conard County. I mean, if any stranger shows up here claiming to be anyone or anything, after what I've done, nobody here is going to believe him, right?''

"At least not until this thing with Alicia is safely settled.''

He nodded. "But then I got to thinking...Alicia isn't here. Which means she has to be someplace else. And if I bail out now, someone else might find her. I can't do that, Hope. I can't take that risk.''

Hope felt herself thaw a little more, although she didn't want to. Having any kind of warm feelings toward this man was far more dangerous than she wanted to think about. She tried to keep her voice cool as she said, "So what are you going to do about it?''

"Well, stupid as it sounds, I'm going to keep looking for Alicia. As long as I'm looking, Harold shouldn't hire anyone else, right?"

Her reaction to that was sharp. "Who do you think you're kidding, Vic? What difference does it make if you find her or somebody else finds her? She'll still wind up back in Harold's clutches."

He shook his head. "It makes a big difference, because I know what's really going on here. If *I* find her, I can make sure she's safe."

She shook her head, not liking what she was hearing. Didn't this man have any scruples? "You can't mean you're going to charge Harold for keeping his wife from him."

"Of course not." He looked seriously offended. "I wouldn't dream of it. I just won't submit a bill when I'm done." He made a disgusted sound. "I guess I deserved that, considering I lied to you. But I'm not like that, Hope. Not at all like that."

She wanted to believe him. It scared her how much she wanted to believe him. But he had lied to her before, so how could she trust what he said now? Except, she admitted, he'd had a reason to lie before. What reason could he have now? He had left, he'd been on his way out of town, and had come back...

But doubt still assailed her. "How am I supposed to know if you're telling the truth *this* time?"

His shoulders slumped a little. "I guess I deserve that, too," he said presently. "And unfortunately, I don't have a wooden nose."

She felt another surge of sympathy for him and wondered why she was being such a bitch about this, anyway. She was more forgiving of the kids in her class, more understanding of a stranger on the street, than she was being of Vic.

But that was the whole problem, she realized. He wasn't a student in her class or a stranger on the street. He was a man who had walked into her life, made love to her, and then turned out to be lying. This was extremely *personal*.

Rising, she headed for the kitchen. "I need a cup of tea," she said. "Want one?" Keeping busy always helped her clear her head, even if it was something as simple as making a cup of tea.

He followed her and sat at the table as she bustled around boiling water, getting out the teapot, laying out some cookies on a platter. Unnecessarily elaborate for this time of night, but it was something to do.

"I'm sorry," he said again as she poured boiling water into the teapot.

She didn't answer, but stood with her back to him, letting the water thoroughly heat the pot. Then she emptied it into the sink, threw in some tea bags, and poured in fresh boiling water. "Do you like milk in your tea?"

"Black with a little sugar," he answered.

She carried everything to the table, realizing that she was going to have to say something to him, but not at all sure what she wanted to say. She felt hurt, and angry with him for hurting her, and yet she understood exactly what had happened. The night they'd gone out together...well, she suspected that she wasn't the only one who hadn't expected it to end that way. In fact, she seemed to remember being very determined that that wasn't going to happen.

Although part of her had wished it would. But she had been in a kind of denial, she realized, wanting Vic but pretending she didn't. Pretending that she was in control and that nothing would happen.

He had probably been telling himself the same thing. Dinner out, no big deal. It didn't have to go any further than that.

And maybe, if she hadn't been deluding herself all along about how much she wanted to make love to him, she would have had the sense not to go out with him that night...or would at least have been prepared for the feelings that had overwhelmed her. Would maybe have raised a few defenses against him.

In all honesty, she didn't think he had planned to take her to bed. That had not been some attempt to cozen her. And he *had* said he'd been planning to tell her the truth before she had stumbled onto it.

She poured tea for both of them and passed him the sugar bowl, watching as he took a quarter-teaspoon of sugar and stirred it into his cup. She preferred hers with just a couple of drops of milk.

"You know," he said, "I hate to say this, because it's probably going to make you furious, but I think I'm going to keep renting my room until you talk to me. Six months, a year? You can keep up this silence however long you want, but I'm going to be in your face."

Annoyance stabbed her. "Is that a threat?"

He flashed one of his devastating smiles. "It's a promise, teach.

And if you evict me, I'll just find someplace else to stay—although I gotta say, the Lazy Rest Motel doesn't look all that inviting."

She shrugged one shoulder as if she didn't care. "It's clean."

"Hmm. Well, it's your choice. Me upstairs, or me at the Lazy Rest, but I'm going to hang around until you forgive me."

Feeling suddenly exasperated, she glared at him. "Why?"

"Because I care what you think of me!" He said it as if the idea upset him. "I can't imagine why. After all, you've made it as clear as can be that you think I'm the scum of the earth. I don't know why the hell it seems so important to change your mind."

"I don't think you're the scum of the earth!"

"Yeah? You give me the feeling that you're afraid I'm going to give you cooties if you so much as look at me."

"Don't be ridiculous. But you lied to me, Vic. You lied to me...." Her voice grew thick, and she looked away.

"I was going to tell you the truth. I know I can't prove it, but I *was*. Just as soon as I got off the phone with Harold Dreyfus, I was going to come downstairs and tell you exactly what I was doing here."

Her throat was tightening, and her eyes felt swollen with unshed tears. "What difference does it make?" she said thickly. "It's water over the dam."

"And that's exactly what's driving me crazy! You won't even let me make amends."

"So what? You're leaving. I'll never see you again, and you'll never see me again. What does it matter what I think of you?"

"It matters. It matters a hell of a lot."

He stood up abruptly, and his chair slid across the floor until it banged against the cabinet.

"I came back to the town because it matters!"

"But..."

She looked up at him and felt a thrill of fear. Some corner of her mind noted that it wasn't an unpleasant thrill at all. He looked furious, frustrated, ready to spit, and for some reason that made her feel good.

"We're going to have this out," he said.

With that, he picked her right up from her chair and carried her back to her bedroom.

Chapter 8

Shock kept Hope silent until Vic set her on her feet and closed her bedroom door behind them.

"What do you think you're doing?" she demanded.

"Getting past your defenses," he replied.

Then, before she could utter another word, he stole her breath, her objections and her heart with a soul-deep kiss.

Some part of her knew she had wanted to provoke this, while another part of her was horrified by his caveman tactics. None of that kept her from melting into his arms as if she was meant to be part of him.

Because the bottom line was, whatever games she had played to push him to this point, this point was exactly where she wanted to be. All her objections had been rational and intellectual, but her wounded heart and soul knew there was only one balm...his love. She had been trying to be wise when it was already too late for wisdom.

His tongue beckoned hers to play, and she responded, clinging to his arms with desperation, more afraid that he would leave than that he would stay.

His hands painted fire on her back, her hips, her bottom, until she was standing on tiptoe, trying to get even closer to him. At some point he reached for the buttons of her blouse, and she heard them pop as they tore from the fabric. The sound excited her even more. There was nothing, absolutely nothing, more delicious than being wanted this much by a man you loved.

Her blouse flew away and was followed by her bra. Feeling almost as desperate as he now, she pulled at his shirt and managed to tug it off him. Several more buttons flew around the room.

And at some point she realized they were both laughing breathlessly, pulling at one another's clothes, gasping with delight when skin brushed skin, giggling when things got tangled.

But finally they were both naked, and they stood looking at one another in the moonlight.

Vic sighed. "God, you're gorgeous." Then he turned, closed the window blinds and drew the curtains. A moment later, she blinked as he switched on the bedside lamp.

"No secrets," he said. "This time there are going to be no secrets between us."

Then he lifted her and laid her down on the bed. A moment later he stretched out beside her and lifted himself on his elbow so he could look down at her.

It was a moment caught in time, a moment she would never, ever forget. Amber lamplight revealed all their secrets, and the look he gave her was so tender it made her throat ache.

"Are you ready to listen to me?" he asked.

"I've *been* listening to you." And listening was not what she wanted to do right now.

"Not really. You've been objecting. That's not the same as listening." Reaching out, he ran his palm across her belly, causing her to shiver with exquisite delight. "I've been trying to tell you that I came back here for *you.*"

"Me?" The word came out on a breathless gasp as his palm brushed over one nipple, then the other.

"You," he repeated. "I was well on the way back home when I realized that my business here wasn't finished."

"Nooo?" Her voice rose slightly as his warm breath fanned her nipple. Then his tongue teased her with several light strokes. "Wha-what busi...ness...?"

A soft, deep chuckle escaped him. "You, sweetheart. You're my unfinished business."

She wanted to ask him what he meant, then completely forgot

the question as his mouth closed over her breast and his hand slipped between her thighs. In an instant she was caught on a hot arc of pleasure that deprived her of every thought but one: him. She needed him. She wanted him. And not one other thing seemed to matter.

His mouth painted hot, wet designs all over her, his hands ignited fires everywhere they trespassed, but finally, finally, he was buried deep inside her.

Where he belonged.

She reached up for him, opening herself as completely as she could, wanting his possession in her deepest being. Each movement of his body seemed to at once soothe her and lift her higher on a spiral of aching need.

"I love you," he whispered. "Can you stand being married to a cop?"

"Married?" The word didn't really penetrate. Her entire consciousness seemed to have become a single pinprick of white heat at her very center.

"I'm asking you to marry me," he whispered roughly, as he rode her to the stars. "Hold on to that thought...."

She climaxed, then climaxed again, feeling as if the paroxysms of delight reached every cell in her body, feeling herself lifted up and flung to a paradise beyond description.

Moments later she felt him erupt inside her, and the feeling filled her with the fiercest joy she had ever known. She held him close to her as they drifted slowly back to earth together, and she couldn't remember ever having felt so protective and so tender toward a man as she felt toward Vic in those beautiful, beautiful moments.

"Marriage?" he said, after they cooled off. They were lying together, as if afraid to lose touch with each other, but reality was beginning to intrude again. Hope heard the sound of the refrigerator turning on, the creak from the attic as it cooled down from the day's heat. She had returned from paradise.

And then she heard him say, "Marriage?"

She looked up at him. "What are you talking about?"

He shook his head and rolled his eyes. "I was hoping you'd remember."

All of a sudden she did. "Oh. Oh!"

"Yes, oh. I asked you to marry me. And I wanted to know if you could stand being married to a cop."

"But..." She hardly knew where to begin. The thought of marrying him filled her with an incredible joy, even if it meant leaving this town she loved so much. But to have him be a cop... "I thought you said you couldn't, because of your eye?"

"Nate Tate offered me a job. He said he didn't think the eye would be a serious problem here. It doesn't pay much...."

"About as much as I'm making."

"So...that wouldn't bother you?"

She thought about it. Having him be a cop here, where a police officer hadn't been killed in many years, didn't sound bad at all. "Would you be happy with the job?"

"Happier than I am chasing down cheating spouses and marital assets. But...hell, Hope, we can figure that out. The main thing I'm worried about is... Damn it! Will you marry me? I love you until I'm out of my mind with it. I'll paint church steeples for a living if it'll make you happy, just please say you'll marry me."

A smile spread slowly across her face, a smile that stretched broadly, as broad as any smile she'd ever smiled. "I love you, too, Vic."

"You forgive me, then?"

She nodded, her heart swelling with sheer delight. "I think I forgave you right away. I just...didn't want to admit it. I was clinging to my anger because I thought you were going to hurt me."

"I damn near did. Hell, I *did* hurt you. But never again, I swear. I've learned my lesson. I'll be a plumber if you want. I'll dig ditches. I really don't care, as long as we can be together."

She caught her breath and touched his face as tenderness filled her. "You don't mind staying here?"

"I actually like it here. Besides, all that matters is you loving me."

"Then...I'd be proud to be married to a sheriff's deputy."

He looked at her, his smile growing, his eyes filling with love and delight; then he let out a huge whoop of sheer joy.

Hope started to laugh, unable to contain her joy another minute. Somewhere in the house, Miss Muffet rapped her cane on the floor to quiet them down, but they never heard her.

Love carried them away.

"Learning to Live Again"
Chapter 1

"**D**id you ever meet Alicia Barstow?" Nate Tate asked Virgil Beauregard. "Or Alicia Dreyfus, I guess she is now."

"I don't remember. I suppose I saw her around when she was living here, but I don't have a clear picture of her. I remember her father, though. Didn't you go after him a couple of times?"

Nate nodded. "For beating Alicia. Never nailed him, though. She always covered for him."

Beau shook his head. "Some people don't deserve to breathe the same air as the rest of us."

"I couldn't agree more," Nate remarked. He shoved a sheet of paper across his desk. "This'll probably jog your memory."

Beau looked down at the photo in front of him on the sheriff's desk and felt his heart slam. He *did* recognize the woman. He remembered her as a shy, quiet child who pretty much stayed out of everyone's way, which was why she had never really come to his attention. As a deputy, he was apt to be better acquainted with the unpleasant and troublesome elements in Conard County. "I remember her. Vaguely. Beautiful woman."

"She's wanted for car theft."

"Whose car?"

"Her husband's. Personally, I think he'd have a hard time making the charge stick, but it gives you some idea how bad he wants to get his hands on Alicia. Keep an eye out, will you?"

"Of course."

The sheriff rocked back in his chair and swiveled so that he could look out the window behind him at the sunny day. The courthouse square looked peaceful, slumbering in the August heat. "If you find her, bring her to me, Beau. I'm going to take personal pleasure in dealing with this turkey she married."

"An awful lot of people probably feel the same way."

Nate snorted. "Yeah, but I get first dibs."

Beau didn't really expect to run across Alicia Dreyfus. He and all the other deputies had been keeping an eye out for her for nearly three weeks, and no one had seen hide nor hair of her. He figured she'd cut out for the Caribbean or some other equally exotic place where she thought she had a better chance of hiding out. Melody Dreyfus might think her sister-in-law didn't have any money, but Beau was inclined to think a smart woman who was planning to leave an abusive husband would have found some way to set funds aside.

Or maybe not, he decided grimly as he pulled out onto the road and began his patrol. Some abused women were never able to get their hands on a dime, because their husbands saw to it that no money came their way. Given that Melody had said her brother had invested all of Alicia's savings in his own name, it was possible the woman was flat broke.

So where might she be? Well, almost anywhere she could find some kind of work, he supposed. By now she could be waiting tables in Bozeman, Montana, or Biloxi, Mississippi. Hell, she'd probably gone to Los Angeles, where she would be harder to find than a needle in a haystack.

He settled quickly into the rhythm of his patrol, enjoying the wide-open spaces and the beautiful August weather. Some people would have found the job boring, little as there usually was to do, but he'd tried big-city police work to satisfy his ex-wife, who'd hated country life, and he'd found he didn't especially like living on a constant adrenaline rush.

The two years in Miami had been hell, as far as he was concerned. No, he'd never gotten bored, but he'd never gotten to know his neighbors, either. Here, even in his Blazer, he was a community cop, a guy who knew most everyone personally. In Miami the only people he'd gotten to know were the small-time street punks who didn't have the wit or the speed to get out of his way.

Worse, he'd found his entire view of the human race was getting skewed in a way he hadn't liked at all. He'd become suspicious of everyone, paranoid and angry. He'd lost touch with the kind of people who gave him faith in his fellow man.

Which wasn't to say he didn't meet bad guys in Conard County, but at least here he didn't need hip boots to wade through the slime.

Besides, he thought as he rounded a curve in the county road and the mountains filled his windshield, you couldn't get a view like that in a city. It was a view that satisfied his very soul.

He came around another curve and stomped on the brakes. Off to one side of the road a black Mercedes sat tipped, two wheels in the ditch. An instant later, he recognized the plate as being the one in the stolen car bulletin.

Alicia Dreyfus! His heart accelerated as he pulled in behind the car. After what her husband and his buddies had done to Tom McKay a couple of weeks ago, Beau was almost afraid of what he might find in that car. Or what he might not find.

He radioed Velma and told her he'd found a car off the road and was going to investigate. He didn't tell her what car. Then he climbed out, drawing his gun and approaching cautiously.

The car was locked, the windows opened just a crack. No one was in the driver's seat, but when he glanced into the back, he felt his heart stop. A woman lay there, curled up on the seat, her face hidden in her arms.

He knocked sharply on the glass to get her attention, hoping against hope that she would respond. Nothing. More concerned now, he banged on the roof of the car.

She sat up with a jolt and looked around in confusion. He recognized her immediately.

"Alicia," he called to her. "Alicia, it's Deputy Beauregard, with the Conard County Sheriff's Department. Are you all right?"

Blinking, she turned and looked at him, and their eyes met for the first time.

Beau noted two things in that instant. She had the bluest eyes he'd ever seen, and she had an ugly green bruise on her left cheek.

Something deep inside him shifted, and concern was suddenly replaced with anger.

"Are you okay?" he asked again.

She nodded slowly, brushing her tangled blond hair back from her face. Then, moving awkwardly, as if she ached all over, she reached for the door latch and opened the car door.

Heat from the inside of the vehicle poured out at him. The sun must have heated the interior up over a hundred, and she didn't look good at all. The only color in her face came from her eyes and the mottled bruise. "Did you get hurt when the car went off the road?" he asked.

"No," she answered uncertainly. "I think...I think I fell asleep at the wheel. I've been driving so much...." Her voice trailed off. "Can you help me out of the ditch?" she asked finally.

Now here was quandary and a half, he thought as he straightened and looked around the empty countryside. This woman was sitting in a vehicle that had been reported stolen. By all rights he ought to put her under arrest and take her back to Nate.

But the bruise on her cheek made him angrier than a hornet, and he had serious doubts about whether a woman could actually steal her husband's car, especially if she'd been allowed to drive it in the past. What's more, the last thing he wanted to do was let Harold Dreyfus know where she was.

Hell's bells!

"Deputy?" she said.

He bent down so he could look in at her. "I can't move the car," he said. "You're Alicia Dreyfus, right?"

He got the impression she wanted to deny it, but finally she nodded.

"Okay." He sighed, straightened and settled his hands on his hips. "Come on, I'll give you a ride to town. You've got no idea how many people are looking for you. Your sister-in-law has camped out in Conard City."

"Melody?"

"The same. She's worried because you don't have any money. Then there's this truck driver who gave you a hand and got beaten up for his trouble."

She drew a sharp breath. "I'm sorry," she said. "Oh, I'm so sorry!"

"Nobody's blaming you," he hastened to tell her. "I guess

what I'm trying to say is there are a lot of people who are very worried about you and want to help you."

She shook her head. "I don't want anybody to know where I am! Nobody!"

He hesitated. "Not even Nate or Carol Tate?"

She pushed herself out of the car and looked at him. For all that she was nearly as tall as he was, she looked fragile, impossibly delicate. "I thought about going to Carol," she said. "But...I don't want to cause anybody any trouble. If Harold finds out somebody helped me, he might..."

"Beat them up?" Beau asked sarcastically.

She paled even more, if that was possible, and looked away. "My husband doesn't like to be thwarted."

"I get that idea. However, he doesn't scare me, and there're laws in this county that he might find himself on the wrong side of."

"He's a powerful man."

"So am I." He sighed, shifted his weight and tried to get through to her. "Let me take you to town. If you don't want Carol or Melody to know where you are, that's fine. I've got an extra room at my place where you can hide out. But I *am* going to tell the sheriff."

"Can't you just let me go?"

He shook his head slowly. "There's a little problem here, Ms. Dreyfus. That car you're driving has been reported stolen. Legally, I can't help you drive away in it."

She caught her breath again, and when she spoke, her tone was bitter. "What did I tell you? He can't have me, so he'll have me thrown in jail."

Beau wanted to reach out and touch her reassuringly, but he didn't dare. She would probably fly into a million pieces at a man's touch after what she'd been through. "Nobody's going to throw you in jail," he said. "At least, not in this county. I'm not even going to arrest you. But if you go driving off into another county, you might get stopped by people who don't know you. It'd be a whole lot better to face this thing with the help of friends."

"By the time he gets done, I won't have any friends."

"I wouldn't be so sure of that. Do you have any suitcases?"

She nodded reluctantly.

"Well, let's get them and head back to town. You can stay in the motel, or you can stay at my place, or you can stay with Nate and Marge Tate. Trust me, we'll get this all sorted out.''

He put her in the front seat with him so she wouldn't feel like a prisoner, and put her suitcases in the back seat. Then he radioed Velma and told her he had a small problem and wasn't going to be able to finish his patrol. He didn't tell her he'd found Alicia Dreyfus, because it was too easy for other people to listen in on the police band, and he was beginning to get the feeling that Harold Dreyfus was going to be a real bear to deal with.

Beau felt his hands tighten around the steering wheel. That was okay, he told himself. He'd dealt with bears before.

Alicia was quiet most of the way into town. Beau suspected there was more to her silence than the fatigue she'd alluded to earlier. She probably felt as if she were walking into the lion's den—or the bear's den—given what she'd said about Harold Dreyfus. She apparently felt that if anyone at all knew where she was, then Dreyfus could find her.

He tried to think of some way to reassure her, but nothing came to mind. He could say all he wanted to about folks around here wanting to protect her, but she was too afraid of her husband's power to believe him. In Beau's estimation, Dreyfus was just a nasty man. In Alicia's mind, he'd evidently taken on the stature of a mythological monster.

Finally he decided he needed to learn more about the dimensions of the problem if he was going to reassure her. "Does your husband know about the Tates?"

Alicia nodded. "I used to talk about them a lot. And I put them on the list of guests I wanted to invite to the wedding."

"So he has their address?"

She nodded again.

"Well, I doubt I was on that list. So you'll stay with me. I have a house with plenty of room. You can have a bedroom and your own bath, and all the privacy you want. And if you don't want anybody to know you're in town, you don't even have to step outside."

She turned her head, and he could feel her eyes on him. "That's an awful lot to offer."

He shrugged. "Seems like the least I can do for someone in trouble."

"You won't... tell Melody?"

"Not where you are. But I feel obliged to let her know you're safe somewhere. She's been worried sick about you. The way I see it, the only other person who has to know exactly where you are is Nate Tate, and he won't tell a soul."

"Why does *he* have to know?"

"Because he's got to help look after you. Believe me, there's nothing he wants more right now than to know you're safe and to nail that son of a bitch you're married to."

Alicia looked away. "I filed divorce papers."

"I heard. Melody said they were served the day after you disappeared."

"I planned it that way."

"I somehow figured that."

"I had to find a lawyer who wasn't scared of him. And I had to save the money to pay for the filing. It took so long...."

Her voice trailed off, and Beau had the feeling she had gone far away from him and into memories that weren't pleasant. "So you found a good lawyer?" he said to distract her.

"Um...yes. I think so. One of the biggest firms in Minneapolis. They seemed almost pleased to get the case. And they told me they'd get their fees from Harold."

"As they should."

"I guess." Again that weary, fading voice. "All I want is to be free of him. My lawyer was the one who told me to hide. He said the most dangerous time is right after the papers are served."

Beau nodded. "That's a fact. What about a restraining order to keep him away from you?"

She looked at him. "You think that would stop *him?*" Her tone was so bitter that Beau felt chilled.

"I guess not," he said finally, thinking of Tom McKay. A man who would stoop to that wouldn't be stopped by a piece of paper. "I'll keep you safe," he heard himself promise. "We'll all keep you safe. You'll see."

She didn't answer, nor did he expect her to. He figured it was going to be a long, long time before Alicia Dreyfus ever felt safe again.

Because Conard City was full of busybodies—after all, without big-city problems and a whole raft of entertainment facilities, gossip was one of the leading diversions—Beau had Alicia put her head down when they approached the outskirts of town. When he reached his own house on a shady side street, he pulled into the garage and closed the door before he let her sit up.

"Come on inside," he invited gently. "I'll get you something to eat and show you your rooms, okay?"

His was an older house, white clapboard with a half-story upstairs. He'd been working for years on remodeling, a little here and a little there, but it was getting into pretty good shape.

He took her and her suitcases up to the second floor, where he'd refinished the bathroom just six months ago, and where there was a large corner bedroom with gleaming plank floors and huge windows that looked out onto the street and the side yard.

He'd almost skipped finishing the two upstairs bedrooms, then had decided it would add to the resale value of the house whenever he decided to move on to another project. In this room there were a double bed and a dresser, but no curtains. The other bedroom was bare.

"I'll get curtains up this afternoon," he told Alicia. "Thick ones, so nobody can see you from the street at night."

"Thank you." Apparently she'd given up arguing. He wasn't sure that was a good sign.

"You go ahead and freshen up," he suggested. "There're towels in the bathroom linen closet. I'll just go down and make us some lunch. Ten minutes?"

She nodded and managed a small, tired smile. He walked away, hoping she wouldn't try to sneak out and get away, because he honestly didn't think she was going to make it very far on her own, not if endlessly driving for several weeks was any indication.

Maybe she was in some kind of shock? he wondered as he went downstairs. Or maybe she was just too afraid to stop running and try to put some kind of life together.

He'd skipped doing his grocery shopping yesterday, when he should have taken care of it, so his lunch options were limited to tuna sandwiches or canned New England clam chowder. He decided to make both, since he had a feeling Alicia hadn't eaten in a while.

While he waited for the soup to heat, he picked up the phone and called Nate.

"I've got her," he said.

"What?"

"I found Alicia. Her car's off the road on County Road 92, just east of the entrance to the Hershorn ranch."

"Well, I'll be damned. You bringing her in?"

"Nope. She's terrified that Dreyfus will find her, so I brought her to my place. She can hide out here."

"Marge and I would take her in a heartbeat."

"That's what I told her. She's afraid Dreyfus will think to look for her there." Over the phone, he could hear a rasping sound as Nate rubbed his chin.

"Okay," Nate said. "I'll report the car found and abandoned. That'll probably bring the sumbitch hotfooting it out here, and we'll take care of him."

"You might want to stop by and reassure Alicia of that fact. She thinks he's all-powerful."

"Ain't nobody that powerful," Nate said grimly. "He's just a man like anybody else."

"Still..."

"Yeah, I'll come by in fifteen, twenty minutes."

Keeping an ear cocked so he would hear if Alicia tried to sneak out of the house, Beau fixed the sandwiches and put bowls of soup on the kitchen table. He was just laying out some paper napkins when she appeared hesitantly in the doorway.

"Hi," he said. He could tell she had brushed her hair and added a dab of makeup for color. "Feel better?"

She nodded uncertainly.

"Have a seat. Lunch is ready. I hope you like tuna and clam chowder."

"Thank you." She pulled out a chair and sat at the dinette.

"Milk, water, iced tea or coffee?"

"Milk, please."

He filled two tall glasses and put them on the table before sitting across from her. "Nate's coming over to see you in a couple of minutes," he told her. "He says he's going to deal with your husband."

A small smile curved one corner of her mouth. "That sounds like him," she said. "He's a very protective man."

"That's right. So let him do it, Ms. Dreyfus."

"Please, just call me Alicia. I'm getting rid of that name just as soon as I can."

"I expect you can get rid of it today, if you want. Call me Beau, then."

"Is Beau your real name?"

He had to smile at that. "It's my nickname. My real name is Virgil."

"That's a nice name."

He shrugged. "I took a lot of teasing until the nickname stuck. I used to wonder why I couldn't just be a John or a Bill."

"And now?"

"Everybody's been calling me Beau since I was about fourteen. It stuck pretty good."

She didn't eat very much, and that worried him. He knew models were supposed to be thin, but this woman looked thinner even than that. Worry and fear had probably been killing her appetite for a long time.

It would forever be a mystery to him how people could hurt their spouses and their kids. As a cop he'd seen enough of both to know it was more common than most people would ever have guessed. He supposed it must be something sick in the human race.

He was just finishing up his own meal, feeling a little awkward about eating heartily when his guest was barely picking at her own food, when he heard a car pull up.

"That'll be Nate," he said, rising from the table and tossing his napkin down. "Be right back."

He met Nate at the front door.

"How is she?" Nate asked quietly, so as not to be overheard.

"Not good. Too thin and very frightened."

Nate's lips tightened. "We'll see about that. Where is she?"

"In the kitchen."

Nate walked right by him, striding toward the kitchen with the purposeful steps of a man who meant business. Beau followed him and watched as Nate greeted her.

"Howdy, Alicia. It's been a while, hasn't it?"

Alicia looked up at him and tried to smile.

Nate squatted and touched her chin with a fingertip, turning her face toward the light that poured in through the kitchen window. When he spoke, his voice was soft. "Did he do that to you?"

She nodded, and an instant later burst into tears.

Chapter 2

"**T**hat's enough," Nate said later as Beau walked him out to the car. "We both saw the bruise, and she said he did it. I'm going to nail that sumbitch. I may not be able to get a warrant, because it didn't happen in this county, but I'm going to call the Minneapolis PD and clue them in. Between us, we ought to be able to get this jackass."

"There's the Tom McKay beating, too. But I'd be really surprised if Harold Dreyfus participated personally in that."

"Hell, no!" Nate agreed. "He hires people to do his dirty work. You can bet on it. But if we can find *them,* we can trace them back to him."

"They'll come back," Beau said. "I'll bet you those guys will come back this way again, looking for Alicia, just as soon as they figure the heat's died down about the McKay thing and soon as we report the car abandoned."

Nate nodded. "That's the way it looks to me, too. You take care of Alicia, Beau."

"I mean to do just that."

"I might let Carol know she's here."

Beau shook his head. "Carol will want to come see her, and

the whole town will start wagging their tongues if Carol starts spending a lot of time here.''

"Good point." Nate stared off up the street, then shrugged. "Okay, I'll just tell Carol and Melody that she's gone to a safe house. But do you have any idea how hard it can be to keep a secret from my daughter?"

Shaking his head, he climbed into his car and drove away.

Beau stood on his front lawn for a few minutes, breathing the warm summer air and thinking about the woman inside his house. He wanted to tell himself that his interest in her was the same as he would have shown any person in trouble, but his heart denied it.

Danger. One woman had nearly wrecked his life, and he'd successfully avoided emotional involvement ever since. Besides, this woman was too young for him. She was what—twenty-four? Much too young for a man of thirty-eight.

Sighing, he ran his fingers through his hair and turned to go back in. He had to go get those curtains so he could put them up before dark.

Alicia was still sitting at the table where he'd left her, staring at her hands. When he entered the room she looked up with a wan smile. "Nate looks good," she said. "Even better than six years ago."

"He's gone on some kind of health kick. It just about drives Maude crazy, the way she can't get him to eat a piece of pie anymore."

Her smile deepened. "That *would* drive Maude crazy."

"That woman's as bad as a pusher, isn't she? She wants to feed us all like farmhands, when the truth is most of us spend too much time sitting these days." He patted his own flat belly. "Maude would add about four inches here if I let her."

"She does make the best steak sandwiches, though."

"I'll bring some back for dinner tonight," he offered. "Meantime, I've got to go get those curtains I promised. You just make yourself at home, hear? I shouldn't be gone long."

She hesitated. "Are you sure your wife won't mind?"

"Hardly. She lives in Miami these days. We're divorced."

"I'm sorry." She looked embarrassed. "I remembered her, and I thought..."

"Natural. But no. She wanted the bright lights and a hell of a lot more money than a cop makes. Married herself some big-time bozo who's rolling in dough.''

"I'm sorry," she said again.

Beau shrugged. "It quit hurting a long time ago." He gave a pretty passable imitation of I-don't-give-a-damn, he guessed, because Alicia stopped looking so embarrassed. "I'll just wash up these dishes and be on my way."

"Let me wash the dishes," she suggested. "It's the least I can do. And really, you don't have to buy those curtains. I'll just stay away from the windows."

He shook his head. "I was going to get them sooner or later. You got any particular color you prefer?"

"You should choose. It's your house."

"Yeah, but I don't use the room, so any color you like is fine by me."

She tilted her head and thought about it. "Royal blue would be really nice, with the white walls and the dark wood floor."

"Royal blue it is, then. And thanks for doing the dishes."

Royal blue, he thought as he climbed into his car. Exactly the color of her eyes.

Damn, he was a sucker for wounded women. Only look at a year ago, when he'd been fancying Esther Jackson, the artist lady with the bum leg. He'd managed to keep clear of her, though it hadn't been easy, until she got herself married to Craig Nighthawk.

But this time could be worse if he didn't watch it. Esther Jackson had lived way out on her own ranch, and he only saw her a few times a month. Alicia Dreyfus was going to be staying right under his roof, which would make the situation all the more dangerous.

But he knew his weakness, he reminded himself. He knew what got to him. And that was half the battle, knowing what to guard against.

Besides, he reassured himself, much as he might find her attractive, she wouldn't be feeling the same way, not with what she was trying to get away from. In fact, it wouldn't surprise him at all if Alicia never wanted anything at all to do with a man again.

Just the way he felt about women.

So it would be okay. Feeling better, he went to get those curtains.

* * *

Alicia cleared the table, taking her time about it. Time was heavy on her hands now, she realized. She'd spent the past few weeks driving endlessly, trying to stay away from any pursuers Harold had sent after her, and at least she'd felt like she was accomplishing something. But now, with nowhere to run to, she felt exposed. Frightened. Like a mouse standing in the middle of a field while an eagle hunted overhead.

But Beau had been right, she realized. With the car reported stolen, the cops would have stopped her sooner or later. And anybody but a Conard County sheriff's deputy probably would have thrown her into jail.

Standing at the sink with a plate in each hand, she stared blindly out the kitchen window, thinking about her situation. What could Harold really do to her? she asked herself. Kidnap her? Kill her?

Those possibilities had loomed large in her mind in the days since she ran away, but now they seemed so remote as to be ridiculous. *Get real,* she told herself. Why would a man with so much to lose go to such an extreme? The worst he could do was try to intimidate her into coming back.

But she knew all about his intimidation. Just thinking about seeing him again made something inside her shrivel.

She rinsed the plates and glasses under the tap, then filled the dishpan with sudsy water. Almost without realizing she was doing it, she cast an uneasy glance out toward the street, fearing she would see Harold. But there was no reason why he should connect her to Virgil Beauregard. No reason at all. Beau was right about that. As long as she lay low here, she was probably safe.

But how long could she do that? Sooner or later she was going to have to get serious about finding work and a place of her own. And once she did that, Harold could find her. All he would need was her social security number, and he had that.

A shiver passed through her, but whether from apprehension or fatigue, she couldn't tell.

Her lawyer had wanted to get a restraining order against Harold, but that would have meant facing him in court, and she couldn't do that. Not yet. Soon, she promised herself. Soon she would gather her resources sufficiently to face him, but for now the memories of his abuse were just too near and too frightening.

Her fingers flew to her cheek, touching the still-tender bruise there. All she had done was laugh a little too brightly at something one of his associates had said over dinner. Harold had accused her of flirting and called her names that were burned into her memory. All because she had laughed in appreciation.

What would he do to her now that she had left him?

Another shiver ran through her, and she hurried to finish the dishes, wanting to run upstairs and hide in the room that Beau had given her. She was suddenly terrified that if Harold happened to drive down the street he would glance in this window and see her. Then what?

Moving quickly, she scoured the dishes, rinsed them and set them in the drain rack. Then, unable to do anything else, she ran up the stairs and sat on the bed, as far as she could get from the window. Oh, she wished Beau would hurry with those curtains!

But as she sat there, feeling frightened, she also began to feel foolish. Whatever threat there was, it wasn't immediate. Harold had to find her first, and it was silly to sit huddled up here as if he were right outside the door. She had to get a grip!

Sometime later, she heard the garage door open and a car drive in. Beau was back. The realization took the edge off her tension, and relief flowed through her. It was wonderful, she thought, not to be alone with this.

A couple of minutes later, she heard him climbing the uncarpeted stairs. He knocked on the door.

"Alicia?"

"Come in, Beau." Beau. Why Beau? She thought Virgil was a beautiful name and wondered if he would mind if she called him that. But it was too soon to presume.

"Could you open the door? My hands are full."

Feeling embarrassed, Alicia hurried across the room and pulled the door open. Beau stepped in with his arms full of curtain rods and packages of royal blue material.

"These are insulated curtains," he said as he dropped everything on the bed. "Nobody will even see your silhouette through them."

He turned to smile at her. "How are you doing?"

"Fighting off a panic attack," she admitted frankly. "I keep trying to tell myself he can't do anything to me, but..." She shrugged, leaving the sentence incomplete.

His smile faded. "He can't do anything to you as long as you're not alone and he can't find you."

She nodded and sat on the edge of the bed, looking down at the packages of curtains. Idly, she ran her hand over the plastic. "It's weird. Even after the last few years, I still have trouble believing he would really hurt me. It seems so...crazy, you know? Why would he risk so much?"

"He's a control freak. At least, that's what Adam Roth says."

"Who's he?"

Beau sat on the straight-back chair beside the dresser. "I guess you've got a lot of catching up to do. I told you your sister-in-law is here looking for you?"

"Melody? Yes, you did."

"Well, when she got here, she was sick. Dehydration. She spent a day in the hospital."

Alicia caught her breath. "Poor Mel! She's okay now, though?"

"Right as rain." Beau leaned forward, resting his elbows on his knees. "She's also engaged."

Alicia's head came up, and her eyes widened at that. "Wow! That was fast. She hasn't even dated since I've known her."

Beau grinned. "Well, Adam wasn't going to let her get away, near as I can tell. The guy's head-over-heels. He was her doctor when she was sick, and I guess she told him a lot about Harold. Adam says Harold is a control freak. The most important thing to him is that other people do exactly what he wants. Apparently it's starting to push him over the edge."

Alicia thought about that. It was true, she realized, that the only time Harold gave her any trouble was when she didn't do exactly what he wanted. At first it had seemed a small thing, but as time went by his demands had grown, until she had felt like a puppet on a string, unable to decide even the simplest thing for herself. "That's Harold," she agreed finally. "He wouldn't even let me decide what to wear."

Beau shook his head. "Don't that beat all."

"At first...at first I thought he was trying to help me." She realized her hands were shaking again, and she clasped them in her lap to hide the tremors. "I mean, I was a small-town girl. You know my roots. I had to be shown the right fork to use and all that. So when Harold started telling me how to dress, I thought it was because I didn't know what was appropriate. The same when he started telling me how to act. He moved with all these wealthy people in society, and I was just a cowboy's daughter who spent a couple of years modeling clothes for magazines and catalogues. When he told me not to talk so much, I thought it was because I was saying stupid things and embarrassing him.''

Beau nodded. "You still think that, don't you?"

She sighed and looked down. "I guess so."

"Well, it's not true, Alicia. You might be a country girl at heart, but you were still good enough for him to marry."

Her head snapped up, and a surprised little laugh escaped her. "I didn't think of it that way!"

Beau shrugged. "This Pygmalion stuff is for the birds. Folks shouldn't go around trying to change other people."

He stood. "I'm going to get my tools so we can get these curtains up. Before you know it, you'll be wanting to turn on some lights in here."

"Can I help?"

"Sure. Just don't get close to the windows."

So she opened the packages of curtains, shook out the wrinkles and inserted the hooks while Beau measured, drilled and put up the rods.

She found herself watching him while she put in the hooks. To her way of thinking, Beau was a very attractive man. He was tall and lean, and weathered by the elements. A Conard County man, not at all like Harold, who was soft from a life spent mostly indoors behind a desk. That had attracted her once, but no more.

Not that she wanted to be attracted to anyone right now, she reminded herself. Her life was in too much of a mess, and she had too much baggage to deal with. Besides, after Harold, it would probably be a long time before she would ever trust another man that way.

Even so, she noticed Beau—but she told herself it was just because he was helping her. Right now she was vulnerable to anyone who seemed to care about her.

Be careful, she told herself. Don't jump from the frying pan into the fire.

"Is there any way I can talk to Melody or Carol?" she asked, wanting to move away from the disturbing direction her thoughts were taking.

Beau paused in the process of putting the rod on the bracket. "I don't know," he said. "I suppose you could call them on the phone, but don't tell them where you are."

"Why not?"

"Because they'll want to come over to see you. And if they do that, either the whole town is going to be gossiping about them spending so much time at my place, or somebody is going to figure out the connection. But I'm sure they want to hear from you. Nate is going to tell them you're at a safe house." He chuckled and finished putting up the rod. "I feel for him. He said I don't know how hard it can be to keep a secret from Carol."

Alicia smiled. "I never could keep a secret from her. Ever. Not that there were too many I wanted to keep." Except for her father getting drunk and beating her. That was one she'd managed never to tell anyone, even people who guessed the truth.

"What happened to your dad?" Beau asked, almost as if he were reading her mind. "He moved away after you left, and nobody ever heard from him again."

"I don't know. I never heard from him, either."

"Hell." Beau stepped down from the ladder and reached for the other rod. "I don't know, Alicia. Sometimes I just don't know about people. Sometimes they do things that are downright unnatural, if you think about it."

She nodded agreement. "But maybe it's not unnatural."

He faced her, rod in hand. "Don't start thinking that way. People who batter their kids and their wives aren't natural. There's something broken in them, sure as I'm standing here. I see a hell of a lot of it as a cop, but as much as I see, I can't start letting myself believe that it's normal. The minute I do that, I might as well turn in my badge and give up."

He moved the ladder and started to put the second rod up. "God knows I saw some awful stuff in Miami."

"Miami?"

"Miami," he repeated. "My ex wanted to move to the big city and a warmer climate. Claimed she was dying of boredom here. Not that I can blame her, I guess. Unless people are your main interest in life, there isn't much happening around here usually."

"We roll up the sidewalks at six," Alicia agreed.

He smiled over her shoulder. "Damn near it. Ellie wanted some nightlife. Restaurants, places to go dancing, the theater—all that stuff. Nothing wrong with that, really. Not my style, but nothing wrong with it. Anyway, I took a job as a cop down there, and she was happy for a while."

"What happened?"

"Oh, I don't know. Maybe I wasn't home enough in the evening to suit her. Probably didn't make enough money. I mean, the salary sounded real good until we got there and discovered the cost of living."

"I can imagine."

"So there we were, living in this little box of a rental house, with window air conditioners that didn't always work, and I was away at night as often as not—and she found somebody who had more money and could be around more often."

"And you didn't want to stay there?"

"Hell, no. I was so busy dealing with bad guys that I never got to meet the good folks. Pass me the curtains, will you?"

She brought him the first one and stood to the side of the window while he put it up. "Too much action?" she asked.

"I guess so." He glanced down at her. "There's a pace to life here that I like. Most of the folks I see on my patrol are good people. I stop at their ranches to check up on them, have a cup of coffee and talk. There wasn't any time for that down there. None at all. The only good guys I got to know were other cops. And not all of *them* were good, either."

"I started to feel like that in Harold's crowd," Alicia said. She went to get another curtain and passed it up to him. "I never got to make any real friends, and everything started to feel plastic. That probably isn't fair, though."

"Maybe not. I suspect Harold didn't want you to have any friends."

"No, I don't think so, either." She glanced out the window, realized she was standing too close to it and backed up. "I guess I should call my lawyer and tell him I'm still alive."

"He might appreciate that. Go ahead and use the phone."

"You don't mind?"

He looked down at her and smiled. "I don't mind at all, Alicia. Help yourself to anything around here, including the phone."

"I'll pay you back." As soon as she could find a job. She *had* to find a job.

"Don't worry about it. Getting you out of this mess is all the payback I need."

Alicia went downstairs, thinking that Beau was one very special person.

Chapter 3

Lew Altares, Alicia's attorney, was thrilled to hear from her. "My God, I was getting to the point of wondering when they'd drag your body out of the river!"

"I'm sorry. I was running too hard to think of anybody else."

"That's all right. I told you to clear out, didn't I? Most dangerous time is right after the papers are served. Hiding is a good thing right now. Although, I gotta admit, Dreyfus's attorneys are getting downright nasty about where you are."

"You won't tell them?"

"Hell, no! Attorney-client privilege. Which they know, so they shouldn't even be asking. Idiots. Anyway, there's nothing you need to do right now. We've served the interrogatories about Harold's financial condition, and they've served us the interrogatories about your financial condition—which is easy, since it's a great big goose egg, thanks to that so-and-so. I *do* need you to answer some of the questions, though, and you'll have to have your signature notarized." He paused. "Let's stall on this a bit, okay? If you get the papers notarized where you are now, they'll know where to look."

"I think they already suspect." She told him about Melody, and about what had happened to the nice truck driver who had helped her.

"Son of a...gun!" She could hear him tapping his pencil on the desk in the background. She had already learned that Lew did that whenever he was thinking, so she remained quiet and let him ponder.

"I don't like this, Alicia. I don't like this at all. Who's investigating what happened to the truck driver?"

"The Conard County, Wyoming, Sheriff's Department."

"I'll give them a call. Maybe we can use this to get a restraining order. Maybe we can use this to keep you hidden until we can nail him with something. I mean, if you're in danger for your life, they can't really expect you to turn up in person for depositions...." He trailed off. "I need to think about this some more. I'm going to find some hook to hang that son of gun on, I promise you. In the meantime, don't worry about the divorce. We've filed the papers, but I can buy as much time as we need on the interrogatories. I realize you want this over with as quickly as possible, but for right now, let's just stall, okay? Once I've got my hook, things'll happen real fast, because he won't want the publicity."

"That sounds good to me, Lew."

"So sit tight and lay low, Alicia. Do you need any money? I'd be happy to advance you some."

"Against what? I barely paid for the filing, never mind your fees."

He laughed richly. "Believe me, Harold's going to pay for it all. Every last little bit, I promise you. You just hang in there. Besides, the court would order Harold to pay your living expenses right now anyway. Hmm. Maybe I'll file for that tomorrow. Wouldn't that wipe the smile off his face?" He laughed again.

When she hung up, Alicia felt a whole lot better.

"Everything okay?"

Beau's voice startled her, and she whirled around sharply before catching herself and remembering that he wasn't a threat. He froze in the doorway and waited.

"I didn't mean to scare you," he said.

"No...no...I'm just edgy." She gave a breathless little laugh and put her hand over her hammering heart. "Sorry."

"No need to apologize." But he remained in the doorway. "The curtains are up."

"Thank you. I'm so sorry," she said again.

He shook his head almost irritably. "It's okay," he said. "I can sure as hell understand why you'd get jumpy when a man comes up behind you. Let me give you Carol's phone number so you can call her. Then I'll take a walk."

She stepped back as he scrawled the number on a pad by the phone, then watched him go. She had the awful feeling that she'd driven him out of his own house.

For long minutes she didn't move, just stared blindly into space, thinking about the person she had become. And she didn't at all like what she saw.

Beau knew he was overreacting. Why shouldn't the woman be scared of men? He'd seen the bruise on her face, and he suspected that wasn't the worst of it. So why was he letting himself get annoyed because she'd reacted with understandable fright when he'd startled her?

Because he didn't see himself that way. Because he would never lay an unwelcome finger on a woman. Because for that instant of time, he had felt as if he were a beast in her eyes.

So even though he knew her reaction wasn't directed at him personally, he decided he'd best stay out of her way. Tomorrow he would be back on the job, and that would help. But they still had the rest of this day to get through, and he wasn't the type who could go down to Mahoney's and hang around for the evening.

Maybe having her stay with him wasn't such a good idea. Maybe he ought to find her somewhere else to hide. But where? If she stayed with someone she knew, it'd be easier for Harold to find her. And why would she want to move in with a total stranger?

Which was part of the problem, he realized. *He* was a total stranger to her. Staying with him was bound to make her uneasy on that basis alone. Add to that the fact that she was a battered wife, and she had even more reason to be on edge.

Maybe it *would* be best for her to stay with Marge and Nate Tate—except for what those two thugs had done to Tom McKay. No way was Beau willing to let Marge run that risk. Marge or her daughters.

So this was it. And he had to get over the feeling that he'd been unjustly accused and convicted simply because he was a man.

Finally, feeling like several kinds of a fool for the way he had reacted, he turned around and headed home.

Hell, he was still wearing his uniform, he realized. Helping Alicia had somehow short-circuited his brain.

He was still shaking his head at himself when he walked back into the house.

She was sitting at the kitchen table, looking lost and alone. When he opened the door, she looked up quickly, then smiled.

"Hi," she said.

"Hi. Look, I'm sorry about storming out of here."

"You didn't exactly storm, Beau. And *I'm* sorry. I'm just so jumpy!"

"That's understandable." He stayed where he was, just inside the door, almost afraid to get any closer to her. "Did you talk to Carol?"

"Yes. Yes, I did." She compressed her lips. "She was so nice to me!"

"Why wouldn't she be? She's your friend."

"But I didn't even invite her to my wedding! Well, I tried to, but Harold—" She broke off sharply. "Anyway, she forgave me for not inviting her and not writing to her, and all she seemed concerned about was whether I was safe. And she even wanted to beat up Harold!" The last came out on a shaky laugh.

Almost in spite of himself, Beau smiled. "I reckon there are a few people around here who'd like to do the same thing. You can count me in."

Alicia's smile became more genuine. "I have to admit, I kind of like the idea. But I don't want anyone to get into any trouble on my account."

"The only one who's going to get into any trouble on your account is Harold." He decided to try coming a little closer. Otherwise he would never be able to get past her and go change.

"My lawyer's going to try to do something about it," Alicia continued. "Lew Altares, so you know in case he calls."

Beau nodded.

"He's going to get a restraining order somehow, and he said he's going to make Harold pay my living expenses." She shook her head. "Boy, that's going to make him furious."

"It's the least he can do, since he robbed you blind."

Color appeared in her cheeks. "You heard about that?"

"Something about it." He pulled out a chair and sat across the table from her. "This is a small town, remember?"

She nodded. "I guess I forgot. But I feel so stupid about it, Beau. He wanted to invest my money. He said I'd get a much better return than keeping it in certificates of deposit. It made sense to me, so I let him have it all. I didn't realize until about a year ago that he'd put it all in *his* name. I can't even touch it. And when I complained about it he—" Again she broke off. "It doesn't matter. Lew says he'll get it all back for me, but that might take six months or a year, depending on how hard Harold fights the divorce."

"I guess he didn't want you to have any way to escape."

Her head snapped up, and she looked straight at him from those incredibly blue eyes. "I didn't think of that! But you're probably right. I would have thought my savings would be a drop in the bucket compared to his wealth."

"It probably was. But as long as you had money of your own, you could go your own way. It all fits, Alicia. Major control freak. He cut you off from your friends, and then he cut you off from your money. I'll bet you didn't even have a joint checking account."

Her eyes widened. "No. He gave me an allowance each month for pin money. He bought everything else."

"How much pin money?"

Her cheeks burned again. "Fifty dollars."

"And no credit cards."

She shook her head. "I canceled all mine when we got married, because he said he was going to put me on his. But he never did." She looked away from him. "At first it didn't seem so outrageous, Beau. I know how it sounds, but...I didn't *need* anything. If I wanted to go out to lunch, I could charge it at one of the restaurants we frequented. I never even needed to put gas in the car, because the chauffeur took care of all that. The housekeeper bought the groceries, and if I wanted something all I had to do was tell her. And everything else—well, he took me shopping, even."

"Sort of like the Queen, I guess, with nothing in her purse but a hanky."

A faint smile flickered over her face. "I guess. It seemed so magical to me at first, you know? As if all I had to do was express a wish and it would happen. I didn't have to worry about anything at all."

"Quite a difference from what you were used to."

"It was. I guess I got blinded. I didn't realize how dependent I was becoming." A sigh escaped her. "I know *now*. Believe me, I know."

"So he reeled you in gently."

She nodded. "I woke up one day and realized I was a bird in a gilded cage. I'd become a cliché."

"Right about the time he started getting abusive, I imagine."

"It's awful to admit I didn't realize what was happening. I feel so stupid! At first I thought he was teaching me things. You know. Better fashion sense, better taste, better manners. But then he started hitting me when I messed up or wanted something different, and that's when I realized I was being trained like an animal."

"I don't know how they do it," Beau said after a moment. "But I noticed a long time ago that abusers are better than psychologists at brainwashing and behavior modification. They seem to be born with an instinct for manipulation and control. A friend of mine had a young daughter get into that kind of situation, and he just about went nuts trying to find a way to get her out. He kept saying it was like she was a zombie, like she was brainwashed. He even talked about hiring a deprogrammer to yank her away from the guy and work her out of it. It was like she was under some kind of spell, he said."

"That's it! That's how I felt, exactly. I'd have these brief moments when I'd look at myself and wonder what was wrong with me, but by then I was...I don't know. Sure that Harold was right and I was just a screwup. Afraid of making him angry." She looked down. "Now I look at myself and I don't like what I see at all."

Beau didn't quite know how to answer that. He could understand how she was feeling, because he hadn't felt very good about himself after Ellie ditched him. Not when he thought about how he'd torn up his life for that woman and busted his butt trying to make her happy, even though it had meant making himself miserable. Not when he had to face the fact that he'd never been and never would be good enough for her.

Nobody could take away those feelings for you. You had to get over them yourself. "Are you thinking about going back to modeling?" he asked finally.

"No. I didn't really like it. I just did it because it was a way to support myself, and I made more than I would waiting tables."

"I thought every woman dreamed of being a model."

That brought a smile to her face. "Every woman dreams of being a supermodel, but there are only seven or eight of them in the world. The rest of us, like me, wind up making a moderate income and feeling like pieces of meat. At least, I did. There's not a whole lot of glamor in modeling clothes for a department store's weekly flyer. And there's so much competition, you wind up getting totally absorbed in your face and body, trying to make sure everything is always just right. I finally started feeling that my body and I were separate things, almost the way I felt about my car. I drove it, took care of it, polished it up and fueled it just right, but it was nothing but a tool."

"I can't imagine that." And he really couldn't. His body was an extension of himself.

"Well, I got hypercritical of myself. I'd stand in front of the mirror making sure my complexion was perfect, checking to be sure I wasn't sagging or getting plump somewhere. I worked all day and spent all evening working out and working on my complexion. It gets to be an obsession."

He nodded, encouraging her to continue.

"I thought when I married Harold that I would put all that behind me but he...wanted me to keep taking care of myself. So all that changed was that I worked on my body and my face for a good part of each day, so I could go out in the evening with him, looking like a model. He even controlled what I ate so I wouldn't gain weight."

"Excuse me for saying so, but a little weight wouldn't hurt."

She didn't take offense. "I lost weight after I married Harold. He was even stricter about what I ate than I was when I was working." She screwed up her face. "See that? I wasn't even allowed to do that because I might get lines. He was worse than a manager!"

Beau felt his simmering anger heat up again. "He should have married a porcelain doll, not a woman."

"He might have been happier." She shook her head, blond hair swinging around. "Oh, well. It's over now. I just have to get myself straightened out and get this divorce finalized."

She was feeling relaxed now, he realized, as if talking about it had eased her anxiety. Well, it hadn't eased his anger any. If he'd been a violent man, Beau might have said that he wanted to bash in Harold Dreyfus's face. "What are you thinking about doing?"

"For work, you mean? I don't know. Maybe I'll go to college eventually, but right now I've got to concentrate on making enough to support myself. I don't suppose there's much available around here."

So she would be leaving again. The thought gave him a strange pang. "Depends on what you want, I suppose. But the first thing is to make sure we get Harold off your back permanently. Then you can work out everything else."

He rose then. "I need to go shower and change. Excuse me?"

"Of course!"

Walking out of the kitchen, he could feel her eyes on him, and he wondered what she was thinking. That was the main reason he needed to go shower and change—because it would get him away from her. Those eyes—well, he couldn't read them, and he had the feeling she was judging him by the only measuring sticks she had: her father and Harold Dreyfus.

But what did it matter, anyway? he asked himself as he climbed the stairs. If life had turned her into a man-hater, it wasn't his problem. His involvement began and ended with keeping her safe from Harold.

Later that evening, Beau's past reared up and bit him on the butt.

He was standing in the kitchen around ten o'clock, thinking about making some popcorn. Alicia had gone up to bed an hour earlier, claiming exhaustion. He figured she would need a week to catch up on her sleep, after what she'd been through.

When the phone rang, he thought something must have come up at work. The last voice he expected to hear was his ex-wife's.

"Hi, Beau," she said, using those throaty tones that had once snared him. "It's been a long time."

Everything inside him froze. It was as if a wave of ice swept through him, shutting everything down. "El."

"Is that all you're going to say?" She laughed.

Suddenly ice became anger. "What do you want, El?"

"What makes you think I want anything?" She sounded pouty now. "I was just thinking about you."

"It's been five years. What am I supposed to think?"

"That I've been missing you, hon."

There had been a time when he would have given almost anything to hear that from her, but he was no longer that stupid young man who'd torn his life to pieces trying to please an unpleasable woman. "Cut the crap, El," he said flatly. "You haven't missed me in all this time. I seriously doubt you're going to start now. So just cut to the chase, will you?"

El was silent for a few moments. "You've changed, Beau."

"Seems like you might've had a hand in that."

"Well, I've changed, too."

"Mmm." He wasn't quite ready to believe that tigers changed their stripes.

"No, I have." Then, "Bernie left me."

Why didn't that surprise him? Even a man who took a trophy wife could eventually get tired of being used. "Sorry, El." It was the most he could manage.

"He found someone younger." Her laugh was almost bitter. "I'm getting up there, Beau."

"You're only thirty-six. Try loving somebody."

"I loved *you.*"

He couldn't even bring himself to answer that. Maybe she *had* loved him at one time, in her limited way. But if she had, it had vanished a long, long time ago—long before he had stopped loving her. Finally he said, "That was a long time ago, El."

"But maybe..." She trailed off. Not even El could quite come right out and ask for this.

"No way," he said flatly. "You hate it here, and I'm never leaving here again. Besides, you hated being married to a cop, remember?"

"Maybe...maybe I've changed."

"Not enough. Sorry. You need money or something?" He figured he could do that much for her, for old times' sake.

"No. No, Bernie's been...generous." Her voice grew waspish. "He can afford it."

Better than I can, Beau thought.

"Would you mind...if I call sometimes?"

"Don't do that, El. Please don't do that." All he needed was this woman wedging her way back into his life with all her problems.

"Okay." She hung up without saying goodbye.

Beau hung up the phone and stood for a second, staring at it like it was a snake. He felt drained, as if he'd been walking a tightrope. Man, he'd thought that was all behind him now.

He turned around and saw Alicia, wearing a satin nightgown, standing in the doorway with her arms wrapped around herself, looking pale as a sheet.

"What's wrong?" he asked immediately.

"I heard the phone.... Sorry. I thought it was...him."

"No, it was my ex. Apparently she just got dumped."

"Oh. Sorry." She started to turn away.

He couldn't let her go like this, he realized. She looked so pale, frightened and lonely. "Alicia? I was just going to make some popcorn, maybe put a movie on. Wanna join me?"

She looked over her shoulder at him. "I...yes. Please." She gave a strained laugh. "I don't know why, but I'm just so frightened! I'm jumping at every little sound."

"Tell you what. I'll get a blanket and pillow for you, and you can stretch out on the couch, and I'll put something funny on."

A little while later, he sat in his recliner while some Chevy Chase movie played, and watched Alicia sleep curled up under a blanket on the couch.

Chapter 4

"How's Alicia doing?" Nate asked Beau a few days later.

"Catching up on her rest, looking healthier, but scared most of the time."

They were sitting in Nate's office while a late afternoon thunderstorm drenched the county. A hollow boom rattled the walls of the old building.

"Well, we got a response out of Minneapolis PD this morning."

"Yeah?"

"They notified Dreyfus that his car was found abandoned. He's sending someone to get it. They were also very interested to hear about Tom McKay's beating. I faxed the description of the assailants, and they're checking on them right now."

"But nothing was said about Alicia's whereabouts?"

Nate shook his head. "Funny thing happened at Bayard's Garage yesterday."

"What?"

"Seems Dirk got a wild hair to clean the Mercedes up. Inside and out. So I guess nobody will ever know for sure who stole the car."

Beau started laughing. "I'll have to pass that on."

"You do that." Nate's eyes crinkled with a smile. "Just us

dumb hicks, you know? Can't even get fingerprints before somebody screws it up. Law enforcement in this county is going to hell."

"Damn shame, isn't it? I guess we need to send everybody back to school."

"Sure enough. We should have lifted those prints when we found the car."

This was one of the things Beau liked about living here. Rules could be bent for a good reason.

"Another thing," Nate said, reaching for his coffee mug. "I got a call from some lawyer in Minneapolis. Says he represents Alicia. Lew Altares."

Beau nodded. "That's his name."

"Well, he was interested in whether I'd be willing to swear an affidavit about the bruise on Alicia's cheek. Suggested you might do one, too."

"Gladly."

"Problem is, if we do that, we're admitting we've seen her. And that ought to bring Dreyfus and his thugs sniffing around."

"Mmm. Well, if they turn up, we can nail 'em."

"That's what I was thinking. Except I want your name out of it as long as Alicia is staying at your place. No point in giving these guys any idea where to look."

"What does Altares want the affidavit for?"

"To use in the divorce. And he said he's going to try to get a restraining order based on our statements. Not that I think it'll do much good."

"Didn't Minneapolis PD want to do anything about the abuse?"

"They were interested but can't do anything without a complaint. The McKay beating is different. It happened here, and we have a complaint, so they can cooperate. But as far as what happened to Alicia...she'll have to file a complaint back there."

Nate rocked back in his chair. "It was interesting, though. I got a feeling the detective I talked to would like nothing better than to nail Harold Dreyfus for something. Which leaves me wondering what the man did to make himself so popular."

"He seems to be real popular with everyone he meets."

Nate snorted. "Ain't that the truth. By the way, Melody wants to talk to Alicia. She's staying at Adam Roth's place, so have her call over there."

"Will do."

Finished with his shift now, Beau headed home. It was still raining cats and dogs, and the gutters were full of rushing water. The day was dark, green-looking, and the clouds looked as if they were skimming the treetops. Nobody was on the street, and he didn't pass a single other car all the way home. A good evening for staying in and playing cards or reading a book.

He expected to find what he usually found when he got home—the house quiet, Alicia napping. Instead he came in from the garage to the kitchen and was surprised to find the lights on and Alicia standing at the stove, cooking.

"Hi," she said with a smile. "I hope you don't mind, but I'm cooking dinner."

"Why in the world would I mind?"

"How about that it's your kitchen and your food I'm using?"

He smiled, glad to see her feeling better. "How about I told you to make yourself at home and I meant it? Besides, you'll never hear me complain if somebody wants to do the cooking. Do I have time to shower and change?"

"Absolutely."

She looked a whole lot better, he thought, as he watched her stir whatever smelled so good in the pot. So much better that he was almost reluctant to remind her why she was here. But he had good news, and it would be wrong to withhold it.

"I talked to Nate a few minutes ago." As he feared, she stiffened, and her face became pinched. He had the worst urge to reach out and hug her and tell her everything was going to be fine. But that meant crossing a line he didn't think either one of them wanted to cross.

She looked at him, the shadows back in her eyes. "And?"

"Melody wants to talk to you. You can call her at Adam Roth's place."

Her face relaxed a little. "Thanks. I'd like to talk to her."

"Your lawyer called Nate and wants some affidavits from us to use in the divorce."

She nodded. "He told me he was going to do that. Is it okay?"

"You bet. Both of us are ready and willing to do whatever we can, Alicia."

"Thank you." But the pinched look remained. "Anything else?"

"Well, that car theft charge doesn't stand a chance in hell, so you can forget about it. Seems Dirk Bayard decided to clean the car yesterday, and there are no fingerprints left anywhere. Nobody can ever prove you were in the car."

She nearly gaped, then started laughing. The sound followed Beau up the stairs as he went to shower. It was good to hear her laugh, he thought. Damn good. The sound warmed him deep inside.

And he didn't want to think about what that might mean.

After his shower, he changed into jeans and a T-shirt and went back downstairs to find that Alicia was serving dinner. Homemade vegetable soup followed by chicken breasts that had been wrapped in ham and Swiss cheese and fried.

"Chicken cordon bleu," she told him, smiling. "Fancy name for an easy meal. Harold's cook taught it to me."

He thought it was delicious, whatever you called it. "I really appreciate you cooking," he told her. "But don't feel you have to."

She shrugged. "I was a single working girl long enough to know what a drag it is to come home after a long day and still have to cook. I don't mind. It's a way I can say thank you."

"No thanks necessary, Alicia."

Her gaze met his. "Thanks *are* necessary, Beau. There aren't many people who would take in a total stranger this way."

He felt embarrassed. "I've got the room. Why don't you call Melody while I wash the dishes? Go ahead and use the phone in the living room, so you can have privacy."

"Thanks."

He didn't know which was worse, having her say she was sorry all the time—which at least had stopped a little—or having her thank him for every damn little thing when it wasn't giving him any trouble at all.

Somebody, he thought, had made this woman feel apologetic for her very existence. Not what you expected in a woman who looked like her.

The thought caught him sideways, and he found himself realizing he was expecting Alicia to act like Ellen. Ellen had been a beautiful woman, too, the kind of a woman who would catch every man's eye the instant she walked into the room.

And El had felt that beauty entitled her to things. Lots of things.

Maybe damn near everything. But Alicia didn't feel she was entitled to anything at all, as near as he could tell.

That bothered him. Nobody ought to feel that undeserving.

Of course, now that he thought about it, he supposed he was guilty of some of that himself. El had sure made him feel he wasn't good enough to wipe her feet on.

He finished up the dishes and leaned back against the counter while he dried his hands on a dish towel. Outside the storm was still hammering the world, but inside his house felt cozy and welcoming—especially since he could hear Alicia's animated voice in the living room. He couldn't make out what she was saying, but it didn't matter. The house felt friendlier with her here.

The thought brought with it a deep, welling sorrow, and he found himself tossing aside the dish towel and going to step out on the front porch. Here the air smelled of ozone and rain. He'd always loved that scent.

It was going to be difficult to go back to his solitary existence, he admitted. Alicia's presence had showed him just how empty his life had been since he split from El. It wasn't that life had been so good with El—God knew it had become purely miserable as her discontent grew—but it had been full. Rarely, at least until toward the end, had he come home to an empty house. Rarely had he felt he was just going through the motions, marking time.

But that was how he felt now. He had no hopes, no aspirations, no dreams. He'd settled back into his safe little rut and made it even safer by refusing to get involved in anything deeper than friendship.

At least during his marriage he'd always had some iron in the fire. Some plan he was working on. Some hope for tomorrow. Kids. He'd always wanted children and had been devastated when he discovered that Ellen didn't. He'd busted his butt to give her what she wanted and had constantly been planning new ways to please her.

So, good or bad, he'd always had something to work toward. And now he was working toward nothing at all.

A gust of wind blew rain up onto the porch, and chilly droplets dampened his face. He wiped them away with the back of his hand. Backing up, he settled on the porch swing and pushed himself aimlessly back and forth.

He had, he realized, been going through his days in a kind of fog, not really thinking about anything except getting through the day. And Alicia had showed him just how empty it was to live that way.

Maybe it was time to stop hiding out. Maybe it was time to start investing himself in the rest of the world again. Maybe he needed to remember how to take a few risks.

Maybe he needed to start living again.

"Did he hit you, Alicia?" Melody asked on the phone.

Alicia closed her eyes, feeling a wave of mixed emotions, sorrow, anger, embarrassment. Why should she feel embarrassed to admit the truth? Why should she feel ashamed because someone else had done something wrong?

"Yes," she said finally.

Melody drew an audible, shaky breath. "I wondered. You were having all those accidents...and I never thought you were clumsy, Al." Melody was the only person in the world who called her Al.

"Not that clumsy, Al."

"No." Silence stretched between them, punctuated only by the quiet hum of the phone line. "Adam says we shouldn't be on the phone when there's a thunderstorm."

"Then you should go."

"No. I've been so worried about you, and now I don't even have a way to call you back. Are you sure you're safe now?"

"As safe as I can be."

"I can't believe Harold did that to you. I mean, I know he's controlling. Adam helped me see that. But why did he have to hit you? He never hit *me*."

"Maybe because you always did what he wanted."

"Maybe." Melody gave a brittle laugh. "He sure had me trained. I didn't even realize how bad it was until I got here. I never did anything without wondering what Harold would think! And I never did anything he didn't approve of, because I knew how mad he'd get."

"I'm glad you're out of there, Mel."

"Me too. I mean, he even had me convinced that nobody would ever want to marry me because I couldn't have kids. And now look."

"Adam knows about that?"

"Adam knows about everything."

Alicia felt a lump in her throat and closed her eyes, trying to hold in the tears. "I'm so happy for you, Mel. So happy."

"Harold had me so convinced that I was utterly stupid and worthless...but he had a lot of time to do it. I mean, he started working on me when I was just a little kid. How did he do it to you, Al? You're so beautiful, and you had everything going for you.... He must have really knocked you around badly."

"It didn't start that way. And regardless of how it looked, Mel, I was...insecure. I was a country kid who didn't know about money and society. And my dad used to knock me around, too, so...it took me a while to realize nobody has the right to do that."

"You? Insecure?" Mel sounded amazed. "Oh, Allie, I never guessed! We should have talked more."

"I guess so. But Harold was always there, it seemed."

"Always. I told him off, you know."

"Really?" Alicia felt herself smiling. "Wow! That takes guts."

"Yeah, when I'm a thousand miles away and he can't get to me. I was afraid he'd find me, but he'll never think to look for me with Adam. And even if he does...well, what can he do?"

Alicia didn't know how to answer that. There were probably a lot of things Harold could do to make Melody miserable.

"He said he was going to cut off my trust fund," Melody continued, "but so what? I saved up a lot of money from my allowance. Adam says he'll take care of me anyway. And I'm going to get a job. A real job. The lady at the library says she can use me for twenty hours a week, and there's a possibility I can work in a dress shop, too."

"That's wonderful."

Melody was silent for a moment. "I've got some money for you, too, Al. I brought it with me because I was worried about you. I know Harold took all yours."

The lump in Alicia's throat grew larger. "Thanks, Mel. But you keep it. You need it, and my lawyer says he can get my money back."

"But you need some in the meantime. And I don't mind sharing it with you at all. In fact, it would make me feel good to share it. I have plenty for both of us."

"Aw, Mel, you're such a sweetheart."

"So are you. I think...I think you gave me the courage to take off on my own."

"Me?"

"That's right. I watched you try to stand up to Harold, and I admired you. Then...well, when you had the guts to file for a divorce and leave town, I got the guts to come looking for you."

"Mel, that had nothing to do with me. That was *you*. Besides, running away was the easiest thing for me to do. What *you* did took courage. You weren't running away."

Melody sighed. "In a way, maybe that's exactly what I was doing. And you were a good excuse to do it. But now we have to figure out a way to make you safe from Harold."

"I'm going to be just fine, Melody. Believe me, you don't want to get involved between Harold and me. There's no need, and he's your brother. I've got a good lawyer, and some people on my side."

"Frankly, I can hardly believe he hired those goons to find you. The ones who beat up Tom McKay. I never would have thought Harold could do something like that, Al." Her voice saddened. "I guess I never really knew what he was like."

"Oh, Mel." Alicia ached for her sister-in-law, and she wished there was something she could say to make Melody feel better. But what? She couldn't deny what Harold had done, and she didn't really feel she could say Harold was a basically good person who had a problem. Right now, she couldn't think of one good word to say about Harold. Period.

"I'll be okay," Melody said after a moment. "I guess I'm just growing up in a hurry. But I'll be fine."

"I'm sure you will. You're a lot stronger than you think."

"Yeah." Melody gave a little laugh. "I'm finding that out. Call me again tomorrow?"

"I promise."

After she hung up, Alicia wondered where Beau had gone to. Then she heard the porch swing creak and guessed he was outside watching the storm. She wished she could go out and sit with him, but she didn't dare take the chance that someone would see her and recognize her. Besides, maybe Beau didn't want the whole town gossiping that he had a woman staying with him.

There was another creak from the front porch, then the sound of heavy bootsteps as Beau walked across the planks. Then the front door opened. Alicia turned in time to see him come into the living room.

"Wild evening out there," he remarked. "How's Melody?"

"Trying to deal with a whole new idea of her brother."

He shook his head. "That's too bad. She's a nice kid."

Kid. The word stung Alicia. She was a year younger than Melody. Did Beau see her as a kid, too? She tried to tell herself it didn't matter, but it did. "She's not a child, Beau." *And neither am I.*

"I didn't mean it in a bad way, Alicia. I just get the feeling that's she's been very sheltered."

"I suppose you think *I'm* a kid, too."

His eyes met hers. "No," he said. "Not at all."

It was suddenly difficult to breathe, but Alicia hardly noticed, so focused was she on making her point. "Why not? I'm a year younger than she is."

"I don't think Carol Tate's a kid, either," Beau said equably. "It's a matter of experience and maturity, Alicia. Not years. You've been to the school of hard knocks. That has a way of making people grow up fast."

She realized she'd been trying to argue with him and felt embarrassed. "I'm sorry. The storm's been making me edgy."

"Maybe you've got a case of cabin fever. Hardly surprising, since you haven't been out of this house in days."

"Not much I can do about it." She shrugged a shoulder and tore her eyes away from him, wondering why it was so difficult not to look at him. "I'll manage."

"I've got a better idea. Why don't we take a drive? If you want to hide until we get out of town, we can drive around the back roads. It might help."

"You don't want to drive in this, Beau. It's a mess out there. Maybe tomorrow, if it's nice?"

"Sure. Tomorrow's fine. And if it's nice, we'll go somewhere you can actually get out and walk and smell the breeze, okay?"

She looked up at him and smiled. "Sounds like heaven. Thank you. I don't mean to be a pain."

He looked surprised. "You're not being a pain. And you probably won't have to be cooped up much longer, either. Nate and I figure the news that the car was found here is going to bring

Dreyfus or his thugs running. Just a few more days, Alicia, and maybe we can wrap this whole thing up.''

She sighed and looked down at her hands.

He came to sit at the other end of the couch, crossing his legs loosely and resting his arm along the back. "Are you missing him?" he asked.

Startled, Alicia jerked her head up. "Harold! Oh, no! I'm not missing him at all. And it's been at least six months since I realized that I'd stopped loving him a long time ago. No, I'll just be glad when he's completely gone from my life."

"Then why the heavy sigh?"

"Did I sigh?" She sighed again. "Oh, I'm just wishing it would all go away. I feel like I'm stuck in limbo, waiting for the other shoe to drop, when all I really want to do is get on with my life. The divorce will probably drag on forever."

"Maybe not."

"That's what my lawyer says. He thinks the threat of adverse publicity will make Harold knuckle under, especially since all I'm asking for is my own money back."

"He's getting off easy, if you ask me. Especially since you quit your career for him."

"It doesn't matter. I just want him to give me what's mine and let me go. I shouldn't have to spend the next year or two fighting for that."

Beau nodded. "Well, things might get taken care of real quick if we can link Harold to the guys who beat up Tom McKay."

"Why should there be a problem? They were looking for *me*, weren't they?"

"Sure, but we don't know that he authorized them to use violence."

"Oh."

"It would really help if you pressed charges against him for hitting you."

She suddenly looked frightened again. "I don't want to do that!"

"Why not? Are you afraid he'll come after you?"

She shuddered. "I don't know. I guess. But...it's so embarrassing."

Beau leaned over and touched her shoulder. "Alicia, you don't have any reason to be embarrassed. You didn't do anything wrong.''

"But it feels like I did, Beau! It feels like I did."

And suddenly huge tears were rolling down her cheeks. Another man probably would have fled, but Beau had never fled from anything. Cursing himself for a fool even as he did it, he gathered Alicia close and hugged her, rocking her gently.

She cried for a long time, soaking his shirt with her tears, but he figured it was good for her. She'd been holding an awful lot inside for an awful long time, and now she was letting it out. He didn't mind that in the least.

But he *did* mind how good she felt in his arms. It had been a long time since he'd held a woman close. He'd forgotten how good it felt. He'd forgotten how good a woman could feel, and how good she could smell. He'd forgotten a lot of things...or maybe had just refused to remember them.

He was in trouble now, he thought. Deep trouble. Headed right down a road he'd sworn never to walk again. And worse, he was starting to feel things for a woman whose life was all messed up, a woman who couldn't possibly have any room for him in the midst of all her other worries.

A woman who was entirely too vulnerable right now, and therefore off-limits.

He should have just gotten up and walked away. But he didn't. He couldn't. So he sat there and held her while she cried, and wondered why he'd never had the sense to jump out from in front of an oncoming train.

Chapter 5

"I'm sorry," Alicia said shakily, a long time later. "I'm sorry."

"Don't apologize." Knowing he was being a fool, he stroked her hair gently and patted her shoulder awkwardly. "You needed that cry."

"I guess so." She moved to sit up, and with greater reluctance than he wanted to feel, he let her go, watching as she wiped her face with her hands.

"Let me get you a tissue," he said. It was as good an excuse as any to get away before he got any closer to her. Before he started thinking too much about how really *good* it had felt to have her in his arms.

"No...no, really, I'm fine." She sniffled and tried to smile. "I was acting like a baby. I made this mess, and now I've got to deal with it. Maybe I should just go back to Minneapolis and face Harold down."

Beau felt his heart slam. "No. Whatever you do, don't do that. Damn it, Allie, you don't want to wind up being another statistic."

"What did you call me?"

He paused and quickly reran his words in his head. "Allie? Sorry."

"No, no, that's okay. It's just that...well, only my mom and

Melody have ever called me that. I like it. Go ahead and call me Allie.''

"Okay." He had the feeling this conversation had been side-tracked, and that she'd done it on purpose. He wasn't so easy to distract. "You can't go back. Not yet. That guy has beaten you, and until he gets used to the idea that he can't have you back, he's dangerous. *Seriously* dangerous."

She tilted her head, looking straight at him. "So if you can call me Allie, I can call you Virgil, right?"

"Virgil?"

"Yes, Virgil. It's a beautiful name. I like it. So if you're not morally opposed to it, can I call you Virgil?"

Almost in spite of himself, he started to grin. There she was, with her eyes all puffy from tears and her face still damp, and she was railroading him. "Yeah. Sure. I guess. I might not remember to answer, though."

"You'll get used to it, Virgil. Now, about Harold. About my soon-to-be-ex. You're probably right." The fleeting smile in answer to his grin faded as quickly as it had appeared. "That's why my attorney told me to clear out of town. That's why I ran the way I did. But it's been three weeks now. Maybe he's calmed down."

"We'll see soon enough." He rubbed his chin and considered scooting back to the far end of the couch, then decided she might misunderstand that. "I'd be really surprised if he doesn't show up personally to get that car, Allie. He's got to believe you're here somewhere."

"But he sent those two men after me."

"He sent them to *find* you. I don't think he told them to snatch you. Kidnaping's a serious crime, and Harold's probably got at least enough intelligence to want to avoid getting into that kind of trouble. No, I figure he wanted them to find you so he could come try to sweet-talk you into coming back."

She thought about that. "He always *did* apologize and get really sweet after he hit me."

"Most abusers do. And you listened to all the sweet talk, right, and gave him another chance?"

She nodded.

"Well, then, he'll probably try the same thing. He'll figure that if he swears to get counseling, swears he'll never lay another finger on you, he can persuade you to come back with him. Why wouldn't he think so? It usually worked in the past.''

She shifted uneasily. "It *always* worked in the past. I don't know why I think I could face him down now.''

"But you'd like to, wouldn't you?"

"I sure would.''

"Well, we'll play it by ear when he shows up. Who knows? Maybe you'll have the opportunity to tell him where to get off. Just as long as you're never alone with him. That's a risk you can't take.''

She turned so she was looking straight at him. "Would you be willing to be with me when I see him? I mean, if he comes to town?''

"Sure.''

"It seems kind of cowardly, though, being afraid to face him on my own.''

"This isn't like getting thrown from a horse, Allie. You might be afraid of heights, but you'd be an absolute fool to try to cure yourself by jumping off a cliff without a parachute. Think of me as a parachute.''

"I guess when you put it that way..." She sighed again. "I keep thinking he couldn't really hurt me now, you know? I keep thinking he'd have to be nuts to try anything.''

"He was nuts to hit you in the first place. You never know what might be going through his head now. If he can't win you back, he might be crazy enough to decide that nobody else is ever going to have you.''

A little shiver ran through her. "He said that once....''

He waited, wondering if she would say anything more. But after a moment she stunned him by leaning over and giving him a gentle kiss on the cheek. "You're a nice man, Virgil. Thank you.''

For the first time in at least ten years, he felt his cheeks grow warm. "It's nothing, Allie. Nothing at all. How about I make some popcorn and we watch a movie? Or we can play cards, if you like.''

"You don't have to entertain me.''

"Hell, I was asking *you* to entertain *me*.''

She laughed, then looked surprised. "You know, I've laughed more in the last few days than I have in the past year.''

He felt a warm glow deep inside, and before he could stop the words he said, "So have I, Allie."

Color flooded her cheeks, and she gave him an almost shy look. Realizing he was treading on dangerous ground, Beau stood up quickly. "I'll go get the cards, okay?"

"As long as you're willing to play rummy. I don't know any other games."

"Rummy's fine."

It turned into a good evening. While the storm continued to hammer the world outside, they sat at the kitchen table playing cards and laughing. Rummy was almost too easy with only two players, so they switched to Hearts, which she picked up quickly, and passed the Queen of Spades back and forth like a couple of kids playing Old Maid. For a little while, in silent mutual agreement, they put everything else from their minds.

But then the phone rang. Beau leaned back in his chair and lifted the receiver from the wall unit. "Beauregard," he said into the mouthpiece.

"Beau, it's Nate. I just had a call from Lucy over at the Lazy Rest Motel. She thought I'd want to know that Harold Dreyfus just checked in."

"I'll be damned. Anything else?"

"Not yet. Just keep Alicia under wraps."

"I was planning to. Want me to go over and talk to him?"

"Hell, no. Let him come to me. He'll probably show up first thing in the morning."

"Probably."

"Be here, okay? I'll get somebody else to cover your patrol."

"Will do."

He hung up the phone and looked at Alicia. Her color was still high, and her eyes still sparkled with good humor. It killed him that he was going to have to ruin her mood, but she had to know. "Harold's in town. He just checked into the motel."

Her face collapsed. There was no other way to describe what happened. Her good spirits fled in an eye blink, and all her nervousness came back.

"He doesn't know where I am?" Her voice sounded strained.

"Absolutely not. Nate just wanted me to be sure to keep you under wraps. And he wants me there in the morning in case Dreyfus shows up. Which he probably will."

"What are you going to do?"

"I don't know. Reckon we'll have a little talk with him about beating his wife."

She nodded slowly. "But Virgil, if you let him know you've seen me, he might guess where I am!"

Beau hadn't thought about that. In his eagerness to tell Dreyfus where to get off, he hadn't considered the possible dangers. "Tell you what," he said after a few moments. "I'll make sure we don't let him know. We'll cover it somehow."

She nodded jerkily, but she didn't look very reassured.

"How about I get Carol to come stay with you tomorrow? Or take you over to stay with Melody at Adam's place?"

"Sure." Alicia gave him a valiant smile. "I'll be fine, Virgil."

He wanted to promise that she would be, but he wasn't one to make promises he might not be able to keep. There was no way to be absolutely certain that Harold wouldn't somehow find out where Alicia was. And if he did...well, Beau couldn't promise it wouldn't get ugly. All he could promise was to make sure she wouldn't be alone.

He had the worst urge to gather her up into his arms and promise he would never let anything bad happen to her, but he didn't have the right. And even if he'd had the right, it wasn't a promise anyone could make.

She drew a deep breath and tried to smile again. "Sorry. I killed the mood, didn't I?

"Harold killed the mood. But it was bound to happen sooner or later."

"Yeah." Her hands twisted together on the table. "I feel... I was feeling as if all the bad stuff was behind me. That I could just be normal again. It's been so long since I could even play cards without wondering if I was going to do something to make Harold mad. You're not like that, Virgil. You even laughed when I rummied your Ace of Spades."

"It's just a card game, for crying out loud." The urge to punch Harold was growing.

"I know but—" she shrugged "—he always had to win. At everything."

"He's not going to win this time, Allie." There was steel in his voice.

"I hope not...."

The words were little more than a whisper, but Beau heard them, and his heart ached. Oh, man, he was getting in deeper by the minute. Part of him wanted to get out of there before he could do something stupid, and part of him wanted very much to do something amazingly stupid, like gather her close and kiss her until she forgot any other man had ever existed. He closed his eyes and willed himself to be smart.

"So," she said after a minute, "it's a night for exes, isn't it? That was your ex-wife earlier, wasn't it?"

His eyes opened, and he almost thanked her for the reminder of why he was never going to be stupid again. "Yeah, it was. Can you believe it? She hasn't spoken a word to me in five years, and out of the blue, she calls."

"How come—if you don't mind me asking?"

He shrugged. It really didn't matter anymore. "I guess her husband is divorcing her. She was probably feeling blue and unwanted, and wanted to salve her ego by twisting me around her finger again."

"It's not going to work?"

"Hell, no! One trip through the wringer is enough for a lifetime. I learned my lesson."

She looked even sadder, if that was possible. "I don't think I have."

"What do you mean?"

"I'd like to marry again. I'd like to find somebody really nice, somebody who really loves me, and have a family. I can't believe all men are like Harold."

"Too many of 'em are."

"Maybe. But you're not, Virgil."

His heart stopped. Did she mean that the way it sounded? He didn't know whether to hope she did or hope she didn't.

"Anyway," she said, going on, "I've still got all these dreams. That's part of what made me leave Harold. Not just that he was mistreating me, but that he was killing my dreams. Did your wife kill your dreams?"

"I thought so." But now he found himself wondering if that was true. Some part of him seemed to be pushing for things he'd sworn off a long time ago—all of them seeming to have to do with a young woman who probably wouldn't give him a second glance if he hadn't rescued her. Not a good situation.

"But now you're not sure?" She sounded almost hopeful.

"I don't know," he said, deciding to be honest. "But I'm thirty-eight...getting a little too old to be thinking about things like that, I guess."

"Old! You're not old at all!"

Too old for you, he thought, and wondered why he was even letting such lunatic thoughts cross his mind. He didn't say anything, for fear of what he *might* say.

"You're not old, Virgil. You seem just right to me."

"And this conversation is getting dangerous, Allie."

"I know." She looked down. "Sorry. I've never been good at keeping my mouth shut. And for the last couple of days I've been wondering why I couldn't have met somebody like you instead of Harold."

"You're just vulnerable right now. Trust me, I won't look so good after you get Harold permanently off your back."

"Okay. Sorry. Didn't mean to make you uncomfortable. I think I'd better go to bed...."

She got up and hurried out of the kitchen. Moments later he heard her run up the stairs.

Oh, damn! What the hell had he gotten into here? And what the hell could he do about it?

And why did the kitchen suddenly feel so damn empty?

In her room, Alicia lay down on the bed and tried to listen to the muted storm sounds, tried to count the seconds between the flashes of lightning and the rumble of thunder, but all she could think about was how she had embarrassed herself.

She was drawn to Virgil in a way she'd never been drawn to anyone before. In the past, she'd always sought excitement from men, but now, for the first time, she was being drawn to steadiness and gentleness. She was being drawn to kindness.

He might be right that she was just vulnerable now, but somehow she didn't think so. It had been a long time since she had felt any love for Harold, and leaving him had not been a painful thing to do. For a while it had even been exhilarating. Frightening, but exhilarating. And frightened or not, she was still very glad she'd left him.

Yes, Virgil made her feel safe, but that wasn't why she was drawn to him. Of that much she was certain.

And it was equally certain from what he had said that he saw her as a child. Not much she could do about that.

The thought saddened her, because she felt that she had been given a glimpse of the way things could be. A glimpse of what it might be like to be friends with a man, instead of just a man's plaything.

She rolled over and hugged her pillow, thinking over what Virgil had said. He was protecting her, she realized. Protecting her from Harold, and protecting her from...what? Himself? Herself? One or the other.

While she appreciated being protected from Harold, she wasn't at all sure she appreciated being protected from herself, or from Virgil. Although, considering the big mistake she'd made in Harold, maybe her judgment stank and Virgil was right to back away.

But his very act of backing away told her she wasn't wrong about him. An awful lot of people wouldn't have scrupled to take advantage of her in these circumstances. She'd learned that the hard way.

Virgil Beauregard was a special man. Of that she had no doubt. As for her own attraction to him... Well, did she really want to start getting involved with someone when her life was such a mess?

She pressed her face into her pillow and fought down the urge to cry. She felt as if the last few years of her life had been stolen from her, along with all her dreams. But her dreams hadn't died, apparently, because she was beginning to have them again. Unfortunately, she was stuck in a situation where they would have to wait indefinitely.

Impatient with herself, she sat up and dashed away her tears. Self-pity. She hated it. She wasn't entitled to it, anyway. She'd made this mess by marrying a man she hadn't known well enough, and now she had to clean it up before she could do anything else.

Deciding a hot bath would make her feel better, she got up and grabbed a fresh nightgown out of the dresser. Just as she was reaching for the doorknob, she heard a knock.

"Allie? Can I talk to you for a minute?"

She hesitated, not wanting him to see that she had been crying, but then decided it didn't matter. She'd embarrassed herself, and he knew it. He probably expected to see tears.

She opened the door and felt her breath catch in her throat. For all that she'd been drawn to him because of his kindness and gentleness, now she was feeling a different kind of attraction. The full force of his maleness struck her like a punch. The urge to reach out for him, to actually feel his warm strength against her, almost overwhelmed her. She'd never felt this way about Harold, she realized in some dim recess of her brain. She'd never had this wild urge to just reach out and grab him and get as close as she could.

"I'm sorry," he said. "I wasn't putting you down, Allie. Honestly."

The ability to speak seemed to have deserted her, and she stared at him mutely, hoping her longing wasn't written on her face.

"I don't think you're a kid. Falling back on my age was mainly an excuse, anyway." He sighed and ran impatient fingers through his dark brown hair. "I made this stupid promise to myself that I was never going to get involved with a woman again, after El."

Her voice cracked as she spoke. "Why do you think that's a stupid promise?"

He shoved his hands into his pockets. "Because I'm apparently not going to be able to keep it."

Her heart slammed. "Um...why not?"

But he didn't answer directly. "After what you've been through with Harold, don't you ever think that you'd be a fool to get involved with another man?"

Her voice quavered as she answered. "No...I mean...he's just *one* man. Not everybody is like him."

"Yeah." He gave a humorless laugh. "Problem is, the problem in my marriage was *me*."

"You? How?"

"I wasn't good enough, Allie. Just look at me. I'm a two-bit cop in a two-bit town. I don't make a whole lot of money, and I'm never going to go anywhere. I'm happy here, and I guess that means I've got no real ambition...well, except maybe to be sheriff someday when Nate retires. But I don't like the city, and I'm damned if I want to sacrifice the quality of my life to go running after money and excitement. So I'm a loser. El was right about that. Women want more from a man."

"*El* wanted more from a man," Alicia said, her heart aching for him. "That's not true for all of us."

"No?" He gave her a crooked smile. "Look at the man you married, Allie. You went for all of that money and success. Good night. Sleep well."

He turned and disappeared down the stairs before she could think of a single argument in response.

Chapter 6

Morning seemed to take forever in coming. Beau sat up half the night thinking about his own failings, then awoke early, impatient to get to the sheriff's office and see what happened with Harold Dreyfus. Finally, deciding it would be best to avoid Alicia this morning, he dressed and left early. Only after he got to the office did he realize how that might look to her.

At least ten times he had to snatch his hand back from the phone so he wouldn't call her and make up some excuse for being gone when she woke. Stupid, he told himself. There was nothing between them that required him to make any excuses.

Even so, he hated to think he might be making her feel bad again. Hell, he would explain later somehow. If he tried to do it right now, he would probably say a whole bunch of things he shouldn't be saying. She was a nice woman and didn't deserve to feel responsible for the mess his emotions were in right now. It wasn't *her* fault his heart was getting tangled up with her.

He'd figured at his age he was immune. Hah. He'd reverted to a kid again, worrying about what she thought of him, worrying about whether she found him attractive, worrying about whether he'd done or said the wrong thing. He hadn't been on tenterhooks like this since Ellie.

Nate walked in the front door and gave him a once-over. "You look like hell warmed over, Beau. Something wrong?"

"Naw. Just insomnia."

"Mmm. Thinking about Dreyfus, huh?"

"Yeah." Easy to answer without lying; Nate hadn't said which Dreyfus.

"Me too. I keep trying to figure out how I can nail that bastard, but we've got so little to go with right now. Alicia's gonna have to file a complaint."

"I don't know if it'd be smart for her to go back to Minneapolis just yet."

"She could go while we stall her husband here." But Nate shook his head. "I'll figure something out. Hell, I hate these slimy bastards, Beau. Always get somebody else to do their dirty work and make everybody so damn terrified of 'em they can get away with just about anything."

"We'll get him." Beau spoke with resolution. "I'm not going to rest until I see his butt behind bars."

Nate gave him a narrow look, but much to Beau's relief didn't comment on his vehemence. He just nodded agreement. "How'd Alicia take the news?"

"Pretty well, considering. She talked to Melody last night."

"Good. Well, let's see how long it takes this jerk to come in here and demand his car and his wife."

Velma Jansen, the crusty dispatcher, walked through the door just then. "The big day, huh? Can I drive a wooden stake through his heart?"

"Just do me a favor, Velma," Nate said. "Don't say or do anything at all. I want this guy to dig his own grave."

Velma shrugged and lit a cigarette, then slid behind her console. "Fine with me, boss. But after he digs it, I'm going to drive a stake through his heart."

Despite his lack of sleep and his edginess, Beau had to laugh. Somehow she always managed to get the last word.

Harold Dreyfus showed up twenty minutes later. He was a large man, a little heavy, but powerful enough to intimidate almost anyone if he wanted to. He wore a tailor-made suit that shrieked money and a pair of shoes that looked both expensive and fresh out of the box.

"I'm Harold Dreyfus," he announced as he stepped through the door, not even waiting to see if anyone else was ahead of him, or carrying on a conversation. "I'm here for my car and my wife."

Beau stood up and leaned casually against the wall. Nate looked the man over from head to foot.

Nate spoke. "I'll need some ID."

Dreyfus frowned but pulled a slim leather wallet out of his inside breast pocket. Flipping it open, he showed his driver's license. "And you are...?" he asked Nate.

"I'm Sheriff Tate." Nate scanned the license with more than ordinary care. Beau suppressed a twinge of amusement. Dreyfus was in for it and didn't even know it.

"You're the one who found the car," Dreyfus said.

"Actually, no. Deputy Beauregard here found it. Abandoned at the side of the road."

Beau nodded when Dreyfus looked at him. He was trying to remain relaxed but found himself folding his arms across his chest.

Dreyfus's lip curled. "I'm supposed to believe my wife wasn't in the car?"

Beau didn't answer. Lying was not his nature, not even under these circumstances.

Nate leaned back against a vacant desk and folded his arms. "What's that supposed to mean?"

"I know you're all trying to protect her!"

"Mmm. Protect her from what?"

Beau felt the muscles in his back tensing. This guy wasn't used to being thwarted.

"Charges of stealing my car!"

"Can a wife steal a car she's been allowed to use in the past?"

Dreyfus's mouth tightened. "She's divorcing me."

Beau spoke. "And property disputes will be settled in civil court."

Dreyfus scowled at him.

Beau shrugged. "When the dust settles, the car could be hers anyway."

Nate spoke. "The Minneapolis police don't want to bother with this crap. They figure it's a marital dispute and don't want to waste the time on a criminal charge. They're not going to do a thing, Dreyfus."

"We'll see about that!"

Nate shrugged.

"And you have no right to keep me from seeing my wife."

Beau straightened. "No one's keeping you from anything, Dreyfus. If she wants to find you, she knows where to look, I'm sure."

"Not if you don't tell her I'm here."

Beau didn't answer that; there was no way he could speak truthfully without giving away Alicia's presence.

"Look," said Nate. "We found the car. Do you want it or not?"

"I want my wife."

Nate sighed. "We also want to question you."

"Me?"

"A couple of thugs beat up a trucker passing through here a couple of weeks ago and put him in the hospital. Seems they were looking for your wife."

"Scum. I wanted them to find her, not beat people up."

Beau spoke. "Really? You hire that kind of dirtball and you get that kind of work. What did you want them to do when they found her, Dreyfus? Kidnap her?"

"Now look!" Dreyfus's color was heightening. "I don't like your insinuations."

"Just asking," Beau said flatly. "Heard you beat her up."

"Where did you hear that? From *her?*"

"More than one source," Beau replied, unable to keep the edge out of his voice.

"Let me guess. My sister's here in town, too."

Neither Beau nor Nate answered that.

"That's what I thought!" Dreyfus swore. "It's a damn conspiracy! Where the hell are they? I want to talk to both of them."

"More to the point," Nate said, "are those guys you hired to find Alicia. Since there's a complaint against them, I want their names and addresses. Alternatively, I can forget your part in it if you go away and never bother Alicia again."

Dreyfus's mouth opened, then snapped shut. "Why the hell should I do that?"

"Because if you don't cooperate with the police on this, we'll have to consider you an accessory."

"Me? I didn't tell them to beat anybody up!"

Beau spoke. "Then you won't mind telling us who they are."

Dreyfus's mouth snapped shut, and he looked as if he wanted

to kill someone. Beau could see why Alicia was afraid of him. Hell, this guy didn't even have to raise a hand to be scary.

"Look, just give me my car and I'll get out of here."

Beau moved across the room, putting his back to the door.

Nate shook his head. "We still need to know who these guys are. Aggravated battery is a serious crime, Dreyfus. They nearly killed the truck driver."

"I didn't have anything to do with that."

"But you know who they are."

"I've had enough of this crap. Keep the damn car! I'm leaving."

He turned around and came face-to-face with Beau, who was planted in front of the door, ready for just about anything.

"Out of my way!" Harold snapped.

"You need to answer the sheriff's question."

"I don't have to tell anyone anything."

Beau felt his eyes narrowing. "You've already admitted you hired them. Now you can either tell us who they are, or we can arrest you as an accomplice."

"That's a load of bull! You can't touch me." Dreyfus whirled on the sheriff. "As for you, I'll have your badge."

Nate shrugged. "Try."

Velma lit a cigarette and blew a smoke ring. "Around these parts, Mr. Dreyfus, reputation means more than money. The sheriff's reputation is solid gold, and your money ain't gonna beat it."

Dreyfus glared at her. "Who asked you?"

"I'm one of the voters around here. Got something to say about who's sheriff."

A vein in Harold Dreyfus's forehead looked about ready to pop. But all he said was, "Just forget it. Forget all of it. I'm outta here."

"No," said Beau, balancing himself to be ready for a shove or punch, "you're under arrest."

"Oh, for..." Dreyfus let the sentence trail off in disgust.

"You have the right to remain silent," Beau began. "Anything you say can and will be used against you in a court of law. You have the right to an attorney...."

Just then the door at his back opened. He broke off and moved, then nearly swore out loud when he saw Alicia.

She stepped in, saw Harold, and froze.

"You lying tramp!" Harold growled.

Beau put himself between them, his back to Alicia. "Go home, Alicia. Please."

He could hear her behind him. She was breathing quickly, frightened.

"I knew you were all lying!" Dreyfus shouted.

"No!" Alicia's voice held sudden strength, and she stepped out from behind Beau to face her husband. "No, Harold. Don't talk to my friends that way."

"Shut up!"

"No, I won't." She was shaking visibly, but she didn't back down, and Beau felt a surge of strong admiration for her. "I had to run from you because you hit me and never listen to me. I'm not running anymore, Harold. I want you out of my life. Completely."

"You're crazy!"

"Not anymore."

Alicia pointed her finger at him, and even though it shook visibly, her determination could not be mistaken. "Get. Out. Of. My. Life."

He took a step toward her and swung his arm, clearly intending to backhand her across the face. Beau leapt forward in an instant, putting himself between them, and catching Harold's arm just before it struck him.

"I've seen enough, Nate," Beau said. "Domestic battery and aggravated battery."

"Hell, no," Nate said. "Battery on a law enforcement officer."

"That too."

Harold, who'd been looking too surprised to move, suddenly went wild, striking out at Beau with his other fist. Beau took the punch in his stomach, let the pain wash through him, then wrenched Dreyfus's arm around until he brought the man to his knees.

"Definitely Batt-LEO," Nate said cheerfully. He pulled his cuffs off his belt and came over to help handcuff Dreyfus. "Couldn't have gone better if I'd planned it."

Alicia had backed up across the room when Harold first swung at her. "Virgil, are you okay?"

"Virgil?" Velma cackled delightedly. "Hon, nobody calls him that."

Alicia's chin came out. "I do. Virgil? Are you all right?"

Beau straightened as the handcuffs clicked closed around Dreyfus's wrists. "I'm fine, Allie."

"Oh, he's fine," Nate said, grinning. "Got a nice big bruise we can take photos of for the judge. Yep. Stepped in to keep this fool from hitting you and got gut punched."

In spite of the ache in his abdomen, Beau felt a grin tug at his own mouth. "Maybe I'd better go to the hospital. Medical reports."

"Good idea," Nate said. "Document it up the wazoo." He looked down at Dreyfus, who was still kneeling with his hands cuffed behind his back, looking as if he wanted to spit acid. "Going up the river for a long time, Mr. Dreyfus. You'll meet lots of nice people who'll treat you the way you've been treating Alicia. Justice, don't you think?"

Then he looked at Beau. "Let's get this guy into a cell. Then you go to the hospital and make sure you don't have any broken ribs."

Dreyfus looked up. "I'll tell you who those guys are."

"Talk to the prosecutor," Nate suggested. "Maybe he'll cut you a deal for the information. I'm through cutting any deals with you."

He and Beau grabbed Dreyfus under his arms and took him upstairs to a cell.

Beau waited outside the cell, hand on his gun, while Nate removed Harold's handcuffs, relieved him of his personal possessions, his necktie, belt and shoes. Dreyfus looked a lot less impressive in nothing but shirt, slacks and stocking feet.

"I'll bring your jumpsuit up in a while," Nate told him. "County orange. You'll love the fashion statement."

Beau wanted to laugh, but it hurt, so he stopped and merely smiled.

Downstairs he found Alicia sitting in a chair, looking pale as a ghost. He went to her at once, squatting in front of her, his concern for her making him forget everything else.

"Are you okay?" he asked her.

She tried to give him a wobbly smile, then threw her arms around his neck and hugged him as tightly as she could. "I'm fine," she said shakily. "I'm fine...."

He hugged her back, tucking her head against his shoulder.

"What ever possessed you to come down here, Allie? What if he'd found you on the street?"

"I had to, Beau. You were gone so early this morning, I thought you were mad at me. Then I decided that if I ran into Harold I could at least tell him off...."

"You sure did that."

"I had to, Beau. I had to. Just once."

Her breath was warm on his neck, and he wished to heaven they were somewhere private. "You did a great job."

She gave a shaky laugh. "I didn't say nearly as much as I wanted to."

"I can imagine."

Nate came down the stairs from the jail and took a look at the two of them. "Take Alicia home, Beau," he said, a twinkle in his eye. "And take the day off. After you go to the emergency room, okay?"

Beau had a feeling that Nate could see right through him. He felt his cheeks growing warm. "There's paperwork...."

"Nothing I can't take care of. Now, outta here, you two."

"I'll drop you off at the house before I go to the hospital," Beau said as he and Alicia walked toward his Blazer.

"No, I'm coming with you." She was determined about that. After all, he'd come to her rescue and had gotten punched for it. Besides, she was worried about how badly he might really be hurt. She knew Harold's strength. "And I'll drive. I don't know if you should."

He opened the passenger side door and smiled down at her. "Nope. Police vehicle, ma'am. I'll do the driving."

So she climbed in the passenger seat, then winced when she saw him wince as he climbed in behind the wheel. He caught her expression and smiled reassuringly. "It's not that bad, Allie. Really. Just a bruise."

"We'll see."

They backed out of the parking space, and Alicia stared out the side window, realizing that she was very close to shattering. First she had awakened this morning to find that Virgil had already gone, well before his usual time, and all she could think was that her behavior last night had made him too uncomfortable to stay in his own home. All she could feel was that she was losing him...and she didn't want to do that.

Even Harold didn't look as threatening beside the fear that she had driven Virgil away. In fact, she had gotten so worked up about Virgil that she'd felt absolutely defiant toward Harold. *Let him try to grab me!* she'd thought as she'd walked out the door. *Just let him try something!* She'd been ready to take on anyone and anything if they got in her way.

And the mood had carried her all the way to the sheriff's office, and had stood her in good stead when she came face-to-face with Harold. Not that it would have accomplished anything if Virgil hadn't been there to keep Harold from decking her...but she felt better for having said even those few words of defiance to him. She felt freer than she had in years.

It was as if she had stepped through the dark cloud that had been covering her life for so long, especially during the weeks of running when she had lived in the car, terrified that Harold would find her. Now he had found her, she had faced him...and she didn't have to worry about him anymore.

Not that that would be the case without her friends, and without Harold being in jail. Right now she didn't want to think about what might happen if he got out on bail.

And she was honest enough to admit that if she had met Harold alone, she would probably be on her way to the hospital right now...or dead. She had done a foolish thing...but she felt better anyway.

She looked over at Virgil as they pulled into the hospital parking lot. "Thank you," she said.

He pulled into a slot and looked at her. "For what?"

"For being there for me. For being there when I faced Harold. That was a stupid thing to do."

He switched off the ignition and faced her. "I won't pretend it wasn't, Allie. Women get killed trying to face a man like that."

"I know. I wasn't thinking clearly." *Because I was worried you were mad at me....*

"If he gets out on bail...well, maybe he won't." He turned off the ignition.

"Why not?" Alicia asked. "I thought everyone got bail."

"Not when they don't live where they're charged." He shrugged. "If he does get bail, it's going to be an awful lot of money. And they might not let him leave the county until the trial."

"Really?" Alicia didn't like the sound of that. The thought of Harold hanging around Conard City for the next several months made her stomach turn over. "Well," she said finally, "if he gets out and has to hang around here, I'm going to get some Mace or a baseball bat or something and carry it with me all the time."

"You're feeling feisty this morning."

She shrugged one shoulder, wishing she felt as brave as she was talking. "I can't live my whole life under a rock."

"No." He reached out and touched her shoulder gently. "You shouldn't have to. But...be careful, please?"

"I will. Now let's get you looked at."

Getting Beau looked at turned out to be a reunion. Carol and Adam were both on duty in the ER, and Carol hugged Alicia the instant she set eyes on her.

"I've been so worried about you!" she said, hugging Alicia as tightly as she could. "So worried. And so has Melody!"

"You're Melody's sister-in-law?" Adam Roth asked. "Hi, I'm Melody's fiancé." He extended his hand to shake Alicia's. "Out of hiding? Good. Come over for dinner tonight...."

Beau spoke up. "What's a guy gotta do to get a little medical attention around here?"

Everyone laughed, but Carol and Adam quickly swept Beau away into a cubicle, leaving Alicia standing alone in the small lobby. There was a tiny waiting room off to one side, so she went in there. If there had ever been any magazines in the room, they were long gone.

But she wasn't alone there long. Carol was back in less than five minutes.

"Beau's okay," she said. "Adam thinks he just has some bruising." She sat next to Alicia and hugged her. "Beau's fine. It's *you* I'm worried about."

Over the next twenty minutes, piece by piece, Alicia told Carol about the last seven years of her life. And by the time she was done, she felt as if she and Carol had never been separated.

"So you like Beau, huh?" Carol asked, having read between the lines. "Well, you go, girl. He needs somebody like you."

"He doesn't seem to think so."

Carol shrugged. "Men never do."

"He thinks he's too old for me."

"Hah!" Carol's eyes sparkled. "He's just scared of getting hurt again. Age makes a great excuse."

Alicia found herself laughing helplessly. She had almost forgotten how positive Carol was about everything, and how willing she was to charge ahead. "I missed you, Carol. Really, really missed you."

"Me too. So we have to figure out a way for you to stay here. I don't want you ever to leave Conard County again."

"I don't want to, either, but jobs don't exactly grow on trees."

"Well, if you want, you can come live with me until something works out. I've got plenty of room."

Alicia's immediate reaction was that she didn't want to leave Virgil's house, even to stay with Carol. She didn't want to leave *Virgil*.

But, in all honesty, she knew that was going to happen. If not today, then tomorrow, as soon as Virgil felt she was no longer at risk from Harold. And it was only right, after all. He'd taken her in because she needed help, not because he wanted a roommate.

He entered the waiting room just then. "I'm fine," he announced. "Just a bruise. Ready to go home, Alicia, or do you want to stay a while and talk with Carol?"

"I've got to get back to work," Carol said swiftly, rising. "You go on home. I'll call tonight, and we can make plans to get together for dinner or something, okay?"

The women hugged once again; then Beau and Alicia headed home. And all the way, Alicia wondered how to bring up the subject of her leaving and couldn't find the courage to do so. Fear that he would want her to go right away held her back. It had to happen, but she didn't want it to happen any sooner than it had to.

Please, she prayed, don't let it happen soon.

Chapter 7

As soon as they got inside, Beau turned to smile at her. "Just let me change into civvies and I'll take you out of here the way I promised to yesterday."

She hesitated, not wanting him to feel obligated. "You don't *have* to, Virgil."

His eyes seemed to darken. "I *want* to, Allie."

Her heart lifted. "Okay. Should I pack a lunch?"

"I'm not sure I have anything that would work for that. Why don't we just stop at the supermarket and pick up something from the deli?"

The deli wasn't as fancy as what Alicia had become accustomed to in Minneapolis, but they made some delicious-looking fried chicken and potato salad. They added some cheese and some soft drinks, bought a foam cooler to put them in, and headed for the mountains.

"Can we go up to the ghost town on Thunder Mountain?" Alicia asked. "Carol and I used to hang out there all the time."

He shook his head. "We had to post it. One of the tunnels collapsed under Carol last week. It's too dangerous."

"She wasn't hurt, was she?"

"No, Tom McKay was there and yanked her away as soon as it started to collapse."

"Thank God."

They found another place, a quiet meadow off a dirt logging road, where a stream gurgled cheerfully and the summer breeze sighed in the trees. Alicia pulled off her tennis shoes, rolled up her pant legs and stepped into the icy water with a shriek. Her toes felt numb in minutes, but the tickle of the moving water against the arches of her feet felt soothing.

Virgil joined her, laughing at the shock of the frigid water.

"Isn't it beautiful?" Alicia asked, opening her arms wide to embrace the forest, meadow and mountains. "I've missed this so much, Virgil! I've been aching for this!"

She closed her eyes and breathed in the fresh pine-scented air, enjoying the prickle of the warm sun on her skin in contrast to the icy cold on her feet. Even the sound of a deerfly buzzing nearby couldn't disturb the wonderful feeling.

"Better get out," he said. "You're going to get frostbitten toes."

She opened her eyes and laughed at him. "It couldn't be *that* cold...." But her feet were numb and aching, so she turned to step back onto the bank.

He reached out instinctively to help her, just in time to catch her when her foot slipped on a wet rock. She started to go down, but he reached out with his other arm and caught her around the waist, pulling her up against him.

She started to laugh, but suddenly there wasn't any air to breathe. Suddenly the whole world seemed to grow hushed and still.

She looked into Virgil's eyes and felt herself falling into those dark depths, felt herself being tugged into a warm place she had forgotten the existence of.

"We'll freeze," he said huskily, then swung her up into his arms as if she weighed nothing at all and carried her up the bank to the warm meadow. For a long time, but not long enough, he simply stood there and held her, looking down into her eyes as if he couldn't look away.

Then, with an almost visible effort, he jerked his gaze away and set her gently on her feet.

"I'm too old," he said gruffly. "Too old for you, damn it."

"No, you're not. I think you're just right." Her heart was hammering in her chest, and she felt as if she were hanging on for dear life to something she would die if she lost.

"What's more, I'm a failure. A great big zero."

"No! Oh, no, Virgil, you're not! You're successful!"

He glanced her way. "Yeah. Right. Big successful deputy sheriff in an itty-bitty pond."

Summoning every ounce of courage she possessed, she reached out and touched his arm. "You're successful," she said again with quiet vehemence. "You've found what you want to do, and you're doing it. What's more, you're living exactly where you want to live. How many people can honestly say that?"

"Don't rightly know," he said, and sighed.

Alicia looked at him, hurting more than she had hurt in a long time, fearing an emotional pain that would far exceed anything Harold had ever done to her. How had she become so involved so fast? And what did it matter, anyway? It just was.

She licked her lips as her mouth turned dry. "Why don't we take another approach to this?"

He finally looked at her and didn't look away. "What approach?"

"Why don't you just ask yourself what *you* really want, and then let *me* decide if it's right for me."

A short sigh escaped him, sounding almost like a muffled laugh. "You're one determined lady."

"I'm just asking you not to make my decisions for me. I've had enough of that in my life."

"I reckon you have." He shook his head and ran his fingers through his hair. "Think about it, Allie. I'm a *man*. You can't possibly want a *man* to touch you ever again."

Her heart was pounding so hard now that she was afraid she might pass out. Anxiety made her almost weak. "We're not talking about *a* man here, Virgil. We're talking about *one* man. I'm not afraid to have you touch me."

"Why the hell not? I'm bigger, stronger...for all you know, I could be just like Harold."

"You could never be like Harold. You're too kind and gentle, and you take care of people. Harold has never done anything in his life like you did for your ex-wife. Harold would *never* have taken in a total stranger, or stood between me and a punch. Heck,

Harold wouldn't even have asked me what color curtains I wanted. You think I can't tell the difference between you and him?''

To her surprise, she saw dusky color rise in his tanned cheeks. He was embarrassed! Emboldened, she stepped even closer. ''Give us a chance, Virgil. Please?''

''Chance? It's too late for that....''

Before she could feel anything at all except a crushing wave of despair, he reached for her and pulled her close to his hard chest.

''Way too late,'' he said huskily, and bent his head until their mouths met.

He was kissing her! Shock held Alicia still for an instant; then joy and need bubbled up inside her all at once. Raising her arms, she wrapped them around Virgil's neck and wished she could crawl right inside him and never have to leave this haven again. She tilted her head back, asking for more, and wondered why she had never before in her life felt this strong a need and longing.

He obliged, drawing her even closer, sliding his hands down her back to grip her bottom and lift her against him. His tongue, warm and wet, accepted her invitation to explore the inside of her mouth, causing deep waves of need to pulse through her. Her feet left the ground, and she reveled in the feeling.

But finally he tore his mouth from hers, making a ragged sound. ''If this keeps up, I'm going to fall over.''

He set her gently on her feet, still holding her close. ''I'm going to get a blanket out of the car....''

This was her chance to say no, but no was the last thing she wanted to say. When he let go of her, it was as if she were suddenly cast adrift in an empty sea. She wanted to reach out to him again but couldn't seem to move. All she could do was whisper one word. ''Yes...''

He brought the blanket from the car and spread it out in a shady spot on a bed of soft pine needles. Then he looked at her, his expression serious. ''You're sure?''

''I've never been surer of anything....'' And that was the honest truth. If all she could have was this afternoon and these moments with him, she would take them and never regret an instant. What she *would* regret was never loving him.

He drew her down beside him on the blanket, then cuddled her close so that they lay face-to-face. Her head rested on his arm for a pillow, and his other hand pressed against the small of her back, keeping her near.

"You're beautiful," he said huskily.

A qualm pierced her. She didn't want to be wanted for her looks alone. Not ever again.

But as if he understood, he smiled. "I mean you're a beautiful person. You're sweet, kind, generous and very, very brave, Allie."

"Me?" She gave a little laugh. "I'm a chicken."

"No, you're not. I saw you stand up to Harold this morning."

"I was more worried about *you*."

"Me?"

"I was worried because you weren't there. I was so afraid you were mad at me.... If Harold had tried to keep me from getting to you, I think I'd have punched him in the nose!"

He didn't laugh. Instead, his entire face softened, growing gentle, and he stole her mouth in another kiss that seemed to sear a path straight to her soul.

Somewhere inside Alicia the beauty of the day blended with the beauty of this man and what he was making her feel. She felt elemental, as if set free of all the constraints of earth and reality, light as a wisp of breeze, eternal as love. Slipping an arm around his waist, she clung to him as tightly as he clung to her.

Yes. This was what she wanted, what she needed as desperately as she needed air to breathe. This man, with his gentle, generous nature. But even as her heart soared, so did her body, and she needed more of him than this embrace and this kiss.

Almost as if he understood, his hand began to roam her back, painting fire everywhere it touched. She arched against him, needing deeper touches and more intimate contact.

Gently he rolled her onto her back and propped himself on one elbow over her. Feeling a sense of loss, she opened her eyes and discovered he was looking down at her.

"You're sure?" he asked.

A nod was all she could manage, but she managed it, bringing a smile to his lips. His hand reached for the front of her shirt.

Oh, yes, please.... Every cell in her body was awakening to the promise of pleasure, the promise of a closeness and intimacy that she wanted with this man more than she had ever wanted it with any other. Her breasts ached for his touch, and her womanhood throbbed with deep yearning.

One by one, he unfastened the buttons on the front of her shirt. The sun seemed too bright now, even in the shade of the tree, and she closed her eyes, filled with impatient anticipation. Here... now...she wished it could go on forever, even as she ached for culmination.

When he reached the waistband of her jeans, he unfastened the snap. The sound, the sensation, was as erotic as anything she had ever felt, and a soft moan escaped her.

Butterfly kisses fell on her face, almost distracting her from the sound of her zipper being pulled down. *Oh, hurry,* she thought helplessly as her body arched upward toward his hand.

"Need you..." She murmured brokenly. "Need you..."

"Lift up, darlin'...."

Her pants disappeared. He lifted her gently and tugged her shirt away...leaving her in nothing but her bra and panties. The breeze felt cool on her skin, but she hardly noticed when she saw the heat in his gaze. And she forgot everything when he started kissing her.

Gently, barely grazing her with his lips, he sprinkled kisses down her throat, across her shoulders, over her midriff and finally on her thighs. Each touch lifted her higher and fueled the growing fire inside her. Feeling almost desperate, she reached out, trying to tug his shirt away, trying to get rid of the clothing that still separated them.

A truncated laugh escaped him, and he helped her, pulling away for what seemed like an eternity to cast his clothes aside. All of them.

Time stood still. She looked at him kneeling beside her and thought that she had never seen a more perfect man. Every inch of him was firm, muscled. Every inch of him appealed to her. She reached up a hand, gently touching the bruise that Harold had given him. He drew a ragged breath of pleasure at her touch, then lay down beside her once more, drawing her close to him.

"Feel so good..." she murmured brokenly as her hands began the joyous task of discovering his angles and planes. Smooth, soft where there was hair, her palms delighted in what they found. She ran them over his chest, feeling his small nipples grow hard, ran them over his back and felt him shudder. Ran them lower and discovered his narrow hips...discovered how much he wanted her.

Joy filled her, riding the tide of pounding desire that was like a roaring surf in her veins.

"Now you," he whispered. Her bra vanished, her panties got tossed away somewhere on the carpet of grass and pine needles, and then he was against her, nothing between them but skin.

And never had anything felt so wondrous or perfect.

He kissed her deeply again, his tongue stoking the fire, building it with each stroke. Then his mouth wandered downward, his tongue tracing teasing circles around her breast until she almost cried out for him to stop.

Then he found her nipple, first with a taunting flick of his tongue, then with a kiss. He sucked gently, rhythmically, finding the rhythm within her as if he felt it himself. With each pull of his mouth, he drew another aching pulse from her womb, made the aching need between her legs even heavier. When she thought she must cry out from need, he moved to her other breast, taking his time, driving her to the edge of madness with longing.

Her hips rocked, echoing the drumbeat in her womb, and his hand slipped down, gently parting her petals, giving her what she so desperately needed. She pressed against him, everything forgotten in her need for fulfillment except...

Except that this was not enough. She needed more, far more. She needed him deep inside her, in the place where a woman made a man her very own. She needed his possession, and she needed to possess him with her deepest being.

She tugged at him, wordlessly begging him, and at last he moved between her legs, offering her the promise of his manhood. She rose up to meet him, and with one long, swift stroke, he buried himself inside her.

The hush filled Alicia again as she savored the utter perfection of their union. This was what she had been born for. This moment and this man. She felt it with all that she was.

Then, with movements at first gentle, then strong, he began to move, driving them relentlessly toward the pinnacle. For a few moments she feared she wouldn't be able to follow him, but then she felt the ache within her bloom, growing harder, deeper... higher....

In the last instant she opened her eyes and saw him looking down at her. His face was taut with desire, but his eyes were alive with warmth and caring. He was waiting for her, she realized....

And then, between one breath and the next, she shot to the heavens and shattered into a thousand falling stars.

Moments later he followed her into oblivion.

Afterward, they didn't get dressed again. They were far enough from the road that no one would see them. He brought her a paper towel dampened in the stream and helped her clean herself. The intimacy both touched and thrilled her. Then they reclined side-by-side and nibbled on fried chicken and potato salad. Afterward they played tag like children in the meadow, and sat by the stream watching guppies.

It wasn't until the sun started to go behind the mountain and the air chilled that they dressed again.

They drove back to town holding hands, the breeze blowing in the open windows of the Blazer. Alicia felt proud to be sitting beside Beau as they drove down the quiet streets to his house.

But as they pulled into the driveway, her stomach sank and her heart darkened. Now it would come. They had made love, but that didn't mean Virgil loved her. The idyll was over, and he would probably suggest that she find a place of her own soon....

She climbed out of the car and looked up and down the street she was really seeing for the first time. Quiet, shaded by elderly trees, it looked so peaceful and welcoming. Back when she had been living on the outskirts of town in a ramshackle three-room house with her dad, she'd dreamed of living on a street like this.

But she didn't believe in happy endings anymore. She had thought Harold was a happy ending, and look what had happened. Virgil had said nothing about a relationship, nothing about staying together, so he probably wasn't interested in her for the long term.

She didn't know if she could survive the loss.

Together they emptied the cooler, storing the leftovers in the refrigerator. Then, with nothing else to keep them busy, there was an awkward pause as they looked at one another.

Finally Beau spoke. "Carol told me she was going to ask you to come live with her while you get on your feet."

This is it. Alicia's throat tightened until it ached. "Yes, she did." She could hear the unshed tears in her voice but hoped he couldn't.

"Mmm." Beau stood awkwardly, staring at her. "Would you...like to do that?"

She shrugged. "Maybe. I guess." But what she really wanted to do was stay right here. If only she could tell him that! But the words didn't want to come.

"I mean..." He shifted as if he were uncomfortable. "If you...oh, hell!"

"What's wrong?"

He threw up a hand. "I don't have any right to say this."

Her heart was racing now, and her throat was so tight that it felt as if there were a noose around it. "Just say it," she managed to breathe. *Just say it and get it over with. Tell me it's been nice, but it's time for me to go. Tell me we have no future together.*

"I know you're coming out of a bad marriage, Allie," he began finally. "You need time to heal, time to find yourself, time to build a new life. I know you don't want to get involved right now."

Her heart climbed into her throat. "I didn't say that, Virgil." How could she? She was already involved.

"You don't have to say it." He sighed and shifted his weight to one foot. "I know how long it took me to get over my marriage."

"But I started getting over mine a long time ago. In fact, I *am* over it. Already."

One corner of his mouth lifted, but he didn't look happy. "Are you really?"

She didn't answer, not knowing quite what she could say to convince him.

"Anyway," he said after a moment, "I know you need time and space right now but...but, damn it, Allie, I wish you'd stay with me."

Her heart began to swell with hope. "Really? Here with you?"

"Don't think I'll misunderstand if you'd rather live with Carol for a while. She's been your friend for a long time, and you hardly know me, but..."

"But?" she prompted, hoping against hope, and trying not to.

He shifted again and sighed. "I'm an insensitive fool, I suppose."

Her heart crashed. This didn't sound good at all. She blinked quickly, trying to hold back tears. "You're not insensitive."

"Sure I am. You're not ready for this."

"Ready for what? Virgil, are you throwing me out?"

He jerked with surprise. "Hell, no!" he said vehemently.

"Asking me to leave? Trying to find a gentle way to tell me to get lost? Feeling bad because we made love and you never want to see me again? What is it, Virgil? Just tell me. Please."

"No, no, it's none of those things! I don't want you to get lost! Damn it, Allie, I'm in love with you!"

Time seemed to stand still. Allie felt her heart stop, felt the world hush again as it had just before they made love. Then joy flooded her, and with it an exuberance that made her fly across the room and throw herself into his arms.

She was laughing and crying all at once as she clung to him and felt him lift her from her feet. "You mean that?" she asked.

"I mean it."

"Love love?" she said. "The kind that means you want me to stay with you forever?"

"Forever," he said. "I don't have the right...."

She looked up and pressed a finger to his mouth, silencing him. "You have every right, Virgil. You have every right because I love you. Love you. Love you..."

A slow smile dawned on his face, and Alicia thought she had never seen anything more beautiful. "Really? Truly?"

"Truly. Forever, Virgil. I'll always love you."

He threw back his head then and laughed, whirling her in circles before he set her back on her feet. When he did, he looked down into her blue eyes, his expression serious.

"You'd be happy living with a deputy sheriff in a tiny town with nothing to do?"

"I'd live with you anywhere, Virgil Beauregard, and here is just fine by me."

His smile returned. "You'll marry me?"

"Absolutely."

"And kids?"

"Oh, yes, please!"

"And what about you, Allie? What do you want? A new house? We can redecorate this whole place...."

Again she touched her finger to his lips. "Just you, Virgil. All I really want in this whole world is you."

He caught her in a tight hug and kissed her soundly, then whispered, "I love you, Allie. You taught me to live again."

It occurred to her that he had taught her the very same thing. Then she gave herself up to the wonder and joy of loving him.

Epilogue

Spring had come to Conard County once again. All the windows in Good Shepherd Church were open, allowing the warm spring breeze to bring its sweet smell indoors, where it commingled with the perfumes of the flowers that decked the church.

It wasn't every day that a man got to give away four "daughters." One by one, Nate Tate walked Carol, Melody, Hope and Alicia to the altar where Tom, Adam, Vic and Beau waited. The brides were resplendent in matching white gowns; the grooms were resplendent in dinner jackets.

The women had wanted to be married together, since their lives were so closely intertwined, and because they had found love all because of one nasty man.

Nate approved wholeheartedly. He'd always felt like Alicia was one of his "girls," and over the past months he'd come to feel the same way about Melody and Hope. As for the men…well, he'd come to think of them as sons.

He got a little choked up when he walked Carol up the aisle, but he managed to keep the tears back. He wasn't losing her, he reminded himself. She was staying right in town while Tom sought a coaching job at the high school.

But when it came to giving away Melody, Hope and Alicia, he

could feel only joy, because these marriages meant they would stay. When he walked them up the aisle, it was with a beaming smile.

As for Harold...well, Nate had to savor that, too. Harold was going to spend the next few years in prison. By the time he got out, he ought to be clear about leaving Alicia alone. And if he wasn't...well, Nate, Beau, Vic, Tom and Adam would be ready for him. But for now, Alicia was safe.

As he turned from the altar, having escorted the last of the brides, he saw his family lined up in the pews. Janet and Wendy were there with their husbands, and Patty, Krissie and Mary sat between them and Marge. Three more to go, Nate thought. He hoped his younger girls did as well as his older ones.

Then he sat beside his wife and reached for her hand, squeezing it gently.

All was well in Conard County. A man couldn't ask for anything more.

* * * * *

Silhouette

SPECIAL EDITION

Stories of love and life, these powerful
novels are tales that you can identify with—
romances with "something special" added
in!

Fall in love with the stories of authors such
as **Nora Roberts, Diana Palmer, Ginna Gray**
and many more of your special favorites—as
well as wonderful new voices!

Special Edition brings you
entertainment for the heart!

SSE-GEN

SILHOUETTE® Desire®

Do you want...

Dangerously handsome heroes

Evocative, everlasting love stories

Sizzling and tantalizing sensuality

Incredibly sexy miniseries like **MAN OF THE MONTH**

Red-hot romance

Enticing entertainment that can't be beat!

You'll find all of this, and much *more* each and every month in **SILHOUETTE DESIRE**. Don't miss these unforgettable love stories by some of romance's hottest authors. Silhouette Desire—where your fantasies will always come true....

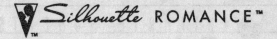
Silhouette ROMANCE™

What's a single dad to do when he needs a wife by next Thursday?

Who's a confirmed bachelor to call when he finds a baby on his doorstep?

How does a plain Jane in love with her gorgeous boss get him to notice her?

From classic love stories to romantic comedies to emotional heart tuggers, **Silhouette Romance** offers six irresistible novels every month by some of your favorite authors! Such as…beloved bestsellers **Diana Palmer, Annette Broadrick, Suzanne Carey, Elizabeth August** and **Marie Ferrarella,** to name just a few—and some sure to become favorites!

Fabulous Fathers…Bundles of Joy…Miniseries… Months of blushing brides and convenient weddings… Holiday celebrations… You'll find all this and much more in **Silhouette Romance**—always emotional, always enjoyable, always about love!

SR-GEN

WAYS TO *UNEXPECTEDLY* MEET MR. RIGHT:

♡ Go out with the sexy-sounding stranger your daughter secretly set you up with through a personal ad.

♡ RSVP yes to a wedding invitation—soon it might be your turn to say "I do!"

♡ Receive a marriage proposal by mail— from a man you've never met....

These are just a few of the unexpected ways that written communication leads to love in *Silhouette* Yours Truly.

Each month, look for two fast-paced, fun and flirtatious Yours Truly novels (with entertaining treats and sneak previews in the back pages) by some of your favorite authors—and some who are sure to become favorites.

YOURS TRULY™:
Love—when you least expect it!

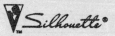

FIVE UNIQUE SERIES
FOR EVERY WOMAN YOU ARE...

❤ *Silhouette* ROMANCE™

From classic love stories to romantic comedies to emotional heart tuggers, Silhouette Romance is sometimes sweet, sometimes sassy—and always enjoyable! Romance—the way you always knew it could be.

SILHOUETTE® *Desire*®

Red-hot is what we've got! Sparkling, scintillating, *sensuous* love stories. Once you pick up one you won't be able to put it down...only in Silhouette Desire.

Silhouette® SPECIAL EDITION®

Stories of love and life, these powerful novels are tales that you can identify with—romances with "something special" added in! Silhouette Special Edition is entertainment for the heart.

SILHOUETTE·INTIMATE·MOMENTS®

Enter a world where passions run hot and excitement is always high. Dramatic, larger than life and always compelling—Silhouette Intimate Moments provides captivating romance to cherish forever.

❤ SILHOUETTE YOURS TRULY™

A personal ad, a "Dear John" letter, a wedding invitation... Just a few of the ways that written communication unexpectedly leads Miss Unmarried to Mr. "I Do" in Yours Truly novels...in the most fun, fast-paced and flirtatious style!